SWORD OF THE DEVIL

SWORD OF
THE DEVIL

Caroline Gray

This first world edition published in Great Britain 1994 by
SEVERN HOUSE PUBLISHERS LTD of
9–15 High Street, Sutton, Surrey SM1 1DF.
First published in the USA 1994 by
SEVERN HOUSE PUBLISHERS INC., of
425 Park Avenue, New York, NY 10022.

British Library Cataloguing in Publication Data
Gray, Caroline
    Sword of the Devil. – (Helier L'Eree Series; Book 2)
    I. Title II. Series
    823.914 [F]

    ISBN 0-7278-4622-1

Typeset by Hewer Text Composition Services, Edinburgh.
Printed and bound in Great Britain by
Redwood Books, Trowbridge, Wiltshire.

CHAPTER 1

"There it is," declared the constable. "The sum owed is two hundred and seventy-one pounds, eighteen shillings, seven pence and three farthings." He looked around my house with a disdainful air. "'Tis not an amount to be raised by a forced sale of anything here. The property will have to go." At this pronouncement, my wife Helga gave a shriek, sank into a chair, and began swearing to herself. As Helga is German, and inclined to relapse into that tongue when agitated, the constable had no idea what she was saying, which was all to the good.

I faced him, hands on hips, and he commenced to tremble. He was only an inch or two over five feet in height, and I am several inches or so above six feet. But he had three stout lads at his back to give him courage. Not that they would have availed him much had I lost my temper. But for the moment I was too surprised at his addle-pated words. "There is no man in the world to whom I owe two hundred and seventy-one pounds," I declared.

He pulled out a list from his pocket, and put on a pair of horn-rimmed spectacles. "Do you deny, Master L'Eree, that you owe Master Short the butcher twenty-seven pounds, six shillings and six pence?"

I scratched my head. "It is possible."

"Do you deny that you owe Master De Garis the baker eighteen pounds, fourteen shillings and three pence three farthings?"

"That is certainly possible," I agreed.

"Do you deny that you owe Master Ozanne the fishmonger thirty-three pounds, sixteen shillings and tuppence halfpenny?"

1

"Is it as much as that?"

"Do you deny that you owe Master Martel the coal merchant sixteen pounds eight shillings?"

"Well..."

"Do you deny that Mistress L'Eree owes Mistress Nicolle the seamstress sixty-three pounds, eighteen shillings, eight pence halfpenny, for labour and materials?"

I looked at Helga, who burst into tears.

"And lastly, but most important, Master L'Eree, do you deny that you owe His Majesty's Comptroller the sum of sixty-one pounds, fourteen shillings and eleven pence Ship Money?"

"That I do deny, Master Ogier," I said stoutly. "The payment of Ship Money for this year has not been authorised by Parliament."

"It was most certainly authorised last year, Master L'Eree," the villain reminded me. "And was not paid then either. As for Parliament, the States of Garnesey makes its own laws, and it has passed the required assessment for Ship Money. The King must have his taxes, Master L'Eree. So there you have it: the sum of two hundred and seventy-one pounds, eighteen shillings and seven pence three farthing."

"Owed to half-a-dozen different people," I pointed out. "You are not going to tell me that all my creditors have banded together against me?"

"No, no," the rascal agreed, replacing the list in his pocket and removing his spectacles. "You will be pleased to know that all of these debts I have enumerated have been paid."

I was so surprised I sat down beside my wife without meaning to. Helga ceased her weeping to stare at the constable with her enormous blue eyes. "Then what is the problem?" I asked, while I wracked my brain in an effort to determine who my benefactor could possibly be.

"Why, Master L'Eree, the problem is simply that you now have but one creditor, and he is desirous of collecting on his investment. Thus I am bid tell you that if by the end of this month the debt is not paid in full, he will sell you out,

2

including the roof over your head. It will be that or the debtor's prison. Or both, if the debt is not met by the sale."

At the sight of my expression he took another step backwards, for I was again on my feet. "You'll name this villain," I demanded.

"That I cannot do, Master L'Eree."

"By God!" I swore, reaching for my sword.

The constable and his assistants rapidly retreated through the door. "The end of the month," Master Ogier shouted. "Or it will be all up with you." He hastened out into the street, while Helga fell to weeping all over again.

Thus it was that two days later, it being the late autumn of the Year of Our Lord 1641, I left my farm, my wife, and my family in the Island of Garnesey, and journeyed to France. The visit was to be a brief and hopefully profitable one. In fact it was to be several years before I saw my homeland again.

Garnesey is an island situated in the Bay of St Malo, and within twenty-five miles of the French mainland, although it, and its neighbours of Jerseye, Sarque, Herme and Jethou all belong to the English crown, such as it now is. Travelling to the mainland was therefore not a difficult matter, providing England and France were at peace, as they happened to be at this time. King Charles I of England had wed the Princess Henrietta Maria, sister to the French King Louis XIII, and it so happened that, some nine years previously, having carried out an important service for the true ruler of France, Cardinal Richelieu, I had, by way of recompense, been granted a small manor and farm in Normandy.

This seigneury should have been sufficient to keep me and mine in comfort for the rest of my days, but sadly my mission, which had involved my participating in that dreadful struggle now known as The Thirty Years' War – and which continued at this time – had made me a host of enemies, while equally involving me in some of the blackest proceedings in history. I had thus felt it appropriate, having survived, by the age of twenty-two, sufficient ad-

3

ventures and misfortunes to fill a lifetime, to flee the mainland and return to my native island. I took with me the beautiful German lady I had accumulated as a wife during my travels.

There were difficulties in the way of this plan, to be sure. I had left Garnesey under something of a cloud, my mother having been burned as a witch. There was also the accusation that I had abducted a young woman of good standing to accompany me upon my flight. However, one of the most remarkable aspects of human nature is the way the bitterest enemy can become the best friend. Providing of course that the object of his animosity possesses sufficient goods of the clinking variety. Silver is acceptable, but gold is preferred. I returned to Garnesey a wealthy man, thanks to my adventures, and thus all was forgiven. I purchased a farm, and settled down to being a good husband to my adoring wife, with the result that during the next six years she mothered four children for me, and that should be enough for any man.

But I did not abandon my Helga, temporarily as I supposed, because I no longer found her embrace satisfying. It was a simple matter of economics. My clinking bag was sadly diminished. In fact, in this Year of Our Lord 1641 all society was going through a difficult time, so difficult that it was about to explode into the most terrifying violence. No one expected this to happen, because England, within its own borders, had been the most peaceful of countries for some eighty years, ever since the abortive revolts in the reign of Queen Mary, she that has become known as 'Bloody'. There had been alarums enough without, chief amongst which had been the expedition of the Great Armada up the English Channel. Not a Spanish soldier had come ashore on that sceptered isle save as a prisoner or the survivor of shipwreck. Equally had English fleets, and armies, ranged abroad, even invading France itself during my youth. But it did seem to the good people of England that at home drawn swords were a thing of the past.

These glittering weapons had been replaced by words. For the past ten years and more the country had watched with amazement the feud between King and Parliament, with the King ever demanding more money and Parliament ever refusing it. These disputes affected trade, and even stretched as far as little Garnesey, an island covering a bare twenty-six square miles, but whose prosperity largely depended upon that of England. When money became tight, all suffered, and when a man cannot meet his creditors they begin to remember disreputable events in his past and ancestry. In a small community everyone can recall everyone else's grandfather. Well, no one could recall *my* grandfather or even my father. Even my mother, who had maintained herself by whoring, had been unable to do that, but they could recall that I was the son of a convicted witch. I was also guilty in their limited conception, of innumerable crimes, and my size left them continually concerned as to whether my father could possibly have been a mortal man – true Garneseymen are somewhat small of stature. In addition to being very tall I am also somewhat large in shoulder and girth and in fact at this time tipped the scales at seventeen stones of bone and muscle, the whole topped by fiery red-brown hair and features more calculated to terrify than attract.

Hence my decision. A quick visit to France, an accumulation of whatever funds might be waiting for me at the manor I had abandoned eight years previously, perhaps even a sale of the place, and thence back to Garnesey once again with my wallet clinking more happily than ever.

It seemed a sensible plan. Additionally, it was the only one which promised salvation.

In preference to landing at the busy seaport of St Malo, where I might have attracted attention, I opted to hire a fishing smack and make the much shorter passage to the tiny haven of Cartaret on the west coast of the Cotentin Peninsular. Here I was set ashore, and quickly managed to hire a horse. I use the word loosely; my mount was the most obvious absconder from the knacker's yard anyone could hope to see. However, he had four legs and a back, and I needed only to travel a short distance. It was a slow business, but before dusk I sat in my saddle above the beautiful valley which belonged to me, feeling a great wave of combined nostalgia and relief sweeping over me.

This was for two reasons. In the first place, it was a relief to discover that my estate was not a figment of my imagination. It lay before me exactly as I remembered it, and even more prosperous in appearance *than* I remembered it. In the second place, when I had fled eight-and-a-half years previously, I had been pursued by a demon. I had no idea what had happened to that foul creature, the most beautiful woman of my experience, who went under the name of Richilde Bethlen, Princess von Hohengraffen. I had supposed her dead at my hands, only to be unable to find her body when I returned to the scene of her demise a few days later. It was of course possible that someone had removed it. But I had also been unable to discover the perpetrator of that deed, and thus had been left a sadly doubtful man. While commonsense tells us that such things as ghosts, goblins, and vampires, are creatures of fairy tale and the imagination, when one's own mother has been condemned for witchcraft there is always room for uncertainty.

Thus it will be understood that my journey had been a matter of looking from left to right and even over my shoulder. Although I am not a religious man and certainly not of the Catholic faith – in my island as in England one needs to be very much a member of the majority in matters of religion – I crossed myself as I passed, at a distance, that churchyard in which I had last beheld her lovely, dreadful, unforgettable visage.

My estate lay not greatly farther on, and so I rode down the drive, feasting my eyes on the evidence of a tremendous prosperity on every side. If in my youth France had been convulsed by religious wars, these had been fought mainly in the south of the country, while if she was now herself a participant in the German struggle, that too was being fought at some distance. Normandy was at peace, and prospering.

A groom appeared as my hooves clattered on the cobbles of the courtyard. He gaped at my clothes, for I had donned my best doublet, cloak and breeches for this journey, wore a feather in my hat, and had my trusted broadsword hanging at my side, all of which went somewhat ill with the sorry mount I rode. Then his mouth drooped open in disbelief, for I am a man who once seen is not easily forgotten, and he undoubtedly recognised his seigneur even after eight years. "My lord!" he cried, hurrying to take my bridle.

"Good evening, Jules," I greeted him, and dismounted.

Now people poured from the door and appeared from round the building. I strode towards them, and was touched by their greeting. "But my lord," gasped Pierre, my steward. "We had supposed you dead."

"Whereas, as you see, I am very much alive," I said, and clapped him on the shoulder. "And close to starving, and thirsty with it."

Fifteen minutes later I was sitting down to a mighty meal of roast mutton, fried chicken, boiled rabbit, and carrots, with a huge flagon of wine at my elbow. I did full justice to this, while understanding that a meal which had been so hastily produced, and yet had been so thoroughly cooked and prepared, had surely not been intended for me, and as there was no other person of my rank in the vicinity, could only have been meant as the supper of my servants. Indeed, they clustered around most anxiously as I ate and drank. "Your bed awaits you, my lord," said Louise the chambermaid. She had been a pretty little thing when last I had seen her, and she was a pretty but somewhat larger thing now, who clearly would also await me were I of that inclination. But I had more pressing matters on my mind.

"Shortly," I promised her. "Now, Pierre, dismiss the servants and sit you down. We have much to discuss."

"My lord?" he asked, seating himself somewhat uncertainly, further down the table, after the menials had left us.

"I am delighted with the appearance of the farm," I told him.

"I but did my best, my lord," he protested, clearly reassured.

7

"While considering me dead. Did you not inform any authorities of this possibility?"

"I never thought you dead, *monsieur*," he declared, having decided to contradict himself. "Whatever the opinion of the servants. I knew you would return, and deemed it my duty to preserve your property to the best of my ability."

"You mean that throughout eight years you have told no one of my absence?"

"No one, my lord."

I knew at once that he was lying, but thought it best to leave the matter for a moment. "And have my affairs prospered, during that absence?"

"Oh, indeed, my lord."

"I am glad to hear it. Then let me see what monies you have accumulated."

"Ah, well, my lord, you will understand that coin is hard to come by in these troubled times. I have dealt mainly in kind, with the result that you will observe the house and grounds are in the very best state of repair, and that your flocks have grown in size."

"Pierre," I said. "You and I hardly know each other. Why, we have not spent more than a week in each other's company. I fear you do not properly understand your master."

"My lord?"

"This goblet," I remarked, draining it and then holding it up. "What is it made of?"

"Best quality pewter, my lord."

"Indeed?" I released the handle and instead wrapped my fingers around the goblet itself, and commenced to squeeze. Here it should be mentioned that I am fortunate enough to be blessed with a strength commensurate to my size, and to the astounded steward's consternation the metal collapsed before my grasp, until the goblet began to resemble a candlestick rather than a drinking vessel.

"My lord!" Pierre gasped.

"Think what I should do to your neck," I recommended, "were you to play me false. Money, man. Show me my

8

money." He leapt to his feet and ran to the wall safe, from which he withdrew several bags which clinked most delightfully. "How much is there?" I asked.

"Why, not less than two thousand francs, my lord."

No doubt he had already hidden the rest in some secure place. But that could wait. Two thousand francs would certainly allay my most pressing creditors. Yet would I need more. And for that I required advice from an altogether more exalted source than he was likely to provide. "Fetch me another goblet," I told him, and when he had returned and refilled it, I asked him, "Now tell me, what of my neighbours, the d'Albrets?"

For the neighbouring seigneury, far larger than my own, was where I had first been taken on originally landing in France, by none other than Cardinal Richelieu himself. It was there I had been taught the arts of a gentleman, that is, to swear and drink and debauch and deflower, and above all to kill. "Well, my lord, as you will know, the old countess died, some years ago," Pierre said.

Sweet Antoinette, I thought. She had not been so old when she had had my virginity. "I knew of this," I said. "I am more interested in her son. And daughter-in-law." For the younger countess was none other than my first love, Marguerite le Gron, with whom I had absconded from Garnesey – she admittedly unwillingly – eleven long years previously. When she had chosen to abandon me in favour of the far more promising position of Countess d'Albret, I had been somewhat resentful. But that also had been a long time ago, and I needed all the assistance I could find.

"Alas, my lord," Pierre said. "Count d'Albret was killed in a duel, some four years gone."

"And his widow? Has she married again?" I could not imagine the beautiful Marguerite, all flaxen hair and flowing figure, not to mention the possessor of a fortune, remaining a widow for four years.

"I cannot say, my lord. Following the count's death, the countess abandoned Normandy and went to live in Paris."

"Then who is the seigneur?" I asked.

"The property is managed by the late count's steward, my lord."

"It appears you have an entirely absentee nobility in these parts," I remarked. "Well, I am for bed. Good night to you, Pierre."

"And tomorrow, my lord?"

"Why, tomorrow is tomorrow," I assured him, throwing my bags of coin across my shoulder.

The girl Louise was indeed waiting for me, but once again I put her aside, bidding her return to her own chamber. I am as libidinous a man as most – indeed, there are many who will claim I am *more* libidinous than most – and she had a most promising body, but I had a great deal to consider. I had no idea how one sold a seigneury, or even if it were possible to do so. I had hoped Marguerite would be able to enlighten me, having spent ten years in the heart of the nobility. Now I would have to make discreet inquiries, while always beset with the need for haste, as the three week's grace I had been allowed by the constable was rushing by.

However, I have always possessed one great asset, the ability to sleep soundly however pressing my problems, whether these have been financial or the promise of a great battle. This is a valuable trait, to be sure, as it ensures continuing good health. Unfortunately, there are times when it is somewhat dangerous. I did not suppose it could possibly be so as I slept in my own bed in my own house for the first time in eight years, but the fact is that I awoke suddenly, startled by movement in the room, opened my eyes to find it already daylight, and also to find that my chamber was filled with eight men, all armed, five of whom were pointing pistols at my head.

Half asleep as I was, I immediately understood my situation. The fact that there were *eight* men awaiting my first movement, apparently with every intention of blowing me apart should I do anything they might construe as aggressive, convinced me that here was no ordinary arrest or even

10

assassination, which is usually entrusted to a single man or at best a pair. These men knew they were confronting one of the great warriors of their times. That ruled out Pierre as the instigator of the assault, however much he had clearly both alerted them to my presence and admitted them to my house; my steward knew me as nothing more than a young man who had mysteriously been granted possession of the seigneury; if he had had an example of my physical strength he had no inkling of the reputation I had gained as a swordsman during my service in the war, or that I had been in the employ of Richelieu himself.

On the other hand, he must have communicated the news of my return to someone who did know me, for these fellows had clearly been instructed. Now their leader presented his sword to my defenceless breast. "Dress yourself, Master L'Eree," he said. "You are to accompany us."

"Am I allowed to ask where we are going?"

"Why," he said. "To Paris. There is someone would speak with you."

Would you believe that I had never been to Paris? But then, I had never been to London, or Vienna, or Madrid, or Rome, or any of the famous cities of the world. Yet Paris I counted greatest, not only because I had served the French, and because of its reputation, but because there I knew I would find the Cardinal, and by now I had no doubt on whose orders I had been kidnapped.

But why? There was the question that taxed me as we rode throughout the next three days. My guards were courteous enough, but they were most certainly my guards, and although as a gentleman they allowed me to wear my sword, they left me in no doubt that they would shoot me down if I made the slightest move against them. When we stopped at an inn for the night we slept all nine to the same room, and they took turns to stay awake in pairs, watching me from behind cocked pistols. Obviously with my enormous strength and experience at every kind of fighting from fisticuffs to musketry I could have taken on even eight men with every prospect of success, but I had thought to

11

put such misbehaviour behind me during the past eight years. Nor did I see that I would be helping myself to any great extent even if I freed myself. Apart from probably having to carry several pistol balls around with me until I could find a surgeon, I had no doubt that Richelieu had allowed for every possible eventuality, and would be able to have me rearrested in very short order, certainly long before I could make my escape from the country he ruled with absolute authority.

In addition, there was the matter of my money, of which my captors had relieved me. Before I could return to Garnesey I must either recover or replace it, or all my hopes were undone, and I could not believe that so paltry a sum as two thousand francs, while a fortune to me, would be of the least interest to the Cardinal, with all the riches of France at his disposal.

Besides, dare I say it, I was curious. I had served this man honourably and well, at great risk to myself, and he had acknowledged this fact. My seigneury had been his reward. That I had chosen to abandon it for a less luxurious life was surely no concern of his. Yet here I was being taken ... not, after all, to Paris, but instead to a château not far from the village of Versailles, where there was some building going on in which apparently the Cardinal was interested.

In the courtyard of this castle we dismounted, and without even being given the opportunity to change my clothes or wash my hands, I was hurried through a succession of corridors and halls, until we arrived at the chamber occupied by the great man.

In the doorway I paused in surprise. The room was large, but gloomy, as the drapes were drawn. To one side there was a desk and chairs and bureaux and masses of papers, to the other there was a tester bed, somewhat tousled, to suggest that although it was late morning its occupant had only recently risen. But it was the idea that the most powerful man in France, and some said in Europe, should be combining his office and his bedchamber in but a single room that astounded me.

Until, as indicated by the officer at my elbow, I advanced to stand before the desk, and the Cardinal himself.

When I had first encountered Armand du Plessis du Richelieu, a matter of eleven years previously, I had formed the impression that he was not in the best of health. Yet he had been tall and well-shouldered, and had carried himself with the arrogance of a man in his supreme position. Additionally, he had been dressed as a gentleman, in all the finery of plumed hat and velvet cloak, thigh boots and kid gauntlets. He had then, as I recalled, been in his middle forties. Therefore the man before me now could not be more than fifty-five. Yet I found myself gazing at a wizened old priest, wearing the red robe and hat of the cardinal he was, as opposed to the finery of the seigneur he had liked to appear, face and hands alike gnarled and wrinkled, and shoulders bowed. However the voice was as crisp as I remembered it. "Monsieur L'Eree," he remarked. "Why, it seems but yesterday when last we spoke."

I removed my hat with a flourish. "I would have come at your summons, Your Eminence. There was no need for kidnapping."

Richelieu gazed at me, his eyes those drops of ice which had frozen the brains of so many men. But I had survived his gaze before, and too much else besides. "Would you?" he remarked. "I wonder." He waved his hand, and I heard movement behind me, and then the closing of the door. Not for the first time in my life I was alone with the ruler of France. "I have a task for you, Helier," he said.

"Your Eminence, when last we spoke, you told me you had no further need of my services, nor would."

"Circumstances change," he observed. "Pour yourself a glass of wine and sit down, Helier."

"And for you, Your Eminence?"

He made a sound which suggested he was blowing air through his nostrils. "My doctors say I should not. They say I am dying, Helier. Can you believe it?" I turned, sharply, the unfilled goblet in my hand. Richelieu smiled, a

13

mere widening of the tight lips. "It will not happen for a while yet. Come and sit down."

I filled my goblet from the decanter on the table, then sat before the desk. "I assume you are familiar with English politics?" the Cardinal asked.

"I endeavour not to be, Your Eminence. As far as we of Garnesey are concerned, English politics appear to be solely concerned with raising taxes, and this is a curse we bear with fortitude, not pleasure."

He frowned at me. "You support the cause of Parliament against the King?"

"Heaven knows, Your Eminence, I have studied neither cause."

"Suppose you had to make the choice?"

"Well . . . the King is the King, Your Eminence. I am no revolutionary."

"Good," Richelieu said. "That is good. You are aware that the Queen of England is the sister of King Louis?"

"I am aware of this, Your Eminence."

"And I will tell you, as you seem to be *unaware* of it, that the war of words between King Charles and the likes of Pym have arrived at a state where words may soon no longer suffice. There was a time when the King possessed a man with sufficient resolution to make him king in deed as well as word. Have you heard of the Earl of Strafford?"

"Wentworth? They executed him last May."

"So you do know something of what is happening across the water."

"It made a great noise at the time, Your Eminence. There were those who claimed he was judicially murdered."

"And they were right. How may a king allow his chief minister to be executed without even a trial?" He spoke with feeling: as Louis' chief minister he had had some uneasy moments in his own early days. "A Bill of Attainder! Ha! I will tell you how it happened, Helier. This King Charles, for all his handsome appearance and claims to possessing a divine right to power, is a weakling. His only virtue is that he loves his wife. I have it on the authority of our ambassador that he was virtually given a choice, by Pym and his Parliamentary friends: Strafford or the Queen. Would you believe it?"

"That sounds *like* revolution," I remarked.

"It does, and it should have been treated as such. But the King chose to sacrifice his strongest weapon to save the woman he loves. Very commendable of him, to be sure. However, what sort of a mess King Charles has got himself into interests me not in the least. What does interest me, what concerns me, as it must concern every Frenchman, is the safety of the Queen. Thus I have summoned you here. Once again you must draw your sword in defence of France."

"With respect, Your Eminence," I pointed out. "I am not a Frenchman."

He glared at me. "You have served me, and this country, before."

"You made it imperative that I do so, Your Eminence, by threatening the life of the woman I then loved. How is the Countess d'Albret, by the way? I was told that young Joseph got himself killed in a duel."

"Indeed, that is what happened. He died defending his wife's 'honour'. Whereas you and I, Helier, both know that the fair Marguerite never had the least understanding of the word. You ask after her health? She is here in Versailles, serving me. Tell me, Helier, would you care to, shall we be vulgar, have her?"

"Your Eminence?"

He smiled. "As I understand it, you kidnapped the young woman from Garnesey, firstly because her father had been the principal accuser against your witch mother, but secondly, because you discovered her to be the most beautiful woman of your then limited acquaintance. However, circumstances conspired to render you unable to consummate your adoration before you found yourself in my hands, and I then prevented such a delicious event until you had carried out a certain duty for me. Sadly, by the time you returned from Germany, she had married, you had sufficient evidence to understand her to be the whore

15

she is, and you had, additionally, lost your heart elsewhere. Correct me if I am wrong."

"You summarise the situation admirably, Your Eminence."

"Yet is she still probably the most beautiful woman of your acquaintance, even now. And she works for me, since the death of her husband left her destitute."

"Destitute, Your Eminence? But she is the Countess d'Albret."

"The Albret Estate belongs to me, Helier. I allowed young Joseph the use of it, and gave him the title, because of the services rendered me by his mother Antoinette, whom you no doubt remember."

"I do indeed, Your Eminence."

"I was sure of it," he agreed, drily, leaving me in no doubt that he was aware of the brief amour I had enjoyed with the late Countess, at a time when she was still his official mistress. "But there it is. When Joseph got himself in the way of a sword thrust, the land reverted to me. Oh, I have allowed Marguerite to retain the title, but it is an empty form. Thus she found herself unable to pay her debts. I was able to do that for her, and thus she is here in this château, bound to do my bidding in all things. Does that thought not excite you?" I am afraid I would be lying were I to claim otherwise. As the Cardinal could discern. "Well, then," he said. "Shall we discuss your mission?"

However, while I may be a libidinous fellow, and the thought of the woman I had once loved sacredly and still did desire profanely waiting for me was most arousing, I am not entirely at the mercy of my carnal instincts. "With respect, Your Eminence," I remarked. "You do not seriously expect me to abandon my home and wife and children and plunge into the midst of English high politics, which we have both agreed is a most dangerous business, for the sake of a fuck, however attractive?"

"My dear Helier," Richelieu said, as urbane as ever. "I had gained the opinion that you had already abandoned home, and wife, and children."

"Briefly, Your Eminence. There is a small matter of some outstanding debts..."

"Ah." The Cardinal glanced at a sheet of paper lying on his desk. "In the amount of two hundred and seventy-one pounds, eighteen shillings, seven pence, three farthings."

"Your Eminence?" I cried. For while I knew he had spies everywhere, it had never occurred to me that he might have them in Garnesey, at least, to the extent of being interested in what he would consider a trifling sum of money.

"Thus you returned to France seeking some funds," Richelieu suggested.

"Well, Your Eminence, as you know so much, yes, that is the truth of the matter. And as it happened I had more than enough awaiting me at my château. Unfortunately, it was stolen by those scoundrels you sent to kidnap me."

"Scoundrels, indeed. I shall have to investigate this."

"I would like the money back, Your Eminence."

"Well, I shall see what can be done. But they have undoubtedly spent it by now."

I preserved my equanimity. "It is also my desire to place my seigneury on the market."

The Cardinal's finger moved to and fro. "That cannot be, Helier. The seigneury was my gift to you. It cannot be sold like a loaf of bread."

"Well, then, Your Eminence, a mortgage..."

"On a church property? Heaven forbid."

"Then, Your Eminence, I must beg you to permit me to go about my business. For it is vital that I raise the amount owed, and quickly. Or be sold up, and incarcerated in a debtor's prison." I knew, of course, that we were playing a game, as was his fashion, and that he not only possessed my two thousand francs, but would also in the course of time tell me exactly what he planned.

"While your wife and children starve," Richelieu said sadly. "I am very much afraid that that is exactly what will happen, if you refuse to serve me." He flicked several other pieces of paper on his desk, which I had previously failed properly to notice. "What have we here? A seamstress, a demand for taxes, a butcher, a baker . . . all that is missing is a candlestick maker."

"Your Eminence?" I leaned forward. "*You* purchased my notes?"

"Of course."

"But why?"

"Simply to bring you to France. I could not risk an international incident by attempting to kidnap you in Garnesey. Nor would I have possessed the necessary means to convince you that your future lies in my service. But now, you see, if you refuse me, you shall indeed go to a debtor's prison, and your wife and children will indeed starve. Whereas, if you carry out this trifling service I require of you, I shall happily tear up these notes and the whole matter will be forgotten. More, I shall bestow upon you sufficient financial reward to prevent such a misfortune occurring again."

I sighed. I knew I was beaten, for the second time. No man could hope successfully to combat someone with all the world at his fingertips. "You wish me to become a bodyguard for the Queen of England, Your Eminence? I feel I should point out that should a Bill of Attainder be brought against *her*, my options would be limited. I may be able to swipe off a head or two before they cut me down, but I can hardly dispose of the entire Parliament."

"You mistake my purpose. I wish you to visit England, obtain an audience with the Queen, persuade her to abandon that useless husband of hers, and then escort her safely to the continent, where she will remain in safety until this business is sorted out, one way or the other."

"Your Eminence, do you seriously suppose Her Majesty is going to listen to the advice and recommendations of a common squire? You would do far better to send one of your great nobles."

"That is not possible. Were any member of the French court to visit England with the avowed intention of calling upon the Queen there would be the most tremendous to-do. A diplomatic incident, no less. I cannot even write to her with any certainty that her mail is not being secretly opened and read. You must bear in mind at all times that Her Majesty is probably the best hated woman in England, because she is French, because she is a Roman Catholic and persists in practicing her religion even in that heathen country, and most of all, because it is perceived that she is a far stronger character than her husband, and that a successful coercion of the King is impossible as long as she remains at his side. But should a Garnesey squire desire to visit his mother country, who could possibly object? You will journey from here to Calais, and from there take ship to Dover – it is the shortest route – and from there travel to London. There will be absolutely no risk of anyone discovering your purpose, for you will have no purpose that can be discovered. My instructions to you will remain locked in your head. You will be travelling upon private business. I leave it to you to determine what this business should be. In London, you will seek an audience with Her Majesty, and there you will deliver my warning and my urgent request, with which you will associate her brother King Louis, and at the same time volunteer to serve her as a faithful servant until she reaches safety."

"You mean, you wish me to return her to France?"

"No, no. That you must not do, under any circumstances. It is quite impractical for the Queen of England to seek refuge in France, even if she herself be French, without causing a diplomatic incident. I have enough to contend with across the Rhine to start worrying about enemies across the Channel. This whole business, as I have attempted to make clear, must be carried out without involving France in any way. You will carry her to the Low Countries. They are already the home of refugees from every royal house in Europe."

This did not make the task seem any the easier to accomplish. "But why should Her Majesty even receive me, Your Eminence?" I asked. "If I can have no official status?"

"Because, when you request the audience, you will do so in the name of God's most faithful servant, and she will know you have come from me."

"Will no one else understand this code, Your Eminence?"

"No one. It was agreed between Her Majesty and myself before she ever married."

Which was a matter of some sixteen years before. I could only hope she had not forgotten. But arguing with Richelieu was a waste of time. He dealt only in facts, as he saw them, and thus I must do the same. "And in the meantime, my debts..."

"Will not be claimed."

"Yet must I leave my wife sufficient to live upon."

"That shall be attended to. Madame L'Eree will receive a monthly remittance, ostensibly from you during your absence."

"And if I do not return?"

"If, by any misfortune, you should die in the service of France, your wife and family become my charge. Should you make the mistake of deciding to abandon them for any reason, then they will of course be put on the street."

"Of course, Your Eminence. However, I am sure you will forgive me if I request some confirmation from my wife that these arrangements have been put into force."

He frowned at me. "Am I to understand that you do not trust me, Helier?"

"By no means, Your Eminence. I am simply a loving and anxious husband."

He gave a short laugh. "Who is also a presumptuous rogue. Very well. You may write to your wife, outlining the arrangements you have made for her well-being while you go about the business of restoring your fortunes, and requesting her to reply to you at an address in London, which I will give to you. I am assuming that she *can* read and write?"

"Better than most, Your Eminence."

"Well, then, from my agent you may receive the letter and have your mind set at rest."

"Thank you, Your Eminence. There is also the matter of my travelling expenses."

"That will be in the care of your companion."

"Your Eminence?"

"You did not suppose I would send you on such a mission all by yourself, Helier? This is both to ensure that you do *not* after all decide to abandon your wife and family, and me, and to provide you with comfort and support in your journey and your task. She will, as I have said, have control of your financial arrangements."

"She, Your Eminence?" I asked, still more uneasily.

The Cardinal rang a little bell on his desk. "Again as I have said, the young lady now works for me."

I leapt to my feet as the door opened, and found myself gazing at Marguerite Countess d'Albret, née le Gron.

My relationship with this woman had ever been decidedly ambiguous. Richelieu had been perfectly correct in reminding me that I had first elected to kidnap her because her father had been the cause of my dear mother's arrest, torture, condemnation and execution. I had then been very young, and Marguerite had been even younger, but innocent as I was I had not been very long in her company – fate had conspired to render us both as naked as the day we had been born – when I had started to have decidedly libidinous thoughts about my captive: even at fifteen Marguerite had been a most attractive young woman. However, despite our mutual nudity, I had been unable to consummate our relationship in the approved fashion, or indeed, in any fashion at all. This had been for three reasons. In the first place, she had evinced from the moment of our first meeting such a dislike for me that sexual intercourse between us would have been the most utter rape. In the second place, as we were fleeing Garnesey in a small boat, rape would have been a most difficult matter, and as she had appeared prepared to resist me to the last breath in her body, might well have capsized us and caused us to drown. And in the third place, despite my antecedents, sexual intercourse was something I knew absolutely nothing about, and my companion had shown no desire to instruct me.

Then, as Richelieu had reminded me, before I had had

21

the time or the opportunity to resolve these three co-nundrums, we had been shipwrecked on the coast of France and fallen into his hands. He had perceived the situation in an instant and realised the great use that could be made of someone of my size and unusual intelligence. He had bound me to him, by physical rewards, to be sure, but also by the promise of possession of Marguerite's delicious white body when I had completed the service he had in mind for me, and equally by the threat that if I failed him or betrayed him he would break that same delicious white body upon the wheel, which is well known to be the most unpleasant fate that can possibly be experienced.

The business had been but compounded two years later, when I had returned from the war covered in glory and success, and fully experienced in the art of woman, having encountered those on my travels who reduced Marguerite to what she truly was, an ignorant if arrogant country bumpkin, to discover that she also had become fully experi-enced. Although married to a French nobleman – I having been supposed dead she was bent on continuing that ex-perience, day in and day out, with whoever happened to be around. In this spirit of great generosity, she had even offered herself to me, my reputation having caused her to forget her original dislike for me, but I had spurned her for what she was, a whore. And now here she was again.

A woman with the instincts of a whore usually retains these throughout her life. In this regard I could not expect my lady to have changed. But even a whore can be well dis-guised. I beheld the most magnificent creature – I use the word advisedly – from the crown of her upswept, pow-dered, golden hair, past the patches on her face, lingering at the swell of her almost totally exposed breasts, considering the small tightness of her waist, and finally attempting to deduce – happy thought – what might lie beneath her flowing skirts, from the hem of which there peeped out a pair of silver-painted shoes. Marguerite's beauty did not rest on her figure alone, as she also owned a most pretty face, a trifle sharp-nosed to be sure but still possessing

22

eminently kissable lips and shallow blue eyes. She also wore rings of obvious value on her fingers, and resting on that white flesh which I instinctively longed to stroke was a rope of pearls which would have ransomed any king.

She was smiling, as she advanced towards me, pearls positively bouncing with the eagerness of her breathing. "Helier!" she said. "Oh, Helier! It has been so long."

This was clearly a rehearsed speech, as her smile was a well-practised one, and I knew that she had not forgiven me for spurning her when last we had met. Thus I looked at the Cardinal for guidance. But he, being a scoundrel, merely smiled at me. "She is all yours," he assured me.

Well, as he was dealing the cards, why should I not pick up whatever jokers might come my way? Would you believe that for all our adventuring together, I had only once ever kissed this woman? This oversight I now corrected, most lovingly and passionately, while my arms pressed her curves against me, and she smiled into my mouth, all searching tongue. "No doubt you are consumed with passion, after such a long separation," Richelieu observed. "There is an inner chamber through there, and in it you will find a bed. Return to me in fifteen minutes."

Hardly long enough for a proper consummation, to be sure, although it did give me an insight into the Cardinal's amatory habits – or lack of them. But I reflected that this was but an *hors d'oeuvre*, so to speak, and made haste. So did Marguerite, who was almost totally disrobed before I even got her through the door. Of course I realised that we were but puppets, dancing to our master's string, and that any pleasure granted by Richelieu had to be paid for many times over, but I had already been informed as to what the payment consisted of, and it did not seem so arduous a duty, while what a delightful dance was preceding the business!

Equally I realised that Marguerite no more loved me, or desired to find herself naked in a bed with me, in preference to any other man, than she might have desired to be ravaged by Richelieu himself – although perhaps I was here still playing the innocent. However, there she was, and here

I was, and play-acting or not she appeared most eager for the fray, so that it was one of the most memorable tumbles I ever had, which even in the short space of fifteen minutes left us mutually gasping while I continued to explore her magnificent mounds, both fore and aft. But she now confirmed all of my suspicions by bouncing off the bed and pulling on her shift. "The Cardinal awaits us," she reminded me.

As she clearly did not intend to dress herself, I donned nothing more than my breeches and hurried behind her. "What an attractive sight," Richelieu remarked. "Can there be anything like a woman straight from a love bed? A man on these occasions always looks utterly bereft. As no doubt he is. Now listen closely. You have your separate instructions. I now give you joint ones. As of this moment you are man and wife ... for the duration of the enterprise," he hastily added, surveying our mutual consternation. "You, Helier, are in command of this expedition, in all matters save financial. You, Marguerite, will obey his every command, at all times, except in financial matters. Is this understood?"

"Entirely, Your Eminence," she said, apparently not unhappy at the idea.

"You, Helier, will apply to Marguerite for such funds as you may require. Just in case you have any odd ideas, I can tell you that she is not going to travel with a bag of coin which may be conveniently removed from her person at any appropriate moment, but will carry only so much as is immediately required."

"Heaven forbid, Your Eminence," I protested.

"Exactly. Marguerite carries in her pretty little head a list of my agents to whom she can and will apply as necessary, and receive such funds as are necessary."

"And my Garnesey requirements, Your Eminence?"

"I have told you, I am sending my agent in St Pierre Port the necessary instructions, and your wife will receive a regular sum of money from that source. She will be given to understand the money is being sent by you, as you are unavoidably delayed in England. No doubt you will write to her in the same vein, and set her mind entirely at rest. As I have promised, once you have removed the Queen from England to safety, and I have been informed by her of her new situation, these notes will be destroyed, your two thousand francs will be restored to you, and I will double it."

This seemed very acceptable to me. I glanced at Marguerite, to see if she also expected a reward, but apparently she did not.

"Now go and prepare yourselves. You may take Helier to your own apartment, Marguerite. Your carriage leaves in one hour, for Calais. There you will find a vessel awaiting you to carry you across the Channel. I will wish you good fortune and a speedy return."

"A bath," Marguerite declared. "I must have a bath before we depart. You may join me, Helier." She hurried ahead of me, having retrieved her clothing but still quite undressed, careless of whom she encountered as she skipped along the corridors. Clearly she knew this château very well, and the Cardinal's servants knew *her* very well. I followed, also somewhat in *déshabillé*. In truth, my mind was in a whirl, as, for the second time, my life had suddenly gone spinning away at a tangent from anything I might have envisaged or planned. And yet, compared with the first mission I had carried out for the Cardinal, which had sent me plunging into the middle of a most bloodthirsty war, this business seemed simple enough. And where my first mission had been undertaken in lonely splendour, on this one I had been vouchsafed a perpetual presence of delightful company. Which is all but an example of how little any of us are able to judge the future.

Of course I cast a thought to my dearest Helga. But I reflected that everything I was being forced to do was designed for her future prosperity, and that she would necessarily forgive the various misdemeanours I would have to commit along the way – if, indeed, she ever learned of them. So for the time being I was content to be Marguerite's faithful husband and lover, and we spent a pleasant half hour soaping each other which in fact entailed that we had to soap each other all over again in order to commence our journey in a proper state of cleanliness.

But Marguerite remained always Marguerite. "This wife of yours," she remarked, when we had boarded the waiting carriage and were bouncing and clattering over the rutted roads towards the seaport. "Is it true that she is a German peasant?"

"In the same way as you began life as a Garnesey peasant, yes."

"Peasant?" she bawled. "I would have you know..."

"That your father possessed a herd of twelve milch cows, while Helga's father owned but a single animal. But these are matters of degree."

"Ha!" she commented. "A German! I'll wager she is as fat as a house."

Well, I would have been telling a lie had I claimed that my Helga was thin, to be sure. "I would prefer to describe her as voluptuous," I suggested.

"Ha!" she remarked again. "You mean her breasts are larger than mine?"

"Indeed."

"I have the best figure in France," Marguerite asserted. "His Eminence himself has told me so."

"And he has undoubtedly had many opportunities for considering that opinion."

"Do you mean to quarrel with me?"

"I beg your pardon. I thought you meant to quarrel with *me*."

"Helier!" She took my hand and pressed it against that portion of her anatomy which had recently been under discussion. "We must not quarrel. We are engaged upon an arduous and dangerous mission."

"I entirely agree. But you will forgive me for being curious enough to inquire what makes you work for the Cardinal, in such a complete fashion?"

"I am in his power."

"How?"

"Well ... " she flushed.

26

"I am aware that when poor Joseph was killed, the Cardinal sequestrated your fortune. But what was to prevent you returning to Garnesey, and your inheritance." I smiled at her. "Those twelve milch cows."

"Bah," she riposted. "Did not Papa marry again, and beget?"

"True. You were still his firstborn."

"Garnesey," she sneered. "A poor, empty place. His Eminence looks after me."

"And employs you."

"I earn my keep," she said with smug satisfaction.

That was all I got out of her, regarding her relationship with the Cardinal, during the two days it took us to reach Calais. As to her relationship with me, we both put quite a lot into *that* on the journey, she having discovered, after eleven years, that I knew what I was about, and was sufficiently well equipped to demonstrate my knowledge time and again. But our dalliance ceased soon after we reached Calais, however. It might have seemed as if it should have continued awhile longer, for we cast off in a very light breeze, which propelled us at barely a knot. As it is some twenty miles from Calais to Dover, this would have seemed to entail a voyage of perhaps twenty-four hours, or perhaps a little more, owing to the strong tides which distort the Dover Strait. I observed, however, that our captain appeared somewhat agitated, and although I found this difficult to understand, the weather being so fair and our ship a well-found barque, it turned out that he was justified in his apprehension: we were literally enjoying the calm before the storm.

Indeed Captain Dinant confided to me that had he not received orders from the Cardinal's agent in the port that he was to sail the very moment Marguerite and I arrived, regardless of the weather he foresaw on its way, he would never have put to sea. Unfortunately, the delay he foresaw could well have cost us several days – as indeed it would have – and he was afraid of the Cardinal's wrath. Thus it was that after having enjoyed a light supper, Marguerite and I, having retired to our cabin in the aftercastle where there was a sizeable bed, and as usual fallen to our favourite sport, were awakened from our sated slumber by a tremendous howling and crashing and banging and heaving and rolling and pitching which tossed us both on to the deck. "Holy Mary Mother of God have mercy on a poor sinner," Marguerite begged in a single breath, for having begun life as the most confounded Calvinist who ever lived she had deemed it expedient to change religious allegiances since becoming acquainted with the Cardinal.

I myself have never had the time to consider religion seriously – except where I have found it necessary to escape various churchmen out for my blood – nor have I been able to persuade myself that God, of whatever persuasion He may actually be, would possibly be interested in the son of a witch who has been forced to commit more crimes than he cares to consider. However, at that moment I was very much inclined to join her in prayer. This was not in fact the first time Marguerite and I had found ourselves in peril on the deep, as in the course of our escape from Garnesey we had been beset by a tempest which had actually caused us to be wrecked on the coast of France and begun the whole madcap adventure which has been my life. Yet I would claim without a moment's hesitation that *that* had been but a gale of wind compared with this monstrous event.

Preferring to die in the open air, if possible, than the confines of a stuffy cabin, I left Marguerite kneeling, hanging on to the bedstead – which was fortunately bolted to the deck – moaning and praying, while I dragged on my breeches, got the cabin door open, and assaulted the companion hatch. This had also been bolted down, but my banging caused it to be lifted by the mate, who regarded me with considerable alarm. "Are we making water?" he demanded.

I was tempted to tell him yes, which would not have been much of a lie, at that, but I was apprehensive of exciting the fellow. "No, no," I said. "I wish to see what is happening."

"At your own risk," he warned me. "And make haste."

I scrambled through the hatch, which was promptly

secured again, and gazed upon a scene of wild wonder. Although it was very dark, the gloom was being regularly pierced by vivid flashes of lightning, which revealed huge, white-crested waves, bubbling and foaming along beside our ship, which was running to the north-east under bare poles. Within a few seconds I was soaked to the skin, but this was principally the result of the rain which pounded down, while my breath was taken by the immensity of the natural forces surrounding me, and I could not understand how the ship remained afloat.

As to where we were going ... the captain himself was grasping the helm, assisted by three of his crew, but their sole ambition – an admirable one – seemed to be to keep the ship running before the wind; clearly we could not head up into such a storm without risking instant destruction. I allowed my mind to give a quick glance over an imagined map of the seas off Europe, and determined that we were most likely to bring up off Iceland. Indeed, I would probably have been right had not the seas begun to abate after some eighteen hours. By the next dusk Captain Dinant was able to put some sail on, and then even to begin thinking of returning us to our course. "Do you know where we are?" I asked.

"Twenty hours, being driven at say six knots, why here," and using his dividers he marked off the distance on the chart, in a north-easterly direction from Calais, which placed us well in the centre of the North Sea. "This is an approximate position," he explained, with remarkable honesty. "When these clouds lift and I am able to get a sight with my sextant, I will know more accurately. But for the time being, why, if we sail due west, we are bound to come to England."

"Where in England?" I ventured.

"Somewhere on the east coast," the villain replied. "I can do no better than that at the moment, Monsieur L'Eree."

I reflected that if fortune was with me, we might find ourselves sailing up the very Thames itself, which would, after all, shorten my journey to Whitehall. Meanwhile I deemed it best to do something about Marguerite, and found I had quite a task on my hands. The poor girl – for all our mutual adventuring, Marguerite was still only twenty-six years old – was in a state of utter collapse, mental and physical, the latter having some unpleasant corollaries. However, cleaning her up was the least difficult of my labours; abating her state of continuing hysteria took a good deal longer. "I want to go home," she wailed, without specifying whether she was referring to France or Garnesey. "I want to go home."

"We shall soon be to land," I reassured her, but as my own stomach was feeling none too strong, I gave her some dry bread to eat – this being recommended by the captain – and left her to return on deck.

To say truth this was hardly more comfortable, as everything was covered in dried salt spray, including my clothes, but the cook managed to produce some hot soup and so we sat out another night, sailing close-hauled, which is to say that the wind still being south-westerly, we were forced to travel in a north-westerly direction, as the ship would point no closer than that. This naturally ended any hopes I may have had of making the Thames, and in fact dawn revealed to us a short, choppy sea which looked more green than blue, to suggest that we were in relatively shallow water, although it was not yet possible to see land. I attended Marguerite once more, and then was called back to the deck by some excitement amongst the crew, our lookout having sighted a small vessel drifting, having been dismasted by the storm. She was low in the water, too, and the three men on board her were bailing as vigorously as they could, although as we approached we could see that they were clearly exhausted. "They will be English fishermen," Captain Dinant said. "Do you speak with them, Monsieur L'Eree."

I was given a speaking trumpet, and used this to bellow at the unfortunate fellows, who had been so busy trying to keep afloat they had not noticed our approach. Now they became very agitated, waving and hallooing, while I assured them of our assistance. Our captain handled his ship with commendable skill, approached upwind so that a rope could be thrown, and thus brought the smack into our lee, to enable the men to scramble aboard, bringing with them such of their belongings as they could, for no sooner had their craft been cast off than she began to fill, and within half an hour had slipped beneath the waves. "You came along at a most opportune moment," remarked one of the men. "Thanks be to the Lord!"

I would have supposed his thanks should have been directed to us, but I was more interested to realise that the men were not, actually, professional fishermen. To be sure they were sodden, miserable specimens, but their clothes were of good quality, and my deduction was confirmed by the man who had thanked us. "Out for a day's fishing, we were," he explained, "when we were set upon by this unGodly weather. Blown out to sea we were, and likely to be lost, had the Lord not taken pity upon us and sent your ship to our rescue."

I was beginning to find the fellow's constant referral to the Deity a trifle irritating, and in addition he was not a very prepossessing-looking character. Although tall and well built, he had a long, overly solemn face, which was not improved by a huge wart close by his nose. However, if he was a resident of that part of England closest to us, and one who knew enough about the coastal waters to go fishing, then I reckoned he, or his companions, must also know something about the tides and the sandbanks in this vicinity, and we were in sore need of guidance, for the water appeared to be growing shallower by the moment. "As you say, friend," I told him, "God must have sent us to your aid, but not less has He sent you to ours, for we are quite lost. Are you able to navigate us to shore?"

"You are on your way to England?" he inquired.

"That is our purpose, sir."

"From whence, may I ask?"

"From Calais, sir. Sadly, the storm blew us off course. However, as you can see, I am not French. I am a Garnesey merchant, engaged in the import-export business, on my way to see one of my clients."

31

He regarded me for several seconds, then cast a glance at Marguerite, who, as the sea had now considerably abated, was emerging from the companion hatch in what can only be described as extreme *déshabillé*, in that she was wrapped in a sheet with which the remaining wind was already commencing to play.

"My wife," I hastily explained.

"You should look to her, sir," he said severely. "However, if you do indeed require pilotage, then my good friend here, Master John Skippon, will see you safe to shore. At which time, sir, God willing, it will be my pleasure to offer you some hospitality in return for the great good service you have done my friends and myself."

"Why, sir, I thank you," I said. "My name is Captain Helier L'Eree, and here is my hand on it."

He looked from my fingers to my face somewhat questioningly. "Did you say, Captain? Are you a military man?"

For of course, in view of the perils we had recently undergone, and the difficulties of keeping one's feet on the heaving deck quite apart from the risk of tripping over a long scabbard, I had left my sword in the cabin. "Tush," I said. "It is but an honorary title now. But in my youth, I had the extreme good fortune to serve in the army of Gustavus Adolphus."

Again I deemed it best to stick to the Protestant side of my past, rather than confess either that I worked for Richelieu or had actually fought for the Imperialists before joining the Swedes, for if ever I saw a Calvinist this man was one. "By the good lord, sir, if you served with the great Gustavus then you were indeed a soldier. And you were a captain?"

"In the King's own bodyguard," I assured him.

"Well, well. Sadly, Master L'Eree, I am but a humble country squire, and have indeed never drawn my sword in anger. But I am right pleased to make your acquaintance, and here is my hand on it. My name is Oliver Cromwell."

CHAPTER 2

Looked at in retrospect, this will readily be seen to have
been a most promising meeting, quite as redolent of either
advancement or disaster as my first encounter with Cardinal Richelieu himself, eleven years before. But I am sure I
can be forgiven for not realising this at the time. Had I done
so, I might have opted to change the entire course of history
by allowing Mr Cromwell to drown.

In this late autumn of 1641 my new friend was forty-two
years old, a country squire, as he had described himself –
only recently, indeed, come into an inheritance which had
made his circumstances somewhat easier – but also a
Member of Parliament, which raised him somewhat above
the common herd. Not that Members of Parliament had
had much to do in recent times, save grumble in their
constituencies, as King Charles had contrived to manage
without their support for some eleven years. However, the
year previous to my meeting with Cromwell, the King had
run out of money, and had thus been forced to summon a
new Parliament. Oliver had again been returned, and
become a somewhat strident member of this aggressive
body. One of its first acts as Richelieu had reminded me,
had been to attaint the Earl of Strafford and cut off his
head, in a most unChristian and indeed illegal fashion.

It had been this same body of men who were reputed to
have told the King that it must be Strafford's head or the
Queen's. It can therefore readily be seen that in view of my
instructions I was not disposed to regard any of these
people as worthy of my friendship, considering as I did that
it might be necessary to despatch one or two of them in the
course of my mission. Just how many of them, or their

33

supporters, I *would* have to send to their Maker I had no idea.

For the time being, however, it was necessary for me to dissemble, and convince Marguerite to do the same; indeed, we were both so exhausted and shaken up by our experience that we were prepared to be friends with anyone who would set our feet firmly on dry land. This Master Cromwell and his companions did in a few short hours, guiding our ship through the shallows and sandbanks into a small seaport – called, oddly enough, Great Yarmouth – where we, or rather, they, were received with a great deal of satisfaction, it having been supposed that they had been lost in the storm.

This was actually the first time that I realised Cromwell was a man of substance in these parts, but the realisation grew when he took Marguerite and myself – our French sailors having put back to sea as soon as their ship was victualled – to his town house, which he owned in addition, it transpired, to a large farm some distance inland from where we had landed. At this house we met Cromwell's wife Elizabeth, as well as his mother, another Elizabeth, and his various children, of whom he had nine, the eldest girls being already married to local gentry, all crowding in to see their strange visitors, and all agog at the story Cromwell told them of the storm. The ladies hurried Marguerite off to see to her bath and toilette, and I was given the same treatment by the gentlemen.

"Garnesey, you say," remarked Mr Rich, when I had been allowed to dress and was sitting down in the parlour with a glass of refreshing ale. Mr. Rich was a neighbour who had ridden over from his farm, a few miles distant, and who, it was whispered in my ear, was a relation of the Earl of Warwick – I realised I was moving in high society indeed. "Yet you bear a French name."

He was all a-bristle with chauvinism, and I gained some understanding of the reason our sea captain had been so anxious to put to sea again. "So do most Garneseymen," I replied, refusing to grant him any sort of title. "That does not mean we are any the less English."

34

"Well spoken," Oliver said. "But tell me, Master L'Eree, how do the Garnesey people stand in the present dispute?"

It was necessary to think very quickly. To disclaim any knowledge of the matter would, I felt, put me at a disadvantage. While to partake in a discussion on the subject might gain me some useful knowledge – providing I did not antagonise these gentlemen. But I had already gathered that Oliver was an MP, and I had just learned that his friends, at the least, were strongly anti-French. "Why, in faith, gentlemen," I said. "While we watch events in England with great interest, we are not directly affected."

"How can that be?" demanded a man named Hampden, a first-cousin of Oliver's. I am bound to confess I did not like this fellow, who had the narrow features and close-set eyes of your perpetual trouble-maker.

But I replied courteously enough. "It is simply that we of Garnesey have our own parliament, which is called the States of Garnesey, and which passes our own laws, and taxes. Thus we are not liable for English taxation."

"Bless my soul," Hampden remarked.

"You do not even pay ship money?" Rich inquired.

"Well, sir, actually, we do," I said. "But it was voted by the States, on a request from the Lord Chancellor, not by any command, or otherwise, of the Parliament."

"Your States would seem to be a spineless lot," Hampden commented.

"John here has been to prison for refusing to pay the tax," Oliver explained.

"Well, sir, I narrowly escaped such a fate myself," I said. Which was perfectly true; I saw no reason to tell these people that my imprisonment would have been for debt, not on a point of principle.

"Sir, that makes me your friend for life," Hampden declared, "even if our entire family did not owe you a debt of gratitude for rescuing Oliver from a watery grave."

"He was sent by the good Lord in Heaven," Oliver said, as usual.

"And now you have business in England," Hampden went on. "Political business?"

"Why, no sir," I protested. "Politics is too dangerous a game for me. I am a man of peace." Well, I had been, for several years.

"There is no business in England today that is not political," Oliver declared darkly. "The good Lord in heaven has set our faces and our feet in the direction of freedom, and we will not be turned back now."

"Forgive me, my friend," I said. "But I prefer not to discuss revolution."

"We plan no revolution," Rich declared. "Heaven forbid. But it is time the King got hold of the problems of this country, and put them to right. He needs money. We need justice. It will be a fair swop."

"It is our intention to present a petition to the King," Hampden explained. "It is being drawn up now. Mr Pym, our leader, calls it the Great Remonstrance. Well, he was ever one for high-sounding titles. It is simply a list of our grievances, of what we have had to suffer, as free men and Englishmen. We have been imprisoned without trial, subjected to barbaric tortures and illegally taxed. Worst of all, there is a move to alter our religion until it is virtually a copy of Rome. As the elected representatives of the people of England, we are entitled to demand redress from the King. He has but to agree to pay regard to our plea, and we will pay equal regard to his requirements. Does that sound like revolution to you, Master L'Eree?"

"Well, sir, the answer to that must depend upon the King's opinion."

"And we know what that will be," Oliver growled. "He apes his father, and attempts to treat us as if we were errant schoolboys. I tell you straight, John, that if, as is most likely, King Charles refuses to listen to us, I shall sell the farm, and everything else I own, and take my family to the Americas. There we may find some free air to breathe."

"Do you not suppose the King's writ can reach you in Virginia or Massachusetts?" Hampden demanded.

"This Great Remonstrance," I said, as Oliver brooded on the last point, "does it in any way involve Her Majesty?"

"Indeed it does," Hampden said, "as she is the main part of the trouble."

"Because she is a woman? Or because she is French?"

"Why, both. A woman's place is to act the wife and mother, not the counseller."

"Has Her Majesty not played her part? She is a mother several times over."

"She stills counsels. And she is French. But worse, she is a Papist, and boldly proclaims it to the world. Not only are her interests across the Channel, but her instincts are for the kind of despotism Richelieu exerts in the name of the King of France. By God, sir, she would have Archbishop Laud as her chief minister. The country would not stand for that. No, no, Henrietta Maria must go."

"What exactly do you mean by that, sir?" I inquired, quietly enough.

"Well ... " he flushed in embarrassment.

"We mean the lady no harm," Rich said, somewhat hurriedly. 'But she must be made quiet, either by restraint, or by returning her to France."

"You would expel her?" This sounded promising.

"No, no," Rich protested. "That would surely cause a rift between the two countries."

"There have been rifts between England and France before, not to our disadvantage," Hampden commented.

"The woman must be *ruled*," Oliver said, emerging from his reverie. "If her husband is incapable, then by some kind of governors. She cannot be returned to France. The good Lord would honour no man who comes between a man and his lawfully married wife."

"Ah," I commented again, unsure at that moment whether what I was hearing was to my advantage or not. But my own thoughts were at this moment interrupted by a great to-do from the upper part of the house.

All our heads turned, to see Marguerite come tumbling down the stairs, fully dressed, to be sure, but still hardly to be considered so when compared with our hostess and her

37

mother and daughters. She was all flying skirts and bouncing breasts, pursued by several ladies, Mistress Cromwell in the van. "Helier!" My charmer shrieked at me. "Save me from these women."

I had to take her in my arms, as she was going there anyway.

"In faith, sir," Elizabeth Cromwell protested. "We but sought to make her decent. She would appear in *déshabillé*."

I looked down from the heaving, and very visible flesh rising against my own bosom, to the wide-collared smock held by our hostess, identical to the one that she was wearing; all her companions were similarly dressed.

"Look to yourself, woman," Oliver growled. "This is not the dissolute Court of St James."

I gave Marguerite a tender squeeze. "It were best to dress as these good people require, dear Wife," I told her. "As we are their guests."

Marguerite was, sadly, not given to tact. She pushed herself away from me and glared at Oliver. "Are you, then, ashamed to look upon a woman's charms?" she demanded. "In faith, sir, I am astounded that you managed to produce any children at all, much less an army of them. Did you do it all with your eyes shut?"

The exchange convinced me that the sooner we left East Anglia the better. The Cromwells apparently felt the same. This was not a result of any ill-feeling for me. Oliver indeed made it plain that I was welcome to stay at his farm for as long as I wished. But at the same time he also made it clear that he found my 'wife' a bit hard to stomach. I in turn found *this* hard to stomach. Sadly, my experiences in Germany during the great war had left me a cynic, with a profound mistrust of human nature. I could not imagine any man, not knowing Marguerite as well as I did, not responding to her physical charms, unless he were an eunuch or a monk, and as she was so close to Richelieu I was not even sure about the latter category. Oliver and his cousin and his friend all looked to me like fairly red-

38

blooded men, and the evidence of this was all about them in their numerous progeny. That they should resent the exposure of a woman's breasts, especially when she was not a member of their family, seemed to me hypocrisy at the very least. I thus found another reason for being unable to like these people.

Nonetheless I dissembled to the best of my ability, and, some horses having been procured for us, shook hands all round and had my back slapped while being assured that I would be remembered and welcome whenever I was in those parts again – pregnant words although I was then unaware of it – and so we parted the best of friends, Marguerite having observed the farewells with total contempt. "What wretched people," she remarked, as we rode away from them. "And they are our enemies."

"Some of them," I observed. "And it always pays to know one's enemies."

This part of England known as East Anglia is singularly flat; indeed in places it is subject to severe inundations from the North Sea. It is also extremely wet from above, certainly as winter approaches, and we made our way south through several heavy falls of rain. However, once we were away from the over-religious Cromwells we were enabled to seek the comfort of each other's arms whenever we halted, and as my accountant possessed sufficient coin we were equally enabled to choose our stopping places with an eye for comfort. It took us two days to reach London Town, and in that time, while Marguerite complained about the whole confounded country and everyone in it, I did some serious thinking.

What I had heard and seen at Cromwell's farm but confirmed what Richelieu had told me. The Commons were preparing to confront the King, and no one could have any doubt of the King's reaction. This man, Charles Stuart, although he was my anointed king, suffered from every possible defect of ancestry it was possible to imagine. One need go back no further than his grandmother, the Queen Mary, known as Queen of Scots. This woman, praised for her beauty in some quarters, had been a total fly-by-night and a menace to everyone with whom she came into contact. For those who fell in love with her feminine charms she was positively deadly.

Mary had only been two years old when her Scots father had got himself killed in battle, and thus, she had been brought up entirely by her mother, who had instilled in her the most absurd notions of monarchical infallibility. She had then been married off to another French king – a successor to the man who had assassinated her brother – just as rapidly as possible. As this gentleman was considerably older than his alluring young bride, he had very rapidly rammed himself to death, whereupon Mary had returned to Scotland as queen, and promptly made war with her own people. Thus her subjects had finally disposed of her by handing her over to Queen Elizabeth of England. Now it has become fashionable in recent years to refer to Elizabeth as a great queen. Obviously this is in part due to the sad lack of greatness in those who have followed her, but however great she may have been, she was a signal failure in the duty which above all else is that of a queen, whether ruling or consort: she did not marry and beget. Thus when she reached an age when even if she did marry she was extremely unlikely *to* beget, her ministers began to worry about the succession, and having looked up the various genealogical tables they made an horrific discovery: next in line to Elizabeth of England was Mary of Scotland. Thus Mary had to go. After imprisoning her for some years Elizabeth finally chopped off her head.

A great deal of catastrophe would have been avoided had this been done many years before. During her brief sojourn upon the throne of Scotland, Mary had contrived to marry twice more. The first of these extra husbands was a cousin of hers, Henry Darnley. He was also agreed by all who knew him to be an imbecile, and Mary, soon discovering this disagreeable fact, had him blown up by several barrels of gunpowder, ignited by the man she then married as her third husband. Sadly, before this happened

40

Darnley had impregnated her, and she had given birth to a son.

Owing to Mary's imprisonment in England, this little lad, named James, the sixth of that title to rule in Scotland, never saw his mother after the age of two. He arrived at manhood – I use the term loosely – having been brought up entirely by men, with the result that he had a pronounced preference for male rather than female genitalia, and a character so timorous he would jump clear out of his boots at the creaking of a door. In addition he had had a lunatic as a father, a fly-by-night as mother, a domineering bitch as grandmother, and knowing that both father, grandfather and mother had died violent deaths, he reached adulthood with a tongue too large for his mouth, so that he dribbled constantly.

The Scots being a dour people to whom misfortune of one kind or another is a daily occurrence, to have such an unfortunate creature as their king should really have had no great effect on either their lives or those of humanity at large. Sadly by one of those concatenations of history which from time to time ruin everyone's plans, this idiot had become King of England!

Actually, this had, at least in the end result, not been quite such an accident as was popularly supposed. It was mainly the doing of a man called Cecil, whom James raised to the peerage as the Earl of Salisbury. Well, he owed him a great deal. A throne, no less. Cecil had been chief minister to Queen Elizabeth, and was well aware that after Mary's death, her son would be next in line. But he undoubtedly presumed that dealing with a timorous half-wit, he would be in complete control of both king and country. Here he was sadly mistaken in his inability to understand human nature. James did not change, as a man, on becoming king; men do not change like that. But he did discover some additional traits, nearly all of them bad. The principal one was a didactic determination to tell everyone, from politician to priest, how to go about his business; this was, of course, coupled with a refusal to accept any such advice from his counsellors, Cecil included.

Even worse, however, James discovered a sense of duty, and despite his inclinations, determined to marry and beget. The tragedy of this was that had he contented himself with his harem of young men, such as Villiers and Carr, there would have been no risk of his line being perpetuated, and he would have rapidly been forgotten. However, not only did he marry an unfortunate princess, Anne of Denmark, but he took her to his bed so successfully that she produced several children. Of these the eldest, named Elizabeth, had married the Elector Palatine, whose ambitions had plunged Europe into thirty years of war, in which, as a very young man, I had both served and gained my reputation. The second, and eldest son, named Henry, is remembered as a perfect paragon of wisdom and virtue, but this is surely because he died too young to do any harm, and because of his successor. For the third child, and second son, named Charles, was the man now on the throne of England.

I must renumerate his antecedents: a father who was at once a coward, a pedant, and given to irregular tastes, and a mother who was entirely bewildered by the situation in which she found herself and spent her time playing childish games; a grandmother who was very little better than a whore but with grandiose conceptions, and a grandfather who was fit only for a lunatic asylum; a great-grandmother whose principal characteristic was arrogance, and a great-grandfather who believed that recalcitrant subjects should be brought to heel by cannon-shot. This was the man I was now committed to serve, at least until I could separate him from his wife.

We entered London Town without difficulty. The roads north of the city, where there were considerable heaths, were reputed to be dangerous, and indeed from time to time we saw mounted men observing us from the shelter of little copses, but only one of the gentlemen was ever unwise enough to approach us. He rode right up to us, we having drawn rein in the most courteous fashion to await his arrival, despite the fact that he wore a mask over his face, and to my surprise, and annoyance, produced a pistol, which he levelled, not at me, but at Marguerite. Apparently this was the accepted procedure, the theory being that any gentleman would hand over all of his valuables without hesitation once his lady was in danger.

Unfortunately for this lout I have never been a gentleman; equally, Marguerite had never been a lady. While she gave a little shriek and appeared to swoon in the saddle her fluttering hands sought to discover a pistol of her own secreted in her wrap: we were, after all, both agents of Richelieu. I whipped my own horse pistol from its holster, and levelled it in turn. "I shall kill your doxy," the fellow spluttered.

"If you do that, be sure I shall kill you," I pointed out. "However, if you drop your weapon, I will permit you to withdraw, unharmed."

It took but a moment's reflection to convince the rascal that that was the best bargain he was likely to get. He dropped his pistol. "Now get you gone," I told him.

He wheeled his horse. "Not so fast," Marguerite remarked, now drawing her own pistol and shooting him in the back. He gave a great cry and tumbled from the saddle, hitting the ground like a sack of coal. I dismounted immediately, but I had seen enough men killed to know that he had been dead before he had ever reached the ground; Marguerite had shot him at a range of only a few feet, and there was a huge hole in his body, through which blood was pouring as wine from a burst barrel.

"I had given him his life," I pointed out.

"Ha!" Marguerite commented. "I wonder I do not shoot you as well, you ill-favoured lout."

"Simply because, if you did that, I would break every bone in your body before I died," I told her. She digested this, while I remounted and we made off. By the time we reached London she was again in a good humour, and we were not again troubled.

In London we fetched up at an inn, and as soon as we were settled Marguerite went off to procure some money. She forbade me to accompany her, and in truth I had no desire to do so; I had no inclination to know more about Richelieu's arrangements than was necessary, and it was far too early to expect any communication from my dearest Helga. I thus spent the afternoon relaxing with a few jugs of ale while I awaited my mistress's return, which took place towards dusk, when to my consternation I saw that she was not alone, but accompanied by half a dozen lads, each carrying two boxes. "Well," she remarked in response to my look, "I can hardly go to meet the Queen without some new clothes."

I reflected that it was she who was going to have to make an financial accounting of our business to the Cardinal. My sole concern was how long it was going to take her to achieve the finery she sought. And next morning, to be sure, a seamstress arrived and got to work, measuring and making notes, while Marguerite stood in the centre of the room in *déshabillé*.

This was attractive enough to look at, but I had not come to London to look at Marguerite. "The dress will take three days," the beldam assured me.

"Three days," I muttered.

"What is your great haste?" Marguerite demanded. "Let us enjoy ourselves."

I am always willing to enjoy myself, where this can be done without inconvenience. Nor, as I have mentioned, was I at all concerned about spending the Cardinal's money. But I *was* concerned about completing at least the first part of our task, getting ourselves into the Queen's employ, as rapidly as possible, for two reasons. In the first place, there was this Great Remonstrance and the possible events which might follow its presentation, and in the second place, Marguerite had a deplorable habit of forgetting to speak English when addressing me. I would be the first to admit that French is the most beautiful of tongues, but I had already discerned that there was a distinctly anti-Gallic mood running through the country, and this was more pronounced in London than even in East Anglia. Our landlord and his cronies commenced giving us sidelong glances and muttering into their tankards, and I could see a crisis looming.

However, Marguerite would not be moved in her intention of appearing at her very best when meeting the Queen, and so I decided at least to reconnoitre the palace and our means of access, and if possible, to proceed on my own. This was clearly going to be a difficult business. The Palace of Whitehall is a rather sombre-looking building situated outside of the walls of the City itself, and hard by the River Thames, which serves it as a thoroughfare, as indeed it does for the City and the adjacent village of Westminster, whenever the roads are too bad for coaches. I approached on foot and to the landward side, through an avenue of rather fine trees, but was prevented from actually entering the gates by a guard of pikemen, who wore scarlet tunics and flat black hats, and clearly took themselves very seriously. They could, of course, see that I was a person of distinction from my clothes, for I was wearing my best yellow tunic and red breeches, but explained that no one could enter the palace without the express permission of the Lord Chancellor. "These are troubled times," their sergeant informed me.

Well, having just walked through the city, I could have told *him* that; never had I heard such revolutionary mutterings as from the apprentices who roamed the street, or even amongst the women. "I seek an audience with Her Majesty," I said.

"You aim too high, sir," he admonished. "In any event, no one may enter the palace without the permission of the King, the Queen, or the Lord Chancellor."

"Then let me send a message to Her Majesty."

"A message, sirrah! Do you suppose Her Majesty is in the habit of receiving messages from all and sundry?"

"I do assure you that she will receive this one," I told him. "I have written it out for you."

I handed him the piece of paper on which I had inscribed Richelieu's words.

The rascal scanned it. "This is in French'"

"Well, of course it is in French, as it is addressed to a

45

French princess. Have you anything against the French?" It had occurred to me that if he was determined to be recalcitrant, one way of gaining entry would be to get myself arrested, which could easily be accomplished by breaking this fellow's head.

"No, no, indeed not," he protested, adding somewhat enigmatically, "Not if it involves Her Majesty."

I returned to Plan A, and gave him a golden sovereign I had extracted from Marguerite's satchel when she was being measured for her new gown. "This is for you," I told him. "Deliver that message for me, and there will be another."

His eyes nearly popped out of his head. "I doubt it can be done for several hours."

"Then you had best commence as soon as possible. I shall return tomorrow."

I was well satisfied with my day's work, and when Marguerite inquired as to where I had been I told her that I had merely walked through the city. She of course was not ready the next day, but I considered this all to the good, and so set off as early as was reasonable. Sadly, it was not early enough. The streets were crowded with people, all reading what appeared to be a pamphlet, and I discovered that the villain Pym had circumvented the difficult business of attempting to present his Great Remonstrance to the King by the far more simple method of having it printed and presenting it to the people. On every street corner there were these knots of men and women carefully perusing the broadsheet which contained the Commons' grievances, and I quickly understood that it represented the people's grievances as well, certainly in London. I quickened my steps, and found the guards on the palace gates redoubled. When I asked for my sergeant, I was asked in turn if I was for King or Parliament.

"I am for King and Queen and Country," I replied, which gave them pause for thought, but before they could come to a decision, my acquaintance had arrived.

"I know this fellow," he said. "He is a faithful servant of

46

Her Majesty." He drew me through the hastily opened gates, which were just as hastily closed again behind me, something of a crowd having gathered. "Have you the other coin?" he whispered.

I showed it to him, but withdrew it again when he would have reached for it. "After I have seen the Queen," I reminded him. "Did you deliver my message?"

"I had it delivered," he said.

"And?"

"Her Majesty will receive you." He seemed surprised by this development, but to say truth, so was I. But greatly relieved, as well.

He made some explanation to his fellows, and then took me to a side door into the palace. We entered, and proceeded along a dark and dismal corridor, so that I loosened my sword in my scabbard, supposing that I might be being led into a trap and that some upstart nobleman might be thinking of advancing himself by arresting me and questioning me as to my antecedents.

However, I was again pleasantly surprised, for at the end of the corridor a door was opened for us, and I found myself in an ante-chamber, and in the presence of a pretty young woman, dark-haired but voluptuous. There were no Puritan smocks to be seen here, but instead a deep blue gown with a rose madder underskirt, with a white collar plunging into a most delightful décolletage – she was trembling with delicious excitement. No doubt she had never seen a man as large as myself, and was thus considering other possible aspects of my size, as women are wont to do. "Captain L'Eree?" she asked in French.

"I have that honour, mademoiselle." One should always assume that's one acquaintances are virgins, unless they are clearly elderly, when to make such an assumption might be an insult. "And yourself?"

"My name is Aimée," she said, with a becoming blush, which, as she was giving me a brief curtsey at the time, I could see extended all the way down to her navel. An entrancing sight. "That will be all, sergeant," she added.

47

Somewhat reluctantly, the sergeant left us. "You have a message?" Aimée inquired.

"For Her Majesty," I said.

She regarded me for a few seconds, then said, "You will come with me, please."

"My pleasure," I told her, entirely honestly, while I considered who the message she had been expecting could have been from, as she had certainly not expected *me*.

She led me across the room, through an inner door, and on to a flight of stairs, mounting in front of me, all rustling skirt and swaying hips. "You are from the Cardinal?" she asked over her shoulder.

"Who I am from is for the ears of Her Majesty," I pointed out.

"Ooh, la-la," she remarked, a trifle disdainfully, and opened a door at the top of the stairs, ushering me into a large, richly-furnished chamber. It was filled with ladies, all, from their dress, of the court party, as was to be expected, as well as two black-robed priests. Two young fellows sat against the far wall strumming lutes, and half-a-dozen dogs of a variety I had not seen before, all big ears, fur, and flopping tails yapped amongst the assembly. But I had eyes only for the woman who waited in the centre of the room.

Henrietta Maria was, at this moment of our first meeting, just thirty-two years old. I knew her background, of course: in many ways it was a tragic one. She was the youngest daughter of the great King Henry IV of France, and the infamous Marie de Médicis, and was thus, as has been related, the sister of the reigning French monarch. However, she had been only six months old when her father had been cut down by an assassin's bullet, and no more than seven when her meddling mother was banished from the French court. At fifteen she was married to Charles of England. This was really a terrible business for a young girl. She could not help but be aware that she was very much a second choice, following the breakdown of the King's negotiations for a Spanish marriage. Equally, she arrived in England within a few weeks of her husband actually becoming King, following the unexpected death of his idiot father, and walked into a court dominated by the late king's favourite, George Villiers, Duke of Buckingham. I am not for a moment suggesting that Charles had any of his father's irregular tastes. Indeed, he seems to have lacked any sexual tastes whatsoever, save for the most orthodox and necessary: I have never even heard the suggestion that he ever had a mistress – a lack which has been more than adjusted by his two surviving sons. However, being an uncertain fellow, he continued Buckingham in his position of chief minister and best friend.

Buckingham himself can best be described as an ambidextrous fellow. He certainly accepted King James' caresses, understanding that this was the way of advancement. But he also had an eye for the ladies, and is reputed to have had an affair with the Queen of France, no less. But this did not make him any the more receptive to Anne of Austria's sister-in-law. In the first place, Anne was herself actually a Spaniard, and had Charles', and Buckingham's, original plan worked, the English queen would have been her sister. In the second place, Anne, whether responsible or not, had certainly been involved in the expulsion of her mother-in-law and Henrietta Maria from the French court, and it may therefore be taken for granted that the two women cordially loathed each other.

To be fair, Buckingham had had certain positive grounds for disliking the Queen. Henrietta may only have been fifteen when she arrived in England, but she was every inch Marie de Médicis' daughter. She travelled with her priests and confessors, as well as her French ladies, and made it perfectly clear that she intended to continue the practice of her religion, despite the understood fact that in England Roman Catholics were regarded as criminals, a national mistrust which since the laudable attempt of a band of Catholics to blow up King James – it unfortunately did not come off – had grown into a national phobia. Worse yet, she refused to attend the King's coronation, or to be crowned herself, because either would have involved

49

a Protestant religious ceremony. Such a refusal had never been known before.

But Henrietta was not a woman to be browbeaten, and Charles was not the man to browbeat. Thus, as I was now observing, sixteen years after their marriage, the Queen still lived as if she were in a French court. This obstinate determination to be her own woman had not endeared her either to her husband's courtiers, or his subjects. As regards the courtiers, her position had improved immeasurably over the years. She had enjoyed the great relief of Buckingham's assassination only three years after her marriage, since when Charles, who ever needed an intimate to lean upon and could not find a male replacement for the Duke, had actually turned to his wife, and was now, by repute and as the Cardinal seemed convinced, deeply in love with her. He was certainly not in love with anybody else, save possibly himself. Her unpopularity with the mob and its representatives, however, had endured and grown, until it had been the head of Strafford, or that of the Queen. Whether he had loved his wife or not, Charles had done the only gentlemanly thing, and undoubtedly she was aware of this. Yet she had changed her way of life not in the least.

She was, every inch a queen. Decidedly diminutive, at least when beheld from my great height, she seemed taller than she was because of her bearing. Her dark hair was worn in the fashionable ringlets of the period. Her features were even enough to be called beautiful, save perhaps for a slight over-largeness of the nose and chin. Her figure was full, as befitted a matron of thirty-two who was several times a mother, but remained attractive; her décolletage was deep. Her hands, one of which she extended for me to kiss, were small and white and well-shaped. "L'Eree," she remarked. "The name has a French ring to it, but it is not one I have heard before." She spoke French.

I knelt, and replied in the same language. "It is a Garnesey name, Your Majesty."

"But you claim to be in Richelieu's employ. Indeed, you know his secret code."

She had spoken in a low tone, but nonetheless I was

uneasy in view of the number of people around us. "He gave it to me himself, Your Majesty," I muttered. "And assured me it was known to you alone."

"Then presumably he has a message of considerable importance to convey to me," she agreed, paying no heed to my plea for caution. "Tell me of it."

"It is for your ears only, Your Majesty."

She regarded me for some seconds, then waved her fan. "Leave us."

"Your Majesty?" Her priests were as scandalised as her ladies, and her lute players ceased their strumming. Even the spaniels seemed concerned.

"I said leave me," Henrietta Maria snapped, her voice becoming uncommonly sharp.

They bowed and withdrew, most reluctantly; the dogs however, remained. "You may leave the door open," the Queen suggested, and smiled at me. "They fear that you may be an assassin."

"Or that I may leap upon you and ravish you, Your Majesty?"

Her smile changed to a frown. "You are very bold, sir."

I have always believed in conquering those I have been called upon to serve. "How may a man be other than bold in the presence of so much beauty, Your Majesty."

Again she considered me for several seconds, before her expression softened. "I must discuss with Richelieu, the quality of his messengers," she remarked. "Rise, and sit. Here."

She patted the sofa, and a moment later I was seated beside a queen. The dogs gurgled a bit, but as I managed to kick one while stretching my legs they slunk off, grumbling.

"You may be sure my people are listening," she said. "So keep your voice low. But do not lean towards me, or that will bring them back. Now tell me what concerns Richelieu?"

"Your safety, Your Majesty." I related what the Cardinal had said to me.

"Bah!" she commented. "No one would dare lay hands on a queen."

"English queens have been executed before, Your Majesty."

"Do you think my Charlie would permit that?"

I preferred not to comment.

She glared at me. "How may a wife abandon her husband?"

"You are surely entitled to leave him for a visit."

"Back to France?" Her face lit up at the prospect.

"Ah ... His Eminence feels that might be unwise, Your Majesty, as he is desirous of maintaining good relations with England. But a visit to Holland..."

"Ha!" she commented. In many ways she reminded me of Marguerite. "And do you suppose these Parliamentary poltroons would permit me to depart the country if they have set their minds on my downfall? The Navy is riddled with sedition."

"Well, as to that, Your Majesty, I suspect it might relieve their minds greatly were you to go freely of your own will. But in any event, you have but to agree to the Cardinal's proposal. Your transference, as well as your safety, will then rest in my care."

She shot me a glance, but it was a soft one. "Would it, L'Eree?"

"I am sworn to defend you to the death, Your Majesty."

"Noble fellow." She rose, and took a turn around the room, all rustling silk. "What the Cardinal wishes is impossible. How may a wife desert her husband, a mother her children, a queen her country? Once I left, would I ever be able to return?" She checked her perambulation. "Would I be able to take my children with me?" Indicating that, like all women, she was quite capable of making a definite statement in one direction while considering a totally opposite line of action.

"We would have to go into details when you have signified your wish to comply with the Cardinal's plan, Your Majesty."

"Ha!" she commented. "I will have to think on it, L'Eree."

"Of course, Your Majesty. But I would but urge you not

52

to take too long over your consideration. There are crowds in the street, speaking treason."

"Is that supposed to alarm me? There are always crowds in those streets, speaking treason."

"I think this is more serious than usual, Your Majesty. Have you heard of the Great Remonstrance?"

"What is that?"

"It is a paper, Your Majesty, being circulated throughout London Town today, throughout the country tomorrow. I recommend that you obtain a copy, and peruse it."

"No doubt it will be shown to the King?"

"And he will refuse to accept it. Then, Your Majesty, I do fear for the future."

"We shall see. Now what of you?"

"My place is by your side."

She raised her eyebrows.

"I meant, as commander of your personal guard."

"I do not have a personal guard."

"Well, then, Your Majesty, permit me to fill that lack."

She came back to sit beside me, and pinched her lip. "You are a most *uncommonly* bold fellow," she murmured.

"I but seek to serve, Your Majesty."

"I can see that. I will have to discuss the situation with the King. Return here tomorrow. Meanwhile ... fetch me yonder box." She pointed, and I hurried across the room to the table she had indicated, returning with an ornate lacquered box. This she took from me, allowing her fingers to brush mine, opened it, and took out a most splendid emerald ring. "This is for your troubles."

"You are too kind, Your Majesty."

"Go now. Aimée!" she called.

The pretty girl hurried in, cheeks pink.

"Aimée will escort you," Henrietta said.

"There is but one thing more, Your Majesty," I said.

She gave me one of her old-fashioned looks.

"I have a companion in this mission," I explained.

"Indeed?" Now she was interested. "Is he of your calibre, L'Eree?"

"He happens to be a woman, Your Majesty."

"A woman?"

"My wife, Your Majesty," I said carefully.

"You take your wife on missions of this nature?" She was sounding thoroughly put out.

"Ah ... " I decided to dissemble. "The lady is an agent of the Cardinal, as am I. Our marriage is purely a convenience. His Eminence felt that for so delicate a mission it were best I be accompanied by a woman. I may say that she is as capable of protecting you as I am myself, and may be perhaps of more ... use?"

"I see. This 'wife', is she pretty?"

"Some would say so, Your Majesty," I said, as deprecatingly as I could.

'Well, well. In that case, bring her with you, tomorrow, that I may inspect her. Good day to you, L'Eree."

I bowed as low as I might, and followed Aimée back down the stairs and the various corridors. "You have pleased my mistress," the young woman remarked.

"What makes you suppose that?"

"Why, we were watching through the doorway. We could tell."

"Then I can tell you that I have some hopes Her Majesty may find me a position."

"That would be capital," she said. "What position did you have in mind?"

"That is for Her Majesty to say."

"She is not as other women," Aimée pointed out.

"I never supposed she was."

"However, I will wish you good fortune." We had reached the outer doorway. "Until tomorrow."

I kissed her fingers, reflecting that if all went according to plan, I might well have my hands full in the not too distant future, quite literally.

"You saw the Queen?" Marguerite demanded, hands on hips and positively swelling with annoyance, which, as she was wearing only her shift, did not cause me any immediate distress. "You went, without me? That is a direct contravention of our instructions from His Eminence."

54

"On the contrary, my sweet," I replied. "Our instructions from the Cardinal were to act with all haste. He said nothing about waiting for gowns to be made."

"I know you for a rogue, Helier L'Eree," she told me. "You are planning to desert me. Be sure the Cardinal shall know of it."

"My dear girl," I said. "Desert you? I have praised you to Her Majesty, and she wishes to see you. Tomorrow."

"*Ooh, la-la!* But my gown will not be ready."

"Then you will just have to wear an old one. Her Majesty is interested in you, not your clothes."

Thus we attended the palace, to find matters had deteriorated overnight. The Great Remonstrance had indeed found its way to the King, and all Whitehall was a matter of whispering consultations, angry denunciations and trembling expressions of fear. I was as before greeted by Aimée, who regarded the cloaked and hooded figure of Marguerite with some amusement. "Does she suffer from an ailment?" she inquired.

"She is nervous in these surroundings," I explained, forgetting for the moment that Marguerite also spoke French.

"I am not the least nervous," she declared, tossing the hood from her head.

The two women regarded each other with undisguised hostility. "Richelieu's creature, in faith," Aimée remarked.

"Who is this person?" Marguerite demanded.

"One of Her Majesty's ladies," I explained.

"Is that so. Well, would you inform her that I am the Countess D'Albret, and expect to be addressed as such."

Aimée gave a somewhat contemptuous curtsey, which reminded me that she need fear comparison with Marguerite in no direction save that of rank. "Then, welcome to Whitehall, milady."

We were taken up to the Queen's apartment, but she was not there. She was attending the King, who with his ministers was in a fine to-do about this latest misbehaviour of the

Commons. Opinion seemed undecided between ignoring it in the hopes that it would go away, or issuing warrants for the arrest of various members of Parliament. Her Majesty was taking a vigorous part in the debate, on the side of dealing harshly with the villains, but unfortunately not all the courtiers were fluent in French and she had steadfastly refused to learn more than a word or two of English, so the whole business was somewhat confused.

Word was got to her, however, that Captain L'Eree and his wife were in attendance, and a few minutes later both King and Queen had withdrawn to an antechamber, and there Marguerite and I were presented to the King of England.

CHAPTER 3

I have already said enough about King Charles I to indicate that I did not hold him in very great esteem. But this opinion was of course based upon hearsay and my own considerable reading on the subject. It is always a different business when one meets someone in the flesh, especially if that someone happens to be a king. I am no believer in the Divine Right as claimed by the Stuarts. I have rubbed shoulders with too many kings and princes, queens and princesses, to hold them in any great awe as human beings. Yet it cannot be denied that there is an aura about such beings which seems to raise them above their fellows.

If I should be required to sum up the King of England in a single word, I would choose 'delicate'. This may seem an odd description of a ruler who made war upon his own people – 'that man of blood', as my friend Oliver later called him – but as I have indicated, this was an inherited trait. At this moment I gazed upon a somewhat small man – all men are small when compared with myself, but Charles was both short and slender – handsome enough with his neatly trimmed beard, a trifle sharp of nose and chin, but this he shared with his queen, thin-lipped and nervously twitchy of movement, and, well, generally delicate of appearance. "C-c-captain L'Eree," he said. "My wife speaks well of you." That he stammered did nothing to enhance his stature.

"Her Majesty flatters me, Your Majesty," I protested, wishing I knew in which regard Henrietta had spoken of me at all.

"These are t-t-troublous t-t-times," the King informed me. 'B-b-but it is g-g-good to know that our G-g-garnesey subjects have our welfare so much at heart that they will t-t-travel so far to b-b-be of service. And t-t-to have brought your good lady with you, that p-p-pleases me. Nothing p-p-pleases me so much as domestic b-b-bliss."

Marguerite and I exchanged glances. She of course had not even had the pleasure of meeting the Queen as yet, and was totally consternated by the whole business.

"You may b-b-be sure that we g-g-gratefully accept your wish to serve," Charles continued. "I have no d-d-doubt that there will be objections, but these p-p-people object to everything. And should a k-k-king not order his own household? You, C-c-captain L'Eree, will as of now be Her Majesty's p-p-personal b-b-bodyguard, whenever she goes abroad."

Henrietta smiled at me, and I bowed in return.

"You, M-m-madame L'Eree, are appointed to Her M-m-majesty's b-b-bedchamber." Marguerite looked even more astounded. Having said this, the King took a pinch of snuff, and Henrietta gave a quick nod to indicate that we should withdraw.

"What is this all about?" Marguerite demanded when we were alone, except for the ever-present Aimée. "I am to be a maidservant, with not even my title recognised?"

"Hard times," Aimée said, shaking her pretty curls.

Marguerite shot her a glance which could have injured her for life.

"My sweet," I said, as placatingly as I could. "Many ladies would give their all to achieve such a position. And in any event," I continued, pressing home the advantage I could see I had gained. "It will only be for a short while, until we can get the Queen safely out of England."

In this hopeful prognostication, I was incorrect, as it turned out. Henrietta Maria joined us soon enough, and dismissed her attendants for a *tête-à-tête*, this being of less concern to her people than on the occasion of our first meeting, because of the presence of my 'wife'. "That went off very well," the Queen said.

"Indeed, Your Majesty," I agreed. "His Majesty was

most gracious. May I inquire as to his reaction to your news?"

"What news?"

"Why, that you intend to have a holiday in Holland, Your Majesty."

"I have told you, L'Eree, that such a step is impossible to take at this time."

"But, Your Majesty," I protested.

"There can be no argument about the matter, L'Eree," she told me. "It would be impossible in any event, but at this moment it is more impossible than ever. There is a crisis afoot. Did you not know this?"

"I told you of it, Your Majesty."

"Well, then, do you not see that His Majesty needs all the stiffening that can be provided? And who, do you suppose, is going to do that, save myself?"

"Then I have failed in my mission."

"On the contrary. You will remain here with me, and be my personal bodyguard, as the King has decreed, only inside the palace as well as outside. And your wife," she smiled at Marguerite, "shall be at my side as required. It will all work out very well."

"I am sure it will, Your Majesty," I said, somewhat uncertainly. It had not been my intention to spend any longer than was necessary in England.

Henrietta Maria could tell that I was not entirely happy with the situation. "Do not fret," she told me. "I will write to Richelieu and tell him of my decision regarding both his plan and yourselves. He will not in any way blame you."

"Thank you, Your Majesty," I said. "But may I ask for how long you wish to employ us?"

"Why, for as long as the crisis lasts."

My poor Helga! But I felt it would ruin my reputation with the Queen were I now to reveal to her that the business of my being married to Marguerite was pure subterfuge.

But Marguerite was by now becoming agitated. "You mean we must remain in this benighted country indefinitely?"

"It will not be for so very long," Henrietta assured us.

"The crisis will end as soon as His Majesty has sorted out this Great Remonstrance."

"May I inquire exactly what he intends to do about it, Your Majesty?"

"Well, as to that, there are several options open, as I am sure you know. But only one will truly settle the matter. Pym, and Hampden and the other three who have appended their names to this pernicious document are guilty of *lèse-majesté* at the very least. But I am sure we can make a charge of treason stick. Then it will be off with their heads." She gave a pretty laugh. "And various other portions of their body as well. I look forward to it."

As we do not have treason trials in Garnesey I had never seen a man hanged, drawn and quartered, but I could well understand that for females with not enough to do to amuse themselves the sight of a man, half dead from being half hanged but still aware of what was happening to him, being castrated before having his head chopped off and his body then dismembered, must be an exciting one. And while my own blood curdled at the thought, and especially that it should happen to a man with whom I had broken bread, I was still more concerned with my own fortune than theirs. "A warrant has been issued for their arrest, Your Majesty?" I asked.

"Well, no, not as yet."

"Ah. But this will happen soon?"

"You are impatient, L'Eree. It cannot happen, yet, simply because all the rascals have gone to their homes for Christmas. It is considered unwise to chase them in five different directions. But directly Christmas and the New Year have come and gone, they will all return to London, and at that time they will all be arrested."

"His Majesty has made this decision?" I pressed.

She glared at me. "He will make it, L'Eree, when the time is right. Now get you about your duties."

I perceived that she was going to be a difficult mistress, although she could never be so difficult as my actual mistress, who became more shrewish with every moment she

60

was required to act the part of my wife. Marguerite undoubtedly liked the sensation of nestling in my arms, and even more of being pierced by my lance, but she did not enjoy the situation of being plain Mrs L'Eree, and having to attend to such matters as my laundry as well as my food when I was off duty. "Be sure I shall make a full report of this to His Eminence," she warned me.

"You are welcome to do so," I said, for I was in the best of humours, having at last received the letter I sought from Helga.

Marguerite of course was both annoyed that I should have received a letter from Garnesey – as she had to collect it from the Cardinal's agent – and that it should be from my wife. Even more was she annoyed that I would not divulge its contents to her. But Helga's words were a great relief to me. While she was distressed that my return had been delayed because of a business matter, she thanked me for the handsome remittance she had received, and informed me further that Master Ogier had told her that the matter of my indebtedness could certainly wait until my return. Thus Richelieu was keeping his end of the bargain, as I had never doubted he would. For all of his continued double-dealing in affairs of state, the Cardinal always dealt fairly with those he employed, providing only they did not attempt any double-dealing themselves. In this regard I could only hope that he would be convinced by Henrietta's letter that I had done all I could to get her out of England, and was continuing to do so.

In the meantime, I was privileged to enjoy the Christmas festivities at Hampton Court with the royal family. This was an intensely happy occasion – the last one for a good many years, although none of us suspected it at the time. In addition to the King and Queen, there were the royal children, who at this time numbered five. The royal couple's eldest son had died after only two hours, but romping around the palace now were Prince Charles, aged eleven, a well-built, lusty lad; Princess Mary, aged ten, altogether more serious in character; Prince James, aged eight, a sly-looking fellow; Princess Elizabeth, aged four;

and Prince Henry, who was a babe in arms, less than a year, and was still at the breast, no longer of the Queen, but attached to a wetnurse.

Prince Henry was of course too small to take any part in the revels save by bellowing as loudly as he could, but for the rest it was a continual round of Blind-man's-bluff and Ring-a-ring-a roses and Pinch-me-quick, in which the numerous royal dogs played a full part, interspersed with long hours of eating and drinking, as if this family had not a care in the world, and certainly no knowledge of dark-visaged men who might be gathering in lonely farmhouses plotting their downfall. Or planning to abandon England together, as no doubt my friend Oliver would do when his cousin was arrested.

In addition to the family amusements, there were elaborate masques performed by various groups of players, all of whom appeared to be well acquainted with Her Majesty – she was passionately fond of this sort of entertainment – and solemn prayers, which from time to time partook of a very Roman Catholic flavour.

There were a considerable number of courtiers present at this long drawn out affair. While some were serious fellows, who stood to one side and pinched their lips while they conversed in undertones, others were somewhat censorious-looking churchmen. I was astounded to discover that the main part of the guests were utterly empty-headed fellows, quite a few of them old enough to have known better, who got down on their hands and knees with the children and barked like dogs when they were not giggling foolishly. Clearly all of these absurdities were desperately in love with their queen, and indeed Henrietta Maria, all flushed cheeks and heaving breasts, presented a most attractive sight.

As did her ladies, who, together with the wives of the guests, were also required to take part in these ridiculous games. Her ladies of course included Marguerite and Aimée, and I watched with indulgence as these delightful creatures were pushed and pummelled and squeezed and caressed by all and sundry as they romped. Sadly I, as the captain of the guard, was not included in the revelry, but I did not entirely miss out. Not only was I wined and fed as the best of them, but on more than one occasion Aimée managed to find herself alone with me in the corridor, where we could indulge in our own variety of Blind-man's-bluff, while I shall never forget when, on New Year's Eve, the Queen herself, before retiring – it was now well into New Year's Day – put her arms round me and kissed me most firmly on the lips. "Oh, L'Eree," she said. "I am so happy."

Happiness is ever a transient business. Three days later, just after we had returned to Whitehall, we received news that the members of Parliament had returned also to London, and had forthwith taken their places in the House.

Her Majesty was at breakfast, served by Aimée and Marguerite, with myself standing attentively by the door, when the King entered. Charles alone of all the royal party had not seemed to enjoy himself over Christmas. He had played in the games, certainly, had allowed himself to be blindfolded and pushed about by his squealing children and his wife's no less squealing ladies, but his smile had been forced, and when not in action, as it were, his face was sombre. He at least had no doubts about the crisis he would soon have to face. Now he looked positively terrified.

Henrietta, on the other hand, remained serenely beautiful, as she listened to what he had to say. "Are all five of them back?" she inquired. "You have no doubt of this?"

"None," the King replied.

"Then have the warrants issued now."

"The warrants have been issued. I have them here."

In truth he was carrying a sheaf of papers in his hand.

"Well, then . . ."

"They have already been served. B-b-by Attorney-General Herbert."

"That is brilliant," the Queen said. "Where are these scoundrels? I wish to see them for myself."

"They are not in c-c-custody."

"What did you say?"

63

"The C-c-commons refused to give them up."

"Then they are all outlaws. Imprison the lot."

"Herbert informs me that if he attempts to enforce these warrants he will be t-t-torn to p-p-pieces."

Henrietta stood up, her good humour quite vanished. "I have never heard such nonsense. Are you to be defied at every turn? Are you King of this land? Or some lackey of the mob? You must show those villains once and for all who is master." She pointed. "You will go yourself, my love. Take your own guards, go to the House, and place those men under arrest." The King gulped. "L'Eree will go with you. Is that not so, L'Eree?"

I did some gulping of my own. I fear no man in the world, should he face me sword in hand. But a mob?

The same thought had occurred to Marguerite, who gave a pretty little shriek and collapsed on the floor. "Oh, really," Henrietta snapped. "Remove that weeping weakling." I hurried forward. "Not you," the Queen said. "Aimée, fetch help."

But Marguerite had by now recovered, not having actually fainted at all; such play-acting was a habit of hers in time of stress. "Well?" the Queen demanded of her husband.

"Ah," the King said. "Well . . . I will have to consider the matter. Perhaps tomorrow."

"May God give me patience," the Queen moaned.

But there it was. Charles wished to consult various people. We spent an anxious day, and an even more anxious night, as Marguerite was concerned. "What shall I do when you are dead?" she inquired, nestling against me in the comfort of our bed to make sure that at that moment, at the least, I was still very much alive.

"Why, return to France," I suggested. "Only be sure to tell the Cardinal that I died in pursuance of my duty to him."

"I shall do that, Helier," she promised. "But Helier, oh Helier . . ."

All in all I did not get to sleep until the small hours, and then was most rudely awakened, and by the Queen herself, standing in the doorway of our small bedchamber, fully dressed, and looking most aggressive. "Do you not realise it is an hour past dawn?" she demanded.

I leapt out of bed, and then leapt back in again, somewhat embarrassed. "Oh, tush," she remarked. "Do you suppose you are the first naked man I have seen? I am a wife and mother. Get up."

Well, obviously, as presumably the only naked man she had previously seen would have been Charles himself, she wished to take a closer look at someone who was better endowed in every way. I obeyed, while Marguerite was by now also sitting up, thrusting her hands into her tousled hair.

"Yes, indeed," Henrietta remarked, apparently to herself. "Get yourself dressed, L'Eree, and accompany me to His Majesty." With that she withdrew, a trifle reluctantly, I felt.

"You go to your death," Marguerite moaned.

"Nonsense," I told her, with more confidence than I felt. And fifteen minutes later I was hurrying behind the Queen to the King's apartments, while guards stood to attention.

Henrietta entered without so much as a knock, throwing the doors wide, and causing Charles, and his attendants, for he was just getting washed and dressed, some alarm. "It is time," the Queen announced.

"Ah," said the King. "Yes. Well, obviously, there are things to b-b-be done."

"What things?" inquired his wife.

"Well, I needs must summon the guard..."

Henrietta marched across the room and threw open the window, not the wisest of things to do in early January, as the room was immediately invaded by an icy blast.

"There is your guard, waiting for you," she announced.

The King went to the window, already shivering. "B-b-bless my soul."

"I had them summoned, an hour ago. Now, Captain L'Eree is here to march at your side."

"Well," the King said. "There are still things to be done, you know, my sweet. There is..."

The Queen slammed the window shut, to my great relief, as I was also beginning to tremble. But now she pointed at the door. She had of course been speaking French from the start, but I cannot convey the heat of the moment without now myself using the Gallic tongue. "*Allons, poltroon!*" is what she said to her lord and master.

We went. I do not suppose there is a man in the world could have looked his wife in the eye after such a command. On the way we accumulated the Prince of Wales, looking very martial and determined. "I will go with you, Father," the stout lad declared.

I was all against this idea. To lose a king to the mob might be a misfortune; to lose a king and his son and heir to the same mob on the same day might well be called carelessness. But Charles seemed delighted to have his son at his side; no doubt he felt that not even a mob would attack an eleven-year-old boy. At this stage of his life, of course, the King had no proper acquaintance with mobs.

We tramped out of Whitehall and down to the village of Westminster. There was no attempt to block our passage to the Parliament Building, although there were sufficient people about. These were indeed gathering all the while, and I, marching beside the King's carriage, perceived that we might have some trouble in regaining the palace.

But we reached the Parliament without mishap, and I threw the doors wide to allow the King and the Prince to enter, while the musketeers filed to either side. The MPs gazed at us, but again in less consternation than I had anticipated, and it began to dawn on me that we were expected.

Yet we were most courteously received. The members rose as one, and doffed their hats, and the Speaker bowed.

For a moment there was a deadly hush, for of course no one knew quite how to proceed, as it was unheard of for the King to visit the Commons in their chamber unless invited to do so. I began to fear that the whole affair was going to end in an acute embarrassment, and did not know how we could possibly face the Queen upon our return to White-

66

hall, when the King seemed to gather himself together, and spoke. "B-b-by your leave, Mr Speaker," he said. "I must b-b-borrow your chair a little."

The Speaker, Lenthall, hastily stepped down, and indeed dropped to his knees, while the King took his place, and the musketeers and myself filed to either side. This unheard of action caused a good deal of rustling and murmuring from the members.

Having seated himself, the King addressed the House; he had prepared a very pretty little speech. "Gentlemen, I am sorry for this occasion of c-c-coming unto you. Yesterday I sent a sergeant-at-arms to apprehend some, that at my c-c-command were accused of high t-t-treason, wherewith I did expect obedience, and not a message; and I must d-d-declare unto you here, that albeit no k-k-king that ever was in England, shall be more c-c-careful of your p-p-privileges, to maintain them to the utmost of his p-p-power, than I shall be; yet you must know that in cases of t-t-treason no person hath a p-p-privilege, and therefore I am c-c-come to know if any of those p-p-persons I have accused, of no slight c-c-crime, b-b-but for treason, are here. I c-c-cannot expect that this house c-c-can be in the right way that I d-d-do heartily wish it, therefore I am c-c-come to tell you that I must have them, wheresoever I find them."

"With respect, Your Majesty," said the Speaker, "Members of Parliament are above the law, when in this House."

"Save in m-m-matters of t-t-treason," the King argued. "The charges against these five m-m-members are of such a nature. Stand forth, Master P-P-Pym."

Silence.

"Master Pym," commanded the Speaker.

"Master Pym has gone hence," someone said.

"Very well," the King said. "Stand forth, Master Hampden."

Silence.

"Master Hampden," commanded the Speaker.

"Master Hampden has gone hence," said another voice.

"Very well," the King said. "Stand forth Master Haselrig."

Silence.

"Master Haselrig," commanded the Speaker.

"Master Haselrig has gone hence," said a third voice.

"Very well," said the King. "Stand forth Master Holles."

Silence.

"Stand forth, Master Holles," said the Speaker.

"Master Holles has gone hence," said a fourth voice.

"Very well," said the King. "Stand forth Master Strode."

Silence.

"Stand forth, Master Strode," said the Speaker.

"Master Strode has gone hence," said a fifth voice.

Silence.

The King looked over the ranks of his opponents, then said, "Well, since I see all the b-b-birds are flown, I do expect that as soon as they return hither, you do send them to me."

Following which, he rose and marched back out of the House. His guards could do nothing more than follow him. Behind us there came shouts of "Privilege! Privilege!"

To my mind the most difficult part of the manoeuvre was now beginning; we had to proceed through a very large crowd, having clearly failed in our task. But of course the Londoners had known from the beginning that we would fail. Now, instead of the stones and curses I had anticipated, they merely followed their MP's in shouting, "Privilege!" That they were hostile could not be doubted. But the King was still the King, and they waited for some sign from him, before initiating action themselves.

Thus we returned to Whitehall.

The King was obviously sorely embarrassed, as well he might be. His reputation had dwindled steadily throughout his reign, but he had remained always the King, and was thus to be feared. Now his authority had been entirely set aside. Additionally, there was the Queen to be faced.

Charles did not appear anxious to face her. We dismissed the troops, and then entered the palace by a side door. However, Henrietta had clearly been watching from a window, and we had hardly regained the King's apartment than we heard her feet on the parquet, accompanied by an immense rustling of skirts, as she marched into our presence, followed by several of her ladies, amongst them, of course, both Marguerite and Aimée. "Well?" the Queen demanded.

"We have b-b-been b-b-betrayed," the King said.

"Are those villains under arrest?"

"We have b-b-been b-b-betrayed," the King repeated. "They were warned. They have fled."

"Fled where?"

"I suspect they are in the city. They cannot have gone far."

"Then they can still be arrested. They *must* be arrested."

"Do you expect me to invade London? I have less than a thousand men. Besides, it would be to start a civil war."

The Queen flung out her hand. "And do you not suppose *they* are going to start a civil war? They have already done so. It may not be a war fought with swords and bullets. That is up to you. But if you do not assert yourself they will dictate peace terms, *their* peace terms, here in this palace. You will become a figurehead. And I ... I will be at the mercy of the mob."

Charles raised his head, wearily. "What am I to do?"

"Show them who is the King! Show them who is their master!"

"They will respect only force," remarked the Earl of Newcastle. Several lords had hurried to be present at this impromptu council of war.

"And we have no force," Charles muttered.

"Then *get* force," Henrietta shouted. "Summon an army. Parliament cannot do that. Only a king may summon an army."

"Armies have to be paid," someone in the background muttered. His name was Edward Hyde, and he was one of the royal secretaries.

69

"If we start to raise an army here at Whitehall, we shall be at the mercy of the mob before it can be assembled," said the Earl of Lindsey, more to the immediate point.

"The mob?" Henrietta demanded contemptuously.

"The London trained bands are a formidable force of militia, Your Majesty."

"Trained bands," Henrietta commented, more contemptuously yet.

"It might be possible to raise an army, were we out of London," said Sir Ralph Hopton.

"And it might be a good idea to leave London, in any event," suggested Lord Goring.

"You mean to flee from these shopkeepers?" Henrietta demanded.

"In order to protect your person, Your Majesty."

"And to be able to pursue our counter-measures in safety," added Newcastle.

"Armies need to be paid for," repeated Hyde.

"They also need generals," said Lord Goring. "We have none. If Lord Strafford were still alive..."

"Does Parliament have generals?" Henrietta inquired.

"Well, no, Your Majesty, but I am sure they can find some."

"Then cannot we, find some? Or at least, one? You, my lord of Lindsey. You have served on the continent."

"Well, yes, Your Majesty ... " Lindsey was blushing. "But never in command of an army."

"The Scots have a general," said Sir Ralph Hopton. "General Leslie. He commanded an army under Gustavus Adolphus."

"But he is a Scot," said Goring.

"And a Covenanter," growled Lindsey.

"You are all afraid," Henrietta declared. "You merely want to run away."

I perceived that this conversation, which might continue itself in circles for the rest of the day, needed to be taken control of, and, incidentally, could be turned to my advantage. I cleared my throat, a sufficiently loud noise to

70

her to her future husband. And secure his support. P-p-prepare yourself to t-t-take ship."

Even Henrietta bowed before this sudden display of mental vigour. "From which port, my lord?"

Charles looked at me.

"That will be my responsibility, Your Majesty."

"You are a smooth rogue, L'Eree," Henrietta informed me, when we had returned to her apartments.

"A man can only do his duty, Your Majesty."

"The question is, to whom is your duty due? England? Me? Or the Cardinal?"

"I would hope to serve all of you, Your Majesty."

"Ha! Well, as I am committed to it, you had best make the arrangements."

"Right away, Your Majesty," and I hurried Marguerite from the room to our own small chambers.

"You run too fast, L'Eree," she panted. "I am inclined to agree with the Queen."

"I am trying to end our assignment as rapidly as possible," I told her. "Do you leave immediately, go to your agent, and tell him what we require."

"What *do* we require? I obtained money only a few days ago."

I raised my eyes to heaven as I wondered if Richelieu had deliberately landed me with a dimwit.

"The ship, sweet Meg, the ship," I said. "This agent will know where the ship will be. And when. He must tell you this, and you must return here with your knowledge."

"Give me paper and a pencil."

"What for?"

"To write the information you require down, goose."

"For Heaven's sake, woman," I cried. "Under no circumstances are you to write anything down. You must keep it in your head. Surely you can remember a time and a place."

"And a signal," she said. "There will have to be a signal."

73

"Very well, a signal. You can memorise that as well. Now off with you."

"You really should not order me about, Helier," she huffed. "You should always remember that I am a countess where you are a bumpkin. I am only pretending to be your wife."

"Pretending or no, if you do not get about our business I shall take my stick to you," I warned her.

"Ha!" she remarked, but pulled on her cloak. "Sending me out into the cold," she grumbled. "A *man* should undertake such a duty for himself."

"Save that I do not know where to go. Nor should I, or I would then have no use for you whatsoever."

"Ha!" she remarked again, tying her bows while she studied herself in the mirror; one would have thought she was going to a ball. To assist her on her way, I went to the door, and threw it open. There was the most tremendous crash and when I stepped into the corridor I found myself gazing at a prostrate Aimée, all flying skirts and exposed stockings.

Clearly she had been listening. In fact, from the way my abrupt movement had upended her, she must have been pressed against the door in her determination to hear what we were saying. Now she cast me a glance of mingled anger and fear, and attempted to scramble to her feet, but hampered as she was by her skirts I had seized her long before she could make her escape. "Let me go, you foul beast!" she shrieked.

By now Marguerite had arrived on the scene. "Whatever are you doing with that girl, Helier?" she demanded.

"I have done nothing with her yet," I said. "But I am going to tear her into two pieces if she does not tell me what *she* was doing, and why."

At this juncture Aimée attempted to bite me, so successfully that I released her with one hand, but at the same time slapped her across the face with the other, so that she collapsed in a heap on the floor, sobbing. "I always knew you wanted to bed her," Marguerite remarked, as usual missing the point entirely.

"Listen," I said. "Put on your cloak and go and do as I have told you."

"While you ram her?"

"I am going to take the young lady to the Queen," I told her. "Now get on with it."

By now Aimée was making another attempt to get up and sidle off, although her head had to be spinning from my blow; her lip was cut. I seized her again, and to prevent further argument – I could see the teeth marks on my hand – threw her across my shoulder and set off along the corridor.

Our progress towards the Queen's apartment was marked by her shrieks, alternated with curses, not to mention attempted kicks and thumping fists on my back, which caused the various guards and courtiers we passed to look at us askance. However, no one was disposed to argue with the Queen's personal bodyguard, especially when he was manhandling one of the Queen's personal maids, and within a few minutes I was being admitted to Her Majesty's boudoir, where she was seated at her desk writing letters. "L'Eree?" she inquired. "Whatever is the cause of this commotion."

I deposited the shrieking Aimée on the carpet before her. She immediately gained her knees. "He assaulted me, Your Majesty, the foul lecherous beast. He would have his way with me."

"Oh, L'Eree," the Queen commented, reproachfully.

"And being thus overcome with desire, I chose to indulge myself before you, Your Majesty?" I inquired.

"Ah," she agreed. "Then tell me what has happened."

"Privily, Your Majesty."

"Very well. Leave us, ladies."

They had already been twittering. Now the racket grew loud enough to drown even Aimée's laments. "You wish to be left alone, Your Majesty?"

"Yes, that is what I wish."

"With this ... this monster?" Clearly they were preparing to take Aimée's side.

"I said out," Henrietta commanded, her voice getting that bite I had learned to respect. "*Allons, allons, allons!*" They scuttled from the room, muttering and whispering. "And close the door," Henrietta bawled.

The doors were closed, leaving me alone with the Queen and Aimée, and, of course, half a dozen little dogs. "Now tell me what has happened," Henrietta said.

"I found Aimée listening at my door, Your Majesty, attempting to discover the port from which you plan to leave."

"Is this true, Aimée?"

"Of course it is not true, Your Majesty. It is a lie. I was passing in the corridor when this madman threw open his door and leapt upon me."

"And then brought you here?"

Aimée bit her lip.

"I would also suggest, Your Majesty," I said, "that Aimée is the person who betrayed His Majesty's intention of arresting the five conspirators in the Commons. It was known to very few people."

"That is a lie!" Aimée screamed. "A foul lie!"

"Be quiet, girl," Henrietta said, in tones that brooked no argument. "I would have you tell me the truth."

"Your Majesty, I swear..."

"Listen to me, girl," Henrietta said. "If you do not admit all, I will permit Captain L'Eree to have his way with you."

An entrancing thought; I hoped Aimée would be defiant. Nor could I suppose that she would really regard it as a threat, in view of our previous flirtations. "As brutally and cruelly as he may," the Queen went on, realising the situation.

That did not sound quite so attractive; whatever my reputation, I have never been very good at being brutal and cruel towards women, a character failing that has landed me in more trouble than I care to consider. "But I am innocent," Aimée wailed.

"If you manage to survive Captain L'Eree's assault,"

Henrietta said, "shall I say, intact, then I shall be forced to accept that you *are* innocent, and I will then punish Captain L'Eree instead of yourself."

"But suppose he kills me, Your Majesty?" Aimée gasped.

"He will not do that, because he will carry out the assault here, before me. Should you kill Aimée, L'Eree, I will take it as an admission of your guilt. But you may commit upon her anything that amuses you, short of death."

I was not at all sure how either Aimée or I was supposed to emerge the victor from these somewhat contradictory arrangements. Aimée was clearly equally confused, as she looked at me, and I looked at her. I at least was looking forward to the coming fray. As, I suspect, was the Queen; I have no doubt that she had already made her decision as to the truth of the matter, and I had equally already observed her interest in my outsize frame and attributes, as she now confirmed. "To save any unseemly tearing of material," Henrietta said, clearly determined to enjoy herself to the limit, "it would be best for you both to disrobe. Now."

I hesitated no more than an instant. It is not every man who is given the opportunity to display himself before a queen. Within a matter of seconds I was naked, and ready for battle.

Aimée had proceeded more slowly, her mind as yet clearly not entirely made up how to achieve salvation, but when at last she removed her shift I was intrigued, because she was a most extraordinarily well-endowed young woman, in every possible sense, quite fit to stand beside my Helga, while at the same time providing a most agreeable contrast, as Aimée was dark where Helga was fair. She also possessed, no less intriguingly, a large mole, just beneath her right breast, which, far from detracting from the beauty of the swelling orb, rather made it more delicious.

These revelations greatly increased my ardour, and thus brought her face to face, as it were, with my weaponry, which is fully in proportion to my size, especially when aroused, a state of affairs which is not true with all men. At this she realised that she was lost, and that I could probably split her open without having recourse to murdering her. "Your Majesty," she cried, falling to her knees, her hands clasped before her heaving breasts. "Spare me."

"Do you then confess that you have betrayed me?"

"They made me, Your Majesty. They made me!"

"Who?"

"Mr Pym and his friends."

"You mean they bought you," Henrietta said. "You? A good Frenchwoman? Why, you were given to me by the Cardinal himself."

Now this, I realised, would require thinking about. Whenever I could find the time.

"Oh, Your Majesty," Aimée wailed. "My mother is so poor!"

"Could you not come to me, silly child?"

Aimée bit her lip; it was possible to suppose that she knew going to the Queen for money would have been a pointless affair; the royal household was at this time operating entirely on credit. "I gave you my trust," Henrietta remarked. "And you betrayed me. Well, you shall suffer for it."

"Oh, Your Majesty," Aimée wailed.

"L'Eree, dress yourself." I obeyed. If I was somewhat disappointed at not being allowed to have my way with the girl, I had in fact somewhat gone off the boil. "Now open the door and summon my ladies," Henrietta commanded.

Again I obeyed. They positively flooded into the room, all agog to see Aimée in nothing more than her shift. I could not help but reflect how much more agog they would have been had they entered but a few minutes earlier. "Take that creature away," Henrietta commanded. "Whip her till she bleeds, and then lock her in her room on bread and water."

They gasped some more, but obeyed. "Now leave us," Henrietta said, to those who had remained.

More twittering, but eventually they filed out.

"You may close the door, L'Eree," Henrietta said. I obeyed.

"Now come here and hold me," the Queen said. "I feel quite faint."

78

Not even I am going to claim that I escorted Her Majesty to bed on such a brief acquaintance, or was even invited to do so. Yet the fact is that the thought crossed both of our minds. The whole incident had been most provocative, and Henrietta had had the opportunity of inspecting me at my best. I had enjoyed no such reciprocal stimulation, but of course the holding of a queen to one's bosom, however briefly, can be a stimulus in itself. Even more stimulating, for both of us, was the consideration that we were about to adventure together, facing heaven knew what perils. I suspect it was this thought that kept us from the ultimate at that moment. The temptation was there, the passion waited only to be summoned, but we were both aware of the immensity of the step we contemplated, and thus drew back, confident that the occasion would soon arise again, when we might no longer be in a royal palace and subject to interruption by ladies-in-waiting – or the proximity of the King!

But it was not a moment I shall ever forget, as I allowed my hands to wander, comfortingly, over the back and sides and at last even the front of that well-filled gown. I doubt Her Majesty has forgotten it either, because she was doing some wandering of her own. "Oh, L'Eree," she whispered. "You will always keep me from peril." And then, possibly recollecting that for a married woman, much less a queen, there are perils not the least associated with exploding pistols or flashing swords, and that I was by no means protecting her from *them* – quite the opposite – suddenly released me and stood up. "Now go, and arrange my departure."

As it turned out, however, we experienced no perils whatsoever in transferring ourselves to Holland, save only those to be expected in travelling anywhere. Marguerite duly visited Richelieu's agent, and received our instructions. The whole thing needing to be done very privily, for the palace was undoubtedly being watched, although there was no overt action against us. This was because Pym and his cohorts definitely wanted the King to make the first move towards the armed confrontation everyone knew was now unavoidable. Equally because they anticipated learning of such a move long before it could be carried out, through the good offices of Aimée. That she did not immediately report to them they no doubt put down to there being nothing *to* report, and knowing the King's difficult financial situation, they assumed that time was most definitely on their side. Meanwhile, we proceeded apace. Great sacks were loaded with all the worthwhile plate and silver, the guards were warned to be ready to move at a moment's notice, and Henrietta took a fond farewell of her husband. This was because Charles would not leave Whitehall until she had already done so, and he could be certain of her safety. The fact is that this odd couple loved each other, although Charles was undoubtedly afraid of his wife, and she equally undoubtedly held him in contempt.

There were of course difficulties in the way of our departure, principally caused by a surfeit of children and dogs, not to mention ladies-in-waiting. In the end Henrietta had to settle for her two favourite canine pets, four ladies apart from Marguerite, half a dozen guards, commanded by myself, and, of course, her brood. Prince Charles remained with his father, not only as heir to the throne but because he was approaching the age where he might prove useful in the field. Henrietta was unhappy about this, as was only to be expected in a mother, but she was a queen and knew such things were to be expected, and at least Prince James and of course Baby Henry were accompanying her, together with her daughters.

Thus off we set, leaving Whitehall in the dead of night to board several small boats, which caused much oohing and aahing amongst the ladies, and even more when the tide, which had been full, commenced to turn and to rush us downriver at a tremendous speed. We underwent a full hour of this exciting experience, amazed at the expertise of our boatmen, who contrived neither to hit any of the ships moored in the river nor any of the other snags which from time to time loomed out of the darkness. In addition, they knew exactly where we were going – to a village named

Erith. Here we came ashore, and there was a carriage and horses waiting for us. Then it was away to Dover, to join a French vessel lying in the harbour. It turned out that this vessel, together with two sisters, had been trading regularly with the port for the past month while awaiting our summons, and each one was fully equipped and ready to receive the Queen of England, who was far more important to the crew as a French princess. Thus carefully had Richelieu's plans been laid.

We boarded, and the captain set his sails. Henrietta refused to retire, but remained on deck, watching the land slipping astern as we passed the pierheads into the Channel, by which time dawn was breaking. "England," she sighed. "Will I ever return, L'Eree?"

I thought, probably not, but deemed it best to keep that opinion to myself. "In the fullness of time and victory, most certainly, Your Majesty."

"With you at my side," she said enthusiastically.

"Ah ... if Fate wills it, Your Majesty."

I had of course lived long enough to understand that there is no such thing as Fate, even if I had experienced some very odd and quite inexplicable events in my time, and was to do so even more in the future. But even these could hardly be put down to Fate, but rather to the machinations of various human and superhuman intelligences and desires. In the present instance, the Fate which would decide whether I should continue to serve the Queen depended upon a battle of wills between Richelieu and myself, and this was a contest I had every intention of winning: my sole desire was to find myself safely back in Garnesey, my debts paid, and my beautiful Helga's arms awaiting me.

We are all inclined to dream.

Reaching Holland presented no difficulty whatsoever. We slipped along in the best of spirits, the Queen and her ladies dining on the raised poop, from whence they could overlook the gently heaving briny without feeling the least desire to add to its content. "You had best see to your friend, L'Eree," Henrietta said jovially. "But remember now, no lewdity."

Marguerite indeed showed some inclination to accompany me, but I shrugged her off and made my way into the bowels of the ship, where Aimée lay, manacled to the mizen mast, which rose out of the keel into the decks above her head. This business of being confined in the very bowels of a ship is not a pleasant one. One's first impression is of constriction, for there is at best five feet between the bilge and the deck above, known as the orlop; for someone like me, this involves virtually descending to one's hands and knees. One's second impression is of a nearness to the sea, for not only do the waves slap constantly against the sides of the vessel, above one's head, which is a disturbing experience, but there is always water in the bilges, and this slurps to and fro with an energy which leaves one wondering whether or not the ship actually does have a bottom.

One's third impression is of an overwhelming odour, as this area is seldom subjected to any cleaning, and there is invariably the odd barrel of salted pork which has seen better days, or lard which is in the last stages of rancidity. And one's fourth impression is of being within the kingdom of the rat, for these areas of a ship are always infested with the horrid creatures, scurrying to and fro, chirping and whistling, and generally making themselves unpleasant. As I had had a severe encounter with these noxious beasts when in Germany during the War, I felt more of a dislike for them than most, even if I knew that to set about myself and slaughter as many of the rodents as I could reach would hardly diminish their numbers while greatly increasing the stench.

To be confined in these surroundings is as severe as the most ghastly torture, and here was the fair Aimée, secured by a chain round her waist to the mizen mast, as I have said. In view of the time of year she had at least been allowed fully to dress herself, while in view of the necessity to defend herself from the rats her hands and feet had been left unbound. But the tightly secured and padlocked chain kept her unable to escape her surroundings, and she presented a

82

most doleful sight, her hair straggling about her face and shoulders, her clothes filthy, and her demeanour desperate. She did not smell so good, either.

But she was still full of spirit. "Have you come to torture me?" she demanded.

"On the contrary, dear lady," I said. "I have been sent by the Queen to inquire after your health and to offer you some wine."

She took the goblet which I had carried with much effort down three sets of ladders, and drank greedily.

"That bitch," she muttered.

"I will tell her that you are doing very well."

Her head jerked. "How long will this interminable voyage take?"

"Why, I understand we hope to be in Holland by tomorrow morning, if the wind holds."

"Thank God for that. But then, Helier ... what will happen then?"

"I believe it is Her Majesty's intention to return you to France, to the Cardinal. As it was he who presented you to Her Majesty in the first place."

"You cannot," she gasped.

"Do you suppose he will be angry?"

"He will tear me limb from limb."

"Yes, I imagine he will do something like that. But then, you should have taken such a possibility into account when deciding to double-cross him."

"Helier," she said. "You are attracted to me. I could tell it the moment we met. As was I to you. Helier! Allow me to escape when we reach Holland, and I swear you may do with me as you wish."

This was of course a typical example of muddled feminine thinking, as if I made free with her now, she had no guarantee that I would then assist her escape, while if I waited until I had assisted her escape, I would obviously be making free with the wind as far as she was concerned. But these matters apart, she was not at that moment the most attractive prospect, when there was so much beauty awaiting me on deck. "I may return to see you later," I suggested.

83

"As to helping you escape, I look forward to escorting you to Paris myself." Because, of course, as I saw it, my mission was coming to an end.

She screamed curses at me as I climbed the ladder.

What would you? She was an utter villainess. Not that she was to be compared with some other villainesses I have encountered in my time. She suffered only from the twin ills of greed and a lack of ethics. But I did look forward to seeing some more of her, in every possible way, on our journey south. But in this, as in so many things, I was to be disappointed, and in fact the event turned out badly for us all.

We entered the Haringvliet without too much difficulty, and brought up at Helvoetsluis. This was my first visit to Holland, and if I had supposed Oliver Cromwell's homeland to be low-lying and featureless, what was I to make of this place, which is not known as the Netherlands for nothing? For as far as the eye could see the country was absolutely flat, the only sights visible above the few trees being windmills. There was also a great deal of water, and I learned that the coastal areas of Holland are liable to inundations from the sea, when the tide is high and the wind is onshore. These unkind physical and climatic conditions have led the Dutch to be a very hard-working people, whether they be farmers or bankers, and thus very eager to do business. In addition they were, as the King had prophesied, overjoyed to receive the future wife of their statholder. The Queen was barely ashore when messengers were arriving from all over the place, inviting her to The Hague, or Amsterdam, or Utrecht, as it was quickly understood that she was not actually on holiday.

As I have indicated, I now imagined that my part of the business was over. I had extricated Her Majesty from England, landed her in a country where she certainly seemed to be welcomed, and was now entitled, I felt, to withdraw gracefully from the scene and claim my reward. Alas, Henrietta saw it differently. "Would you desert me now, L'Eree?" she cried. "I need you more than ever. Do

84

you not suppose those villains will send behind me to assassinate me, once they know where I am?"

I did not suppose this in the least. From what I had seen of Cromwell and Hampden I had never met men who looked and talked less like assassins, and in any event, the more radical Parliamentarians had surely had sufficient opportunities during the last dozen years to assassinate both king and queen without having to wait until they had left England. The important thing was that she *had* left England, which was what they actually desired more than anything else.

I endeavoured to explain these self-evident facts, but explaining things to queens who have got an idea to the contrary in their heads is never a profitable business. "You do not know these people as I do, L'Eree," she declared.

Actually, she had never met any of them at all. "They are after my blood. And now you wish to desert me?"

"Your Majesty," I protested. "My wife and I were contracted by Cardinal Richelieu to get you out of England. This we have done. You must understand that we have our affairs to attend to, our children..."

"You have children, L'Eree?"

"Several, Your Majesty."

"You did not tell me this before. But that is very good. I had put you down as a fly-by-night when it came to women."

"Far from it, Your Majesty. But as you undoubtedly understand..."

"Your children are perfectly safe, as they are in the care of the Cardinal. So are your affairs. Do not fret so, L'Eree. I will write to His Eminence, praise your industry and loyalty, demand that whatever he is paying you shall be doubled, and inform him that I require your services for awhile longer. You see? You have nothing with which to concern yourself. The letter will go off today with Aimée's escort."

"You are truly sending Aimée to the Cardinal?"

"Of course. That was always my intention."

"You are sending her to her death, Your Majesty. A very unpleasant death, I will wager."

She frowned at me. "She is a traitor. Are you, a veteran of the Thirty Years' War, squeamish about unpleasant deaths? I will wager in turn that you have sent many a good fellow to his doom."

I could not argue with that, although I had never deliberately ill-treated anyone, to my knowledge. My opinion of the Queen dwindled somewhat, and more as I realised that I was trapped. I wrote the Cardinal myself, begging him to relieve me from a duty which had become burdensome, and entrusted the letter to one of the escort who was to accompany Aimée south. Then I visited the prisoner herself. She had been allowed to bathe and a change of clothing had been found for her, and she appeared in a far more salubrious light than when last we had confronted one another. But, contrariwise, her enmity had grown.

"I shall survive even the Cardinal, L'Eree," she told me. "And you and I will meet again, one day."

"You had best hope it will not be soon, milady," I said.

Then she was off, southbound, and we were off, eastbound, for the bankers of Antwerp. Marguerite had been a somewhat petulant observer of all that was going on, but of course she had no such urgent need as I to return to France. Yet even she felt called upon to comment, "I do believe we have commenced a life's work, here, Helier. On the other hand, it could be worse. It is at least, you and I, together."

"Who could ask for anything more?" I agreed, knowing that she liked such comforting.

Thus we removed ourselves to Antwerp, and much activity. The Dutch are a peculiar people in their attitude to politics. They have never actually had a king, although from time to time they admit the authority of a member of the House of Orange, whom as I have mentioned they call statholder, and, again as I have mentioned, they seemed delighted that this prince should be marrying into the House of Stuart, although the two systems of government, and indeed, religion, were as far apart as it was possible to be. Once the province of the Dukes of Burgundy, who in their prime were very nearly as powerful as kings, they had found themselves, by marriage, part of the huge Hapsburg domains, which controlled, at least through cousins, a large part of Europe. But the Hapsburgs were Catholics, whereas the Dutch were soon infested with Calvinism. As the Catholics believe that the Calvinists can only be properly treated by burning at the stake, and the Calvinists believe that the best way to deal with a Catholic is to shoot him first and negotiate afterwards, the situation could not endure. The Dutch, indeed, had been fighting the Hapsburgs long before the Thirty Years' War erupted, and thus far at least the Dutch had been the only gainers, as their practical independence was by now recognised on all sides and under their republican government they had become exceedingly prosperous. In fact, the situation had so far changed that the good boors feared the machinations of Richelieu far more than those of Olivares, on the very sound principle that Richelieu was much closer to hand than the Spanish minister, and thus more dangerous.

However, the fact that it was the sister of the King of France with whom they were dealing did not affect their eye for business – no doubt the handing over of Princess Mary had a good deal to do with this – and Henrietta was soon engaged in lengthy conferences from which the clink of silver was never long separated. In fact, in very short order she succeeded in raising eighty hundred and forty-five thousand guilders from the merchants of Amsterdam, sixty-five thousand from those of Rotterdam, one hundred and sixty-six thousand from those of The Hague, while in addition she pawned her pearls for two hundred and thirteen thousand, and six rubies for four thousand. When all of this was converted into sterling, she had accumulated two million pounds! No one could argue that she was not throwing everything she possessed into her husband's cause.

Meanwhile we eagerly awaited every piece of news from England, the main part of which was of the gathering crisis.

King Charles had duly reached his safe haven at York, where, having rejected a Parliamentary proposal that it should have control of all armed forces in the country, he had been joined by thirty-two peers and sixty-five members of the Commons. He also, of course, had the Great Seal, which effectively meant that the country was divided into two, with Parliament in the south-east passing laws which lacked the monarchical authority, and the King in the north and west denouncing their machinations. An appeal to force was obviously about to happen, and thus the King's letters to his wife took on an extra urgency. Henrietta was continuing to work hard, and not merely in conferring with bankers. She also let the situation be known far and wide, and soon began a recruitment of her own, not of an army, as such, but of officers of experience, men who had fought with Gustavus Adolphus or Bernard of Saxe-Weimar, the great generals of the early part of the war which still raged in Germany.

These gentlemen she supplied with the first fruits of her financial negotiations to enable them to cross to England and offer their swords to the King, for they were nearly all strapped. However, in the course of this transaction, she netted an enormous fish, although perhaps we did not realise it at the time. It was the end of May, and the Queen was, as usual, interviewing people in the parlour of the modest house we had rented, with her secretaries making notes, her ladies, amongst them Marguerite, twittering in the background, and myself, as always, standing guard at the door. There was a tremendous racket at the street door, and the man on duty there retreated at haste into the house, wailing, "I have been bitten. Bitten, Master L'Eree!"

True enough, he was followed by a little white dog, all yapping tongue and gnashing teeth. But the dog was certainly little, and did not look large enough to have reached above the sentry's boots, while the distraught fellow was clutching his upper arm. My first reaction was that the animal was afflicted with rabies and his unhappy victim gone mad from the bite. Then I observed that draped round his neck there was another furry animal, this all arms and legs and small, aggressive face equipped with sharp white teeth clearly preparing to bite him again.

I leapt forward, prepared to defend my comrade, when a voice said, "You naughty girl, behave yourself."

The creature, which I now recognised to be a small species of monkey, wearing a red jacket and a blue hat with a red tassel, immediately transferred itself, by means of a short leap, from the terrified sentry to the shoulder of a man who was at that moment entering the open door, followed by several others. This principal newcomer was a fine looking fellow, swarthy, with dark hair – like myself he wore no wig – and hatchet-like features, clean-shaven. He was no more than average height, but seemed larger, both because of the way in which he carried himself, and his clothes, which were dominated by a red tunic, slashed with cloth of silver, across which there was stretched a deep blue baldric, from which hung a most serviceable looking sword. Beneath this, his breeches, stockings and shoes were black, and in faultless repair. He was not very old, indeed, I was to discover that he was some eight years younger than myself, but yet carried himself like the soldier he was. If unsure, on this our first meeting, whether I would like him or not, I formed the immediate opinion that he was no man to cross.

And yet cross him I must, as he was entering my Queen's house without her leave, and accompanied by several others, not to mention his ferocious pets. Thus with my usual speed I whipped my sword from my scabbard and presented it. "You are too bold, sir," I informed him.

At this the little dog took offence, and advanced up to me, teeth bared. I pointed with my blade. "I must inform you, sir," I said, "that if that dog attempts to bite me, I shall strike off his head."

We gazed at each other, his face somewhat contorted with anger, and I realised that it might well come to sword-play when he looked past me, and I realised that the inner door had opened, and Henrietta Maria had emerged to discover what the racket was about. At the sight of the Queen, the intruder whipped his hat from his head, and gave a deep bow. This was to be expected in the presence of royalty. But it was his words surprised me. "Why, Auntie," he said. "How good to see you looking so well."

"Rupert?" Henrietta inquired. "Can it truly be you?"

"All the way from the Rhine," the young scoundrel said. Thus informing me that he was King Charles' nephew, the son of his sister Elizabeth by her husband the Elector Frederick Palatine: he went by the name of Prince Rupert.

CHAPTER 4

Prince Rupert of the Palatinate, or as he was more generally known, Rupert of the Rhine, was born 17 December 1619, which is to say that, like Gustavus Adolphus, his birthday was within a few days of my own, and we shared the star sign of Sagittarius. As I endeavour not to be superstitious – although heaven knows I have sufficient reason to be – I merely offer these facts for consideration, rather than as any attempt to explain events. But certainly Rupert had much of the great Swede in him. The difference was that he suffered to a large extent from the hereditary drawbacks of his Uncle Charles. His mother, as I have explained, was that Princess Elizabeth who was Charles' elder sister. She, perhaps the leading Protestant princess in Europe, had been married to the Elector Frederick of the Palatinate, who was regarded as the natural leader of the Protestant faction in Germany, then about to begin its struggle against Catholic domination. Prince Rupert had been not yet a year old when his father's ambitions had been shattered at the Battle of the White Mountain outside Prague, and all central Europe had been convulsed in war.

For Frederick and Elizabeth, it had been a disastrous war, which had very rapidly reduced them to penniless fugitives, existing on the generosity of Elizabeth's father, King James, who was well known to be the meanest king in Christendom – except to his male favourites – and then her brother, who never had two pennies to rub together. Frederick had died, of despair it was said, some time ago, and Elizabeth and her children had made their home in these very United Provinces, and when Rupert, at the age of sixteen, had visited his uncle in London in 1636, he had captivated the court with his handsome face and outgoing personality.

Since then his fortunes had not been so high. He had returned to Holland, and now being a man, had felt it his duty to take part in the war which had made his father an exile. Although all the great names such as Gustavus and Bernhard, Tilly and Wallenstein and Pappenheim, were dead, this war continued to drag on, and was now being stoked, with both men and money, by Richelieu. Rupert of course had drawn his sword upon the Protestant side, and had promptly been taken prisoner at Vlothe on the Weser in what had virtually been his first action. This had been in 1638, and for the next three years he had been held a captive in Austria. Being of royal blood his captivity had not been an arduous one, save that the very fact of being a captive is arduous. He had in fact been released only a few months previous to our arrival in Holland, and had only been back in his adopted country a few weeks, before learning of the arrival of his aunt-in-law, and hurrying to offer her his sword.

It may be supposed that this particular nephew was not the one the Queen most wished to see at this juncture. Rupert was an ardent Protestant – insofar as he was ardent about religious matters at all – and Henrietta was an even more ardent Catholic. But Rupert was a difficult fellow to put down, and now he swept Henrietta from the floor and gave her a hearty hug, while her ladies looked on in scandalised astonishment. "I am hearing the most absurd rumours from England, my dear Aunt," he said.

"I only wish they were absurd," Henrietta grumbled, when she had got her breath back. "Why do you think I am here?"

"I was told you had fled for your safety."

"Ha! That is a foul calumny." She paused for a moment to glare at me as if daring me to interrupt. "I have come to Holland to buy arms for the King, so that he may teach his subjects a lesson."

"There is going to be a war?!" Rupert's entire body became animated. "Then I shall fight for my uncle."

"You?"

Rupert was of course at this time only twenty-two years old, and his principal experience of warfare had been that Austrian prison. But I immediately saw in him the answer to all our problems, including mine. "Your Majesty," I said, "the Prince is the ideal man."

Rupert looked at me for the first time since our difference over the behaviour of his dog. "Who is this large fellow?" he inquired.

"My faithful bodyguard," Henrietta said proudly.

"Indeed, Aunt, I had observed that. Well, send him hence. I do not discuss matters of importance before bodyguards." He chuckled. "Unless you consider that you need protecting from *me*, Your Majesty."

"Captain L'Eree is a veteran of the War," Henrietta pointed out.

'Indeed? And on which side did you fight, fellow?"

"Your Highness, I was with Gustavus Adolphus at both Breitenfeld, where I was wounded, and at Lutzen, where in my capacity as the King's personal bodyguard, I was first to find his body." As with Cromwell, I considered it wisest to confine myself to a limited number of relevant facts, and not confuse the poor boy by revealing that owing to circumstances beyond my control I had actually fought on *both* sides, but I had certainly hoped to make him realise that my worth as a fighting man was somewhat greater than his own. In the event, I was totally surprised by Rupert's reaction. As if a mask had been whipped from his face, all the bantering and even contemptuous humour left his expression, and he stared at me with the most piercing eyes I had ever seen, since those of the great Swedish king himself.

"You rode with Gustavus?" he demanded, and before I could stop him he had seized my hand and was shaking it most vigorously. "Then I owe you every apology possible. You must tell me of him. Oh, indeed, we have much to speak of. Good Aunt, you must release this man from your service that he may enter mine, and ride with me as well."

"Well ... " Henrietta said.

"My lord ... " I protested.

"I go to fight for your husband, and yourself, and your children, and the monarchy," Rupert declared, with tremendous aplomb. "I need every experienced fighting man I can get."

"Well, in that case," Henrietta said.

"Your Majesty," I protested.

"Have you lost your stomach for a fight, man?" Rupert demanded.

"By no means, Your Highness, but I took on a specific task, that of escorting Her Majesty to safety, which I have done, following which I was promised a return to my family and business."

"Surely you can postpone that for a few months?" Rupert asked. "It will take us no longer to deal with these Parliamentary scoundrels."

"Of course it will not," Henrietta agreed. "I give you my permission to accompany Prince Rupert, L'Eree. More, I insist upon it."

I was not prepared to surrender so easily. My plan had been to distract the Queen with the Prince, not involve myself in his ambitions. "I take my orders from another source, as you well know, Your Majesty. It will be necessary for me to ask His Eminence for permission."

"His Eminence?" Rupert frowned. "Are you a confounded Papist?"

"By no means, Your Highness. I am a soldier of fortune who offers his sword where it can be put to its best use."

Rupert digested this, as the statement was not so different a description to his own. "Richelieu has my welfare much at heart, Nephew," the Queen said. "He also has the interests of my husband at heart, which is why he has supplied us with this formidable fellow. Very well, L'Eree, write to the Cardinal. It will be a few weeks yet before my transactions here will be completed. You will remain with me for that time, Rupert."

"It will be my pleasure, Aunt."

"It would be quickest, Your Majesty, for me to visit the Cardinal myself," I said. Things were getting out of hand.

"You mean to desert me," Henrietta grumbled. As if she had not just sent me from her side!

"I must obey my master, Your Majesty. I will put the situation before him, and if he commands me to serve Prince Rupert, then I will do so."

"This is a confoundedly independent fellow," Rupert remarked.

"Yet is he right," Henrietta said. "And it would be to our advantage to keep the Cardinal on our side."

"Aunt, would you have me sup with the devil?"

"Oh, come now," Henrietta said. "You are splitting hairs. L'Eree, I would speak with you privily, before you take your leave."

I joined her in her boudoir, wondering if we were about to regain that most promising situation we had shared in Whitehall. But sadly, there were several ladies present, including Marguerite, who was in a very excited state. "Now, L'Eree," the Queen said, "I am letting you go for a variety of reasons. You have several matters to put to Richelieu. First is his support for my husband. This is essential. I quite understand that it cannot be done openly. Money is what I need. Understood?"

"I understand, Your Majesty."

"Secondly, there is my own position. I have every intention of rejoining the King just as soon as is possible. But it is also possible that circumstances may conspire to prevent my doing so. In which case I should not like to have to spend the rest of my days in this dismal place."

"I understand, Your Majesty."

"My final message is for your ears alone, L'Eree. Leave us, ladies." There was the usual considerable twittering, and some loud harrumphs from Marguerite as the women filed from the room. "Close the door, L'Eree."

I obeyed, and returned to her side, conscious of a considerable emotion, which was shared, I could tell. "Kneel beside me, L'Eree." I sank to my knees beside her chair. "You and I have adventured together, L'Eree," she told me. "And yet, I feel there is so much more for us to do."

"Oh, indeed, Your Majesty," I said most fervently, and without invitation, clasped her hand.

She lifted it, and therefore mine, to press it against the bodice of her gown; beneath the swelling softness against which I was lodged, I could feel the beating of her heart. "Come back to me, L'Eree," she whispered.

"Your Majesty," I said, adding my first hand to the one she held, and about to seek a way to heaven.

But she either lost her nerve or recalled herself, for she rose, and my hands must perforce return to my sides. "Return to me," she said again. "I bid you adieu."

I got to my feet, seized her hand again to kiss it, and went to the door. Both the Queen and I received a considerable shock, for on opening it, I discovered Marguerite standing there, wearing coat and hat and boots, and carrying the small carpetbag which contained all of our worldly possessions – at least, all those we had with us. "I am ready, Helier," she declared.

"Ready for what, my sweet?"

"Ready to accompany you, of course. Back to France."

I personally had no objection to this plan, as my principal aim in life was to get rid of her, and no matter what decision Richelieu came to he could neither send me off to war accompanied by a woman, nor send me back to my wife in a similar condition. But we had not reckoned with Henrietta's habitual distrust of all around her. "Oh, no," she said. "Oh, no, no, no. Your wife remains here, L'Eree. How else would I be certain that you will come back to me?"

How indeed? Marguerite and I looked at each other, the same thoughts passing through each of our minds, I am certain. "I hate to threaten anyone, L'Eree," the Queen continued, "but I must warn you that if you do not return, it may well go hard with this delightful creature, as I will be forced to conclude that you have betrayed me, and a betrayal of the Queen of England means a charge of treason. I am sure you know what is the penalty for treason in England."

Well, she had herself reminded me, and not so long ago.

96

However ... "A sentence which is difficult to carry out on a woman, Your Majesty."

"I agree. More's the pity. However, a female traitor can certainly be hanged. Think upon this as you journey south."

"Oh, I shall, Your Majesty," I promised, and smiled at Marguerite. She obviously remembered as well as I how my earlier adventures had been caused by a similar situation, the Cardinal having promised to execute her did I not carry out his wishes. But that had been a long time ago, when I had considered her the purest and most beautiful woman on earth, and was quite prepared to die for her. She would also have realised that such a situation no longer obtained.

"Your Majesty," she declared, "it is time for this play-acting to cease. I am not Captain L'Eree's wife. I never was, and God willing, I never will be. I hate and despise him for the bumpkin he is, and have always done so. I am the Countess d'Albret, owner of vast estates in Normandy."

Well, that was a bit of an exaggeration, for a start, even if she had actually owned them, which she did not – they belonged to the Cardinal. Henrietta remained quite unconvinced. "Really, my child," she said, "do not make yourself absurd."

"But it is true!" Marguerite bawled. "I am employed by the Cardinal, as is L'Eree. It was deemed best that we should travel as man and wife. That was the Cardinal's idea, not mine."

"Yet you seem to have fallen in with it very willingly," Henrietta pointed out. "From what I have seen, you have played the wife in every possible way. Are you that lacking in morality? Faith, it does not go well with your claim to be a countess." Clearly the Queen did not know many countesses very well.

"I was forced to it by His Eminence!" Marguerite wailed.

"Enough. I am thoroughly disappointed in you, Marguerite, attempting such a shabby trick. And I am sure Helier is disappointed too. You will remain here with me until your husband returns for you ... or until I am convinced he is not going to do so in turn, at which time we will reconsider the situation."

"Helier!" Marguerite screamed. "Tell her the truth."

I kissed her forehead, and gently removed her arms from around my neck. "I can understand your reluctance to be separated from me, dear wife," I said, "but I agree with Her Majesty that you have chosen a disappointing, dishonest and downright dishonourable way of going about it. I shall of course return to you." And I bent my head to kiss her cheek, at the same time, whispering, "have faith in the Cardinal." With which I left them.

It was with a tremendous feeling of release that I rode my hired horse south from Amsterdam, along the various bridle paths that bordered the canals with which this pretty little country is inundated. Truth to say, I had found the company of Henrietta Maria and her ladies, however from time to time delightful, so cloying as to be almost stifling. While as to the King and his asinine advisers, I gave them no chance at all of surviving the coming fracas, even with the assistance of Rupert of the Rhine, who was clearly a hothead and would require a great deal of control. I was thoroughly glad to be shot of the lot of them.

From the above reflections it will be understood that at this juncture I had absolutely no intention of returning to Holland, and even less to England. I had carried out my part of the bargain, and now sought only to go home to Garnesey. As for Marguerite, I wished her no harm, and was quite sure that Richelieu would be able to extricate her from Henrietta's clutches – after all, he was vital to the Queen's future, and she would have to accept his decree. Thus I rode along with a merry song on my lips, stopped at the various inns which suited me on the way, and clattered into Paris without a care in my heart. Nor did I have to do more than make my name known and I was admitted into the Cardinal's presence. My good humour changed to concern as I perceived that his remark the previous autumn, to the effect that he was dying, and which I had taken as a jest, was apparently all too near the truth: never had I met a man with cheeks so sunken, body so bent, whole demeanour so sickly. But yet with eyes which shone like beacons, and illuminated the acute brain behind.

He waved his attendants away, and then bade me sit and tell my story. When I had finished, he flicked some of the papers on his desk. "You understand that I have received letters from Her Majesty, written soon after her arrival in Holland?"

"Yes, Your Eminence," I said, somewhat uneasily; I had by now learned enough about Henrietta to know that she could be quite as two-faced as any politician when it suited her.

However, to my enormous relief, the Cardinal said, "They confirm in every way what you have just told me."

"Well, then, Your Eminence..."

"Civil war in England," the Cardinal mused, chin in hand. "It is nigh on two hundred years since last there was a civil war in that benighted country. And do you know, for that ancient period of some thirty years, while the English were hacking at each other, we enjoyed a period of peace here in France. What a delightful thought! You are a soldier, Helier. Tell me how this war will go."

"As to that, Your Eminence, the King has no money."

"Will the Queen not raise some in Holland?"

"She is doing this, Your Eminence, and as I have just intimated, she hopes that you also will dig deep into your pocket to help a princess of France." I paused here for a comment, but he made none, merely waving his hand for me to continue. "But any money made by means of loans or gallant gestures, Your Eminence, can never equal that available to a body which controls the principal resources of an entire country. Parliament not only possesses London, but also controls the Navy, so it is said, which will hamper the Queen's efforts to succour her husband. But it is the money which matters. Parliament will be able to raise more men, and keep them in the field longer, than the King."

"Do you have no regard to the quality of the men,

Helier? You, who have served with both Tilly and Gustavus?"

"I agree that discipline and *élan* are essential to victorious troops, Your Eminence. However, I am bound to confess I observed little of either in England, on either side. And discipline and *élan* can only be created, and then properly used, by commanders. As far as I was able to discern, there is not a general, not a colonel, not a captain, in England at this moment, fit to serve Tilly as a stable groom, much less Gustavus. Scotland, now, abounds with good men, veterans of the War. But it is impossible to say which side, if either, the Scots would support. They hate the King for his attempts to impose episcopacy on them. But Parliament hates them for their determination to impose Presbyterianism on England. It is a sorry business."

"As you say. You are surely not suggesting that I send the Prince of Condé to King Charles? Now *that* would cause an international incident. What of this fellow Rupert?"

"A tearaway, Your Eminence, entirely lacking in experience."

"So it is your opinion that the English monarchy is about to be overthrown, and replaced with a republic? Then we would have a republic across the Channel to set with the republic to our north? No, no, that would be quite unacceptable."

I began to perceive that perhaps I had been a little too forceful, as well as honest, in my estimation of the situation. And my apprehensions were confirmed by his next words. "It occurs to me, Helier, that you have been too modest in describing England as entirely lacking in expert soldiers. Surely you do not include yourself in that description?"

"I am a Garneseyman, Your Eminence."

"Nonetheless, you owe allegiance to the English crown. Can you stand idly by and see it roll into the gutter?"

"Your Eminence, they would have none of me. I actually did suggest that they might make use of me, but those fops

... unless you have a title or a reasonable expectation of one, they hardly know you exist."

"That is the way of kings, and courts. By the way, how is the Countess d'Albret?"

"She is being held as security for my return."

"Ah. Tell me, have your relations at all improved, during your several months as man and wife?"

"I do not think it is possible for our relations to improve, Your Eminence."

"She is a difficult woman," Richelieu agreed. "But you *are* accepted as man and wife?"

"Yes, Your Eminence."

"Thus you cannot really consider abandoning her to whatever fate the Queen may have in mind for her if you should not return. Do you have any idea what that fate would be?"

"There was some talk of hanging, Your Eminence."

"Well, then, we cannot possibly permit that pretty little neck to be stretched. I have been considering your several points, Helier. Let me put one more question to you: when you say you and Marguerite are considered man and wife, how exactly are you known?"

"Why, Your Eminence, as Captain and Mrs L'Eree."

"Marguerite has never laid claim to her proper title?"

"Well, she has, from time to time, Your Eminence. And has been treated with contempt."

"And there is the source of all your problems," Richelieu said. "But it is a matter easily solved. Helier L'Eree, I of this moment endow thee with the château and lands of Albret, together of course with those of L'Eree, which you already hold. As these two demesnes are situated close to each other, it is even possible that in the course of time they might become linked. Then indeed would you be a great landowner. Thus as of this moment you will be known as Count d'Albret."

Heady talk indeed, for a man who had begun life as a humble gravedigger. But I perceived difficulties. "If I am to be Count d'Albret, Your Eminence, where does that leave Marguerite?"

"As what she already is, Countess d'Albret, save that she will now again have a count to keep her company. You will make it understood that your previous *nom-de-plume*, that of Captain Helier L'Eree from Garnesey, was adopted simply for expediency."

"But we are not married, nor can we be: I have a wife in Garnesey, and even if I did not, I would never consider marriage to Marguerite le Gron."

"Tush, Helier, you do split hairs. All the world that matters in this context, that is, the English court, regards you as man and wife. So you continue this play-acting for awhile longer. You will return to Holland as the Count d'Albret. I will provide you with letters patent to prove it, as it shall be true. You will accompany this Rupert to England, and the pair of you will take command of the King's army, and put an end to this proposed insurrection. I will supply you with some funds as well, to help in the purchase of munitions. You will triumph, and your reward will be, as I have promised you, Albret."

"And Marguerite?"

"At the end of the business, you will be quietly divorced. I will find some other reward for her."

"And my Helga?"

"Awaits your return to Garnesey. I suggest you write to her and inform her that you have again been unavoidably delayed. Do not tell her why. She will be sad, but she is in a very good state, with your remittance arriving punctually every month, her debts suspended..."

"You promised me they would be forgotten, once the Queen was safely delivered to Holland, Your Eminence."

"And so they are, all but." We gazed at each other. Of course I knew that I was being duped, but only in the sense that events had gone beyond the Cardinal's original estimation. While to say truth, there were powerful factors at work to encourage me to do what I was going to be forced to do anyway. I had undertaken the first part of this mission in order to escape the consequences of being in debt. But now I was being offered far more than that. I was to be a count! How proud would that make poor Mama! Not to mention Helga!

In addition, I am bound to admit that the prospect of again going to war was a powerful impulse. Man is a fighting animal; this is well known, and those who attempt to deny it are flouting the laws of nature. To be sure, the reality of war is always a good deal less pleasant than our expectation of it, and my experiences in Germany had at the time convinced me that I wished to have no part in any further maiming, destroying, and killing. But that was now ten years in the past, and I knew that I had been steadily growing more and more discontented, not to say bored, in Garnesey. A man can milk only so many cows and catch so many fish and hoe so many rows. Sadly, he can also find solace in the same pair of arms only so many times. It had been necessary to remain faithful to my Helga, with my body as well as my heart – I would always remain faithful with my heart – for the very good reason that in Garnesey adultery is hardly a practical proposition, on two counts: firstly, the island is so small that everyone knows everyone else, and everyone else's business as well, and secondly, it is regarded as a crime and severely punished.

Thus the call to adventure touched a ready chord in my mind, especially where there was so much reward being offered. Against this was only a slightly longer separation from my wife and children. "I will have the letters patent drawn up now," the Cardinal said, having been observing my expression. "Then we will visit my treasury and see what can be spared, and then you must be away. Haste, Helier, haste."

"There are two other matters, Your Eminence."

Richelieu, in the act of rising, sank back into his chair. "It is possible to try me too far, Helier. What is it now?"

"These matters do not directly concern me, Your Eminence," I protested. "But Her Majesty will certainly inquire of them when I return to Amsterdam."

"Well?"

"Firstly, there is the business of her future residence,

should matters not go well in England. The Queen desires to return to France."

"As I have made clear, that is impossible," Richelieu said. "Certainly while she is Queen of England, and even more, I may say, were she to be so unfortunate as to become the *exiled* Queen of England. Because that would mean you had been defeated, Helier, and I would have to see what sort of relations I could achieve with these round-headed Parliamentarians. I do not see what I could do if it was known I was giving shelter to the man they had expelled. If, by any chance, the King were to die before this business is resolved, then it might be possible to reconsider the situation."

"Is that what I must say to Her Majesty?"

"It were best the facts were put to her plainly."

"She will not be pleased."

"I am not in the business of pleasing people, Helier. I am in the business of ruling France."

I inclined my head.

"You mentioned another matter."

"Yes, Your Eminence. May I inquire what has become of Aimée Hubert?"

Richelieu raised his eyebrows. "Do I know this person?"

"She was sent to you, Your Eminence, by Her Majesty, along with her first letters. You received the letters."

"But not the young lady. I assume she was a young lady. Was she some kind of gift? I am a little too unwell for coping with nubile young women."

"On the contrary, Your Eminence: Mademoiselle Hubert was a gift from you to Her Majesty, some years ago."

"Is that a fact? Her name quite escapes me. And she has offended Her Majesty?"

"Offended her, Your Eminence? She has turned out to be Parliamentary spy. Her Majesty sent her back to you that she might be dealt with in an appropriate fashion."

"As she managed to avoid such a fate, she would appear to be a resourceful young woman."

"Did her escort not speak of her?"

"They did not."

"Then they must be found, and required to give an explanation of how she escaped their custody, and where she is to be found now."

"You sound uncommonly agitated, Helier? Can a great lout like yourself be afraid of some chit of a girl?"

"Well, as to that, she has certainly sworn to kill me," I agreed.

"In that case, I suggest you kill her first. I give you my permission to do so. However, I do not give you permission to go hunting for her. Your business is saving the English monarchy."

An enormous responsibility. And one which the Cardinal clearly underestimated. "Your Eminence, this woman is dedicated to the downfall of that monarchy, and what is more, she knows our plans. Or most of them, certainly."

The Cardinal stroked his chin. "Then I will endeavour to have her found, and disposed of. But I refuse to accept that any one person, and a woman to boot, can possibly be of any great importance to our purpose. Now come with me, my lord Count, and we shall equip you for the fray."

Well, I could hardly refuse such an invitation couched in such terms. But I also could not help reflecting that the Cardinal, in so dismissing the so-called gentle sex as irrelevant in men's affairs, was revealing all the weaknesses of his calling.

For the moment, however, I was totally concerned with current events, seeing as how they all concerned me and were to my advantage. Ill he might be, but the Cardinal had lost none of his energy, or his authority. My letters patent were drawn up in a matter of hours, and I became a member of the Second Estate of France. Equally was I provided before nightfall with an order upon the Cardinal's agents in Antwerp, commanding them to grant me credit worth one hundred thousand English pounds. Best of all, I was also given a list of all the Cardinal's agents in England – I was astounded at their number – and the right to call upon any one of *them* to supply me with up to one hundred English pounds for my own personal use, as necessary. This meant that Marguerite was now completely irrelevant, which was a reassuring thought.

These vital requirements met, the Cardinal dismissed me. "You will leave at dawn," he said, "to return to Amsterdam and your destiny. I have chosen a suitable lodging for your night. I own the inn, and you will be well looked after. Tomorrow morning I will send along a suitable escort for a count, to see you on your way. I will wish you Godspeed, Helier, and every possible success."

I bowed, at the moment once again caught up in all the anxious anticipation of going off to war. Thus I was the more at ease as I made my way towards the address he had given me, a youth I had employed at the flip of a coin carrying my as yet scanty belongings. My thoughts were concerned with the future, not the present. I was therefore the more taken by surprise, as I followed the directions given me, to hear a cry of alarm and the sound of a scuffle from near at hand, and, rounding a corner, I came upon one man desperately defending himself against two. All had swords, and I realised at once that it was an assassination attempt, at the very least, for the defender was in every way better dressed than his assailants. Equally was he much smaller, and although obviously skilled in the use of a sword, unable to do more than defend himself against the swings and thrusts of his opponents. My porter promptly dropped my parcel and took to his heels, but I have never been one to consider the niceties, or the dangers, of any situation where I can be of assistance to a weaker party. Without a moment's hesitation I had whipped my own sword from my scabbard and charged the two attackers, giving a bellow to alarm them. They certainly seemed alarmed, cast a hasty glance at me, and made off as fast as they could, feet slipping on the cobbles.

I was tempted to follow them, but then realised that the man I had assisted had fallen, and for a moment I thought he had been wounded at the least. Thus I stooped beside him, to discover that he had merely been winded and slipped, for there was no sign of blood upon his white coat or doublet. He was also, I now realised, as I peered at him in the gloom, remarkably young. True, he wore a thin black moustache, but there was no evidence of any beard. In fact he was a very handsome fellow, with small, delicate features, although his body was also small and seemed somewhat undernourished. Intriguingly, there was something familiar about him, although at that moment and in the semi-darkness I could not recall where we might have met, nor could I suppose it was at all possible.

"I owe you my life," he said, as I assisted him to his feet. His voice was low, and musical . . . and also faintly familiar.

"Could you not have dealt with them yourself?" I asked, for he had seemed to know the use of a sword.

"They were gaining the advantage," my young friend admitted, and held out his hand. "You have my everlasting gratitude, *monsieur*. Now I must repay you. My name is . . . Charles Le Brock."

The name did not suit either the clothes or the demeanour of the gentleman, who now stooped to retrieve his hat and place it upon his somewhat ruffled but surprisingly undisarranged wig, which was made from the most splendid curling black hair. Well, no doubt the scion of a noble house – as I was certain he was – would not wish to reveal his name to a chance acquaintance who had just saved his life. As I suffered no such inhibitions, I grasped his fingers and said, "Helier L'Eree, at your service." Only then remembering that I had actually just gained a much grander title.

"No, no," he said. "I am at *your* service, Monsieur L'Eree. Will you dine with me?"

Well, I thought, why not? The Cardinal had told me I must be ready to leave at dawn. He had given no instructions or indication of how I should spend my evening. "It will be my pleasure," I agreed. "I am on my way to the Horn Tavern. Can I but find it."

"Why, I know it well," declared Monsieur Le Brock, as for the moment I had to consider him, and led the way to the very tavern, where we were welcomed by the landlord, when my host had produced several silver coins. I felt a bit

107

put out at the way he was taking over the evening, but had no wish to inform either of them that I had been sent to this inn by the Cardinal, and so kept my tongue. "We wish a private room," Le Brock said.

"Of course, *messieurs*, of course." The patron rubbed his hands as he hurried in front of us, taking us up a short flight of stairs from the taproom, which was already crowded, and into a small private chamber, where there was a table, set before a well-cushioned bench seat and with two other chairs as well. Sconces burned quietly, and the place was very cosy. "Now, *messieurs*," the landlord said, continuing to rub his hands together.

Charles Le Brock waved his hand in my direction. "You have but to say, Monsieur L'Eree."

"Why, sir," I protested, "As you are hosting..."

"I may do as I please," he agreed. "And it pleases me that you should order."

Who was I to argue? And it was some time since I had eaten. "I think some lamb chops," I said. "And a couple of chickens. And a pork roast. And some tarts. And a gallon of your best wine."

The hand-rubbing had by now reached the fire-starting stage. "And some company, perhaps, *messieurs*?"

"Why not," I agreed, for in common with most men, having had my dander raised, as it were, by the prospect of action, I was aroused in every possible manner. "Is that satisfactory, Monsieur Le Brock?"

"If it is what you wish, it is satisfactory," the young man said. "But allow me to ask you a question," he continued, when the landlord had left us for the moment.

"Anything," I agreed with a wave of the hand. Obviously I had not agreed to answer his question, but still it seemed ingenuous enough.

"I cannot help but feel, from your accent, that you are not a native of these parts," he remarked.

"Why, no, I am not," I acknowledged. "My estates are in Normandy."

"Estates, indeed!"

"Why, sir," I told him. "Although my family name is L'Eree, my title is that of Count d'Albret."

"Good *seigneur*, my most humble apologies. I knew you immediately for a gentleman, but had no knowledge of your nobility." At this juncture the patron returned with an enormous pot of wine, which I immediately investigated, for in addition to being hungry and aroused, I was more tremendously thirsty. Sadly wine, while delicious both as to taste and effect, does nothing to quench the thirst. Indeed, one goblet, when thirsty, immediately calls for another, and then another, and I was on my third when my host made his next remark – I had not previously considered it necessary to reply to his flattering observation. "And yet," he said, "as I have spent some time in Normandy, I would swear that your accent is not that of the Norman either, but rather suggests someone who never spoke French as a native tongue."

I gave a little hiccup, my hasty intake of wine having trapped some wind. "Why, as to that, sir," I said, "you are absolutely right." And why should I not confide in this very pleasant fellow, and more than that, for having had the opportunity to study him in the light, I reckoned he had to be about the most handsome man I had ever seen in my life. "My home is an island called Garnesey."

"Ah, Garnesey," Charles remarked.

"You do not know it, *monsieur*?" I was astonished, for truth to tell, very few people outside of the Channel Islands have ever heard of them.

"I have never been there, to be sure," he said. "But I know of it, certainly."

"You amaze me, *monsieur*," I confessed.

Further conversation was ended by the arrival of our dinner, which was to be served by two extremely attractive young women – I would hesitate to describe them as maidens. But they were certainly buxom, as could immediately be discerned from their décolletages, which were as deep as any noble lady's, and even more willing, as they displayed by putting their arms round our necks and sitting on our laps as they conveyed various delicacies to our lips. I am

109

bound to confess that I allowed myself to be served in every possible sense, being a libidinous fellow in any event, and in addition being in the mood to celebrate my sudden elevation to the nobility as well as the understanding that I was again going off to war. By the time the meal was finished, perhaps an hour later, I was very nearly as naked as the girl in my arms. By that time I was also extremely drunk.

But not yet so drunk that I had not observed that my new friend clearly did not approve of my behaviour. True he had the other girl on his knee, and he seemed happy enough to be kissed by her and to play with her appurtenances, but any suggestion of being undressed by her was firmly rejected, somewhat to her discontent, so much so that at some time during the evening she abandoned the prudish Charles in order to join the assault upon myself. With this sort of fighting I was more than familiar, but with the room reeling about me like a ship at sea, I was relieved when my two charmers informed me that there was a bedchamber right next door, where we could disport ourselves to our hearts' content in more comfort. Of course this would have to be paid for, but then, the ladies would have to be paid for as well. Yet they had timed their approach to perfection, as by then I was past caring who was going to pay for what and how much.

Thus we staggered into the inner room and fell to. I naturally assumed that Charles would accompany us, and that I saw little of him did not seem to me out of the ordinary. In fact I am not sure that I achieved anything worth remembering with either of my charmers – I certainly do not remember anything – because I very rapidly fell into a deep sleep.

And dreamed. At least, I supposed it was a dream. In my dream I most certainly had a sexual encounter, of an intensity I had not known for several years. But the succubus who lay on my exhausted breast was most definitely neither of the barmaids, who, while fine specimens of rampant femininity, were all too obviously of the lowest social order. This ethereal creature, alike from her slender but voluptuous body, her delicious scent, her refined yet practised and even wanton movements, was most definitely a lady. Indeed, I had known, in this Biblical sense, only one woman in the past to match her, and she had been the vampire-princess Richilde Bethlen, Princess von Hohengraffen. And as, in my dream, we wrestled in each other's arms, it came upon me that it was indeed Richilde with whom I was coupling, as I had done before on so many unforgettable occasions.

Small wonder that I awoke in a cold sweat, gasping for breath.

CHAPTER 5

For some moments I was not even sure where I was. Far worse, I was not even sure I had been dreaming. I could still feel every contour of Richilde's body against mine, and although I was alone, I almost felt I had heard the bedroom door closing, as if someone had just left. I sat up, driving my hands into my hair as I tried to calm the heaving of the bed and the room, the spinning of my head, and the throbbing explosions inside my brain. Gradually the horrors within me settled down, and I looked left and right, blinking in the gloom, for the curtains were drawn across the single window.

I got out of bed, swayed like a flagpole in a strong breeze, fell across the bed, and forced myself up again, reaching for my clothes and more importantly, my sword. But it was not there, and neither were any of my garments. I was naked, and alone, in a strange place ... The door opened, and I turned towards it, gasping, but determined to sell my life dearly if I had to, even if beset by demons while unarmed.

But to my enormous relief it was my companion of the night before, Charles Le Brock. He was fully dressed, and did not look the least to be suffering from our night's debauch. But then, as I recalled, he had taken very little part in it. But as I recalled him, so the events of the evening began to return to me. Up to a point. I remembered very little after taking the two barmaids to bed. Except my dream! "You are quite a fellow," Charles remarked.

"My sword?" I asked.

"It is here, with your clothes. Do you always think of your sword, first, on awakening."

"In strange surroundings, yes. Thus, you see, I am still alive. But this morning, just."

"I have had some water sent up," Charles said. "Can you make it to the other room?"

I managed this, and immersed my head in the bucket for so long I all but drowned. Then a vigorous towelling restored some of my senses, but not all. "What happened?" I asked.

"You mean you cannot remember?" Charles sat down at the table, legs crossed, looking as composed as could be possible. "Perhaps some breakfast would help." He gestured at the basket of fruit and bread which sat before him.

"In the name of God, do not even mention the word," I said.

"Then I shall not," he agreed, although whether he was referring to the Deity or food I was not certain. 'Well, last night. You saved my life from some cutthroats."

"Oh, I remember that," I said, sitting down myself, and despite myself taking a bite out of a croissant. "And coming here, and dining. There were two wenches."

"Indeed," Charles agreed, gravely.

"Who we..."

"Who *you* tumbled until they collapsed from exhaustion. But by then you were also collapsed, from exhaustion. Thus I sent them away, to let you sleep. Which you did, most thoroughly."

"Did I not cry out?"

"Why, yes, so you did, once or twice." He frowned at me. "You mean you were *not* asleep?"

"Oh, I was asleep," I said. "But dreaming. My God, what dreams!"

"Tell me of them."

I glanced at him, and started on my second croissant. By now the room had stopped heaving and trembling, and so had I. "You would not enjoy them. They were the most hideous nightmares. I fear I have lived an uneven life, and from time to time memories return to haunt me."

"Ah, to have lived long enough, and well enough, to have memories," my young friend philosophised. "Still, I hope to achieve that, at your side, my good Helier. When do we start?"

"Start? Start what?"

"Why, your mission for the Cardinal."

I finished my second croissant, and began to dress, attempting as I did so to get my brain into working order. "How do you know I am on a mission for the Cardinal?"

"Why, you told me so, Helier."

"Did I?" I scratched my head.

"Last night, while we were drinking."

I could not deny that this might be true; I am given to loquacity when in my cups. "Then you had best forget everything I said."

"Oh, I shall. My business is but to follow and obey. But we should make a move. There are some fellows downstairs waiting to accompany us."

The Cardinal's escort. But ... "Us?"

"Have you forgotten inviting me to serve you?"

"Serve me where?"

"Why, Helier, as to that, you did not tell me. Merely that you were following the path to glory, and that you would be happy to lead me along that path."

I scratched my head. This too was entirely possible, as I had taken quite a liking to this young man, while feeling somewhat guilty as I did so, because he was the prettiest boy I had ever encountered. In view of some of my experiences in Germany, I should of course have known better than to accept him at face value. That I did so must be put down to the combination of euphoria at my recent sudden elevation, which left the entire world my oyster, or so it seemed to me at that moment, and the amount of wine I had consumed during the preceding twelve hours, which left my brain in a still very fuddled state. As is not unusual in these situations, my mental processes fastened upon a single point of view, that if indeed the boy knew that I was working for the Cardinal, it might well be best to have him along in preference to letting him roam the streets, no doubt resentful, and thus complaining to all and sundry. Especially, dare I say it, when his continued presence perhaps promised future pleasures. Am I not an unmitigated rogue? But there it was. The only alternative was to kill him there and then, and on a more serious note, I greatly looked forward to his company.

The Cardinal's guards were only required to escort me across the border into Holland, and they had no objection when they discovered that I had accumulated a travelling companion; indeed, they had been surprised that a chevalier like myself lacked a servant. But this duty young Charles seemed happy to undertake. I remonstrated with him, feeling that menial tasks were beneath his dignity, but he would have none of it, and I must say that his care for me was as tender as that of a mother for her babe. Yet, anxious as I was to regain the Queen and my future, I continued to find nothing amiss with the lad, not even to the extent of remarking his extreme privacy, for he would never undress before me, nor, on the occasion that evening when my entire cavalcade stopped by a babbling brook and doffed our clothes to bathe, did he avail himself of the facilities, although he sat on the bank and watched us with considerable interest. "He is a dirty fellow," remarked the captain of my escort. "What say you, Count? Shall we have some sport? Shall we strip him and bathe him, willy nilly?"

I was tempted, but decided against it, and was heartily glad of my decision, for as it was late afternoon, I decided to make our camp in these delightful sylvan surroundings, and continue with our ride the next day; we were already within a few miles of the border. We had managed to purchase some chickens in the last village through which we had passed, and these were soon roasting away, while my people disported themselves on the grass. With the meal went some flagons of wine, also recently purchased, following which we retired early, as I at least was still suffering from the previous night's debauch.

As an experienced campaigner, I of course set a guard, and arranged for him to be replaced in rotation. Whereupon I retired to my bivouac, which was close to that of young Charles. I was asleep instantly, only to be awakened,

115

it seemed, an instant later. But I could tell from the air that several hours had passed, and indeed it was beyond midnight. Then what had disturbed me? I moved my head a fraction, to allow myself to inspect the situation, and saw immediately that Charles had left his blanket and was making his way out of the camp. To be sure, he was challenged by the sentry, and replied. Both men spoke in low voices, and I could not tell what was said, but the sentry seemed satisfied, and Charles continued on his way.

I sat up, and looked at his roll. His sword was still there, as were his cloak and boots, so he was obviously not deserting. I got up and followed. "Is something amiss, Count?" asked the sentry.

"Where has the boy gone?"

"He said something about his necessaries."

"Stay alert," I told him, and went past him.

He made no comment, and a moment later I was virtually out of sight of the camp as I gained a stand of trees, some hundred yards upriver. Now I could hear the sound of gentle splashes, and a few moments later I came across Charles' discarded clothing, lying on the bank. The night was dark, but I could yet make out the sliver of white that was his body, as he disported himself in the water. I had no desire immediately to disturb him, so seated myself against a tree, close beside his clothing, and awaited his emergence. When he at last did so, I received a great surprise. Any readers of this manuscript will no doubt have long deduced the situation, and as I have indicated, I should have also but for the many distractions that had crowded upon me during the thirty-six hours since I had first met this delightful ... maiden? Hardly that, I suspected. But there she was, slowly emerging out of the darkness, while my wits tried to gather themselves. It was now that I realised her wig was not a wig, but her very own hair, and was hardly more magnificently luxuriant on her head than elsewhere. Equally, as indicated by the role she had chosen to play, her breasts were not large, at least when compared with those of Marguerite or the Queen, or indeed, Aimée Hubert, but they were most delightfully shaped. Her legs were long and

116

slender, and these added to the rest of her, made up a quite entrancing whole, even when it was considered that she still wore her false moustache, firmly glued to her upper lip. It may be imagined with what a feeling of rapture did I realise that I was not, after all, going to have to play the sodomite to enjoy this magnificent creature, although, being a villain, I did not, to be sure, put the idea entirely from my mind, understanding as I did that *anything* I might choose to do with her could hardly be less than a delight. After all, it had been her decision to ride with me.

For her part, Charles, or Caroline, as for the moment I had to consider her, had advanced right up the bank to her clothes before she realised she was not alone. Her reaction was instantaneous, and in keeping with the character she had taken on. On observing the figure awaiting her in the shadows, she threw herself full length at her clothing, delving for, and finding, a long, slim-bladed knife she had concealed in a sheath on the inside of her breeches. However, as quick and decisive as had been her movement, I was there before her, kneeling beside her and closing my hand on her wrist even as she closed her fingers on the haft of her weapon. She struck at me with her other hand, but to do this had to roll on her side, which left her even more at my mercy, as I simply pushed her on to her back, and knelt astride her, an entrancing position to be in, to be sure, save that I had my breeches on, and seized her other wrist in turn. She heaved against me with her thighs, but was of course helpless beneath my bulk, and after a moment subsided, the quicker as she now recognised who I was. "Helier," she muttered. "I nearly killed you."

"Now you have the advantage of me," I suggested.

She licked her lips. "We have much to discuss."

"When you have released the knife, *mademoiselle*," I said politely. "If you do not, I shall be forced to break your wrist."

"Which I am sure you could do with the simplest ease," she agreed, and opened her fingers. The knife fell out, and I released her in turn, in the same movement picking up the weapon, and retaining it, returned to sit against my tree.

The situation was singular, to be sure. But yet it was one I had encountered before, in the forests of Germany. This makes my earlier inability to understand the true nature of my strange companion the more inexplicable, perhaps only to be interpreted in terms of witchcraft. But having now arrived at the truth, I was even more mesmerised, for my earlier companion had proved, in addition to being the most delightful of bedwarmers, a support of great strength in time of need, and I had already seen that this young woman could defend herself. She watched me resume my seat, having risen to her elbow, then sat up and looked down at her mudstained body. "You have rolled me in the dirt when wet," she pointed out.

"Then why do you not wash it off," I suggested. I was in no hurry. I had long learned that all things come to he who waits, and this was most certainly worth waiting for.

She considered me for a moment, then returned into the water and gave herself a thorough rinse, including her hair, which had become as dirty as the rest of her during our brief tussle. She clambered back up the bank and stood before me, dripping most entrancingly. "I owe you an explanation," she observed.

"I am thinking that you owe me more than that," I countered.

"Who do you suppose exhausted you last night?" she asked.

"By God! And the barmaids?"

"They were but the *hors d'oeuvre*," she remarked, contemptuously.

"And I can remember nothing of it," I said regretfully. "You will have to refresh my memory, *mademoiselle*. Have you a name?"

"What is in a name?" she asked. "What would you like mine to be?"

"I am perfectly easy on that score," I said. "So, Caroline it shall be. But whatever your name, you must have had a purpose."

"To serve you."

"Then the two men who assailed you . . ."

"I paid them to attack me as you approached."

"You are singularly free with other people's lives, *mademoiselle*. I could easily have killed one of them. Or both."

"They had but to run away. As they did."

"Very good. So you wished to take service with me. Thus you wished to find out what I was about. Who sent you?"

"Is that important?"

"Very. Come here."

She hesitated, then came forward, and knelt beside me. This enabled me to touch her, which was what I wished to do more than anything else in the world at that moment. But I had more pressing matters to consider than her flesh, or mine, for that matter. I certainly touched her, but having stroked her breasts, slid my fingers down to caress her thighs, and then slipped my left hand between her legs to grasp her left buttock firmly, from underneath and behind, at the same moment putting my right hand behind her, to bring her against me, and seizing her right buttock, equally firmly. A fascinating business, but I was still not entirely after pleasure. She gave a little gasp, but whether of fear or delight I could not be certain.

"Do you understand," I said, "that with a twist of my hands as they are presently situated, I could tear you into two pieces?"

Her face was very close to mine. "Do you not suppose I would scratch out both of your eyes in return?" she asked, placing her hands on my shoulders, perhaps in readiness.

"I doubt you would succeed," I said, "and even if you did, while I might be blind, you would be dying in the utmost agony."

"What is it you wish to know?" she asked, proving herself to be a very sensible young woman.

"I have told you. I wish to know who sent you."

"If I am to tell you," she said, "you must either move your hands or use them to their best advantage. They are most distracting in their present position."

I was tempted to adopt her second suggestion, but reflecting that duty must always come before pleasure, and that she would not be going anywhere until and unless I

119

sent her, I released her, and with a little sigh she sat beside me. As she remained naked, and my eyes had by now become accustomed to the gloom, it was I who was being powerfully distracted, as no doubt she intended. I could not help but wonder why she refrained from at least donning a shirt, for although we were in the month of June the night air was by now uncommonly chill, although of course, from the point of view of a spectator, this was all to the good. "You could say I was sent from the grave," Caroline remarked, quietly.

"Eh?" My distraction vanished in the instant. Quite apart from my nightmare, I had too many memories from beyond the grave.

"Do you remember a woman named Jeanne d'Ailly?"

"Jeanne?" I cried. "I knew her only as Jeanne. D'Ailly? That sounds like a noble name." My brain was doing handsprings, as I tried to relate the rough and ready female soldier with whom I had campaigned ten years before with a noble lineage.

"It is indeed a noble name," Caroline agreed.

"But she never used it, or gave any indication of her background, save to say she had served in the army for five years."

"That is exactly so. But why do you suppose she was forced to abandon home and family, and don man's clothing, in the first place?"

I frowned at her. "Because of you? By God, you'll not pretend Jeanne was your mother."

"I do not pretend anything," Caroline said. "My mother formed an unfortunate liaison when she was but a girl, and when her condition became known, was expelled from her house by her father. She took refuge with a peasant family, gave birth, and then abandoned me to seek her fortune as a man."

"By all the saints," I muttered. "My Jeanne. Do you realise she also mothered a child for me? A son?"

"My brother," Caroline agreed. "But he is dead, is he not? As is Mama?"

By now a glimmer of sense was starting to flicker in my

brain. "You could not have known of it. Your brother was born in the castle of Hohengraffen, which has since been burned to the ground."

"I know of it, because my mother wrote to me of it."

"That I can never believe. I was forced to leave your pregnant mother in the care of the Princess von Hohengraffen while I went off to war."

"And the Princess would never had permitted Mama to write to me? You are right, of course. But she did, and smuggled the letter out of the castle. Thus I learned that she had given birth, and that you, her great love, had returned wounded from the field of Breitenfeld, but yet covered in glory, and would recover. She also told me that should anything happen to her, and from the tone of her words I assumed she felt that her life was in danger, I should look upon you as my father, seek you out, and give you all the love and support in my power. She seems to have had no doubt that *you* would survive whatever danger was hanging over the Hohengraffen Schloss. And she was right, was she not?"

I scratched my head. Her story was so shot full of holes it could have been a Gruyère cheese. "Permit me to ask you one or two questions."

"Of course." At last she put on her shirt, I assumed both because she was chilled and because she had determined that our sexual relationship had also cooled, at least for the moment.

"You say your mother abandoned you immediately after your birth, and went off to the wars."

"That is correct."

"From which she never returned. Thus she never laid eyes upon you, except for the first few days of your life."

"Yet she always loved me, and hoped to come back to me," Caroline insisted, and anticipated my next question. "And of course she knew the name of the people with whom I was lodged, and who brought me up."

"I see. Then she wrote you, as you say, from Schloss Hohengraffen, after the Battle of Breitenfeld. That would

121

have been around Christmas 1631. How long did her letter take to reach you?"

"Some months."

"Shall we say the summer of 1632. And you were born...?"

"In the summer of 1623," she answered with total equanimity.

"So you were nine years old. Yet you were able to make all of these interesting deductions?"

"I read the letter for the first time when I was nine years old, to be sure, Helier. And then I kept it, and read it again and again as I grew older."

"Until having reached the great age of eighteen, you determined to carry out your mother's wishes, and seek me out. Knowing that she was dead. Did she also write you from beyond the grave?"

"You should not joke about matters of which you understand so little, Helier," she said, a young girl rebuking a gnarled old warrior like myself. "Anyway, should I not know my mother was dead, having not heard from her in nine years?"

"There was no means of your knowing whether I was alive or dead. Yet you knew exactly where to look for me, in Paris, when I visited the city for the first time in my life and then unexpectedly, and for exactly one night. You try my credulity a trifle too far. I think you had better bring your backside back to me that I may commence tearing you into two pieces."

She knew, of course, that if I was not exactly jesting, she was in very little danger, as she had quickly discerned my susceptibility to feminine beauty. Nonetheless, her continued equanimity was amazing. And her next words were disturbing. "Do you then, consider that you know all the secrets of the universe?" she asked.

I gulped. This too was familiar territory. But one on which I had sworn to turn my back forever. "You cannot deny that I know as much, no, more, indeed, about Jeanne d'Ailly than you do yourself," she continued. "How could I, and indeed, *why* should I be interested, were I not her

122

daughter? As to how and where you were to be found, that is my business. What matters is that I have found you, and that I am sworn to serve you, in every possible way, for the rest of my natural days. Or yours."

A singular statement. But one which contained so much promise, I can hardly be blamed for overlooking her last, brief sentence, which indeed I scarcely heard, as she dropped her voice as she uttered it. I can, of course, be blamed for a great many other things. I was bound upon a mission of great importance and great secrecy, known to myself and Richelieu alone. This beautiful girl already knew too much of it. Had I been truly your born secret agent I should have strangled her there and then. But I did not.

I was a happily married man, unfortunately separated from my wife. This beautiful girl had already imposed herself between me and my memory of my wife. Had I been an honest husband I should have sent her about her business there and then. But I did not.

I was pretending, in the course of my business with the Cardinal, to be married. This beautiful girl could only be a cause of discord between myself and my pretended wife and thus could only be regarded as a danger to my mission. Thus again I should have put her aside. But I did not.

Most important of all, I had at an earlier stage in my life come into the closest possible contact with the powers of the Devil, quite apart from the misfortunes of my own dear mother. I should thus, at the very first suggestion of witchcraft by this beautiful girl, have sent her on her way.

But there was the problem: this beautiful girl, kneeling virtually naked beside me. In addition to being a libidinous rogue I am also an incurable romantic – some would say a fool. Although Caroline d'Ailly did not in any way resemble the woman she claimed to be her mother, there were certain things about her that were familiar, and as she had pointed out, she certainly had her facts right. She *could* be Jeanne's daughter, and Jeanne I remembered as the best and truest of companions, who had saved my life as I had once saved hers, and who had remained ever trustworthy, even after being exposed to the foul pestilence of witchcraft herself. Besides, this girl possessed a beauty her mother had entirely lacked. And if it had indeed been her in my arms last night ... but this gave me pause for thought, for if I am a libidinous man, I yet endeavour to be an ethical one.

"So will you not tell me how my mother died, at the least?" Caroline asked, having observed that she had won the day.

I sighed. "She died when I was attempting to rescue her from the witch-hunters, pierced by a pike. I buried her myself."

"Thus proving that her judgement of you as the best and truest of men was entirely correct," remarked my charmer.

"Perhaps," I agreed. "But the fact is that she was murdered, as were so many good men and women, by the foulest witch who ever walked the face of this earth: the Princess von Hohengraffen."

"Is that so," Caroline remarked. "Was the Princess then present at the death of my mother?"

"No, she had fled before then. But it was she directed the witch-hunters to her castle, and Jeanne."

"Knowing they would both be destroyed," Caroline mused. "She seems to have been an odd woman."

"I have told you, she was a witch."

"Was? Then she too has paid the penalty for her crimes."

I shuddered. "I would prefer not to discuss it."

Caroline regarded me for some seconds. "You were in love with her," she observed.

"Me? In love with the foulest witch and vampire who ever walked the face of this earth?"

"The margin between love and hate is often so slender as to be impossible to discern," pointed out this girl, who by her own admission was not yet nineteen years old. "I have heard of this Princess von Hohengraffen. I have heard that she was the most beautiful and alluring of women."

"Maybe she was," I agreed. "But none the less, a black-hearted sorceress."

"And you dream of her still," Caroline chided. "When you were mounting me, last night, you cried out her name."

"Aye, there you have it. In my drunken stupor I thought you were she."

"I am flattered."

"You should not be. And there is another point. You have just admitted you knew me for your mother's lover, yet you came to me without hesitation."

"My mother is dead," she said, with charming simplicity.

"She bade you regard me as a father!"

"She was writing to a nine-year-old girl," Caroline reminded me, at the same time unbuttoning her shirt. "Would you *really* like me to treat you as a father?"

What would you? For the second time in my life I allowed myself to be seduced by beauty and apparent devotion, nor, on this occasion, were the consequences to be any the less dreadful. But at that moment I cared nought for possible consequences. The next morning, having crossed the border, I dismissed my escort, somewhat sleepily, to be sure, as I had had very little rest, and then Caroline and I made our way north towards the windmills.

"Riding at your side," Caroline observed, "I can experience at second hand something of what my mother must have felt, when you rode together, two against the world."

Well, she had already sampled a good deal of what her mother must have felt, on various occasions, and, if I remembered correctly, far more enthusiastically than Jeanne had ever done. I do declare that my erstwhile mistress had been so long a soldier, required to conceal her sex from her companions, that she was no longer sure whether she was man or woman, and was thus the more tremulous in intimate situations. Those of you sweet ladies whose entire lives have been spent attending to domestic duties and in the security of your own home and village may consider such matters as almost beyond comprehension, when the time involved is a matter of years. But the fact is that your average soldier, when campaigning – and the

Thirty Years War was one unending campaign – is neither very fastidious nor very clean, seldom strips to the skin, and quickly learns not to take too close an interest in the personal habits of his comrades unless invited to do so. Your female soldier soon enough finds a bosom companion with whom to share her secret – often she joins up merely to *be* with her beloved through thick and thin – and who stands guard while she performs her necessaries, as I had done often enough for my dear Jeanne. Additionally the fact of sharing one's blanket with someone who is also quite capable of guarding one's back when in battle doubles a man's strength.

I had discovered all of these things with Jeanne, and now I looked forward to discovering them over again with Caroline. But there was more. I had been very fond of Jeanne, but I had never been in love with her, in the sense that a man's mind can be distracted by the very thought of the object of his adoration. I had only previously felt such a compelling emotion for one woman, and she had turned out to be a witch. Now I was enjoying such a transport of delight for the second time, for if I could not remember enough of my first tumble with Caroline, my second, on the banks of that stream, left me certain that this was the woman to whom fate had been directing my feet from the day of my birth. As to my wife, I had no doubt that I could come to a satisfactory arrangement in that direction without too much difficulty. After all, I was now the owner of a vast property in Normandy as well as a small one in Garnesey. Should I not divide my time between the two, in proportion to their sizes, and equally between my wife in Garnesey and my squire in Normandy?

That my only previously similar surge of emotion had been with a witch, and that Caroline had virtually admitted herself to have some knowledge of the unspeakable, never crossed my mind, at that moment. I was indeed, bewitched, or at least, suffering from an extreme case of the disease known as hubris. But at that moment, the happiest man in the world, as Caroline seemed equally delighted, laughing and singing as we rode along, to the amazement of the boors we from time to time passed.

Yet there remained questions to be answered. "How did you learn the use of a sword?" I asked.

"I took lessons."

"They must have been from a very early age."

"I was thirteen when I first handled a blade."

"A thirteen-year-old girl, taking fencing lessons? What did your foster parents think of that?"

"They were happy to indulge my fancy."

"And the expense? You spoke of them as peasants."

"Well, so they were, regarded from the station of Mama's family background. But actually Papa Le Brock was a baker, and a successful one. By the time I reached womanhood he owned several bakeries, and was a relatively wealthy man."

"They had no children of their own?"

"Sadly, no."

"And thus they released you to do as you pleased, at a very tender age."

"I have told you, they were indulgent to me."

"And you love them dearly."

"Of course. But I love you more, Helier." And as we had stopped for dinner, she proceeded to demonstrate her affection.

A most singular situation. But I defy any man who is not a monk at heart to have refused such a gift from the gods, even if *in* his heart he might know that she had to come from the very opposite direction. But in addition here was I, two yards and more of solid bone and muscle and experience of the worst that god or devil could hurl at my head; was I going to be frightened of a young woman who wished to adore me, however certain I was that she had told me very little that could be true of her background?

I was more concerned about the future. "You will, of course, continue to play the part of my squire," I told her.

"Of course, my lord."

"Are you aware that I am married?"

"But your wife is in Garnesey."

127

"Unfortunately, no."

It was the first time I had seen anything even approaching concern in her expression. "The German woman is in Holland?"

Fool that I was, I did not even pause to consider how she knew that Helga was German, as I had not accumulated her until after Jeanne was long dead.

"For the purposes of my mission," I explained. "I am married to the widowed Countess d'Albret. Which is why I bear the title, Count d'Albret."

She considered this. "And this 'wife' awaits you in Holland?"

"She is not twelve hours away. However," I hastily continued, "we have already agreed that you will continue your transvestite subterfuge, and in any event, I have no intention of taking Marguerite with me on the campaign, so it will only be for a short while. But for that short while, you will have to conduct yourself with propriety."

"Campaign," she said. "Is that what we are about, sweet Helier?"

"What did you expect? I am a soldier. Does the thought frighten you?"

"Not in the least. But ... " She frowned. "You do not mean we are to go to Germany?" Which was where most of the campaigning was currently being carried on.

"There are, or will be, wars in other places beside Germany," I pointed out. "You will just have to be patient. However, there is another matter. In addition to my wife, I have an interest elsewhere."

"You mean you have a mistress," she remarked, a trifle tartly.

"I have hopes of a mistress, certainly."

"You amaze me, sir. Can you not be satisfied with two women? Three, in fact, if we include your wife in Garnesey."

"You mistake the situation. This lady is the Queen."

Her mouth made an O. "You aim so high?"

"Or she aims so low. However, it is my intention to let events take their course. You will also."

"You will hardly have time for me at all," she grumbled.

But she accepted the situation, as she had no choice, and the next day we regained Amsterdam, where I was immediately shown into the Queen's presence. With her were her ladies, including Marguerite, as well as Prince Rupert, who had with him an even younger prince, who I gathered was his brother Maurice. All seemed very pleased to see me, although in a state of great agitation, and although we were in such public conditions Henrietta Maria actually embraced me before the throng. "Stout L'Eree!" she declared. "I never doubted you would return. What news from Paris?"

I glanced to left and right. "What I have to say were best kept as privy as possible, Your Majesty."

"I am sure you are right." She waved her fan. "Leave us."

"Your Majesty," Rupert protested.

"L'Eree is the bearer of secret intelligence," Henrietta said severely. "If it is something you should know, nephew, be sure that I will tell you. Now be off with you."

The ladies were already filing out, each in turn casting a curious glance at Caroline, who stood just within the door. Marguerite's glance, I may say, was a good deal more than curious. But even she was not as interested as Rupert, who stopped to gaze at the handsome 'boy'. "And who are you, my pretty fellow?" he asked.

"I serve the Count d'Albret," she replied, in her invariable low tones.

He tweaked her ear. "You'll be aware there are severe laws against sodomy in this land," he said, and left the room.

"What is this, L'Eree?" asked the Queen.

I had already decided to stretch a point for safety's sake. "This young man is an agent of the Cardinal's, Your Majesty. Sent to support me and make sure all goes well."

"All what?"

"That I am about to tell you."

129

She nodded. "Come forward, boy. I assume he has a name, L'Eree?"

"I am Captain Charles Le Brock, Your Majesty," Caroline said, making a leg.

Henrietta gestured her to stand straight, and I could tell at once that she was interested, if for all the wrong reasons. "You are very young," she remarked, "to be employed by Richelieu."

"His Eminence does not find me very young, Your Majesty," Caroline replied, in a most enigmatic fashion.

"Hm," Henrietta remarked. "Very well, Captain. Run along. Captain L'Eree and I have privy matters to discuss."

"With respect, Your Majesty," Caroline said boldly. "If the matters pertain to His Eminence, then I am bound to remain. The Count and I can have no secrets from each other."

Henrietta looked at me, and I shrugged. "Insofar as they do, Your Majesty..."

"Oh, very well," Henrietta snapped. "Let the fellow remain. Now tell me, L'Eree? *Count* d'Albret?"

I explained that I had been elevated, and then showed her the Cardinal's order upon his Dutch agents for funds. This entirely distracted her. "Thank God," the Queen muttered. "Thank God! I have pawned my pearls, sold my plate, and still have not raised sufficient money. But now..."

"What is the news from England, Your Majesty?"

"The news from England is black, L'Eree. You will know that the King betook himself to York? Well, once there, he sought to raise a force for his protection from the mob. But armies need munitions, and weapons of war, and he had none. However, there was the arsenal at Hull. He therefore sent to Sir John Hotham, governing the place, demanding the surrender of all weapons of war and munitions in the arsenal. Would you believe that the scoundrel refused? And when His Majesty sought to gain possession of the place by force, this despicable lout took up arms and drove our people off."

I was aghast. "You mean there has been fighting?"

"It is depicted as a civil clash. But it is a sign of things to come. Did you know that Parliament then sent a deputation to His Majesty, outlining their demands? I will not bore you with the traitorous details, but the two main points were, one, that His Majesty hand over command and control of all armed forces in the country, and secondly, that he also hand over his children to the care of Parliament. Can you believe it?"

The demands certainly seemed extreme. Acceptance would put the King, and indeed the Crown, under Parliamentary control, for more than a generation, at the least.

"His Majesty refused, of course," Henrietta went on. "Whereupon those villains declared the nation was in danger and formed a Committee of Public Safety."

"But that is virtually a declaration of war," Caroline observed.

"Of course," Henrietta agreed. "And it was too much for some of them. I believe better than sixty Members of Parliament and quite a few peers have left London to join His Majesty."

"Then what exactly is the situation, Your Majesty?" I inquired.

"Why, Parliament issues laws and decrees in London, and His Majesty issues them in York. However, as His Majesty has the Great Seal, and they do not, their laws do not amount to a bag of beans. Unfortunately, they are now issuing calls to arms. These will have to be met with arms. Thus you see why your return, with French funds, is so timely."

"No one must know of this, Your Majesty," I reminded her.

"I can hardly spend money without revealing that I possess it, L'Eree."

"I meant, no one must know the funds came from the Cardinal."

"No one shall. But we must set about buying everything we need. And then ... " she sighed. "I have no choice but to place the matter in the hands of Prince Rupert. Indeed, as I made the mistake of informing the King that Prince Rupert and his brother had joined me and were anxious to help, he has commanded me to send the pair over to England as rapidly as possible. He appears to regard those boys as being great soldiers. Whereas you and I know better."

"Great soldiers they shall be, Your Majesty," I declared. "The Count D'Albret shall ride at their shoulder."

"You, L'Eree! You would risk so much, for England?"

I kissed her hand. "I would risk so much, for England's Queen. Besides, did you not command me to do so?"

"Oh, L'Eree!" she said, and glanced at Caroline. "Leave us, boy. Leave us!"

Caroline, whatever her personal feelings, had the wit to obey, and a moment later the Queen and I were alone. By then Henrietta had regained some of her composure. "You are, of course, instructed by Richelieu," she said. "Tell me what his interest can be?"

"Why, Your Majesty, His Eminence has commanded me to do nothing more, or less, than serve Your Majesty's best interests, in whatever way I can. Publicly, I can think of no better way to do this than to destroy your husband's enemies and replace you, safely, upon the throne of England."

"Oh, L'Eree," she said. "I should be forever in your debt. And privately?"

I knelt beside her chair. "I am yours to command, Your Majesty."

"Oh, L'Eree!" she said again, and as was her wont, took my hand to hold it against her heart. "Were I not a queen..."

"Are queens not women, Your Majesty?" I asked, and held her chin to turn her head towards me, and kiss her on her parted lips.

I am well aware that this was villainous of me. I did not love this woman, who was in any event somewhat older than myself, and while I was not concerned about adultery, having, through circumstances beyond my control, had to indulge in it once or twice in the past, it is a considerable business to seduce the wife of a king, especially when one is about to risk all for that king. But there was the point: there

132

is something about a queen which raises her above the common folk, even though she may lack any outstanding beauty or personal qualities. For that, one would indeed risk all, and indeed, for a few brief moments I thought to have succeeded. Certainly she allowed me to conquer her mouth, and to make free with those splendid orbs which were her principal claim to beauty, at least in so far as I could deduce, never having yet beheld her legs. But these too were within my grasp, quite literally, when she gave a kind of gasp, and suddenly remembered who she was. "No, L'Eree, no," she whispered in my ear. "It cannot be."

I released her immediately, of course. Appearances to the contrary, I have never actually committed rape in my life, and I was not about to begin with a queen.

She held my hands. "Serve me faithfully, L'Eree and who knows, but one day..."

"One day, Your Majesty," I agreed, and rose, to bow and take my leave.

Caroline was waiting in the corridor. "What a bill and coo," she remarked.

"If I thought you were listening, I would put you across my knee," I told her.

"Sodomy is punishable with death, in Holland," she reminded me.

"But the Dutch, I think, do go in for good old-fashioned chastisement," I suggested.

She put out her tongue, suggesting that for all her airs, and her undoubted sexual prowess, she remained in some ways still a small girl. "I do not see what you can find attractive in a middle-aged frump," she grumbled.

"Patience, my sweet," I advised. "You will one day be a middle-aged frump yourself, and then you may find out."

"I shall never be middle-aged," she announced, and it seemed in no way a boast, but merely a statement of fact. But I had no real time to consider it at that moment, for I had a far more immediate crisis at hand. Marguerite was also waiting for me.

"Just what is going on?" she demanded, hands on hips, as I entered our bedchamber.

I was of course accompanied by Caroline, who had not yet been allotted anywhere to sleep. The fact is that the Queen, although she had rented a large house, had accumulated an even larger band of would-be helpers and plain hangers-on, quite apart from the entourage she had brought from England, and Marguerite and I were very lucky to have this small room to ourselves. There was no prospect of Caroline being granted any privacy, and being at that stage of a love affair when one is consumed with both passion and jealousy, it was not my intention to allow her to be placed in a barracks with a dozen hairy and undoubtedly libidinous men, who might well find much to please them in a pretty young man, long before they discovered he had even more attractive qualities. To that extent, therefore, I needed to temporise with my 'wife', and thus smiled at her benevolently. "What is concerning you?" I asked.

"What is this Count d'Albret nonsense?"

"Why, I have so been created by the Cardinal." I opened my wallet. "Here are the letters patent, if you are in any doubt."

She snatched them. "You mean D'Albret has been returned to me?"

"Ah . . . no. It has been given to *me*."

"What did you say?"

"What I said. However, His Eminence has given me to understand that you will be amply rewarded when you return to Paris."

"And when will that be?"

"When we have completed our mission."

"And when will *that* be?"

"When we have defeated the forces of Parliament, and replaced the King, and therefore the Queen, securely on their thrones."

"My God! That could take years."

"No, no, it will be a trifling matter. For the time being,

134

you will remain in the Queen's service, guarding her with your life if need be."

"Oh, yes? And where are we going to be?"

"Right here. Under no circumstances must Her Majesty be allowed to return to England until Parliament is disciplined."

"You will have to tell her this yourself."

"I shall not be here, my poppet."

"What?"

"I am to accompany Princes Rupert and Maurice to England as their chief of staff, to command the King's army."

"But ... " she turned her glare upon Caroline. "And he goes with you?"

"Of course. He is my servant."

"Ha!" she commented. But she had other things on her mind at the moment. "You will leave me sufficient money, Helier?"

"As of now you are in the Queen's charge, my dear."

"But you are my husband."

"And at the moment, a trifle short. Now, space must be made for Charles to share this room with us."

"*What* did you say?"

"There is nowhere else, my pet."

"Sometimes you try me too far, Helier," she grumbled, and then took another look at Caroline. "But I suppose, if there *is* nowhere else."

Caroline rolled her eyes.

Someone else who was not entirely happy with the situation was Prince Rupert, who, however much he may have been impressed at learning I had ridden with Gustavus, yet regarded me, with reason, as being too familiar with the Queen. Well, to be frank, I regarded him as the most difficult part of my mission. But in the event I was pleasantly surprised, at least up to a point. "Well, Count," he said, "we had best get to know each other. Come to my chamber, and let us discuss things."

I went readily, only regretting that Caroline had to be

excluded: Rupert had taken a profound dislike to my servant. Caro indeed was also going through a difficult period, as she and I were quite unable to get together owing to a complete lack of privacy. I could only assure her that this unsatisfactory state of affairs would end as soon as we embarked for England.

"Now," Rupert said. "You claim to have served with Gustavus Adolphus. In what branch?"

"In every branch, Your Highness," I told him, and continued while he digested this. "I began as a pikeman, to be sure, but then I became one of his cavalry, and at the end rode at his side as an aide."

"What is your belief in the use of cavalry?" he demanded.

"To charge at the gallop, sword in hand. Which is not to say that I do not have an acquaintance with the Spanish method, from an earlier campaign."

I was not of course going to confess that I had actually ridden with the Imperialist cavalry of Gustav von Pappenheim. And he was too excited to worry about details, for here was the great debate of the day concerning cavalry tactics. The Spanish system, as practised by the Imperialists, was for the cavalry to advance in good order, with swords sheathed and pistols cocked, until within range of the enemy battle – and we are talking here of a matter of a few yards – when they would level their pistols, fire into the opposing mass, and retire to reload, before commencing another advance. The object of this exercise was to cause disarray in the enemy ranks, and force openings, into which one's own infantry could advance. The Spanish cavalry was only ever loosed at the gallop upon broken and fleeing opponents. Gustavus had entirely reversed this, and reinstated cavalry as the principal arm on the battlefield, leading them himself, sword in hand, against the enemy ranks, even against pikemen, after using his artillery to create the gaps.

"How are the English trained, do you think?" Rupert asked me.

"I do not think they are trained at all, Your Highness.

But the King's supporters, being mostly drawn from the gentry and their retainers, will all ride to the hunt. I fancy you will command the finest heavy cavalry in Europe."

"Aye," he breathed. "That I will."

"Providing they are disciplined, Your Highness," I added. "Undisciplined cavalry are as much a menace to their own side as the enemy. Teaching your men to obey your commands, whether expressed by word of mouth or by trumpet blast, must be your first consideration."

He grinned. "No, no, L'Eree. That must be *your* first consideration, as you will be chief of staff. Now, artillery?"

"Massed before the infantry, Your Highness."

"Again in the Swedish fashion, eh?"

"Exactly, Your Grace. All you need is enough of it."

"That is the Queen's responsibility. But she assures me there will be cannon. And infantry?"

"Pikemen in the centre, musketeers on either wing, Your Highness."

"You seek an entirely Swedish formation."

"Properly led, Your Highness, the Swedes have never lost a battle."

"Hm," he commented. "And what of the opposition, Count?"

"This will be a war, if there is a war, Your Highness, of amateurs. England does not maintain a standing army. What professional soldiers there are, guard the King. There is an army in Ireland, which has been in being now for some dozen years. This is a formidable force. As to whether it would be politically expedient to bring this force to England ... it was a consideration of this possibility that cost Strafford his head."

"If it comes to blows, Count, it will be a matter of all of our heads. What is politically expedient will have to take second place to what is militarily necessary. Reckon this: the King, and his generals, can only be brought to book for employing Irish troops if they are defeated. But if they are defeated, will they not be brought to book in any event?"

It was the first time I had felt any respect for this tyro; the

137

knowledge that he understood how to separate the wheat from the chaff was a reassuring one.

"So you think," the Prince went on, "that we will be opposed by amateurs."

"As we will command amateurs, Your Highness. It would not do to underestimate our enemies. They will have great qualities of tenacity and stubbornness, and some of them are inspired by deep religious feelings. But I still do not think there will be any proper soldiers amongst them."

"Which makes our task the easier. Providing, as you say, we do not underestimate them. Well, Count, I look forward to having you at my side when we ride into battle. Tell me, what talents do you have, apart from those of the soldier, and, shall I say, the lover?" Proving that he was an observant fellow.

"Why, Your Highness, I doubt I have any qualities, save for those two most important ones." I can be as modest as the next man.

"Have you never dabbled in the unknown?"

Not another one? I asked myself. "In what sense, Your Highness?" I asked, cautiously.

"I mean, simply, have you never been curious enough to investigate the secrets of nature."

"Ah ... " I could not be sure whether or not he was laying a trap for me.

"These are matters which should concern any intelligent man," the Prince continued, clearly another youth who enjoyed lecturing his seniors. "Come in here, Count, and I will show you a little secret that I have discovered."

I followed him somewhat uneasily, into an inner chamber, which was crowded with a variety of odd-looking containers and instrument. Two men, middle-aged and poorly dressed, wearing leather aprons, apparently working diligently, looked up and bowed as their master entered. "Science is my hobby," the Prince explained. "And although I knew I would be here for only a short while, I had some of my equipment sent down, especially as what I am working on at the moment may be of great use to us. Look here."

I stood beside him at the workbench, where the Prince's assistants had taken their cue and were prepared to show me their latest invention. Very carefully one melted a large piece of glass over a flame, while another prepared a cold box, made of tin, lined with straw, and packed with ice. "Now," Rupert said. The melted glass was poured into the ice box, and the lid clamped on. "It will not take long," the Prince assured me. "But while it is freezing, tell me what you think of this."

On the far side of the room there was a wooden frame, a solid construction, and bolted to the wood, were eight steel tubes. "Now, you see," Rupert explained. "Each of these tubes is loaded with a ball, packed down with powder, and each has a touchhole, here, you see. Thus your musketeer simply stands behind his weapon, and touches each hole in turn, and *voilà!* You have a discharge of eight bullets in a matter of ten seconds. Thus one man does the work of eight, you see."

"It is an ingenious weapon, Your Highness," I agreed. "But it is not very manoeuverable."

"Well, it could be mounted on wheels, of course," Rupert agreed. "But its principal application would be in defence, certainly. Now, Johann, is my teardrop ready?"

"I think so, Your Highness."

"Now, Count, look at this." Rupert gestured, and the lid of the icebox was removed. From its interior, Johann lifted what indeed resembled a huge, frozen teardrop. "Brace yourself," Rupert commanded.

I had no idea what he meant, but I was to find out. Johann, holding the teardrop in both of his gloved hands, turned, and cast the object into a bucket of water waiting on the far side of the room. Instantly there was a loud explosion, and the bucket burst, inundating the floor. "What in the name of the Devil . . . " I cried.

"The Devil has nothing to do with it, Count," Rupert said. "It is a simple scientific experiment. The glass itself was not actually frozen, you see; there was only a thin shield of ice surrounding it. But the glass within had actually contracted because of the cold. When the ice was

139

broken, that contracting process was reversed, with sufficient pressure to cause an explosion." He stroked his chin. "All I need now is to find a practical use for it."

My regard for the Prince grew enormously from that visit to his laboratory, but of course we were engaged in a more serious business than scientific experiments. Only a week later the wind was in the east, and we were ready to sail. We embarked in a single vessel; the main part of the armament that the Queen was raising would follow in several ships behind us. "They shall be there in a month," she promised us, regarding me at the least with tears in her eyes. "Give my love to His Majesty," she said. "Assure him of my undying devotion, both to him and to the cause."

I bowed.

"And come back to me," she whispered.

"Not all the Pyms in the world shall keep me away," I promised.

Marguerite was less eager for my return. Although Caroline had behaved herself with perfect decorum throughout, and as we had had to be three in the bed, had insisted upon keeping both her shirt and her breeches on. Although in all the circumstances I had insisted upon sleeping between my squire and my wife, Marguerite, with her well-known libidinous tendencies, had managed to become quite fond of the handsome boy, so that I had been almost afraid to leave them alone together. Caroline, however, was perfectly capable of taking care of herself, and on one occasion, when Marguerite's hand had slipped down his/her breeches, had slapped my wife's face so severely that her lip had bled. Marguerite was therefore perfectly happy to see the back of us, and was now dropping heavy hints that she wished only to return to Paris, no doubt to work on the Cardinal in my absence.

For the time being, however, her endeavours were proving unsuccessful, as Henrietta Maria appeared to feel that my return to her side would be more likely were I also to be returning to my wife. "So, complete your campaign, cut off all the heads of the Parliamentarians and hurry back," she told me. "If possible, leaving that scurvy rogue behind."

Would that her instructions had been possible to carry out!

CHAPTER 6

Our voyage to England was a hazardous one, and not only on account of the weather; the ships of the Royal Navy were reputed to be entirely against the King. However, most of them were in the Channel and we were crossing the southern North Sea. And the weather, amazingly, stayed fine, as did the wind in the east, with the result that we bowled along. But it would have been most unwise of us to make for the nearest English coast, that part of the country dominated by people like Cromwell and his friends, and thus we had to steer farther north. But here again, our captain considered it unwise to put in at the Humber, in view of the quarrel that had erupted between the King and the governor of Hull, Sir John Hotham. So we had to steer farther north yet, and finally came ashore at the little village of Whitby, of some importance in religious history, four days after leaving Holland instead of the two that might have been anticipated.

As I have intimated, I had at that time never been a sailor of note, whatever distinction I might be going to gain at sea in the future, and four days bouncing on the briny was far more than my stomach could accept. In a word, I was as sick as a dog. However, I did my best to be cheerful, in order to match the spirits of the two princes, who appeared to adore every moment of the journey, and whose only disappointment was that no Navy ships did heave into sight, as they were anxious for a fight. My admiration for the young men grew with every moment I spent in their company, even as I realised that my principal task was to keep their enthusiasm under some kind of restraint. In an exactly opposite way, I was astounded at the behaviour of

Caroline, who at the sight of the sea came over in what can only be described as a fit of the feminine vapours, not a failing I had previously observed in this most enigmatic of transvestites. "You knew we would have to cross the water," I reminded her.

"Yes. Yes, I did. But I am mortally afraid of drowning, Helier," she confided, trembling from tit to toe.

"Most people are," I agreed, recalling how I had once tried to drown someone, and what a dreadful event it had been. "But this is a stout ship, and the weather is fair. We shall be in England before you know it."

But as I have already related, this turned out to be an optimistic exaggeration, and for the entire four days Caroline never left her hammock. This was the more surprising as she did not appear to suffer, as I did, from sea-sickness. She just refused ever to go on deck and gaze at the waves. I was forced to wait on her like a wetnurse, and though in the case of someone like Caroline, as my duties involved rubbing her chest and back from time to time, not to mention her nether regions, this was no great hardship, it was nonetheless disconcerting.

The princes of course were amused, and loud in their contempt. "He may be a pretty boy," Rupert commented. "But by God he will never make a soldier, Count." What this had to do with the poor girl's dislike for the sea quite escaped me.

Caroline certainly regained her spirits quickly enough when finally we came ashore. We purchased the best horses available, which is not saying a great deal, and galloped off to York, where we hoped to find the King. Of course we did not; events had travelled too quickly, and upon learning that Parliament had passed a Bill of Attainder against the Queen herself the King had realised that he must bestir himself, and had ridden south with his supporters, to Nottingham we were told. It had apparently been discovered that she was raising men and munitions on the continent, and a Committee of Public Safety had been appointed which in turn had appointed the Earl of Essex as commander of an army of twenty thousand foot and four thousand horse.

The King had not even waited for his baggage and supply train, which was about to leave York when we arrived. We exhorted it to make haste, and then galloped as fast as we could to Nottingham, arriving on the day before King Charles raised his standard and followed the precedent of his great-grandfather in declaring war upon his own subjects.

We reached Nottingham on 21 August 1642, to find the city abuzz with rumour, the fatal step having not yet been taken. But that it would have to *be* taken, was obvious to everyone, unless His Majesty would tamely surrender himself to Parliament and hand over his Queen to be executed and his children to be educated. The King was as usual surrounded by his great lords, men such as the Earl of Newcastle, the Earl of Lindsey, Lord Goring, Sir Ralph Hopton and Sir Jacob Astley, all of whom I had met, and for whose military capabilities I had as much respect as they had for mine as a gentleman. He was overjoyed to welcome his nephews, as, in common with everyone else, he assumed that Rupert at the least, by the mere virtue of having fought in the continental war, was a born commander of troops.

However, he did possess a born commander of troops, even if he did not appear quite so pleased to see me. "C-c-captain L'Eree?" he inquired. "I had supposed your d-d-duty was g-g-guarding Her Majesty."

"Her Majesty being in a place of complete safety, Your Majesty, she and I deemed it my premier duty to assist in your victory."

"As he shall, Uncle," Rupert declared enthusiastically. "The Count d'Albret rode with Gustavus Adolphus, and will be of enormous assistance to our cause."

Charles did some harrumphing at this. "Count d-d-d'Albret?"

"That is my title Your Majesty," I told him. "When I came to England previously, it was deemed best that I suppress my true rank, for fear of giving offence."

"Hm," commented the King. "Hm." His courtiers looked even more sceptical. "What of the Queen?" he continued. "Has she raised any more funds?"

"Her Majesty does well, Your Majesty," I assured him. "Another shipment of arms will shortly be on its way."

"Well, then, let us raise the Royal Standard, and summon all good men and true to the support of their lawful Sovereign."

This declaration was greeted with acclamation by the lords, but when it was read to the people of Nottingham, there was no great rush of enthusiasm. Nor was Caroline impressed. "We are fighting for a losing cause, Helier," she told me that night, as we sought our lodgings. At that we were fortunate to have a tiny garret room to ourselves, so crowded was the city. But at least we were alone for the first time since leaving the ship, and she had entirely regained her spirits.

I thus did not seek to argue the matter for some minutes, until we were both somewhat breathless. Then I ventured, "Yet is he our king, and it is our duty to fight for him and die for him if need be."

She raised herself on her elbow. "He is not *my* king. And is he truly yours?"

I was not in the mood for a genealogical argument. "He is all the king I happen to have at the moment, and if you intend to ride at my side, then he is all the king you have at this moment, either."

"You are my king, Helier," she assured me, and with that proceeded to make me content.

The next morning all the lords and the King's guards assembled, a-bristle with red tunics and gleaming swords and pikes and muskets. Prince Rupert mounted with his beastly monkey sitting on his bridle and his equally beastly little dog yapping at his horse's heels, to watch the standard being raised. A goodly crowd had also assembled, including men as well as boys, women, girls, ancients, dogs, cats, chickens, goats, geese and cattle – this being, thoughtfully, market day – and the recruiting sergeants were already seated at their desks hopefully waiting to enroll the multitudes anxious to follow my example and die for their king. There was also a huge bag of shillings, one of which would be given to each recruit, it being felt that this would be a powerful incentive to would-be volunteers; no one knew when they would see any further pay, but this was not a matter into which anyone wished to go at that moment.

Unfortunately, while man, even a king, may propose, it is God who does the disposing. The morning had begun with a gusty wind, raising dust and leaves and generally causing a great deal of inconvenience. No sooner had the standard been raised than the wind became a gale, the gale became a storm, the storm became a tempest, and the tempest became what I believe is known in certain remoter quarters of the globe as a hurricane. This all happened in the space of an hour, while His Majesty and his lords were still making speeches intended to whip up the people into a patriotic fervour. My own reflection, as Caroline and I were forced to dismount to stop ourselves being blown out of the saddle, was that we should thank God this had not happened a few days earlier, while we had been at sea. Some idea of what might have overtaken us was indicated by the flagpole, which promptly blew down, while the standard itself was shredded. Men hurried forward to raise the timber again, and attempted to bend on a new flag, but this too was shredded in a matter of seconds, while the pole was ripped from their grasps and hurled against the wall of a house, shattering in the process.

By now the lightning was flashing and the thunder was crashing and the rain was teeming down; the entire day had turned into a disaster. Even had we succeeded in re-establishing the standard, and keeping it up, it would have done the King no good. The assembled populace had decided it was no day to be out, and had departed to the various taverns on the sound principle that when it is very wet without the only sensible action to take is to become equally wet within. Needless to say, they did not succeed in taking all their animals with them, and the square became a dangerous place as neighing asses, barking dogs, and hissing geese all seemed to lose their senses at the same time.

This tempest blew for three days, and made the most utter mess of the King's plans, not to say his prospects. For naturally there were enough people to mutter that if the elements were against the assertion of monarchical authority then God must be too. "This campaign," Caroline remarked, "is a shambles before it has even properly begun."

I couldn't help but agree with her, even though I would not have said so. But the fact was that a most profound depression had overcome the royal forces, and more particularly the royal commanders. This was not merely a result of the tempest in itself: there had been very little recruitment from the people of Nottingham, the baggage train from York had not yet arrived – obviously it had merely been delayed by the bad weather but when one is depressed these slight mishaps are always mentally magnified into imminent catastrophe – and to cap it all news was received that Essex with fifteen thousand men was on his way to do battle.

From the above strictures I must except the two princes. Rupert was as filled with energy as ever, and was for sallying forth with what we had to face the foe. The rest of the King's advisers were less sanguine. "We do not muster five thousand men, Your Majesty," Newcastle protested. "How may five thousand hope to face fifteen?"

"We have five thousand *men*, my lord earl," Rupert declared. "Essex has fifteen thousand farm boys and shop assistants. It would be no contest."

The King meanwhile was stroking his chin and wringing his hands. I am of course aware that His Majesty has come to be regarded as the most dishonest of men, giving his word in one direction today, breaking it to give another solemn promise in another direction tomorrow, and generally displaying himself as utterly untrustworthy. This is certainly how his actions presented themselves, and as the good book says, one should judge a man by his works.

However, my own personal opinion is that the King was not so much duplicitous as simply unable to make up his mind resolutely in any direction. Granted he was beset with contrary advice between the princes and his lords, but he was our commander, it was for him to make firm decisions, and adhere to them. Well, he finally did make a decision, but it was the wrong one: he sent Sir John Colepepper to London to hear what terms Parliament wanted. As if he did not already know what Parliament wanted, and as if he could not understand that by sending to treat on the approach of a hostile army he was merely betraying his own weakness.

But there it was. Colepepper rode off with his escort and his flag of truce, and our gallant lords were mightily relieved, because, in view of the negotiations, Essex ceased his advance. Prince Rupert was furious. He stamped into the inn where Caroline and I were having our midday meal, bent his usual censorious glance upon my squire – he had no doubt at all that we were the most rampant sodomites in Europe, a not entirely incorrect conclusion – and threw himself down beside me, drinking my mug of ale. "God's truth, what terrible muck," he growled. "But the wine is hardly better. Count, if we remain so we are undone."

My instincts told me that he was referring to our military situation rather than our dinner; in which case I couldn't argue with his prognostication. "But there are some of us with fire in our bellies," the Prince went on. "We need men, and arms, and money, and food ... and wine, by God. Will you ride with me to obtain these things?"

"Ride where, Your Highness?"

He waved his hand. "To wherever we can find what we require. I am told there is much wealth in Coventry. And an arsenal."

"You intend to attack Coventry, Your Highness?"

"I intend to *visit* Coventry, Count, at the head of a regiment of horse, and, in the name of the King, demand a contribution to our cause. As I assume they are loyal citizens, I do not anticipate any great difficulty."

"And if they refuse your demand, Your Highness?"

148

"Why, then, they will obviously be Parliamentarians, and we will take what we need."

"By attacking them."

"I did not come here to indulge in a contest in semantics, Count. I intend to requisition our requirements; if that involves the use of force, then it involves the use of force. Are you with me, or not?"

"Is this chevauchée authorised by His Majesty, Your Highness?"

"I have not the time to waste in applying to the King, Count. More, he has not the time to waste, either, although he does not seem aware of it. It would take him a week to make up his mind. We need to act now, if only for the very good reason that we need to show Essex and his Parliamentary poltroons that we have no intention of sitting on our asses while they string a noose round our necks."

"Such an action will upset a great many people, Your Highness."

"God's truth, Count, I came here to win a war, and I have never heard of any general who accomplished that without upsetting one or two people. Will you ride with me, or no?" He glanced at Caroline. "You may leave your servant, if you feel he may be at risk."

Caroline's answer was to rise and clap her hat the more firmly on her head. I could do no less.

So off we set, at dawn the following day. Rupert had rounded up, as he had said, some three hundred of the younger and more enthusiastic of the King's assembly. We made a merry company as we clattered along, all great boots and feathered hats and swinging coats and brilliant doublets, armed with sword and pistol and mounted upon the best of horses. Even Caroline and I were at last well off in this respect, for if the good people of Nottinghamshire had been less than responsive to their King's summons to arms, the farmers and lower gentry of the county had immediately perceived the possibility of a profit from such a martial proceeding in their neighbourhood. They had produced their horseflesh in great numbers, for sale at

149

exorbitant prices, to be sure, but thanks to the Cardinal's generosity I was well heeled at that moment, and so had purchased us each a splendid mount, although I might sigh for any horse equal to my great Hannibal, who had carried me throughout the German war, and who was at that moment enjoying the life of a stud on my farm in Garnesey.

However, I was immediately concerned with the evidences of how this war was going to be fought. My only experience of campaigning had been in Germany, and I had arrived on that horrendous scene when the conflict had been in progress for more than ten years. That is to say, every town or village worth pillaging had been pillaged, most thoroughly; every source of wealth or sustenance had been looted, most thoroughly; every man capable of raising arms against the prevailing army had been hanged, most thoroughly; and every woman or girl worth raping had been raped, most thoroughly.

These unhappy conditions had not obtained in England for many hundreds of years. Even the Wars of the Roses, of which men still spoke in whispers, had in the main been a gigantic tournament between knight and knight. The common folk had often been dragooned, certainly, but when not engaged in combat – and there were only half-a-dozen proper battles in the whole of those thirty years – were generally left to themselves. Life, property and chastity had been on the whole respected. Indeed, I have heard it said that one reason the English were so eager to draw swords for either King or Parliament was simply because it had been so long since they had experienced a domestic war that they were eager to find out what it was all about.

Well, they were about to.

It is not for me to say that Prince Rupert precipitated the whole mad business. This is certainly untrue. So far had relations between King and Parliament become estranged that there was bound to be a lot of bloodletting before any sort of agreement could be reached. But Rupert certainly set the ball rolling as we galloped behind him across the countryside, hallooing and firing our pistols for all the world as if we were engaging in some gigantic hunt. Which, indeed, we were.

As nothing like this was known in England, people came out of their houses to gaze at us, and even to cheer us. We clattered through villages, the princes out in front with their standard bearer, Caroline and I close behind, and the rest strung out behind us. However, when we had ridden some fifteen miles, and our mounts were all but blown, Rupert called a halt at the next village, and we crowded into the yard of the inn. "Ale!" Rupert bellowed at the landlord. "Ale for my hearty fellows."

"Ale it shall be, my lord," the landlord agreed, and his tapsters began working. Our thirsts were slaked, but by now our danders were up, with the exception of Caroline, who of course did not possess one, and I could see our initial welcome diminishing as there arose a series of screams from the various serving wenches who found themselves being tumbled. To be sure, the screams were not very convincing, being more of the Oh-sir-please-do-not-be-quite-so-rough variety rather than your full-blooded cry for help, but of course the menfolk were offended. Although it was easy to see they were even more offended by the sight of their fowls being pocketed for our dinner. The fowls, I may say, made considerably more noise than the women at being ravished. However, they swallowed their anger in anticipation of a fat profit, and mine host presented his account.,

"A pen," Rupert shouted. "Have you not a pen, man?"

"A pen," the landlord agreed, totally mystified. He became even more mystified when, a pen and inkwell having been found, Rupert scrawled across the account: *In the name of the King.*

"Indeed, my lord," the good fellow said, "we are all supporters of the King, to be sure. But the account requires settling in coin."

"Coin?" Rupert demanded. "Do you suppose I am a common cutpurse, sir? I do not carry coin. My name is Rupert of the Rhine, and the King, God bless him, is my uncle. There is his name on your account. Present it to His Majesty's Treasurer, and you will be paid."

The landlord goggled at the paper. "May I ask where His Majesty's Treasurer is to be found, Your Highness?"

"When last I saw the fellow, he was at Nottingham. But you must make haste, landlord. I doubt he will be there much longer. Haha!" And off we rode again, leaving a sorely troubled group of people behind us.

They were only the first. We requisitioned food and ale, and a certain amount of company, at every stop, to the continuing discomfort of the yokels. And not only them. "These men disgust me," Caroline remarked. I couldn't argue that her presence was entirely superfluous, as she ate little, drank less, and appeared to be totally unstirred by the sight of heaving breast or ruby-red lips ... but this of course was hardly surprising. My misfortune was that with her along I could not indulge to any great extent myself. But by late afternoon we had arrived at our destination, and were clattering down the main street of the town of Coventry.

This brought the people out in their thousands to see us, and I felt a little uneasy, because there were, literally, thousands of them, to our three hundred. But a large proportion of the onlookers were women and children, and only a few of the men were gentry; the remainder were unarmed. We rode straight to the town hall, where we dismounted and Rupert and his brother went inside. I remained outside, placing our men in a position of defence, although at the moment this did not appear necessary: the onlookers were more curious than hostile. Soon one of the clerks came scurrying out, looking very hot and bothered, followed by the princes, who stood at the top of the steps and surveyed the mob, which had now grown and was clustering upon us, although still seemingly over-awed by the heavily armed dragoons with whom they were confronted.

Rupert waved his arms, and as this had little effect, I commanded our trumpeter to blow a blast, which he did, following which the Prince was able to make himself heard. "Good people of Coventry," Rupert bellowed. "You have no doubt learned how certain traitorous villains in London, who call themselves Members of Parliament, have determined to depose the King, murder the Queen, and subject the princes and princesses of the royal house to perpetual imprisonment. Thus, it will not surprise you to learn that the King's friends have determined that this shall not happen."

He paused, and the crowd rustled, having heard nothing of the sort: very little of what the Prince had said was true. "Now," Rupert went on, "as I am Rupert of the Rhine, and have the honour to call the King uncle, I have been placed in command of those who would defend His Majesty's person. There are many of us. What you see here is but a handful. And we are well armed, as you can see. But we need more men to complete our task. And we need more arms and ammunition. And we need supplies of food and money. I have thus come to your fair town, certain of your loyalty, to obtain this very necessary support. Now then, who will first volunteer to serve the King?"

There was no immediate rush forward. In fact, I perceived that there was a distinct movement the other way, quite a few people beginning to hurry off, no doubt in order to secure their valuables. It was at this moment that the Mayor, who had been summoned by the clerk, arrived. He was a heavy-browed fellow with a red face, and wore a tall hat and a puritan collar. I knew at once that we were going to have trouble with him. "How now?" he inquired, loudly. "What means this tumult?"

Rupert went through his speech again, and more people slouched off. "Has His Majesty authority for such a requisition, from Parliament?" demanded the Mayor.

"Of course. From the Parliament sitting in Nottingham," Rupert replied, with great patience.

"The only Parliament I know of sits in Westminster," the Mayor declared.

Rupert's patience evaporated. He seized the unhappy fellow by the doublet and shook him. "You are a traitorous rogue," he remarked, loudly. "Now, I make a demand of you. I wish men, money, and food. But most of all, I need the keys to the arsenal. I will have these within the hour, or by God I shall hang you above these very steps."

The mayor did not lack courage. "By God, sir," he retorted. "I will set my town about your ears." With which defiant statement he called to his fellows, "To me. We are beset. To me."

Instantly all was confusion. Some of the townspeople surged forward. I countered this by commanding a volley to be fired over their heads; I might have campaigned with the worst of the Imperialist generals but there was no way I was going to fire into an unarmed mob except as a last resort. This gave them pause. Some ran away, others began to throw stones. I and my men drew our swords, while at the same time endeavouring to recharge our pistols and muskets, a lengthy process.

While this was going on, the Mayor had thrust Rupert to one side and dashed into the hall. He was pursued, but knew the various passages better than we, and was not seen again. "By God, but he has tricked us," Rupert declared. "Very well, gentlemen. This town has declared for the Parliament. I give it to you."

What followed can only be described as chaos. In the course of my earlier soldiering I had been forced to take part in more than one sack. That which stands out most vividly in my mind was Magdeburg, where an entire city of thirty thousand souls was torn apart by the rampant soldiery. But in that case the soldiery had also amounted to roughly thirty thousand ... well, I would hardly like to call them souls, even if I was of their number. Coventry was an entirely different matter, as here was a town of several thousand souls being given over to a sack by three hundred!

However, we had the advantage of surprise, and for a little while all went well. That is to say, we ransacked the town hall, but found very little of value, so we turned our attention to the houses and shops to either side, and here we found a great deal. To his credit, Rupert had told his men before entering the town that there was to be no rape and no wanton destruction of property, but these things take on a nice distinction when someone wants something and someone else is reluctant to let him have it. Certainly there arose a most tremendous hubbub. "It is the arsenal we really want," Rupert said. "And that rascal of a mayor has run off with the key. Count, you must break down the door."

I was happy to undertake this task if only to avoid joining in the general guilty procedure, which I was sure would have unfortunate repercussions. I beckoned Caroline, who also had little interest in rape and pillage, and a dozen men, and we mounted our horses and rode to the arsenal, which was situated just outside the town. But here we encountered the Mayor again, who was also accompanied by a dozen fellows, all armed. To be sure, they would not have caused us any difficulty, save for the fact that several of them carried flaming torches. The door was open, and we could see a powder train laid and waiting. "Advance but one step further," declared His Worship, "and I will blow this building sky high."

"And yourself with it," Caroline pointed out.

"Aye, but you will be accompanying me, lad," was his retort.

"I think he is bluffing," the stout girl said.

"And I do not think it is worth the risk," I pointed out. "Bluffing or not, all it takes is for him to drop that torch, and we are all in perdition."

"But we shall be travelling together, Helier," she said, most disconcertingly.

"Unfortunately, so will all the arms and ammunition," I reminded her. "Which will thence be of no use to anyone." And I commanded a retreat.

It was just as well I did. We rode back to the town hall amongst people gathering from every direction, and these were in the main armed men. Indeed, we had to gallop the last quarter of a mile, hurling people left and right as we did so, to gain safety. By now it was quite late, and beginning to darken, and our situation was grave in the extreme. For the gathering human storm had been overseen by Rupert, who had called his people together. So there we were, three hundred strong, now surrounded by an armed mob of at least a thousand, and possibly a good deal more; it was difficult to be sure in the gloom.

"They want war, do they?" demanded the Prince. "Then they will have war. Prepare to charge."

"With respect, Your Highness," I said. "To charge those people would be an act of war."

"That is what I just said," he pointed out, with his usual impatience.

"You have authority to start the war, Your Highness?"

"Do you not suppose they intend to start one, Count?"

"Then let them, Your Highness. I would ask you this: suppose you charge those people, and we return to Nottingham to discover that His Majesty has made his peace with Parliament? Then we are cutthroats and robbers, and will all hang."

"Confound you for a lawyer, sir!" Rupert went very red in the face as he spoke, and no doubt reflected that as the King's nephew he was unlikely to have to suffer the ultimate fate. But my words had been overheard by most of our men, and they nodded their agreement, realising that *they* enjoyed no such royal immunity.

"And do you think these people will let us depart, with what we have taken?" Prince Maurice asked.

"I believe they may well do so, Your Highness," I said. "Providing we leave now, and in an orderly manner. They will know as well as we that to start a fight will result in lives being lost. On the other hand, if they do attack us, then we are entitled to defend ourselves."

"By God, you are right," Rupert said, and gave the command. We formed column of fours, with drawn swords and cocked pistols, and rode away from the town hall. At first a cry went up to watch out, they are about to charge, but the more sensible of our antagonists realised that we did not intend violence, and after some hesitation, they parted before us and allowed us through.

"In truth, I shall never understand you, Helier," muttered Caroline, as ever at my side. "Did you not come here

156

to start a war? You will never have a better opportunity than that."

"I came here to *win* a war," I corrected her. "It is somebody else's business to start it."

In fact we returned to a realisation that the war had indeed started. Parliament, as I had expected would be the case, had merely upped the ante when the King had asked them to repeat their terms, and the King, as equally was to be expected, had refused. However, I have no regrets for preventing Rupert from engaging in a battle with the people of Coventry; on the one side it could have been a massacre, on the other we could have been very roughly handled. Not that my action prevented the Parliamentary pamphleteers making the most of it, describing in graphic and quite untrue details how the King's dreadful German general had brought the methods of waging war practised by the hordes of Wallenstein and Tilly into the heart of peaceful England! Well, they hadn't seen anything yet.

Unable to discover a great deal of support around Nottingham, the King now departed for the West Country, where he remained popular, and made his headquarters at Shrewsbury, while we set about recruiting in earnest. People flocked to the royal banner, while His Majesty made great speeches about suppressing both Papism and Puritanism. This while instructing the Earl of Newcastle to consider the best ways and means of bringing the army of Ireland, which was composed in the main of Papists, across the water to fight for him! He also managed to raise a good deal of money by selling baronies, at six thousand pounds a time. I have to confess I was tempted, as a title such as Baron L'Eree of Torteval – a parish in Garnesey where I had my farm – would I thought have sounded even better than Count d'Albret. Unfortunately, I did not have six thousand pounds on me at the moment.

However, by these and other methods the King raised both men and money, and by the end of September he possessed an army, equipped and ready to fight, of some eleven thousand men. Whereupon he summoned the usual conference of his commanders to decide what should be done.

I was of course present at this, although Caroline, much to her disgust, was excluded. We had both spent a very busy time during the preceding month, training our people. This was obviously not what Caroline had expected to have to do, and she had become somewhat disgruntled, while always anxious to please me when we were alone together. My own feelings towards her grew more ambiguous with every day. Sexually, she was a delicious bundle of joy, and there is obviously something which appeals to the devil in all of us about retiring to a privy bedchamber with a handsome young man who strips to reveal himself as an even handsomer young woman. But as I came to know her better, so I more and more became certain that she was never my poor Jeanne's daughter. Actually the consideration was in reverse – I could not accept that Jeanne could possibly be Caroline's mother. I had of course felt from the first that it was extremely difficult to accept that Jeanne had ever been a member of even the minor nobility; for all the physical charms that were to be discovered when one managed to delve beneath her masculine clothing, she was one of the most uncouth human beings I had ever encountered: the concept that she could once have known how to handle a fork or had ever sat before a mirror while her hair was dressed was absurd; she had not even revealed any ability to read or write – save for that mysterious letter to her long-lost daughter!

These obvious discrepancies between what Caroline claimed and what had to be the truth had lain at the back of my mind as an irritant from the beginning. But in the mere presence of the beautiful girl, and the great events that were whirling around our heads, they had remained no more than irritants. The month we spent at Shrewsbury while the King formed his army was the first occasion on which we had come to rest, as it were, and thus the first occasion on

158

which I had had the time to study my charming companion with any closeness.

She again indicated the reverse sign of the coin, for she was every inch a lady, which did not entirely go with her claim to have been brought up by a country baker: it was as if mother should have had the daughter's manners and demeanour, and daughter the mother's. But there was more. There was a remote possibility that the good Baker Le Brock, aware of the true identity of his foster daughter, might have got hold of some lessons in etiquette and general behaviour of the upper classes and instilled these in the child. But he could not have instilled in her the *arrogance* of one conscious of noble birth, and this my Caroline possessed in the fullest measure. More, it was not merely the arrogance of the *petite noblesse*, but that of the *grande dame*. It shone through in many little ways, not least in the way she constantly had to recall herself to her station when she unthinkingly sought to be the first to eat or drink, or indeed when she looked around herself at table, as if expecting to be served. And while she worked hard at being domestic, it was very easy to tell that she was a complete stranger to the management of a household: when, seeking to make life easier for her, I purchased her a laundry tally, she merely looked at the various revolving numbers as if they were some kind of game, never having seen such a thing before.

Most disturbing of all, however, was her complete lack of anything which might be described as fear, not only of injury but even of death, as typified by her willingness to challenge the Mayor of Coventry and his powder train. This was so much at odds with her behaviour when on the ship. It will therefore be seen that there was growing in my mind a steady concern that a young woman who was so patently not what she appeared, might have some entirely ulterior motive for serving me than the adoration which she professed, and which, I had to admit, she displayed at every opportunity. Doubt is probably the most debilitating affliction that can overtake any man, and it would soon have begun to ruin our relationship had events not now started to move with a rapidity which drove personal matters from my consideration.

At the conference the King made his usual harrumphs and considered this plan and then that; there were the usual suggestions that now we possessed an army it might be possible again to approach Parliament and attempt to reach terms with them; and the usual declaration by Rupert that, now we had an army, our business was to seek out Essex and destroy him – and *then* discuss terms with Parliament. This last certainly was the only suggestion that made any sense, but it also had its weaknesses. As was expressed by Lord Goring. "Oh, indeed, my lord Prince," he said sarcastically. "Seek out Essex. And do you suppose that will be a matter of snapping our fingers? Why, we do not even know where Essex is."

"Ah, my lord," Rupert said. "But I do. He is at Worcester, and preparing to go into winter quarters there. I know this because I took one of the patrols up there but last week, and encountered a Parliamentary outpost. I assumed that they too were but a small force, but when I pressed them, I suddenly found myself confronted by the entire rebel army. Thus I withdrew."

"And no doubt Essex has done the same," Sir Ralph Hopton remarked.

"We shall find him," Prince Charles declared, fired with the resolution of his cousin.

"With respect, Your Highness," Newcastle protested. "We would wear out our people tramping to and fro, and with winter coming on? There is only one thing that is certain here, and that is that Essex will only fight us when he is good and ready, not simply because we prance up to him and challenge him. Far and away our best plan would be to follow the example of the Earl and go into winter quarters. By next spring, who can tell what may have happened?"

"Bah!" Rupert declared. "You are always following other people's example, my lord earl. Is it not time you set an example of your own? I can tell you what will have happened by next spring, if we do nothing. They will have grown stronger, and we will have grown weaker. That is what will have happened."

Newcastle bristled, and clearly we were on the verge of a serious difference of opinion. I deemed it necessary to give a loud cough. "Yes, L'Eree?" asked the King.

"Your Majesty," I said. "Prince Rupert is absolutely right. We have raised an army. We must use it, while it is bright and keen. To sit here for the next six months will but see it dwindle. And the only proper way to use the army is against the enemy. But," I added, as I could see the various officers preparing to shout me down. "The Earl of Newcastle is also right when he says that the Earl of Essex will only fight us on his terms, knowing as he does that time is on his side."

"Faith," Goring remarked, "this fellow is a master of stating the obvious."

I ignored him. "However, Your Majesty, the answer to our conundrum is a simple one: we must make it *imperative* for Essex to fight us."

"And how is this to be d-d-done?" asked the King.

"Very simply, Your Majesty. March on London."

That did cause a commotion.

"March on London? With eleven thousand men?" Newcastle demanded. Even Rupert was stroking his chin.

I was not disconcerted. "I appreciate that we can hardly attack London with eleven thousand men, my lord, much less hope to hold it. But can my Lord of Essex dare let us try? Supposing he did nothing, and it were left to the trained bands to defend their city? It is almost certain that they would come out and meet us on an open field. We would equally certainly defeat them. After that, we would be faced with a problem, because of our lack of numbers. But Essex would be faced with a far greater problem, if he permitted us to advance, and win a victory, without raising a finger to help the people by whom he is employed. He would be charged with high treason, no less." I looked around their faces. "No, no, my lords, the Earl of Essex has, by adopting Worcester as his headquarters, placed himself in an invidious position. From Shrewsbury to

161

London is no further than from Worcester, saving only that we needs cross the river before approaching the city. However, Essex must still follow us, and stop us, as soon as possible. Therefore, I would recommend that we first of all march north-east, until we are north of the Thames, and then turn east with all despatch. Essex will have to respond."

"And if we first of all march north-east, he will have the *time* to respond, and to catch us, too," Newcastle protested.

I smiled at him. "But is that not what we want, my Lord? For him to catch us?"

There was a roar of approbation. And so I had, after all, started the war.

CHAPTER 7

My estimation of the situation was proved correct. Essex felt bound to chase behind us, and as we were deliberately moving slowly, caught up with us at a place called Edge Hill, in Warwickshire. We knew of their approach, of course, from our scouts behind us, and had halted and placed ourselves in a state of preparedness, so that when on the morning of 23 October Essex resumed his advance, he found us drawn up on the next rise, waiting for him. This gave him pause for thought, and he drew up his men in turn. The Parliamentarians disposed of some fifteen thousand men, horse and foot, which meant that they outnumbered us to a considerable extent, but it appeared that they had no great intention of attacking us, having, as they thought, fulfilled their duty by bringing our easterly march to a halt. However, I at the least had every intention of attacking *them*, as did Rupert, even if the same could hardly be said of Lindsey who, having arranged our people in battle array, proceeded to order an early dinner.

The King, by this time, was dressed in full armour and looking exceedingly warlike, but when asked when we would commence hostilities, replied, "You will have to ask the Earl."

But the Earl, when applied to, said, "Whenever my lord of Essex makes a move."

When I remembered the way Gustavus had always struck his enemies at the earliest possible moment – he would have attacked the Parliamentarians while they were still forming up – I felt quite despairing. Rupert was more sanguine. "We will have them yet, Count. Do not give up hope."

And he set to work on his uncle. I returned to be with the horse, while studying the enemy as best I could. They were a motley crowd, to be sure, arranged in the most orthodox of fashions, pikemen and musketeers in the centre, horsemen on each wing, artillery out in front. But then, so were we: both Essex and Lindsey had had their experience on the continent. I was more interested in the various component parts of the enemy force, and I found myself staring in particular at one of the cavalry commanders on their right wing, which was of course on the far side of the field from our right wing, where Caroline and I were situated. Thus he was a considerable distance away, and it was quite impossible to make out his features, but yet there was something familiar about him, and his movements, as he walked his horse up and down in front of his people, clearly as impatient to be about the business as myself.

"By God," I said. "I would swear that is Cromwell."

"Who?" Caroline asked.

"A fellow I met on my last visit, a year ago."

"A Parliamentarian?"

"Oh, indeed, that he is. But I had not thought to see him here. He was on his way to America when last we spoke."

"Well, no doubt he will soon wish he had gone," she commented. For dinner having been eaten, and much wine consumed, Rupert was returning with his uncle and several lords. By now the Parliamentarian artillery had opened fire, not very effectively, and as our lords gathered round our batteries, it was clear that we meant to reply. No doubt with the encouragement of his nephew – I was out of earshot – King Charles himself somewhat delicately applied a slow match to the touchhole of one of the cannon, springing briskly back when it exploded. The ball bounded towards the enemy, and at the same time, our pikemen began to advance down the hill, long poles thrust to the fore, while the drums beat and the bugles blew.

At the sight of the Royalist mass advancing towards them behind their wall of pikes, a great tremor rippled through the Parliamentarian ranks, but then they moved forward themselves, confounding several of our officers who had felt that the enemy would turn and run at the first shot. Clearly there was going to be a severe encounter in the centre, as Rupert saw, when, accompanied by Maurice and Prince Charles, he cantered back to our position. "We must do something about their flanks, Your Highness," I said.

"My own thoughts entirely." He rose in his stirrups as he turned to look back over his eager men, scarce able to keep their mounts under control. "The regiment will charge," he called.

"With respect, Your Highness, in which direction?" Caroline asked, drawing her sword.

"Why, my little fellow, straight ahead," Rupert said. "There is our enemy." And he pointed his sword at the Parliamentarian left wing, composed, like ourselves, entirely of cavalry.

"Those are unbroken, Your Highness."

"Then we shall break them."

"What of the Prince of Wales, Your Highness?" I asked in a low voice. "Even the Black Prince was sixteen before being sent into battle."

"By God, but you are right. You'll withdraw, Charlie."

The Prince would have demurred, but Rupert sent him off under an escort, and then again rose in his stirrups. "Blow, bugler." The trumpet sounded, Rupert pointed his sword, and away we went, quite ignoring the tremendous clash of arms that was coming from our left. We anticipated a similar clash from in front of us, but the Parliamentarians, although many of them were well mounted and armed with sword and pistol as ourselves, did not hang about. To be sure a few of them were bold enough to spur towards us, as we careered down into the shallow valley that separated the two armies, and then surged up the far side, carried on by the sheer impetus of our downward movement. But these were swept aside in a moment, horses and riders flung to the ground to be trampled, while we chased after their weaker brethren. In a matter it seemed of a few minutes we were clear of the field, the Parliamentarian horse were galloping for their lives to the west, and the sounds of conflict were receding behind us.

By now our horses were blown, and so we reined in. Very few of us had blood on our swords, but that we had gained at least a tactical victory could not be denied. However, from behind us there came the sounds of the most determined struggle, in which exploding gunpowder, clashing swords, and screaming voices were all to be discerned. "We must return, Your Highness," I said. "A charge from the rear will put the enemy to flight."

"When our horses have regained their wind, Count," he said.

His decision made sense, and thus far so good; a delay of even half-an-hour would be worth it if we could deliver our charge with the fullest possible momentum. But at that moment one of his cavaliers rose in his stirrups and pointed. "And what have we there, Your Highness?"

I looked in the direction of his pointing finger, and my heart sank. Only half a mile away was the village of Kineton, and parked by the houses were several wagons. "Essex's baggage train, by God!" Prince Maurice shouted. "We must have it." And he rode towards it, followed without hesitation by nearly our entire force.

"Your Highness," I begged Rupert. "The battle..."

"Our horses need time, Count," he reminded me. "And Essex will rue the loss of his train." Saying which he rode off behind his men, leaving Caroline and myself quite alone.

"That man will be the ruination of our cause," Caroline remarked.

"We must make sure the halt is no longer than can be avoided," I told her, and rode off in my turn, she following.

Alas for my hopes, the baggage train was considerable, and our men were already at work, the guards having fled at our approach. Essex being a Parliamentarian and thus a Puritan general, there were no women to be found, which sorely disappointed our young bloods, but there was a good deal of fine stuff, including coin, not to mention wine and substantial food. It took me two hours to get our people back into the saddle and riding east, from where the sounds of battle still rose skywards.

As it happened, we were in time. Just! The King's centre was hard pressed by the push of pikes, and if he was hanging on to his standard, he had lost his standard-bearer, Sir Edmund Verney. His flanks were being assailed by the Parliamentarian right wing horse, who included in their ranks, as I had supposed, my friend Oliver, who had after all determined to remain and fight for what he believed to be the right. Indeed the Prince of Wales, who had so reluctantly rejoined his father, was now in far greater danger than if he had charged with us.

Into the rear of this mass we hurled ourselves. On this occasion we were less effective, as the enemy heard us coming and turned some of his people to face us. Horses charging unbroken pikes are at a disadvantage, but we caused sufficient disorganisation amongst the opposing ranks for the momentum of *their* attack on the King to be lost. We rode round them, and rejoined the Royal Standard, where everyone was looking very hot and bothered. "I had supposed you c-c-commanded my c-c-cavalry," the King remonstrated to his nephew.

"I do, Your Majesty, and we have carried the day," Rupert assured him. Remarkably, he was right, although everyone else was somewhat sceptical at the time. But as it was now dusk, the Parliamentarians had withdrawn, in good order, to be sure.

"Depend upon it," the Earl of Newcastle grumbled. "The whole business will have to be done again tomorrow. And then, my lord Prince, I do beg you to keep your men in hand."

I went off to see to the wounded, following Caroline, who seemed most solicitous. I was not at all sure that a surgeon's tent was the place for a young girl, but of course I could do nothing about it as to everyone else she was a young man, and had every right to be there. And in fact, she seemed fascinated by the gruesome goings-on, standing close as the bloodstained Hippocrates used a rusty saw to cut his way through the thigh of some unfortunate who had been hit by a cannon ball in the knee. Clearly amputation was the only answer to his problem, but yet it brought back my own horrid memories of my experiences after the Battle of Breitenfeld, when I had shared such a tent with similar unfortunates. My wound had been on the body rather than the limbs. Normally, this is even more immediately vital, and that I had survived after being thrown aside as certain to die was entirely due to the black arts practised by the Princess von Hohengraffen. It will therefore be understood that there was more than one reason for me to stumble from the tent, hands held to my mouth, and as I knelt, close enough to a row of groaning men, waiting to regain my manhood, Caroline knelt beside me.

"Why, Helier," she said. "You are all overcome."

"And you are not," I replied, somewhat irritably, as no man likes to be found in want by his mistress.

"I was unfortunate enough to spend a season in the Convent of Our Lady of Mercy in Bourges," she explained. "At a time when the plague was raging. There I saw, and tended, many worse sights than these."

Another revelation of her past which had previously been unknown to me. But now came the most terrifying of all, for the man lying close to us uttered a horrible groan, and commenced to writhe in a positively obscene manner. "He is dying," I muttered.

"Probably," she agreed, and knelt beside the injured man. "But possibly not. He has simply been neglected."

I forced myself to look more closely, and saw, protruding from the man's upper right chest, just beneath the collarbone, a pikehead which had snapped off, leaving some four inches of steel embedded in the flesh. "That should have been removed long ago," Caroline observed, and without further ado removed it, by the simple process of grasping the offending metal and pulling it out.

The man uttered a great shriek, and blood began to gush from the wound. Consider my consternation when I watched my companion of many a midnight tumble lower her head and commence to suck at the wound, nor did she ever trouble to spit out the blood she took into her mouth, but rather swallowed it with every suggestion of enjoy-

168

ment. I was appalled. But if most people would have been similarly afflicted, consider *my* situation. For the last time I had seen anyone appearing to enjoy the taste of human blood had been when I had knelt at the side of Richilde Bethlen, Princess von Hohengraffen, the woman I had condemned to death for witchcraft and vampirism.

Now suddenly the entire truth of the matter dawned on me, a trifle late, it could be said. But at the same time, not the *entire* truth. Richilde was dead. If I had been unable to find her corpse where I had left it, I was still certain I had slain her. What I had fled from, abandoning my Normandy seigneury to seek refuge across the water in Garnesey, had been her ghost. But this was no ghost. Time and again I had been reassured on that score. Yet if Caroline was not a ghost ... My charmer at last raised her head, presenting a horrifying if exciting sight, for her mouth was still filled with blood, although this she rapidly enough swallowed. Nor did she seem to find anything exceptional in what she had done. "He will live now," she said.

"From your saliva?"

"Providing the saliva comes from a healthy host, it is the best of medicines," she assured me.

"And will you now suck the wound of every man in this encampment?"

"Would that I could," she said.

I turned and walked away from her. My senses were sufficiently confused to have caused me to do something irretrievable, and certainly stupid at that time. But if this woman was in some way a vampire, as Richilde had been ... ? and I had fallen as much in love with her as I ever had with her predecessor. I heard her footsteps beside me, as I stood in the dark, away from our campfires.

"Now I have betrayed myself," she said softly.

"That you have," I agreed. "Will you not tell me the truth of the matter?" I could have added, before I throttle you, but I did not.

"You knew my mother," she said. "Nay, you *killed* my mother."

I turned, fiercely and desperately. "You claim too many mothers, *mademoiselle*."

"Come now, Helier, you knew my original story was false."

"And this is the truth? Richilde? She was a girl of twenty when I knew her."

"Do you really suppose so? Did you ever inquire after her age?"

I bit my lip, for if Richilde Bethlen had had the body of a girl, I had never doubted that she had lived a long time. I had considered it better not to think about it, at the time. "Then the Prince von Hohengraffen was your father? You are a princess?"

She smiled; her teeth gleamed in the darkness. "Would that I were, Helier. But not by that snivelling madman. I do not know who my father was. That part of my story was true. I do know that, like Jeanne, my mother would have had it be you."

"Jeanne," I muttered. "Your mother killed her."

"She did not, Helier. You yourself have admitted this. She left her to the witch-hunters, that is true. But if I cannot deny that I have inherited her unnatural taste for human blood, am I to be held responsible for every crime committed by my mother? In any event, did you *not* slay her in turn?"

I was caught up in such a moral morass my head was spinning. On the other hand, there were realities, to which I needed desperately to cling. "You claim I killed your mother? How can you know this? No one was there, but she and I."

Another smile. "Have you not just admitted it? But of course I knew, long before I first laid eyes upon you. Did I not warn you, months ago, that there are things about which you know nothing? How do you suppose I knew so much about you?"

"You are saying that your mother communicated with you from beyond the grave?"

"Do you really want me to answer that, Helier?"

"No," I said. "No. I do not wish you to answer that. But

I wish you to tell me why you have attached yourself to me." Because it hardly made sense to suppose that she had sought me out merely to avenge Richilde. She could have done that on a thousand occasions since our first meeting, including, indeed, our very first night together.

"I have told you, my sweet. I did not lie about *that*. I regard you as all the relative I have left in the world. Would you have me wander that world, alone?"

It may seem incredible, but I determined to believe her. For consider my alternatives? I could have strangled her without further hesitation. Undoubtedly, looked at in the cold light of reason – and hindsight – this would have been the best thing to do. But this would have required explanations, and possibly caused investigations. Someone with a background such as mine, a mother burned as a witch and close relations with another witch, might find it difficult explaining that my apparently masculine servant was actually a female, and a witch herself. Because clearly this had been known to me for some time, and I had done nothing about it. While to many people, the mere fact of a woman wearing man's clothing at all is evidence of witchcraft, and those who associate with witches are regarded as being equally guilty. Then I had the comforting thought I have already revealed, that if she meant me ill she was taking a very long time about it, to which was added a certain relief, that at last all was out in the open, as it were, and the various suspicions which had haunted my midnight hours were now proven to be correct, and at the same time had been allayed.

But uppermost in my decision was my wicked, wanton wish to continue our relationship. If I had finally exploded into anger and disgust at the machinations of Caroline's mother, I had yet loved her more than any woman before or since, in or out of bed. When I had considered her dead, however much I had feared her ghost, I had yet wept to think that I would never again feel those sinuous limbs wrapped around mine. But now she had been reincarnated in the form of her daughter, just as sexually compelling, just as attractive a personality, and more, one who, if she

171

claimed a certain knowledge of the Black Art, had not yet revealed the slightest desire to dabble in it, or indeed, to do anything other than serve me. Her mother, as I recalled, however much I had adored her, had never left me in the slightest doubt that I was serving *her*. As for the morality in bedding a daughter after having bedded the mother, which might have been expected to cause me a good deal of mental distress, that was as water on a duck's back compared with the other moral problems I was carelessly casting aside.

Thus I took her back to our bivouac, and, most of the Royalist encampment being asleep, took her beneath my blanket as well for a most thorough joust. My mind remained confounded, and I do believe it was my intention, on the morrow, to perform the most amazing feats of derring do, and perhaps get myself killed into the bargain, as the one certain way to put an end to my dilemma. But when I awoke it was to find my intentions again confounded, for the Parliamentarian army had disappeared.

To say truth, we had been aroused during the night by various noises from across the valley, and had stood to our arms, but as a thick mist had descended we had no idea of what was happening, and certainly the noises were not approaching. Thus we had stood down again, but now we faced an empty hillside. Naturally we represented the event as a victory, in that the enemy had quitted the field. But the fact was that we had been outmanoeuvred. Essex had completed the first part of his task in checking our advance. Now he needed only to throw himself between us and London. And this he accomplished. I am bound to confess that Essex, although a much reviled man by history – history being written in the main by his personal enemies or Parliamentary pamphleteers – was a much more accomplished politician than he is given credit for. His mistake, as it was perceived at the time, was that he fought for limited objectives, that is to say, the establishment of a constitutional monarchy.

Certainly there were some doubts as to how thoroughly

172

he wished the King to be beaten. Essex was a complicated character who had lived a somewhat remarkable life. Son of the earl who had loved Queen Elizabeth and been executed by her, he had been restored to his father's estates and rank by James, and had also been given in marriage to the most beautiful woman in England, so it was said. Unfortunately this female, Frances Howard, was also about the most evil woman in England, Caroline Bethlen not having got there as yet. As the couple had been a trifle young when married, Frances had been left a ward of court while her husband made a Grand Tour. He returned to discover that his wife had become the mistress of one of the King's favourites, another ambidextrous fellow named Robert Carr, whom the besotted James had made Earl of Rochester. Frances wished to marry Rochester, and Essex had had no objection to having his marriage terminated. Unfortunately there were those who were against the union, notably one Sir Thomas Overbury, an old friend of Rochester's, who now threatened to reveal all manner of unpleasant knowledge that he possessed about the young couple. Frances therefore had him poisoned, and was very fortunate to escape the gallows when the whole thing came out in a huge scandal that is still spoken of. The event finished her socially, and her second husband as well.

One would have supposed that these goings-on would have put Essex entirely off courts and royalty, but in fact he had been a faithful supporter of Charles down to a few years previously, when he had been refused command of the army the King was unwisely sending against the Scots for declining to accept his religious convictions – and which had been the cause of the deep financial problems which had enabled Parliament to gain the ascendancy. Thus the Earl had opted to command against his King, at least at the start of the conflict. He was to be succeeded by an altogether more ruthless and reckless group, of whom my friend Oliver was only the outstanding protagonist, who sought much more sinister ends. And what is the result, after nearly two decades of bitter fighting which has cost a

173

great many lives and an untold amount of property? We have a constitutional monarchy!

At the same time one is bound to admit that attempting to attain this desirable end while Charles I was king was rightly regarded by a good many people as being impossible. The events following the Battle of Edge Hill prove this. Having determined that the Parliamentarian forces had withdrawn, the King rallied his own people and resumed our advance on the capital. No one could take exception to this, as it was his avowed intention, as recommended by myself, although I had always understood that the occupation of a hostile city by an army of some ten thousand men was quite impossible. Now that we had failed to destroy Essex's army, I would have sought an alternative course of action. Our advance, however irrelevant in military terms, and however delayed by the necessity to see to our wounded, bury our dead, and accumulate some fresh supplies of powder and ball, yet caused the greatest excitement. Essex might have stolen a march on us by his adroit disengagement, but as no one knew precisely where he was or what he was doing, and as we were trumpeting to the world that we had won a great victory, it seemed to many people that the Rebellion was about to end, and in a victory for the King. Thus it was that we approached the capital, none of us knowing precisely what to expect but all of us praying for a miracle. This miracle occurred.

The first obstacle to our march had been expected to be the fortified town of Reading. But as we prepared for battle our scouts reported that the Parliamentarian garrison had fled, and that the road to the capital was open. This was a great, and bloodless victory, enhanced the following day when a deputation arrived under a white flag, headed by the Earl of Northumberland. The King received him graciously, surrounded by his officers, amongst whose number was myself. Northumberland indicated that it was Parliament's sole wish to come to some accommodation with the King, and Charles replied graciously that it was his sole wish to spare his subjects the catastrophe of war. All he required was a resumption of the *status quo antebellum*, with, to be sure, a guarantee by Parliament that they would always provide him with sufficient funds to continue ruling the kingdom as he chose.

Northumberland promised to relay the King's wishes to London, and we sat down to wait. We could hardly believe our eyes or our ears when the next day Sir Peter Killigrew arrived to inform us that Parliament had instructed all its commanders to cease hostilities while terms were discussed, and begging His Majesty to agree to do the same. Now, there has been some debate since as to which side was the more dishonest at this time. Parliament were aware that Essex, having to march round us, had all but achieved his objective. The Earl himself was actually in London, and his men were near at hand, but not yet sufficiently organised to give battle. It has therefore been represented that Parliament was but stalling for time to enable Essex to assemble an overwhelming force against us. This may well be so. But the fact is that the King agreed to the truce proposed by Killigrew – and he was the one to break it.

For it so happened that the next day arrived with a thick fog, and the King's generals devised that it would be possible for him to evade the patrols watching us, march into Westminster, and be in possession of Parliament before they knew what was happening. In this madcap scheme Prince Rupert naturally was supportive. I was not, less on the moral grounds that the King would be breaking a solemn truce without notice, than because I had fought a battle in fog once before, on that fatal day at Lutzen in November 1632, when although the Swedes had eventually gained the day, it had been a most fortuitous event, and had cost us the life of Gustavus Adolphus.

I was of course overruled, and off we set, to disaster. Our movement was easily detected, even in the mist – a large body of men, armed and accoutred and mostly mounted, does not move without a great deal of clanking and grunting, neighing and shouting – and when we arrived at Brentford, having determined to enter the city from the north, we found our way barred by a body of horse commanded by

Denzil Holles. This was not a very large force, and we brushed them aside without difficulty, but all was at sixes and sevens in the mist, and our generals took the totally absurd decision that, having commenced our manoeuvre because of the concealment afforded us by the fog, we should now wait for the fog to lift in order that we might see what we were about, before continuing our advance.

Well, the fog lifted the next morning – and we found ourselves, at Turnham Green, confronted by Holles' horse, Essex's army, and the trained bands hastily assembled and marched out of London, a small matter of some twenty-four thousand men in total. Obviously there was nothing our ten thousand could do but retreat, with utter ignominy, the fruits of Edge Hill entirely dissipated and what is worse, the King's credibility as a man of honour totally diminished. At that we were lucky to get away. We later learned that the bolder Parliamentary commanders, as soon as they heard of our forward movement, wished to despatch a sizeable force behind us, to cut off our retreat. Had this been done the Great Rebellion might have ended several years early, and again with an enormous saving of life and property. However, while I have just praised Essex's political objectives, I am bound to confess that he was an utterly incompetent military commander. Even if he outnumbered us by better than two to one, the concept of dividing his army reduced him to a gibbering wreck, and thus we were allowed to withdraw and go into winter quarters at Oxford.

I may say that Oliver took no part in these debates and mistakes. As I was soon to discover, he had taken himself home after Edge Hill, disgusted at once with the Parliamentarian leadership and the quality of its soldiers. Principally had he been disgusted with the way the left wing cavalry had fled every which way before the impetuous charge led by Rupert and myself, and he had realised that the war could never be won, at least militarily, until Parliament could put into the field horse of at least an equal quality. The gulf between the two sides, when mounted, was indeed enormous. Our people were nearly all the sons and servants of the gentry, men who had been in the saddle since childhood and who had ridden to the hunt since then as well. The risk of being thrown and breaking several bones and perhaps even one's neck was merely part of the game to such bloods. To clerks and apprentices, quite apart from their inexperience at controlling their mounts while galloping at speed over broken ground, the fear of a heavy fall was almost greater than the fear of an opponent's sword. But Cromwell thought that the gulf could be bridged, with training and discipline, and in the event, he was proved right.

Of this sinister development we were at that time unaware. Yet looked at from any point of view, the development with which we *were* faced and of which we *were* aware was sinister enough. As I had realised from the beginning, and had pointed out from time to time, the only war we could win was a short one. For all the efforts of Henrietta Maria, Parliament had the greater resources of money, and therefore of men and munitions. It was also bound to have, in the long run, the support of a majority of the people. The King could only survive by levying taxes. Without the granting of such taxes by Parliament, they were all illegal. Well, the King had lived by levying illegal taxes for a dozen years before the rebellion, but then men had conceived they had no alternative but to pay or accept imprisonment. Now they did have an alternative: they could support Parliament, composed in the main of men they had themselves elected to office. And Parliament did not have to rely on taxes entirely; it could also sequestrate the property of the Royalist supporters. The King could hardly do this, simply because the majority of those who supported Parliament *had* no property to sequestrate. Most dangerous of all, to my mind, was that insensibly the country, discovering that it was surviving, if hazardously, without a king ruling in Whitehall, would come to ask whether it was necessary to have a king ruling in Whitehall at all, whatever the outcome of the war.

Charles, of course, understood most of these things, and understood too that London was the key to his fortunes.

He thus settled down to draw up plans. He was encouraged by all of his generals, for with the exception only of Rupert – who was quite the reverse – they were to a man far better at drawing up plans than of carrying out such plans to a proper conclusion.

In the event their plan was ludicrous. It consisted of a grand design, in which the King and Rupert with the main Royalist army were to confront Essex in the Midlands, while Hopton marched a separate force from the west, approaching London south of the Thames, and Newcastle led a similar body down from the north. The concept was that either Essex would have to give battle, and everyone was quite confident of again 'defeating' him, or that the armies of Hopton and Newcastle would meet, athwart the Thames and below London, and thus cut off the city from its shipborne trade and supplies, and force its surrender. This clap-brained scheme – which appeared so simple when constructed on a map – might just have worked if the royalist commanders had had some means of keeping in instant communication with each other, whereas the simplest message from one to the other took several days, and if they had had any means of blockading the river, which they did not.

Equally it might have worked if the Count d'Albret had continued to ride beside Prince Rupert at the head of the King's cavalry. But circumstances now arose to put an end to that aspect of my career, at least for a season.

The plan was to be instrumented in the spring of 1643. Both sides were happy to go into winter quarters, and accumulate men and munitions, while denouncing the other by means of pamphlets. And, incidentally, quarrel with and about their commanders. It was represented on the Parliamentary side that Essex did not have his heart in the war, and should be replaced by Sir William Waller, who had obtained some trifling successes against the King's people in the West Country. On our side it was equally represented that Lindsey had been incompetent. No doubt both charges were accurate enough, but while Essex survived his critics, at least for the time, Lindsey had not. He was replaced by Rupert, an appointment that everyone realised must either very rapidly be proved an outstanding success or an outstanding failure. In fact it would have been an outstanding success, had I remained at his shoulder. But as I have said, I was not to be there again until the cause was lost.

Caroline and I had found ourselves some comfortable lodgings in Oxford, and were looking forward to a winter of connubial bliss, as it did not appear that our military duties were going to be excessive over the next few months, when we were assailed by the most unfortunate news from France: Richelieu was dead!

Well, to be sure, when he had recalled me to his service, just a year previously, he had claimed to be dying. But it is always best not to accept such a statement from a man in such a position of power and authority. Equally, when last I had seen him, earlier this very year, I had been distressed at the deterioration in his appearance, but as I have recounted, he had seemed to possess all his old energy. Now I felt as if I had been kicked in the stomach by a mule. My personal position was not immediately affected, although I could not doubt that my mission had ceased to exist along with the Cardinal: I was at least certain of employment as long as I continued to serve the King. But what of my family? All the many agents Richelieu had scattered round Europe – and Garnesey would be no exception – had answered to the great man alone, not the French Government. As was my own case. Thus, like me, these men would know that their positions and instructions were also terminated. There would be no more funds paid to Helga at the beginning of every month. I could hope that my debt had also died with the Cardinal, although as this was a matter of figures on paper rather than in the mind I could not be confident of it. But certainly Helga would be in a fair way to starve if I could not get back to her – and quickly.

"We must leave," I told Caroline that night.

"Because of the death of a French minister? He was a

179

villain." Again, no doubt, she had received some kind of transmission from her dead mother.

"He was my employer. Without him, I am a broken sword, and my family is destitute." And I explained the situation to her.

"So," she said. "You will return to your Frau and desert the only woman who loves you."

Well, I had no doubt that Helga loved me, although of course after ten years of marriage there are many women who consider their husband's faults as more important than his virtues. And the biggest fault that a husband can develop, in the eyes of his wife, is a failure to provide sufficient funds for whichever style of living she may have become accustomed to. But I could still do this for Helga, could I regain her side in time, and could I but remove her to my French estates, and make sure that they were, still, my estates. I was confident of this, however, as Richelieu had promised to record my letters patent and my title deeds. All that was necessary was to be there. Which meant getting there. "My own dear love," I said. "I adore you and value you above all other women. Nor will I ever desert you. But we are speaking of my children, not to mention the woman who once saved my life and to whom I have sworn certain oaths. Would you have me break them?"

Well, obviously, to a woman like Caroline Bethlen the odd oath or two was totally meaningless. But she could see I was very agitated, and besides, she had no interest whatsoever in the war being carried on in England. "Very well," she said. "I will ride with you to succour your wife. If you will swear to me that you will never leave my side."

I swore willingly, which is but a further example of the baseness that is man. But swearing a false oath was the least of my problems. Even deserting the King's army was no difficulty; people were doing it every day. It was getting back to Garnesey with the greatest speed that taxed me. But equally, there was no great point in regaining Garnesey without sufficient funds to satisfy any additional creditors my Helga – I was aware of her extravagance – might have accumulated. Now, to regain Garnesey regardless of any other considerations, the quickest way was to reach the south coast and charter a ship, providing this could be done without encountering opposition, which, once the fact of my desertion became known, could arise from either Parliamentarians or Royalists. But to regain France the quickest way lay east, to the East Anglian ports. This had the merit of being a shorter distance, and, as I considered it, less hazardous. It might be well known that a Frenchman named the Count d'Albret was fighting for the King, but no one could possibly connect the Count d'Albret with the Garnesey merchant Helier L'Eree, whose feat of rescuing Squire Cromwell from a watery grave would, I was certain, be well remembered, and thus honoured in those parts. I had, of course, no idea that Oliver himself was in those parts; as I had seen him at Edge Hill I felt sure he had remained with Essex.

As to wishing to regain France in preference to Garnesey, it was my opinion that a visit to both Albret and l'Eree, both to make sure these were undoubtedly mine and to accumulate whatever funds might be waiting for me there, would be a wise step before I again set foot in Garnesey. I did not anticipate the sidestep consuming more than an extra fortnight, and even if Helga had so managed to mishandle our affairs as to wind up in prison for debt before that time had elapsed, I reckoned it was surely better for me to appear with sufficient funds to extricate her from that predicament than for me to appear in great haste but penniless, when we might both find ourselves behind bars. This was my decision. Naturally, like most men who make bold decisions, I did not stop to consider the proportion of proposal/disposal: man/God ratios which have turned out badly. Caroline raised no objection to my plan: she had the utmost confidence in my judgement when it came to human matters.

Thus we stole out of Oxford that very night. I was of course sorry to be abandoning my comrades of the past six months, and even more, the two German princes, for whom, despite their excesses, I had formed a genuine attachment. On the other hand, I had entirely lost faith in the honesty of the King, or in the chances of his victory, and wished only to wash my hands of the entire business, regain Garnesey via Normandy, collect my family, and then return to France, and spend the rest of my life at ease. The necessary adjustment that would be required to accommodate both Helga and Caroline did not appear to me to be insurmountable. We thus walked our horses through the night, and a chilly drizzling rain, while I made certain suggestions to Caroline. The principal one was that as we were now abandoning all pretence at being soldiers, she should resume her natural state. I must confess that I wished her to do this even more from a libidinous point of view than from the practical desire of confusing any pursuers, who would be looking for two men rather than a man and a woman. Especially was I anxious to behold her without the false hair which was so firmly glued to her upper lip.

She agreed willingly enough. "Only provide me with some skirts, Helier," she said. But being Caroline, she had more immediate ideas as to how this should be done than I. I had supposed we would make a town, and she would remain discreetly out of sight while I procured the necessary feminine garments. But when, soon after dawn, we found ourselves close to a high road, somewhat discomforted by the drizzling rain, she quickly discerned an approaching coach. "There is our target," she declared.

"You mean to play the highwayman?" I asked. "That leads to the noose."

"Helier," she said patiently. "Desertion also leads to the noose. Does it matter who ties the knot? Our business is to avoid nooses and knots altogether, by escaping this land with all possible haste. And as you have convinced me, disguising ourselves is an important part of our prospects of survival."

She had this gift of reducing problems to their essentials, and providing the answers, too. Thus I added highway robbery to my other crimes.

I had much in mind the fate of the unhappy fellow who had

tried to waylay Marguerite and myself, and while I rode out in front of the coach I told Caroline to approach from behind. But in fact there was no resistance, and we were more fortunate than we could have hoped, as, the coachman having brought his vehicle to a stop and raised his hands, and his guard done likewise after throwing away his blunderbuss, we found three people anxious to dismount from the interior to avoid any mistreatment. At that they were the unfortunate ones. They were a mother and a father and a daughter. Caroline perfectly purred with pleasure, for the daughter was of a size very similar to herself, and their clothes were very rich. "I'll trouble you to strip," she told the girl, who promptly looked ready to faint.

While her father looked ready to explode. "Would you add rape to your crimes?" he demanded.

"Why, we may well do so," Caroline agreed, "when we have seen what the young lady has to offer."

At which the mother swooned, requiring her husband to catch her before she measured her length in the mud.

"Haste, girl, haste," Caroline commanded. "We are all getting wet. Get into the coach, and there disrobe."

The young woman, who despite her initial reaction was clearly not so distressed about the immediate future as her parents, obeyed, but then, even if rape *were* involved, Caroline was a most handsome young man. Hastily she clambered inside, Caroline entering behind her. Once protected from the rain she proceeded to undress, but I was too busy watching the coachmen and the father – busily fanning his wife's cheeks – to appreciate her finer points. However, we were all arrested by a squawk from our victim, and for a moment I almost thought that Caroline was indeed assaulting her, which, knowing Caroline, was not impossible however unnatural, but it turned out that she was only carrying her demands to the ultimate. "Everything?" the girl demanded, her voice high.

"Every last stitch," Caroline told her. "Or I shall give you to my companion here, and I assure you, your maidenhead will disappear in a puff of smoke."

At this exchange both coachmen climbed down from their seats to discover what was going on. "Keep your hands up," I told them, and this they seemed quite willing to do provided they could also keep their eyes open. Nor were they disappointed, as a few minutes later the door was opened and their young passenger was evicted, as naked as the day she had been born.

This caused her mother to faint again, while even I became interested, because she was a most comely maiden, and the rain was chill. But even tumescently naked, she immediately sank into insignificance beside the startling beauty of Caroline, now emerging from the coach dressed as a woman and pulling on her victim's discarded pelisse, following which she adjusted her broad-brimmed hat over her eyes. "How do I look?" she inquired at large.

"Magnificent," I said. "Save for the moustache."

"We shall attend to that as soon as possible. But not here." She then mounted, being forced to continue sitting astride as we had no side-saddle, and thus presenting another entrancing sight, totally confounding the coachmen, who could not determine whether to look at her legs or the bereft young woman she had just robbed of her all, who was now kneeling in the mud and attempting to use her hands to cover her various appurtenances, an impossible task, as she only had two hands.

"What am I to do?" she wailed.

"Try my breeches," Caroline recommended, and cantered off. I followed, reasoning that the coachmen's weapons were entirely clogged with mud. I was right, and no shot was sent behind us, although this may have been because they were preoccupied.

"Do you not suppose they will remember that you began as a man?" I inquired, catching Caroline up.

She gave a delicious laugh. "They will have so much to remember. In any event, they were going south, and we are going east. But I must get rid of this moustache before we encounter any more people."

We found ourselves a stand of trees which provided us with some shelter, and from her saddlebag Caroline removed a bottle of some kind of solvent, with which she proceeded to coat her upper lip. The business took some time, and required several applications, leaving, at the end, her flesh somewhat pink and irritated. But all trace of the moustache was quite gone, leaving me with very mixed feelings, for while Caroline's beauty had been redoubled, the removal of the facial fungus left absolutely no doubt that she was Richilde Bethlen's daughter. In fact, the resemblance was so striking that for a moment I felt myself to be once again in the presence of that most terrible of demons.

This was impossible, of course, or so I told myself. And Caroline herself dissipated my sudden apprehensions with a merry laugh and a loving kiss. "Now let us find a bed," she said. "And I will come to you as a woman."

We found a bed, quickly enough, in an inn at the next village, where we determined to stop for the night, the weather showing no sign of improving, and we having had a long day. Having made the decision, and had a hot bath and a long lie, we equally determined to eat and drink our fill, greatly relieved at being no longer soldiers. But we were somewhat confounded, on descending to the taproom following a most satisfactory tumble, to find our landlord, who had seemed a cheerful enough fellow when we had first appeared, wearing a very long expression. I immediately sought an explanation for this *volte face*, and supposed it would be simple enough. The country over which we had ridden all afternoon had clearly never seen the passage of an army, either friendly or hostile. Therefore ... "You are approached by an enemy, mine host?" I inquired.

He replied in no more than a whisper. "The enemy is already here, sir."

I cast a hasty look out of the window, not wishing to see any of Rupert's dragoons so soon on my trail. But the yard was empty, of horses, although there was a fair number of people on the street, causing quite a commotion. "You have not, I hope, acquired the plague?" Caroline asked.

"Would that we had, mistress. 'Tis Master Hopkins. He

rode in this afternoon while you were resting. There has been an accusation."

I had no idea what the fellow was talking about. "Who is this Mr Hopkins?"

He frowned at me. "You have not heard of Matthew Hopkins, the witch-hunter?"

Caroline and I exchanged glances, no doubt the same trend of thought careering through our minds. "You say there has been an accusation?" I demanded.

"Aye, the Widow Litchen. Well, she is a strange woman to be sure, but I would not like to say anything against her myself. But then ... Oh, the good Lord have mercy upon us," he gasped.

Both Caroline and I went to the window, to see a group of men, and several women, entering the yard and approaching the inn. Four of the men were half forcing, half carrying, a woman between them. This was clearly the Widow Litchen. But our attention was more taken by the man leading the group, who was tall and thin and cadaverous, wore a tall hat, and simply reeked of Puritanism, and more besides. It was this man who now threw open the door, while mine host and his scullery maids retreated against the wall with every expression of terror, as did their customers, ourselves excluded. "Clear the bar," the new arrival declared, while his henchmen dragged in the unfortunate woman, who continued to endeavour to resist them, without much success, and to the total disarrangement of her clothing, while, her cap having fallen off in the struggle, it could be seen that she was by no means old, and was indeed quite comely, with a wealth of yellow hair which curled about her shoulders.

At his command, the other customers ran for the door. I will confess that I was inclined to do the same, save that Caroline now returned to our table, seated herself as coolly as if she had been in her own house, and remarked. "Faith, sir, your boorish manners bid well to interrupt our meal."

The stranger glared at her, and receiving a smile in return, looked at the landlord for an explanation.

"Travellers, Master Hopkins," the host gabbled.

I perceived it was time I took my part in the conversation and determined that aggression was the best policy. "I am Captain L'Eree," I informed him. "And this is my wife. And you are Matthew Hopkins. By Heaven, sir, I have heard of you. What deviltry are you up to now?"

Hopkins was for the moment quite taken aback by our boldness, while the other people who had crowded into the room, including the captive woman, goggled at us. But then the witch-hunter recovered himself. "Deviltry, sir? do you then, claim an acquaintance with the unholy?"

"Only through people such as yourself," I told him. "I have an acquaintance with Benedict Carpzov."

Well, this was perfectly true, as I had all but slain the most famed witch-hunter in Europe while escaping his clutches. Beside me I heard Caroline draw a sharp breath. But Master Hopkins, as I had expected, was totally confounded. "Carpzov," he muttered. "You have an acquaintance with Carpzov? Well, then, Captain L'Eree, you shall be witness to my duties here."

"Witness?" I demanded. "Duties?"

"This woman has been accused of witchcraft, Captain. It is my painful duty to ascertain the truth of this accusation. But it must be done before witnesses, and these people, being acquainted with the accused, are of little value. L'Eree, sir. Is that not a French name?"

"It is a Garnesey name, sir," I told him.

"Ah. Well, that is better yet. I have heard that in the Channel Islands they know how to deal with witches. Clear the room," he repeated. "Save for Captain L'Eree." He gave Caroline a brief bow. "Perchance you would care to withdraw as well, Mistress L'Eree. There will be nothing pretty here."

"I will remain," Caroline said. "Like my husband, I am not unacquainted with witchcraft."

Hopkins gave her an appraising look, as if wondering what it would be like to have so much beauty at his mercy, then allowed her another short bow. "As you wish. Is the room cleared?" The last of the customers had been ushered out, and the last of the inquisitive women, as well. There remained only the four men who held the victim, and of course the landlord, who had shown his women from the taproom, but remained himself, a mixture of terror and titillation. "Very good," Hopkins said. "Strip the witch."

"With respect, Master Hopkins," Caroline interjected. "But you do not yet know she is a witch."

"Why, madam, you are entirely right," Hopkins agreed. "I meant, the accused. Mind you, I would say she is a witch. I can smell them a mile away. Let's have her."

Caroline tossed her head at his last remark, which made me quite anxious, but I was more concerned about the unfortunate woman, for whom I could tell the coming minutes were going to be most unpleasant. And so they were, as Hopkins' men removed every one of her garments, not without a good deal of manhandling, exposing a sturdy and well-formed body which they lifted, again with much obvious enjoyment, and deposited on the bar counter, while she screamed her outrage and indignation and attempted to fight them until she ran right out of breath. "You will observe, Captain L'Eree, Mistress L'Eree, that we have offered this woman no insult whatsoever," Hopkins said.

"You would not call so exposing her, an insult?" Caroline inquired.

"It is necessary, mistress. How else may we seek the Devil's mark? It will be there, for sure. But I will find him out." And from his satchel he drew a long steel needle, fitted with a handle for the easier holding.

At this my anger threatened to overwhelm me, as I recalled such an instrument being used upon my own dear mother. But as my hand dropped to my sword hilt, Caroline's closed on it, giving me a warning squeeze. Obviously it would be fatal to our ambitions to become involved in a tumult which might result in our imprisonment. Certainly everyone in the village seemed afraid of Hopkins, and would thus probably obey him.

Thus I allowed myself to be restrained, and watched while scissors and water and a razor were brought, and the unfortunate women was stripped of her hair, both on her body and on her head, as she had been stripped of her clothing. Again, as Mr Hopkins was careful to point out, there was no lewdity, and when one of his people was guilty of even a lascivious grin he was most severely reprimanded. But they were clearly enjoying their work, and to deprive a woman of her hair, her crowning glory looked at from any angle, is surely as humiliating an injury as rape itself. And when it was done she was subjected to the needle. "What exactly are you seeking?" Caroline asked, as if she did not know. But the fact was that while I was reduced to a trembling wreck by what I was witnessing, she was most interested, and seemed not a whit affected, even if, by her own admission, this was an ordeal she had to expect herself one day to endure.

"The Devil's mark," Hopkins explained, bending low over his victim's quivering flesh. "It is well known, you see, Mistress L'Eree, that when the Devil accepts a disciple, he kisses her, or him, for that matter, upon some intimate part of the body. Now where this kiss is implanted, there is always left some mark, and this mark is invariably quite insensitive to pain. Our first business must be to find that mark. Aha, this looks promising."

What he had found was a mole situated just above the unhappy woman's left buttock. Into this he now thrust his needle, eliciting a terrible scream, and a fresh set of writhing movements. "That is obviously not it," Caroline remarked.

"We must persevere," Hopkins said. "I would not have you suppose that my life is an easy one."

I considered that, easy or not, his life had been far too long, already, but I kept myself under control while he continued with his prodding, leaving the heaving white flesh beneath him dotted with red pin-pricks, until he returned to the same mole as he had first assailed. This time there was no answering scream, or even a twitch of movement. Well, I could see that his victim was at that moment entirely out of breath and exhausted by her torment, but Hopkins was satisfied. "The mark has been found," he declared. "Do you tell them outside, landlord."

189

Mine host ran to the door and threw it open. "The mark has been found!" he shouted.

There was a chorus of oohs and aahs, and someone actually clapped. "What happens now?" Caroline asked, interested to the last. "Is she burned?"

"No, no, Mistress L'Eree," Hopkins protested. "The mere possession of the Devil's mark is no proof that she is a witch. Is it now, eh?" he asked his victim jovially, giving her a hearty slap on those buttocks he had so recently been misusing. "It merely means that she has had an acquaintance with the Devil. Up you get, Mistress Litchen, and dress yourself. We'll have no lewdity here."

The woman, for all her obvious discomfort, rolled off the counter with great alacrity and began pulling on her clothes, some of which had been sadly torn by the men. "You mean she goes free?" Caroline was astonished. And perhaps relieved. I know I was.

"Well," Hopkins said, "Of course she cannot go free. The mark having been found, we must now discover whether or not she *is* a witch." The Widow Litchen, in the act of tying her bodice into place, paused in consternation. "But first," Hopkins continued, again opening his satchel and taking out a sheet of parchment, "I wish you, Captain L'Eree, and your good lady, to append your signatures at the appropriate place, to attest that no lewdity was used upon this woman, nor was she made to suffer any unnecessary discomfort."

"By God, sir," I said, but was interrupted by Caroline.

"Of course we will be pleased to sign your paper, Master Hopkins," she said, in tones that left no room for argument. I reflected that after all she was not so very different in character from her mother. But I signed.

"That is very satisfactory," Master Hopkins said. "Now then, all that remains is to arrive at the proof. The woman will be ducked."

At this Mistress Litchen gave a shriek, and ran for the door. But she was easily enough prevented from escaping by the eager throng which had been admitted by the earlier calls that the Devil's mark had been found. Now she was seized by all and sundry, led by Master Hopkins and his minions, and carried off in the direction of the village pond. I watched them go with a growing sense of anger, yet retained sufficient hold of my senses to understand that whatever my repugnance for the machinations of Master Hopkins and his helpers, I must not become involved. Indeed, I wished only to be rid of the lot of them. "Let us cast the mud of this place from our shoes," I told Caroline.

"We must see the woman to her fate," she insisted.

"You, of all people, wish to do that?" I demanded.

"You are a soldier," she retorted, enigmatically, "And are you therefore afraid of watching men die?"

A disturbing comparison. But I allowed myself to be led from the inn and to the banks of the pond, where we watched the unhappy Widow Litchen, screaming her outrage throughout, have her left thumb tied to her right big toe, and her right thumb tied to her left big toe, and in this humiliating and most helpless situation be hurled into the pond. Down she sank, and a few seconds later up she came again, gasping for breath. The onlookers cheered. But no one made any effort to assist her. Down she sank again, and up she bobbed again, spluttering and coughing. "How long does this continue?" Caroline asked.

"The third time is the decisive one," Hopkins said.

Down went the widow the third time, and some of the villagers actually waded into the shallows preparatory to grasping her. As they did, when she re-emerged for a third time.

"Is she now proved innocent?" Caroline inquired.

"Not necessarily," Hopkins explained. "If she has survived three sinkings, then she must undoubtedly be a witch."

"And if she has not?" I demanded.

"Then she is innocent, of course."

The Widow Litchen was most undoubtedly innocent: she was utterly devoid of life.

"I must kill that man, if it is the last thing I ever do," I muttered to Caroline.

191

"Here and now it *would* be the last thing you would ever do," she assured me. "These people regard him as some kind of magistrate."

"Then let us away from here with all possible despatch," I said.

"We will leave at dawn," she promised me.

She was not the least concerned with what had happened, and proceeded to eat a hearty supper, regardless of the fact that we were joined by Master Hopkins and his minions, the witch-hunter well satisfied with his day's work. "I am paid two shillings per witch," he told us, proudly.

"Thus you must need to work hard for a good living," Caroline suggested.

"Indeed I must. I scarce ever have a day's rest. But it is rewarding labour, Mistress L'Eree, and no man can ask for more than that. Garnesey, is it? Are you on your way there now?"

"Indeed we are," Caroline said. "We have seen too much mayhem and misery in this misbegotten country."

"Amen," Hopkins agreed piously. "There is a witch hiding round every corner. But I have heard that they are also numbers of these foul creatures in the Channel Islands. Do you think it would be a good idea for me to pay them a visit?"

"I do not recommend it," I said, most earnestly. "I doubt you would find the Channel Island air good for your health." Certainly not if I am there, I silently vowed.

He considered this, without taking my meaning. "Well," he said at last. "There is enough to be done here, to be sure."

We left early the next morning, and never have I been so glad to see the back of any community. "Tell me the truth," I asked Caroline. "You are aware that one day you may be tried as a witch?"

She gave a soft laugh. "I understand that it is possible."

"Then tell me what are your feelings at the supposition

192

that you may be stripped by lusting hands, and have a needle thrust into your most intimate parts?"

"Why," she said carelessly, "I have no doubt I would enjoy it."

I shuddered. "And then to be drowned? Or if fortunate enough to survive that, to be burned at the stake?"

"I am contemptuous of those who so accuse and mistreat poor old women, Helier," she said. "Even if I can understand the urgings of those who may enjoy so mistreating poor *young* women. However, can you not see that you, and they, are entirely missing the point? For if a woman is indeed a witch, and in league with the Devil, would she not be able to feel pain, or not, as she chose? Would she not be able to summon up her hellish friends and accomplices, at will, to dispose of those who would torment her? Would she not be immortal?" She laughed. "As am I."

She was joking of course, and yet the hair on the nape of my neck rose up in consternation at the very idea. But it was later on that day that all thoughts of witches and witch-hunters had necessarily to be driven from my mind, as we encountered a Parliamentarian patrol.

We had had dinner at another village hostelry, and were proceeding at no more than a walk, feeling very comfortable if perhaps a trifle drowsy, when there was a musket shot. That brought us both up very sharp, reaching for our swords, but before we could properly adjust our thoughts we were surrounded by a dozen rustics. The only indication that they were soldiers was that they were singularly well armed, and this observation determined me against acting rashly. Besides, my objective was to gain the coast, and this would be uncommonly difficult to do were I to have to fight my way there through an entire Parliamentary army. For their part, they were impressed by our clothes, even if Caroline's were beginning to look a little the worse for wear. "Cavaliers, by God!" said their sergeant.

"What makes you say that?" I inquired, most courteously; I knew that this was the term, intended as an insult, by which the Parliamentarians referred to the Royalists.

"Do not try to hoodwink me," the fellow declared. "I can smell a cavalier a mile off. And his lady." Accompanying this with a leer at Caroline.

Shades of Hopkins. But Caroline, as always, was not the least put out. "Well, then, your nose is blocked," she remarked. "We are Garnesey folk, seeking a way home."

"Garnesey folk?" He looked thoroughly confused. "And where might Garnesey be?"

"It is an island in the English Channel," I told him.

"Ha! You mean Jerseye," he suggested.

For it is a sad fact that for some reason, I cannot explain why, more people have heard of Jerseye than of Garnesey. "I do not mean Jerseye," I said. "Garnesey lies to the north. However, you will understand that we seek the coast, and a ship."

"Ha!" he remarked again. "You will have to answer to our colonel, first."

"Indeed? And who may your colonel be, fellow?"

"Why, Colonel Hampden, of course."

It was my turn to say, "Ha! Well, then, lead on, my good fellow."

"Do you know this man?" Caroline asked in a low voice as we were escorted to the neighbouring encampment.

"Indeed I do, he is an old friend," I promised her.

"Let us hope he remains so," she observed.

In fact Hampden was utterly astonished to see us, and somewhat suspicious. He had no idea that I was actually the Count d'Albret, of course. But he was confounded to find Helier L'Eree still in England a year after our first meeting, and accompanied by a young woman who was even more attractive than the one I had claimed as a wife on that occasion.

I was at pains to put him at his ease, Caroline having the good sense to leave the talking to me. "This country of yours has gone to wrack and ruin," I told him, as we enjoyed a mug of ale. "Finding my debtors, much less extracting any money from them, had been a most lengthy task."

"Have you not been involved in the war at all?" he inquired.

"Heaven forbid! As I told you last year, Mr Hampden, I have turned my back upon violence."

"Yet you wear a sword, I see. And carry another in your baggage, as well as four outsize pistols."

"Well, sir, a man needs to defend himself in these troubled times."

He could not argue with that, but now turned his attention to Caroline. "And how is your good wife?" he asked.

"Why, as far as I know, in the best of health. She returned to Garnesey some time ago."

"And so you found yourself another travelling companion," he observed, severely.

"Sir, you speak rashly," I riposted, just as severely. "This young lady is my niece, whom I am sworn to return to the safety of Garnesey, away from the strife that consumes this land."

He did some harrumphing at his mistake. "So now you seek a ship, eh? Well, I will provide you with an escort to Great Yarmouth. But be sure you call upon cousin Oliver on the way. He would be sadly regretful to think that you had been in these parts and not visited him."

"Cromwell is here?" I was astounded.

"He is at his home, to be sure. Training men. Depend upon it," Hampden said, "by next summer we shall have an army fit to put into the field against even Rupert."

"Well, well," I commented, somewhat sceptically. "I shall be right pleased to make Mr Cromwell's acquaintance again." I certainly did not anticipate any difficulty in this business. Indeed, I considered that our path would be that much easier, with Hampden and then Cromwell to look after us. The only inconvenience that lay ahead was the requirement that I and my niece should sleep separately, but I reasoned that this too was for but a brief period.

We ate well, slept soundly, or at least, I did. Next morning I emerged from my tent in the best of spirits, disturbed by the sound of hooves. The new arrivals were just dismounting, and amongst their number were several women.

This interested me, in a Puritan encampment, and so I went closer to discover who they might be. They were certainly dressed as Puritans, with their high bodices, wide collars, and tall hats. But as I approached, one of them turned directly to face me, and I checked in consternation: it was Aimée Hubert.

CHAPTER 8

Aimée recognised me in the same instant as I recognised her, and it would be difficult to estimate who was the more surprised. But I could be in no doubt who was in the greater danger from this quite unexpected meeting, for she immediately uttered a piercing shriek. "Arrest that man!" she screeched. "He is a Royalist spy, and a French agent."

Consternation! As everyone was in a totally confused state, I could have drawn my sword, leapt upon the nearest horse, and no doubt made my escape. Unfortunately, I was not a free agent, as I could not possibly contemplate abandoning Caroline. I therefore realised that I would have to bluff my way out of my predicament, and so stood my ground and smiled at the men who surged around me. "Tush," I said. "Would you take the word of a madwoman?"

"Shoot him down!" Aimée was recommending, loudly. "He is a monster."

By now the entire camp was awake, and Hampden had emerged from his tent, to be rapidly brought up to date by his aide-de-camp on what was happening. Caroline was also appearing, looking somewhat bleary-eyed and as amazed at the noisy developments of the morning as anyone. I could only pray she neither said nor did anything rash. "What is this all about?" Hampden inquired, approaching. "Do you know Mademoiselle Hubert, Captain L'Eree?"

Time for a hasty decision. Absolute denial? Or an attempt to twist facts? I was a little short of thinking time,

197

and therefore made a perhaps unwise decision. "I have never seen her before in my life, Colonel," I said.

"He is lying," Aimée declared. "His name is Helier L'Eree, and he is a Garneseyman in the pay of Cardinal Richelieu, whose sole mission is the protection of the Queen and the furtherance of her evil designs."

"What nonsense," I remarked.

"Yet she knows your name, Captain. And that you hail from Garnesey."

"Then no doubt she has been to Garnesey, and heard of me."

At this moment we were joined by Caroline, who, sensible girl, had lingered just long enough to gather the gist of what was happening. "Is something amiss, uncle?" she asked, in the most dulcet of tones.

"Some absurdity, my dear girl," I said. "Tell me this, have you ever beheld this woman before?"

"Indeed I have not," Caroline said, bending upon Aimée a look which indicated that if she *had*, the question of seeing her again would never have arisen.

"There, you see?" I asked Hampden. He was looking sorely confounded. "Ask him where he has spent the past year?" Aimée commanded.

"Are you sure there is no mistake?" Hampden asked. "We are much beholden to this man."

"Listen," Aimée said. "I saw this man in the Queen's employ. He it was had me arrested as a spy, and sent me to Richelieu. I escaped and returned here. You know this, Mr Hampden."

"Hm," Hampden commented. "Hm. And the young lady?"

"I have never seen her before," Aimée said, honestly enough.

"And you, Captain L'Eree?"

I had to stick to my story. "I repeat, Colonel, that I have never seen this woman before. You know why I came to England."

"That was a year ago. You have been here ever since?"

"By no means. I completed my business and returned to

Garnesey. But when hostilities commenced, our family determined that it was necessary to get our niece out of the country, and I was appointed to accomplish this."

Hampden looked at Caroline. "My uncle is telling the truth," she said without batting an eyelid. "I will swear it on the Bible."

Which, as far as Caroline was concerned, was of course totally meaningless. Yet Hampden was impressed, as he knew nothing of her background. "Hm," He commented again. "Hm."

"Hang him," Aimée insisted. "And her."

"The woman is demented," I repeated, while attempting to assess our chances of escaping. But as by now the entire camp had gathered round there was no possibility of making a run for it.

"Well, Captain," Hampden said, arriving at a decision to postpone the necessity of making a decision, "I am afraid there does seem to be a case to be answered. But I am sensible of the great service you did for our cause a year ago in rescuing my cousin from a watery grave. I think I will send you to him for judgement."

"You mean you will send me to the Army?" I demanded. That did not go well with my plans, as so far as I knew the Army was somewhere in the centre of the country, from whence we had just come.

"No, no," he said. "I am sending you to Cambridge-shire, where Oliver is recruiting men. Your niece will accompany you. And should Oliver be satisfied that you are not what this woman claims, why, from one of the east coast ports you may obtain a boat to take you home."

I was obviously going to find nothing better, so I said, "That seems an entirely agreeable decision, Colonel."

"And what of me?" Aimée demanded. "I wish to see him hung. He is a scoundrel who betrays our cause and ill treats women."

I felt this last was an exaggeration, but preferred not to say so. "You will write out a deposition, Mistress Hubert, which I shall send to Colonel Cromwell along with these people," Hampden said. "Then you had best continue on your way."

"Without me there to face him he will connive to escape his just desserts," she grumbled.

"This is not a matter of personalities, mistress," Hampden said sternly. "It is a matter of facts. Write down what you believe to be the truth of the matter. Colonel Cromwell will decide. And you, Captain L'Eree, prepare to leave."

"Nothing would give me greater pleasure, sir," I said. And an hour later Caroline and I were on our way again.

"Are we in danger?" Caroline asked softly, as we rode along in the centre of a platoon of a dozen men, armed with muskets as well as swords, which meant that attempting to escape them would be a most hazardous business.

"I do not think so," I told her. "This man Cromwell owes me his life, and is aware of it."

"Cromwell," she remarked. "You saw him at Edge Hill."

"Yes. But he gave no indication of having seen me."

Nor, it appeared, had he. "Captain L'Eree?" Oliver asked incredulously when we reached Huntingdon and were taken to his house. "By God's will, it is good to see you." He frowned at Caroline, who was of course still wearing the clothes she had taken from the girl in the coach, and was therefore as immodestly dressed – by his standards – as Marguerite had been when last we had met. "You never seem to lack the company of a beautiful woman."

I went through the niece routine, while the cornet in command of our escort became restless. "I have letters for you, from Colonel Hampden," he said when he could get a word in.

"You have been with Cousin John?" Cromwell asked.

"I was with him yesterday."

"Well, well. Sit you down, man. And Miss L'Eree. Lizzie, tea for our guests."

Even Mrs Cromwell looked pleased to see us, and her daughters, as usual, were gawking. But I was observing

200

that a great deal had changed over the year since last I had been in this house, or indeed, in this district. The whole area had taken on the appearance of an armed camp. From the blacksmith's shop there came the screech of tortured metal as ploughshares were beaten into swords, reversing the process recommended in that Bible of which Oliver was so fond. On the village green men drilled ceaselessly, and interestingly they were all dressed in the same clothes, a red tunic, buff breeches, and black boots; their armour was also the same for all – breast- and back-plates, together with a morion, and every man carried a sword and musket.

More disturbingly yet, while these fellows drilled and wheeled and presented to the commands of their sergeants, others, similarly dressed, armoured and equipped, were mounted, and also performing intricate exercises – which included charging at the gallop, swords to the fore. "You are creating an army here, Oliver," I commented.

He had been studying Hampden's letter and Aimée's deposition. Now he raised his head. "Well, a regiment, at the least. I call them my Ironsides. They will be the finest cavalry in the world."

"Have they yet been tried in battle?" I asked, perhaps sceptically.

"They will win their battles," he asserted. "Because they are God-fearing men, who neither swear nor drink nor fornicate, and who fear *only* God." He gave a grim smile. "And myself, to be sure. There is a deal to be done, but we shall be ready for the coming year. Now this ... " he threw the papers on to the table. "What is your answer to these charges?"

"As I told your cousin. They are all false. I do not know who this woman is, or can be. Perhaps it is she who should be investigated."

"She is a loyal servant of our Cause," Cromwell pointed out. "Employed by Mr Pym himself." Someone for whom he obviously had the greatest respect. "Equally," he went on, "there can be no doubt that she was detected by *someone* in the Queen's service, kidnapped and taken to

Holland, and from there sent to the Cardinal. She claims that you are that person."

"I can only deny it."

He stroked his large chin. "You will understand, Helier, that this puts me in something of a quandary. You saved my life, and I am proud to call you friend. But this woman had proved her loyalty to our cause over and again. The point is, you see, why should she accuse you, if she had never seen you before?"

"I have long ceased to understand the whims of women," I said. "But does this mean you are calling me a liar, Oliver?"

Well, of course he was. But he sought to temporise. "it is not my judgement alone here," he grumbled. "I am but a humble colonel. I do not suppose you can prove where you have been this last year? I mean, prove that you were not in the service of the Queen?"

"Certainly I can," I said boldly. "But let me return to Garnesey, and I will produce all the witnesses you could possibly require."

"I am not a total fool," he remarked, a trifle acidly.

"However, I have the perfect solution. I shall find a stout ship and a trustworthy captain, and place your niece on board, with instructions to the captain not only to deliver her to Garnesey, but to await her return here, either with the required witnesses or with signed statements made under oath." He smiled. "These will be acceptable to us, because the States of Garnesey have declared for Parliament."

"The States?" I cried. "But what of the Lieutenant-Governor?"

"Oh, to be sure, he has declared for the King, and has locked himself up in Castle Cornet. I understand he exchanges shots now and then with St Pierre Port. But as he is on a very small island, and the States control the larger island, you will appreciate that they have the advantage. Exactly the reverse obtains in Jerseye, where the Lieutenant-Governor has declared for Parliament, while the States have declared for the King. But we will sort them out, when

202

we have sorted out matters over here. Now, are you satisfied with my arrangement?"

I was not in the least satisfied. However much I adored Caroline, I did not like to contemplate a meeting between Caroline and Helga without my being present ... quite apart from the fact that without me there she would probably be quite incapable of bringing back any support for my claim to have spent most of the year in Garnesey. Besides ... "I cannot do this," I said. "My niece has a mortal fear of sea travel."

"Yet you were about to take her to sea."

"Well, with me at her side to reassure her, it might be all right. But by herself..."

"I suspect this niece of yours is given to play-acting," Cromwell observed. "And by keeping you here, I may be preserving you from mortal sin."

His tone indicated that he already suspected me guilty of it. But I was yet extremely put out. "You mean I am a prisoner," I remarked.

"I would not like you to think of it in that way," Cromwell said. "What I am doing is recruiting you to assist me in the creation of my new regiment. I need such assistance, because I am actually attracting more recruits than I can handle. And could I possibly seek anyone more capable than yourself, who rode with Gustavus Adolphus?"

There was little left to be said. Apart from explaining the situation to Caroline. She listened with grave attention, then asked me – we had been allowed these moments to ourselves – "What would you have me do?"

"It is a serious problem," I told her, having determined to make the best of the situation. "You will have to act as my agent in this. But once the business is explained to Helga, you should receive sufficient help."

"Your Garnesey advocates will swear a false oath?"

"If they are sufficiently encouraged to do so."

"But we have no money. And you say your wife is probably in debt."

"I said it is a serious situation."

203

She smiled, and blew me a kiss. "Leave it with me. Obtaining money is no problem."

"I would not like you to be hanged, Caro."

"I will not be hanged. I consider there is a yet more serious matter. Your wife will know that you do not have a niece."

"Ah. Well, can you overcome that as well?"

Another smile. "Of course. I will brood on it during my voyage. But give me written *carte blanche* to tell her whatever I wish. And of course, to do whatever may be necessary, to procure the affidavits you require."

And I, being still a besotted fool, willingly did so, only reiterating, "You understand I am trusting you with everything I hold dear. Do not fail me in this, or I shall follow you to the ends of the earth to exact vengeance."

"As you followed my mother across Europe for a similar purpose," she remarked. But then removed the sting with one of her smiles. "I shall not fail you, Helier. You have my word."

And with that I was content. In my circumstances, I had to be. And yet . . . "Are you not afraid of the voyage? I shall not be there to comfort you."

She smiled, bravely. "Then I shall have to manage on my own. I will dream of you, constantly."

"And I will pray for you."

Now her smile was mocking. "To God, or the Devil?"

"How soon do you expect to return, Mistress L'Eree?" Cromwell asked, as we assembled on the Great Yarmouth quayside for her embarkation.

"Within two months," she promised.

"Well, then, we shall spend an impatient winter."

As we were surrounded by these beastly strait-laced people I could do no more than plant a chaste kiss on her forehead. "Do not fail me," I whispered again.

"Then would I be failing myself," she replied.

I looked into her eyes. It was like peering into a pool of clear green water . . . but a pool without visible bottom. "Then, Godspeed."

Again her smile was contemptuous, and she descended into the boat. "You are blest with a most comely family," Mrs Cromwell remarked.

"No man is blest with a family at all, in time of war," her husband growled. "They are but hostages to fortune. Let us to work."

And work we did, with scarce a pause for Christmas. It was hard, and from my point of view, somewhat counter-productive labour, as I had to continue to view these men as possible enemies I might have to face in the field; clearly, if Caroline were in some way to fail me, I would have to attempt to make my escape and rejoin the King's army. And as the new year dawned, and she had been absent for the two months she had anticipated, this probability began to increase. I was naturally a prey to the most unfortunate reflections, whether they be of a purely carnal variety – as Oliver had pronounced, there was no casual fornication where he was in command, and even the prettiest village maiden was not to be tempted for fear of incurring his wrath – or of loving concern as to what might have become of her. Which increased as every day passed and I missed her more and more on both accounts.

Meanwhile, I worked, to Oliver's great pleasure. And in fact, although as I have said I undertook my duties with a heavy heart, to mine. Training men to fight is always an enjoyable pastime – where the men wish to be so taught. These men were eager. Indeed, Oliver, who, as he had told me, had set out to raise a regiment, soon found himself thinking in terms of a brigade. This was an ambitious programme, as it involved not merely the men, but the mounts. And then the remounts, which could hardly be less than two to a man. In a community such as East Anglia, devoted to farming, this last was not as severe a problem as it might have been elsewhere, but he was planning to take his Ironsides elsewhere. In addition to finding horses, it is of course far more difficult to train a man to fight mounted than it is on foot, where it is simply a business of teaching him to shoot a musket or advance – or stand fast – behind his pike. But it was amazing how enthusiasm could take the place of inbred skills. I have previously stated that the main problem with the Parliamentary cavalry was an inability to contemplate the injuries risked in charging across broken ground. Cromwell's volunteers regularly fell off, and broke this and that, and yet were quick to get back into the saddle and try the whole thing over again. This is most gratifying to an instructor, but most upsetting to an instructor who, through no fault of his own, is also a turncoat, and whose only real hope of salvation was to rejoin the opposition, if that could be accomplished.

My experience of Charles, and Lindsey, and now Rupert, as army commanders, had not inspired me with the least confidence in the Royalist cause. But even in those early days my doubts had arisen from their incompetence and divided counsels, rather than any fear that they could not defeat the Parliamentarian trained bands as and when they chose. But here I was helping to create a weapon which was clearly going to be as far superior to the trained bands as a sword is to a wooden club. It therefore seemed to me that the defeat of the King was certain, unless a way could be found to end the war before the armies commenced their summer campaigning. In this situation I was confounded by the news, late in February, that Henrietta Maria was again in England, having returned from Holland, and with a squadron laden with munitions and no doubt men as well.

Cromwell was furious. "The French bitch," he declared, "is determined to strike us down. But she works for the Devil, and ours is God's work." This was of course a point of view. While I felt that the Queen had acted rashly, there could be no arguing with her courage in returning into the lion's den, and just how dangerous this was was immediately revealed when Parliament renewed the Bill of Attainder against her, which, in effect, meant that she was an outlaw and could be killed on sight.

This action, unique against a woman, also revealed how terrified Parliament was of her. I, naturally, could not help but wonder if Marguerite was still in her entourage? In any event the Queen treated the pronouncement with her usual contempt, slept and ate amongst the soldiers she was rallying to the King's cause, and pronounced herself the She-Majesty Generalissimo. This was equally calculated to raise Cromwell's blood-pressure, but what really annoyed him was when we received news that Sir Thomas Fairfax, commanding the Parliamentarian forces in the north, had actually offered Henrietta a safe conduct from one place to another, on the grounds that gentlemen do not make war upon women, much less queens.

This was in the best traditions of knightly chivalry, but Oliver did not see it so. He was, in truth, a man of enormous contradictions, far more, indeed, than I had ever suspected, but as I was soon to find out. He was, as he declared and demonstrated almost every day, the most God-fearing of men, and he expected those close to him and serving under him to be also. His home and domestic life was conducted upon the most gentle and Christian of principles, and no man could have been more kind and even generous to his own people. As he had shown in my own case, he hesitated to condemn and sought only to do the correct thing. But by the same token, when he conceived that God had directed him to the destruction of a heathen or an idolater, he could turn into a veritable demon of destruction. I received an example of this early in the spring, when he determined to lead his first regiment out on a patrol in lands which could at best be described as neutral; that is, they were not definitely under the control of either side.

I say first regiment, because so many recruits had flocked to his colours that the brigade he dreamed of was almost in being, but a large proportion of these men were still in the training stages. "You will ride at my side, Helier," he said.

This was very flattering, although I understood that he really did not wish me out of his sight. He still could not condemn me, because Caroline's failure to return might have been caused by an accident, but I still had not been able to prove my innocence. So off we set, myself, as may be imagined, with decidedly mixed feelings, as I feared I would be called upon to fight some of my erstwhile comrades.

Sharing my place immediately behind our colonel was a young man named Henry Ireton, who was captain of the second squadron. He was a protégé of Oliver's, and indeed had an understanding with one of the great man's daughters, thus he was every bit as devout a Puritan, while also being something of a firebrand.

It was late March, cold and crisp, with a thin covering of ice on such standing water as we encountered. But the skies were blue and it was most splendid weather. We were thankfully travelling somewhat farther north than the route Caroline and I had followed on our journey in December, pausing for the night at various villages, where everything was carefully paid for in coin in strong contrast to Rupert's behaviour, and where Cromwell invariably sat down with the more important members of the community seeking information. On the third day of our chevauchée he joined me for our evening meal, decidedly agitated. "O'Connell House," he said. "It lies not far from here, and is a Royalist nest, so I am informed."

"Possibly the landlord merely dislikes the owner," I suggested.

"With reason," Oliver growled. "He is an Irishman, as his name is O'Connell. Sir Rory O'Connell. I will wager you anything you like that he is not only Irish, but a Papist as well. We will pay this fellow a visit."

"You mean to attack this house?" I inquired.

"If it does not surrender, yes."

"And when it surrenders? You propose to garrison it?"

"By no means. If it is indeed a nest of Irish Papists, I intend to burn it to the ground."

Not even Rupert had actually proposed that kind of behaviour.

We were off at dawn, and within sight of O'Connell House three hours later. In fact it looked a very substantial dwelling, for if it was by no means a fortress, it was easy to see that the walls were thick and strong, and it was surrounded by a good many outbuildings, which were also capable of defence. "They are expecting us, Colonel," said the sergeant who had ridden out ahead to reconnoitre. "There is not a man nor a beast to be seen."

"The Lord will strike those who oppose His work," Cromwell declared, and waved us forward. We arrived at the gates and found these securely locked. Cromwell peered through for a while, studying the distant building, for the drive led straight up to the huge front doors, which were also shut. To the right the stables were shuttered and beyond the farm also looked either derelict or well locked up. "Force the gates," Cromwell commanded.

This was the work of minutes, and the drive was open to us. Whereupon our colonel remounted and led us, at a walk, towards the house. We must have made an impressive sight, for we were some two hundred strong, and the morning sunlight was reflecting from our polished helmets and breastplates, not to mention our scabbards. Our hooves clicked on the driveway and our accoutrements jingled as we proceeded up to the door, now aware that we were being overlooked from the upstairs windows. These had all been shuttered, as were the lower casements, but one or two of the upper ones had been left slightly ajar, and now we saw them move. "Muskets!" I snapped.

"Regiment will scatter," Cromwell shouted. Immediately we split up into squadrons, riding for the trees to either side, and just in time, for several muskets and blunderbusses exploded. None of our people was hurt, but Cromwell was exceedingly angry. "Open a hot fire," he commanded.

We dismounted, and while one man in each section held the now thoroughly excited horses, the rest of us levelled our muskets and commenced firing at the windows. But this was slow and ineffectual work, as it takes some time to load a musket, and our balls mostly bounced off the thick shutters. "This is a waste of time," Cromwell fumed. "We must force an entry. How many men do you suppose are inside, Helier?"

"Half-a-dozen fired at us." I replied. "But that may be because they have no more firearms than that."

"Then only half-a-dozen shots can be fired at an assaulting party. If we were to charge the side door, it may be possible to force an entry. Volunteers!''

I stepped forward immediately. It was not so much that I had any desire to play the hero, but that I had every desire to remain as high as possible in this man's esteem, and equally to prove my loyalty to his cause. "Noble L'Eree," he acknowledged. "Who will follow my Garneseyman?"

A dozen stout fellows immediately joined me. "Good men," Oliver declared. "Do you force the door. We will be right behind you."

Thus encouraged, we mounted, another volunteer joining our ranks to take charge of the horses. We loaded our muskets and our pistols, loosened our swords in our scabbards, and at a signal from our colonel, issued from the trees at the gallop, charging round the house to attack the butler's pantry. We were received by a volley, which sent one of my people tumbling from his saddle, then we were at the steps, leaping from our saddles and running at the door. Now some pistols were discharged into our midst from the windows, and another of our number fell, but then we were at the door and hurling our shoulders against it. Unlike the front doors, this was of a single panelling, and very rapidly gave way before our impetuous assault, although not before we had lost a third man writhing in pain, he having been struck by a chamber-pot – unfortunately full – hurled from the window immediately above the door.

Then we were through, and into a narrow corridor. Here we were confronted with several people armed with muskets and pistols, which they discharged at us, and we lost a fourth man. Thus I gave the order to fire in reply, whereupon the hallway became filled with smoke and screams and shouts. Throwing down both pistol and musket, now empty, I drew my sword and charged ahead of my men, to check in consternation where the passage debouched into a pantry, and where there were three people writhing on the floor. One of these was a man, and the other two were women. Nor, even in the heat of the moment, did it escape me that the man was somewhat elderly, while the women were hardly young. However, I had to expect more serious opposition, and so I ran behind the surviving women, who scattered, three running into the kitchens while the others chased into the downstairs dining hall, where there was a large table and some ornately-backed chairs, not to mention several full-length family portraits on the walls.

I directed half of my men into the kitchen, and myself went into the dining-room, three troopers at my heels. Here we found the maidservants scuttling up the great staircase, seeking the protection of the lady of the house, who stood at the top, some more women at her back. These were armed with pistols and muskets, which made me pause to consider, for despite my antagonism to Richilde Bethlen I had never actually made war upon women before, and the sight of the two earlier struck by our bullets had been most depressing. However, I was saved from the ultimate, at least immediately, by Lady O'Connell herself, who now threw her pistol down the stairs to have it clatter at my feet. Her action was followed by her companions. "We yield," Lady O'Connell said. "To your masculine superiority."

Thus, as I supposed, saving me from an embarrassing situation, for my men had become fairly hot. "What of your other servants?" I inquired.

"Betty, ring the bell," Lady O'Connell commanded, and came down the steps towards me. She was a handsome woman, in early middle-age, with graying fair hair and soft features, as well as a formidable décolletage. At her shoulder was a much younger woman, clearly a daughter although her hair was reddish-brown, but equally well endowed, and she was breathing heavily. The appearance of these two extremely attractive ladies somewhat distracted me from the noises off, for there was a good deal of swearing and screaming and cursing and banging from the kitchen, but now the remainder of my men came into the hall, following several more women, clearly scullery wenches, a couple of whom had been stripped to their shifts. But there were no men.

Before I could investigate this odd phenomenon, matters were taken out of my hands. There was a tremendous clumping of boots, and Oliver stamped into the hall, followed by Ireton and some twenty troopers, with drawn swords. "Faith, sir, but it seems we are over-matched," Lady O'Connell remarked.

"Faith, is it," Oliver remarked. "Where is your husband?"

"My husband rides with the King, God bless him."

"Papist bitch," Ireton growled.

"Are you a Papist, woman?" Cromwell demanded.

This was surely a rhetorical question, for the house was filled with crucifixes and representations of the Virgin Mary and Child. "I am of the true faith, yes," Lady O'Connell replied.

"Then you will have a priest on the premises. Summon him forth. And indeed, all of your menfolk."

"There are no menfolk," Lady O'Connell declared. "What you see before you is my entire garrison."

Ireton gave a short laugh. "You expect us to believe that we have been opposing a clutch of women?"

"And my butler, to be sure, whom you have murdered."

"Madam, four of your women are guilty of attempted murder, at the least," Cromwell said. "Four of my men are lying out there grievously wounded, and one is like to die."

"My women are guilty of nothing more than defending my home, on my instructions. As to your people, I shot one of them myself, as I would shoot anyone who attempted to break into my house."

Cromwell had gone very red in the face, and I could see that he was enduring a good deal of pent-up anger. But even I was totally unprepared for his next command. "Then, madam," he said. "You are condemned out of your own mouth, as a foul traitor to the Commonwealth of England, and as a murderess to boot." He turned to me. "Take her outside and hang her."

I goggled at him. "With respect, Colonel Cromwell, I have never hanged a woman in my life, and I am a little old to start learning new tricks."

If I had hoped, as indeed I did, that by giving him a moment's pause I might civilise his feelings, I was greatly mistaken. "Fie on you, Helier," he said. "But then, I have long suspected that your experiences have made you half a papist yourself. Henry, see to this woman."

It was Lady O'Connell's turn to goggle, as her arms were seized by two of the troopers; clearly it had never crossed her mind that she was actually in any danger. "Mama!" screamed the young woman, who had remained on the stairs during the conversation, but now came running down, with such haste that she lost her footing and tumbled to the floor at my very feet. Hastily I scooped her up, but she ignored me as she continued to shriek, "Mama!"

She had virtually no effect on what was happening, save to attract lascivious glances from the troopers, but we were now arrested by a shout from the gallery at the head of the stairs.

"Wait there!" We turned our heads to look up, and saw a man clad all in black save for his white collar, beginning his descent. "It is I you seek," he declared.

"Well, well," Oliver remarked. "You'll be the priest."

"An emissary of the Devil," Henry Ireton growled.

"I am Lady O'Connell's confessor," the priest said, speaking with a broad brogue.

"And Irish with it," Cromwell pointed out.

"I have that honour, sir. And by what right do you break into a household which has always been law-abiding, and seeks only the peace of this land?"

"Are you for King or Parliament, man? Speak!"

The priest crossed himself. "I am a loyal subject of His Majesty."

"And a Catholic priest! And an Irishman." Cromwell pointed. "Hang him beside his mistress!" The priest gasped his disbelief as he in turn was seized by the troopers. Lady O'Connell uttered a faint shriek. Her daughter had fainted, draped across my arm like a bolt of cloth. The female servants gaped at the catastrophe which had overtaken their employer, not yet understanding the catastrophe which was about to overtake *them*. For as Lady O'Connell and the priest, too stunned to resist, were dragged through the door Cromwell turned to one of the girls and snapped, "Your name! Speak!"

She licked her lips and trembled. "Molly, your honour."

She too spoke with a pronounced brogue. Yet would Cromwell be sure, as was his wont. "Your surname, girl!"

Another lick of the lips. "Molly O'Rourke, your honour."

"You are Irish!"

"Well, yes, your honour. But I am presently in England." A statement which entirely proved her nationality.

"And these?" Cromwell flung out his arm to encompass her fellows. "Are they all also Irish?"

"Well, your honour, they are," Molly explained. "But they too..."

Cromwell turned to his sergeant. "They are yours. Have them and kill them. Half an hour. Then we burn this evil place." For the past few minutes he had ignored me as an indication of his displeasure. Now he turned to me. "I put you in charge of this duty, Captain L'Eree. No man is to be prevented from wrecking his worst upon this Papist crew. And you, sir, either take that woman and then knock her on the head or give her to my people. I will await you outside."

Saying which he strode from the room.

For a moment there was absolute silence, while I looked at my troopers and then at the women, who appeared paralysed with fright, and the troopers looked at me and then at the women. But the Colonel had given his command, and these were men who had for too long been forbidden the least misbehaviour; with a whoop they rushed forward, discarding accoutrements and clothes as they did so, wishing only to come to grips with the buxom Irish ladies.

These appeared to be still too terrified to attempt to escape, and were quickly overborne, the more so as for each woman there were half a dozen men. I was quite as transfixed as they, not from fear, to be sure, but from a mixture of anger and disgust.

In a matter of seconds the maidservants and gentle ladies were stripped to the skin, thrown to the floor, and raped, time and again. This was sufficiently bestial, but the morning was rendered the more horrific by the plea of one of the maids, for mercy on the grounds that she was pregnant. The human wolves surrounding her gave a whoop, drew their knives, and proceeded to rip open her belly and deliver the child there and then, following which they dashed out its brains while the mother screamed and bled to death. These events took place with a speed which exceeded my ability to determine what I should do about the situation. I too had been given specific orders by my colonel, and I knew that he was none too pleased with my refusal to hang Lady O'Connell in any event. To my everlasting shame, I do believe I might have acquiesced in the tragedy being enacted about me, had not these blood-lusting madmen, who a few minutes previously I had called comrades, turned their attention to Miss O'Connell.

I had laid the young lady on a settee while I considered my next move, and thus they presumed that I had discarded her. With another of their whoops four of them descended upon her, and with a simple exercise of their masculine strength ripped away gown and petticoats and stays and shift, to leave her wearing only her stockings. This awoke her from her swoon, and her shrieks joined those of her companions in distress, if in slightly more modulated tones. She was, as I have indicated, an extremely well-endowed young woman. Indeed, of all the women I have known – and there have been a few – only my Helga had a more Junoesque appearance. But I should hate anyone to suppose my reaction was caused entirely at the sight of so much pulchritude about to be rolled in the dust, as it were. Her maltreatment merely hardened the resolve that had been insensibly growing within me for the past few minutes, that this company was not for me. Indeed, I had not sought it in the first place. Now I had to be rid of it, and quickly. And if I was going anyway...

I leapt forward, grasped the shoulder of the first lout who was unbuckling his breeches, and hurled him into a corner. The others looked up in alarm, for Helier L'Eree when aroused is a fearsome sight, and I scattered them left and right with a few sweeps of my arm. "This woman is mine," I told them.

They muttered a bit, but I was not only bigger than they, I was their captain. And so I picked up the girl, threw her across my shoulder, and proceeded up the stairs. "He seeks a bed," someone sneered.

I ignored them, and hurried along the gallery. In fact, I sought somewhere to think for a moment. I knew, of course, that simply emerging from the house would do me no good at all. Certainly while carrying a naked woman. Cromwell would immediately appropriate her, and if he did not hang her, would hand her over to some more of his men. I had to make my escape, and this was clearly going to be difficult, as, peering from a window as I passed it, I could see troopers roaming all over the estate, chasing the horses and pigs out of their stalls, before setting fire to the outbuildings. I thus opened the door to one of the first floor withdrawing chambers, and placed my captive in a chair.

She gazed at me with enormous eyes while seizing a cushion to hold against her belly and breasts in an endeavour to conceal her charms from my gaze. "I beg of you, sir," she said.

More and more she reminded me of Helga, not only on account of her buxomness but because she had big blue eyes, as well as remarkably well-formed limbs; only the colour of her hair was different – Helga's was golden. "I mean you no harm," I told her. "Indeed, I would save your life, if you can but tell me how to get out of here without being seen."

"It amuses you to tease me," she said, beginning to weep.

"Listen," I said. "Things are not as they seem. I would take you with me."

Her head came up, and through the tear mist her eyes grew larger yet. "You are not a Puritan devil?"

"I serve the Queen."

She gasped. "Then, sir, there is a secret passage..."

"Let's get into it."

For while the shrieks from downstairs had abated, they had been replaced by barked commands, and I knew that

216

the house was about to be fired. "I must have clothes," she said. "Please, sir, I will lead us out."

She discarded the cushion, held my hand, and led me up another flight of stairs. I had to reflect that we were following a most dangerous course, but I have never been able to resist being led by the hand by a beautiful naked woman – indeed, this was the first time I had enjoyed such an experience. "Perhaps you would tell me your name," I suggested as we reached the upper landing.

"Maureen," she replied, and opened a door. This was clearly her own bedroom, and while I looked around me she put on a shift and a gown and a pair of shoes, added a pelisse, and thus once again the height of modesty, seemed ready to face the world.

Just in time; I could smell smoke. "This secret passage," I reminded her.

"It is from Mama's bedroom. Oh, Mama!" Suddenly she seemed to recall her parent's fate, and burst into tears.

I hurried her along lest she also look out of a window to see her mother swinging to and fro. We entered a much larger and more elaborate bedroom; as we did so, I heard someone calling my name, Cromwell obviously having suddenly realised that his drillmaster was missing. "Haste," I told my guide. "Or we are lost."

I could even hear the crackling of flames now, and smoke was seeping up the stairwell behind us. "Help me!" Maureen O'Connell panted.

She was wrestling with various knobs on the surround for her mother's fireplace. I hastened to lend my strength, and slowly a panel swung in to reveal a staircase set into the outer wall of the house. Maureen stepped into this without a moment's hesitation, although it descended into darkness which would have put any pit to shame. I could do no less than follow. "We must close it behind us," I suggested.

"It cannot be done from the inside," she said.

I could only hope that those seeking me would not risk the upper floors with the house already alight, and indeed this was the case, but our descent was equally perilous because the building was burning fiercely, and the walls became hot to the touch, while from beyond the stonework there came a great deal of clattering as various ornaments collapsed.

I could see absolutely nothing, so rested my hand on the girl's shoulder as we went down. I realised that we had passed beneath the earth when the heat began to abate and was replaced by an increasing coolness. Soon after this the steps ended, and I followed her along a passageway. Now at last she spoke again. "This was built to enable our priest to escape, during the persecutions," she explained. "Or to hide, until the ungodly had departed."

I preferred not to comment: presumably she would include me in the ranks of the ungodly. And before long we were climbing another flight of steps, although this was brief compared with that inside the house. Now she halted, so suddenly I ran into her. "We must be careful," she admonished.

I entirely agreed with her. Above our head there was a trap, and to this we pressed our ears, listening to a variety of sounds. But the trap itself was hot, and through it there filtered some smoke. "Where are we?" I asked.

"Just behind the stables."

"And these have been set alight. We will have to wait some time before we can leave."

I sat on the step, and after a brief hesitation she sat beside me. "I had supposed you were going to rape me," she said, "and then slit my throat."

"And you were wrong," I said. "I never had the slightest intention of slitting your throat."

CHAPTER 9

Well, what would you? I had had an exciting morning, and the adrenalin was bubbling through both our veins. In addition, I had not had the solace of female company since Caroline's departure, and that was now a very long time in the past.

Besides, it was no rape. Maureen O'Connell might have shrunk from being debauched in front of a squadron of soldiers, but she was a grateful girl and, as it turned out, not a virgin. I naturally did not pursue such a private matter very deeply, content only that she was willing, and that I was committing no crime. "They called you L'Eree," she remarked, when I was clearly a spent force and she was fumbling about in the darkness, for her clothes amongst other things. "Are you then, French? Riding with the Roundheads? We understood they hate the French worse than the Devil because of the Queen."

"The Roundheads?"

"That is what we call them, because they wear their hair so short."

It seemed appropriate, and I recalled that Richelieu had similarly described them, some time previously. "No," I told her. "I am not French." And I told her about Garnesey, omitting only any reference to my domestic situation, as I reckoned that she was an innocent child who might be shocked at the realisation that she had conspired to make me commit adultery.

"Now you must tell me of yourself," I suggested.

"You have seen the destruction of my home and family."

"But your father?"

"Is with the King."

"Then I shall take you to him," I promised her.

She wept tears of joy as she nestled in my arms, causing us to renew our earlier affection. At the end of which I was utterly exhausted. I pressed my hand against the underside of the trap, and found it much cooler.

"I think we may now leave this place," I said. "But remember, caution."

I put my shoulder to the trap and slowly raised it, allowing a thin mist of still warm white dust to filter downwards until I could see out. This was not very informative, as I merely gazed at the blackened timbers of the burned out stables. But more important, I could hear, and if there remained a variety of sounds, at least there did not appear to be any human voices. Thus relieved, I threw the trap right back and scrambled out, to gaze at a scene of the most utter desolation. The stables and the farm had burned to the ground, and beyond, the house still glowed, although the roof and upper stories had fallen in and the walls looked about to do the same.

Of animals and humans, however, there were none. At least, alive. Cromwell had clearly driven off all the livestock he could find, including of course the so valuable horses. All that was left, apart from the burning buildings, were the two figures dangling from the branch of an oak tree, some distance from the house. I bade Maureen stay where she was while I went forward to investigate. Not that I expected to find either Lady O'Connell or her confessor alive: they had been hanging for several hours, and indeed presented a pretty revolting sight. But I had thought one or two of the serving maids might have survived. In the event, none were to be seen; either they had all been burned in the house or they had been carried off.

I heard footfalls and saw that Maureen after all had disobeyed me. "Fiends!" she exclaimed. "They spend their time praying to God, but they do the Devil's work."

"Amen," I agreed, and as she now fell to her knees to pray before the body of her mother, I felt I could do nothing less than join her. Following which I cut the bodies down, and after hunting around, found a spade which if blackened was still serviceable, and buried the pair of them together, in a flower bed off the front drive.

Maureen watched me, still kneeling. "You are a good man, Helier L'Eree," she said. "Are you of the true faith?"

"Sadly, Miss O'Connell," I said, "I am of no faith whatsoever. And as for being good, there are many who would claim that I am descended from the Devil himself."

"Then am I his disciple from now on," she said, and rose. "I shall bring my father here," she said. "To watch Cromwell hang from that same tree." I reflected that it is always worthwhile to have an objective in life, however difficult it may be to realise our ambitions.

It is also, fortunately, difficult to destroy any community, no matter how hard one tries. Cromwell, perhaps from a sense of guilt, had not tried all that hard. True, he had killed all the inhabitants of the manor, as he supposed, and he had burned all the buildings, and he had driven off all the livestock that he could find. However, he had not even considered catching all the fish in the stream which ran past the property, and in the house, when the flames had burned themselves out and the charred wood- and stone-work had somewhat cooled, we were able to find items of food, such as loaves of fresh-made bread which had been in the previously unlit oven. They now resembled toast, but were none the less edible, the stout oven walls, intended to keep the heat in when the fire was lit, having done a good job of keeping the heat *out*, when the building had been lit. Fashioning a rod and a hook was no trouble at all, and we enjoyed a good supper of roasted carp on the banks of the stream, following which, as it was now dark, Maureen fell into a deep sleep.

For me, however, it was time to consider my position, which was as uncomfortable as at any time in the past. On the credit side, I had escaped with my life and my sword, and I had escaped the Roundheads, which I was more and more considering a most apt name for Cromwell and his crew. And I had accumulated a most pleasant travelling companion. On the debit side, I was absolutely destitute, save for my sword. I did not even possess a horse, and I had lost my musket and pistols, not that I would have had any means of charging them even had I been able to find them. I had also lost any possibility of Caroline ever being able to find *me*, supposing she was ever going to reappear at all. And that meant I would have to rethink my plans for returning to Garnesey.

I was also lumbered with this young orphan. Well, she was very attractive, to be sure, and appeared to be entirely willing. But the fact was that she was just as destitute as I, at this moment, and when it came to nubile young women, I had too many of them hanging about my neck, in a manner of speaking, not to mention a very nubile wife waiting for me at home. Sometimes a man finds himself sinking beneath an accumulation of burdens, however delightful.

Fortunately, I am a logical fellow, able to discern the obvious steps one needs to take to achieve salvation, or in my unhappy case, even to place oneself in a position to begin to *think* about salvation. Clearly, I was going to do Helga no good by getting myself killed, or permanently incarcerated, and I could not help but feel that to make my way to the east and attempt to rejoin Cromwell, with some story of how I had escaped the conflagration, might lead in one or the other of those directions; he had not been very pleased with me when last I had seen him. Equally, such a plan would bode no good for Maureen O'Connell, and I could not contemplate her suffering a fate similar to that of her mother.

I therefore came to the decision that my best bet was to regain the King's company, hopefully deliver Maureen to her anxious parent, and then revert to what might be called Plan A, and make my way to one of the southern ports to gain a ship for Garnesey. By returning to the King, I also hoped to be able to obtain some arrears of pay, which would finance the journey. There was of course the small matter of my disappearance some six months before, but I had little doubt that I could overcome this, especially if, as I imagined would be the case, Henrietta Maria had by now joined her husband.

But I could not prevent my heart from becoming heavy as I understood that I was now perhaps two months from gaining Garnesey, and in that time my Helga and my children might have to suffer. It was just as well that I did not then know the truth of the matter, and was able to convince myself that everything would be set to rights when I finally regained my home.

Thus off we set the next morning, very much two fugitives, moving with great care and taking cover whenever we saw a body of horsemen, for the Roundhead patrols were now becoming very bold, in the absence of any Royalist troops. Being on foot, our progress was slow, and painful. We were also entirely dependent upon my skill as a fisherman, and not every stream was filled with fish. This was very depressing, and twenty-four hours after we had left the O'Connell estate, having spent another night upon the open heath beneath a drizzling rain, we began to resemble a pair of half-drowned, and more than half-starved, rats.

I had acquainted Maureen with my plan, and she had seemed satisfied enough. She had, additionally, proved herself to be in every way the best of travelling companions, in her eagerness to be of comfort to me quite reminding me of Caroline, although I had perceived in her none of the fiery spirit of the vampire-child. But now she surprised me. "Captain L'Eree," she said. "Is that not a church steeple in the distance? And houses? Oh, what would I give for a hot bath and some warm food."

"I entirely understand," I agreed. "But I am afraid that we will have to forego those pleasures until we can regain the King's encampment. And your father."

'May I ask why?"

"Very simply, because I have no money."

She considered this for some minutes. Then she asked, "How many days do you expect we will take to reach the King?"

"Three or four, I would estimate."

"By that time, sir, we shall either have starved or frozen to death."

Having been forced to exist in these circumstances before, in Germany, I was less pessimistic. But as I did not wish to buoy her spirits unduly, I merely replied, "We must do the best we can."

"There is a saying, is there not," she persisted, "that the Good Lord helps those who help themselves?"

"That is true enough," I agreed. "This is what we are endeavouring to do."

"I am sure we can improve matters. Will you allow me to try?"

"In what way?" I asked, somewhat uneasily. This young woman was beginning to remind me more and more of Caroline. "If you are considering highway robbery, this is difficult to accomplish without horses."

"I would never dream of robbing anyone, certainly on the highway," she protested. "Do you rest here, and allow me to go into the town. I will need several hours. After which I suggest that we meet again on the far side of the town."

I did not inquire what she had in mind, although I suspected it well enough. And sure enough, when we made our rendezvous, myself by then a very hungry and lonely man, she was carrying a sack over her shoulder, containing a leg of mutton and a bag of turnips, all cooked, as well as a purse which clinked as well as any I had ever known. "This will buy us a horse at the next village," she said, and proceeded to bathe herself in the stream beside which I had been waiting. Indeed, she spent a very long time in the water, as if quite unable to make herself clean, while I sat on the bank and watched her.

Maureen's ability as a harlot stood us in good stead. By allowing her to go into the next town, again on her own, we soon possessed two horses as well as money to spare, although we had no furniture and were obliged to ride bareback. When one remembers that these animals cost at least five pounds apiece, it will be understood that her efforts were prodigious. But Maureen proved an adept horsewoman, and we were able to travel as man and wife, which she did most willingly, her tasks during the day in no way dulling her appetite for the less enervating business of coping with but a single man at night. Thus we progressed steadily, and a few days later encountered a Royalist patrol not far east of Oxford. Their captain had been at Edge Hill, and regarded me with consternation, for while he recognised me easily enough, he could hardly reconcile my torn and tattered clothing, my unshaven chin, and my bare-backed mount, with my appearance the last time he had seen me. Even more was he, and his men, inclined to goggle at Maureen, who of course was forced to ride astride and was therefore revealing a good deal of very white leg, while her gown was sufficiently tattered to be revealing an equal amount of the rest of her, also remarkably white. "Count d'Albret?" he cried. "Why, man, we had supposed you dead. Or deserted," he added, beginning to think too much.

"Do I look as if I have deserted?" I inquired.

"Nevertheless, my lord, I must place you under arrest. You will surrender your sword, if you please."

I had already enjoined Maureen to leave the talking to me, but now she could not help but remark, "Count? You never told me you were a count."

"You never asked me," I pointed out, handing over my sword. I needed these people if I was ever to regain Garnesey.

We were taken straightaway to the local provost marshal, where Maureen also made herself known. This good fellow realised that he was dealing with people superior to his authority, and despatched us to Oxford itself. Word having been sent ahead, we were greeted by quite a crowd, not all of whom were friendly, but a way was cleared for us and soon enough I was standing before the King, who was surrounded by all the familiar faces I remembered so well, although Prince Rupert was not amongst them; I learned later that he was away besieging Bristol, and truth to tell, I was not sorry about this, as I regarded his intelligence as far sharper than that of any other of Charles's advisers – or indeed of the King.

However, Charles himself was not looking very pleased to see me, while his gentlemen were positively glowering. But then, they had never actually liked me. "It seems to me, C-c-count," Charles remarked, "that you have a d-d-deal to answer for. You are a d-d-deserter, sir, in time of war."

"He should be shot," growled Sir Jacob Astley.

"No, no, shooting is too good for him," said the man Hyde. "He should be hanged."

"What have you to say, sir?" the King demanded.

"Simply that I can explain everything, Your Majesty."

"Then d-d-do so, sir. If you c-c-can."

"Why, Your Majesty, as I understood you were going into winter quarters, Mr Le Brock and I took it into our heads to carry out a reconnaissance into that part of the country controlled by the rebels."

"You t-t-told no one of this d-d-design."

'Well, no, Your Majesty. We considered it necessary to undertake our expedition in absolute secrecy." I allowed myself a glance at the faces around me; at times like this the only possible safety lies in attack. "Lest we be betrayed."

"By God, sir . . . " began one of the gentlemen, allowing his hand to drop to his sword hilt.

"Your courage does you credit, sir," I said. "Seeing that I am unarmed."

"So, you went on a reconnaissance," the King remarked. "With Mr Le B-b-brock. But the young gentleman has not returned with you."

"Sadly, Your Majesty, the young gentleman is no more. We encountered a Roundhead cavalry squadron besieging the home of Sir Rory O'Connell, and endeavouring to assist the defenders, Mr Le Brock was killed." This did not seem an unreasonable approach to the situation. I was by now seriously concerned regarding Caroline's safety in any event, but if she did come back, it would have to be as a woman.

"Sir Rory O'Connell, you say? The rebels attacked his house?"

"And burned it to the ground, Your Majesty. Lady O'Connell they hanged."

"The devils," someone growled.

"But I managed to assist Miss O'Connell to escape."

"Indeed? And what have you d-d-done with her?"

"She is outside, Your Majesty, awaiting your pleasure."

"By Heaven, sir, you mean the lady is here? Unharmed?"

"Save for a few bruises and much sorrow, Your Majesty."

"Hyde, you'll inform Sir Rory immediately, and fetch him here. B-b-bring the girl in, C-c-count. B-b-bring her in."

I did this immediately, Maureen looking most appealing, and somehow more tattered than I even remembered. "D-d-did this man truly rescue you from the rebels, miss?" Charles inquired.

"I owe the Count my life," she said, more appealingly yet.

"Hm," the King commented. 'Hm. And your mother is d-d-dead, you say."

"Hanged by a foul brute named Cromwell, Your Majesty. I crave vengeance."

"C-c-cromwell?" the King asked at large. "Do we know this fellow?"

"There was one such sat as Member for Huntingdon, Your Majesty," said Hyde. He had returned after sending a messenger in search of Maureen's father.

"Ah. Well, b-b-be sure that he will b-b-be hanged, young lady. Now, withdraw and find yourself some d-d-decent clothing. Your father will soon b-b-be here."

Maureen performed another curtsey which had more eyes rolling, and turned to withdraw, only to encounter the Queen, sweeping into the room, followed by her ladies. "L'Eree?" Henrietta demanded. "Is it really you?"

"In the flesh, Your Majesty." I bowed.

Henrietta gazed at Maureen, who was busily performing another devastating curtsey. "You are a rogue, L'Eree," the Queen announced.

"Quite the c-c-contrary, madam," the King interjected.

"C-c-count d-d-d'Albret has saved this poor child from a fate worse than d-d-death." Henrietta gave him a glance to indicate that in her opinion if he believed that he would believe anything, so he hurried on. "Not to mention d-d-death itself."

"I am sure she will soon die in any event," Henrietta snapped. "From exposure. You ... " she pointed at one of her ladies. "Take her away and put some clothes on her."

"Her father is coming, Your Majesty," Hyde protested.

"He will hardly wish to see her in *déshabillé*. Off with her." She turned her attention to me. "You are scarce an improvement, Count. I will send for you, when you have attended to your toilette."

I looked at the King, somewhat uncertainly, but he waved his hand. "Her Majesty is right. C-c-clean yourself up. Then report to me. Reconnaissance, indeed."

I appeared to be back in the fold.

Finding clothes to fit a giant like myself is never an easy task, but after some discussion with the commissariat I was equipped as one of Rupert's dragoons, all red coat and vest and breeches, with a new sword belt and even a pair of boots into which I could just squeeze my feet. That done, I attended the King, the Queen not having yet summoned me. There I told him of Cromwell's endeavours to create his regiment of cavalry.

The King and his gentlemen listened with undisguised contempt. "Do you suppose, Count, that putting a group of yokels into a uniform type of clothing, and mounting them upon farm horses, immediately transforms them into cavalry?" Goring asked.

"Not immediately, my lord. Everything depends on the training they receive afterwards. In this regard, these men are cavalry, yes."

"Trained by whom? This fellow Cromwell? Does he know anything about soldiering? Attacking undefended manor houses, now, that is one thing. Standing up to the rigours of a battle, that is something entirely different."

I was not about to confess that I had played an important part in the training of the Ironsides myself. So I contented myself with repeating, "They struck me as being well-mounted and disciplined troops, my lord."

"And you have ridden with the Swedish c-c-cavalry," Charles observed, revealing that he was not quite the dunderhead that has been supposed. "We thank you, C-c-count. We shall inform you in due course as to what other d-d-duties we require of you."

I withdrew. There were a thousand and one questions to which I required answers, of course. But I would clearly have to be patient. As it happened, I did not have to be *that* patient, for that evening the Queen sent for me. "L'Eree," she said, when she had dismissed her ladies. "They told me you had deserted! I had not thought ever to see you alive again."

I went into the same rigmarole I had with the King, but I could tell Henrietta was not quite so gullible. "You are the most complete rogue I have ever met," she commented when I had finished.

"Your Majesty?"

"You have not thought to ask after your wife, L'Eree. Surely that should be a husband's first concern?"

"Well, Your Majesty..."

"But obviously you did not consider it necessary, as you know she is alive and well and living in Garnesey."

I swallowed.

"As for Marguerite, obviously there is no necessity to ask after *her*," Henrietta continued. "As she was no more than a plaything for you."

"The Countess is no longer with you, Your Highness?"

"I decided to let her go, when she had told me the entire truth of the matter."

"You believed her?"

"Much of what she said made sense, L'Eree. And I had always known there was something amiss between the pair of you. But I cannot say I entirely believed her. I merely found I could no longer give her employment, and so let her return to France. What convinced me that she had all the

229

time been telling the truth was when I learned the simple fact that you had deserted."

"Your Majesty..."

"L'Eree, you departed the King's camp, upon your 're-connaissance', within a few days of news of the Cardinal's death being received. Now, is that not a fact? The truth of the matter is that you have no loyalty to me or my cause, only your paymaster, whoever he happens to be at the time."

I hung my head. "You are an incorrigible rogue," she said again. "As to your relationship with that handsome young man ... is he truly dead?"

"Alas, Your Majesty, I shall never see him again."

"Then I am sorry for it." She glanced at me. "Did you really, well ..."

"We were very fond of each other," I said, carefully.

"Yet the moment he was dead, you leapt into the arms of the nearest available female. You are worse than an incorrigible rogue. You deserve to be hanged."

"So it has been said, from time to time, Your Majesty. However, the sequence did not go quite as you described it."

I was not of course the least concerned by her apparent anger. It is a remarkable thing that the more a female considers a man to be a villain, at least in sexual matters, the more she begins to consider the possibility of having some of his villainy rub off on her, quite literally. Henrietta had always been powerfully affected by my presence. Now that she considered me the ultimate roué into the bargain, she was finding me practically irresistible. As I could tell from a glance at her flushed cheeks and heaving breasts. I had to press home my advantage; quite apart from my personal feelings, this woman was the ultimate safeguard of my survival. "Indeed, Your Majesty," I went on, "my adventures have been quite remarkable. Would you like to hear them?"

"Oh, yes," she said.

I glanced at the doors. "Are you certain we will not be interrupted, Your Majesty?"

230

"Well, no, I cannot be certain of that. These ladies, they are confoundedly suspicious, especially where you are concerned."

"I should hate to have my story interrupted, Your Majesty."

Now I was in control, and she was all of a twitter. "I shall send for you, when ... when we are less likely to be interrupted."

"I shall await your summons, Your Majesty, with an anxiously beating heart."

She pointed. "Until I do send for you, L'Eree, I absolutely forbid you to speak with, or even to see, Miss O'Connell."

"Why, Your Majesty," I protested. "Nothing could have been further from my mind."

In fact, I was quite interested to discover what might have become of Maureen, especially after being reunited with her father in circumstances which could only be described as distressing. But *in* the circumstances, and having regard to my ambitions, I deemed it best to let her handle her own affairs for the moment. My judgement was proved correct, for within a few minutes of having dined and retiring to my quarters, grudgingly assigned, I was disturbed by a knock on the door, and opened it to a pretty little maid – although perhaps I was being optimistic with regard to her actual condition. "Well, hello," I said, drawing her into the room.

"I am from Her Majesty."

"What a delightful gift."

"You are to come with me, Count."

"Why, that will be a pleasure."

It will be gathered that I still did not take her at face value. But there it was. I was guided through the narrow streets of Oxford, taken up secret passageways in the heart of Christ Church College, which was serving as the royal palace, and delivered into the very bedchamber of the Queen. Here the young lady gave a quick curtsey in the direction of the tester bed which occupied the centre of the room, and then withdrew.

231

Now it is time for me to make a very formidable confession. Here I was, Helier L'Eree, Count d'Albret, a man whose weapons, of various sorts, had carried him from one end of Europe to the other with complete success, now reaching, and being granted, the ultimate prize ... and I was quite overcome. Immediately, however, this did not concern me: I had no doubt my reactions would follow their proper course once I held the Queen naked in my arms. Nor was I to be delayed in reaching that goal.

"Helier?" she asked from the confines of the bed.

"I am here, Your Majesty," I said fervently, and advanced, the curtains were drawn and I hesitated.

"I am waiting for you, Helier," she informed me.

I drew the drapes and gazed upon the most magnificent of sights, the Queen of England, clad as she would have been upon her first day on earth, only grown considerably. Indeed I can say without fear of contradiction that of all the women I had then known, only my Helga and possibly Maureen O'Connell bore the least comparison when it came to the size of her pulchritude, in every direction. "Helier," she said.

"Your Majesty."

It was then I became aware of that most sinking feeling, a certainty that I would be unable to rise to the occasion. At least without considerable stimulation, and I did not know if I could rely upon a queen to provide that: she would surely be used to service rather than serving. "Is something amiss?" she asked.

"I am overcome by your beauty, Your Majesty."

"You say the sweetest things, Helier. But time is fleeting."

Thus commanded I undressed and got into bed beside her. One would have supposed *this* the most stimulating of experiences. But she could tell at a glance that things were not as she would have wished. "You are troubled, Helier," she said.

"I have never sought to fly so high, Your Majesty," I confessed. "Thus I feel a veritable tyro."

"Do you not suppose I feel the same?" she asked. "It is treason to cuckold a king."

"Oh, my dear!" In view of the rumours concerning a certain fellow named Jermyn, who was one of the Queen's most constant attendants, it had never occurred to me that it might be the first time for her as well. I folded her in my arms, hugged her tightly, and kissed her lips. Her body moved against mine, her legs twined themselves round mine, and I felt the surge of manhood which indicated that the deed was as good as done . . . when we heard a considerable noise in the antechamber. There was a stamping of feet, a rumble of voices, and above all, a yapping of dogs.

Henrietta sat up with such violence that she threw me off. "The King!" she gasped.

That caused me to sit up as well. "We are betrayed!"

"No, no," she protested. "He is merely . . . attending me. He does this, sometimes, without notice. He is so impulsive!"

Well, I could have wished she had told me this before. I scrambled out of bed and began to dress. "There is no time for that," she said.

And to confirm her words there came a knock on the door. "M-m-madame? Will you p-p-permit me to visit you?"

"Under the bed!" Henrietta whispered. "Hurry! Why, my lord," she said in a loud voice, "what a very pleasant surprise."

I dived beneath the drapes and wormed my way into the land of the chamberpot, hastily checking that I had brought everything with me. The door opened, and then closed again. "Charles," Henrietta said. "I had been hoping you would come to me tonight."

"Were you, my dear." His feet had by now arrived at the bedside. "B-b-but . . . you have nothing on."

"Because I was dreaming of you," Henrietta said, somewhat enigmatically, I felt. However, Charles seemed to find her answer satisfactory, and a moment later his clothes were where mine had been only seconds before, and he was where I had been only seconds before.

Only somewhat more satisfactorily, as it turned out. Before the summer was out, it was announced that the Queen was pregnant.

Naturally I would like to claim that I had a hand in this, even if the word hand is not at all appropriate. But I cannot claim to have fathered a princess. I was interrupted before I had even gained an entry, while the King gained several entries, as I could tell from my situation beneath the bed.

It was in fact a harrowing experience, but fortunately His Majesty finally withdrew and took his departure before daybreak, and I was able to make my escape. Henrietta swore she would send for me again, but she never did; presumably she felt that our escape had been too narrow to permit a repetition, and by the time she regained her nerve the facts of her condition were apparent. Whereupon the King determined to remove her to a position of safety for her lying-in: Exeter. Truth to tell I was not too sorry about this: I was absolutely shattered by the whole experience. Even with Maureen O'Connell, who, having been reunited with her father soon paid me a call, I was unable to work up much enthusiasm.

Meanwhile, what of the war in which I was again involved? My ambition, as I have made clear, was to be as little involved as possible, and make my departure for the south just as soon as could be done. But obviously this would have to be carefully planned, as again to be accused of desertion might prove too much to be defended, especially as I no longer could look for the Queen's support: she was several hundred miles away.

The war itself had degenerated into a series of skirmishes, mainly because both sides were preparing vast schemes: the King had at last determined to bring his Irish army over, even if he was aware that it would alienate the majority of his people, and Parliament, with equal carelessness of public opinion, was negotiating an alliance with the Scots, who had arguably the best army in the kingdom, at least in so far as was known at the time.

In the field there had been some important events as well. Rupert had succeeded in capturing Bristol, one of the major seaports in the country, and thus of great importance for the supply of the Royalist forces. Having accomplished this, he returned to the main army. I anticipated his coming with some apprehension, but he seemed pleased to see me, and even more pleased to discover that my friend Le Brock was dead. He appointed me Quartermaster-General. Equally he was interested in what I had discovered as a result of my 'reconnaissance', but sadly he did not take my suggestion that Parliament now disposed of a formidable body of horse any more seriously than did the other Royalist generals. In fact, the Royalists were well pleased with the way the war was going. They were still in the field after a year, they had secured Bristol and most of the west country, they also had York and thus dominated the north – they were as yet unaware of the treaty between Parliament and the Scots – and thus conceived that their enemies were penned into the south and east of the country. That this was the richest part of England did not seem to concern them unduly.

They were also gaining successes in the field, their principal achievement coming in a skirmish at Chalgrove Field, where the redoubtable Hampden received a mortal wound and expired some days later. There was great rejoicing in the Royalist camp when this news was received, Hampden, one of the signatories of the Great Remonstrance, being regarded as one of the arch-enemies of the Crown. I could not help but reflect that his untimely death would but steel the determination of his cousin Cromwell down in Cambridgeshire. But I did not suppose it was going to be any great concern of mine, as I had every intention of being away before there was any more campaigning, especially as autumn drew on. I laid my plans carefully, played the fullest part in training the King's people and in formulating *his* plans, while I prepared myself for my departure, when I received the most horrific shock of my life, at least to that time.

Part of the business of preparing for war is a constant attention to recruiting. This is not only to swell the numbers of an army, but also to replace those who might have fallen in battle or been taken ill, or who had deserted. The fact is that soldiering, while an attractive prospect in the abstract, is an unhappy business in the particular. It is a matter of marching and counter-marching, of sleeping under skies which more often than not are raining, of eating at odd times and whatever happens to be available, of suffering severe punishments for the least infringement of military law, and of being, every so often, subjected to the risk of sudden death. Small wonder that a good many men, having joined the forces, either from loyalty to the King or from the glamorous idea of wearing a uniform, rapidly came to reflect that they would be much better off at home, and took themselves there as quickly as possible. Replacing these desertions was an unending task, and it often had to be accomplished by the use of force. That is, we would march a regiment into the nearest village and requisition every male of military age we could find, whether he wished to be a soldier or not. This business was attended by some resentment on the part of the populace, but there was nothing for it, and we seldom encountered any open resistance. The deed having been done, it was my business to train the recruits as they were brought in.

On the whole they were a sorry lot, not a whit better than those I had trained for Cromwell in East Anglia, but I reflected that as I had succeeded with those I would succeed with these. My way had always been to get to know my recruits, to be able to call them by name, and in fact almost to treat them as friends, while never letting them forget that I was their superior. Thus it was that late in the year I was overseeing the first drill of a bunch of recruits we had appropriated from a neighbouring town, when I became aware that one of them was staring at me with his mouth open. It also occurred to me that there was something familiar about his face, but I did not pursue the matter, and it was he who sought an interview with me, when the day's work was done. "Captain L'Eree?" he asked, on being shown into my room. "Can it really be you?"

His accent betrayed him. "You are a Garneseyman," I said.

"Indeed I am, sir. Jonathan Martel, at your service."

"By God," I commented. "I knew your father. And what are you doing here?"

"Well, sir, it is a sorry story," said the lad. "My father inherited some property through his mother, an English-woman, a year gone, and in view of all the trouble he felt I should come to see what could be done about it. And now I find myself pressed into the King's army."

"It will happen, in time of war," I agreed, my mind already ranging to possibilities. I had just about accumu-lated sufficient funds to get me passage on a ship, and was indeed considering the best opportunity for leaving, for my anxieties had grown with every passing month and it was now all but a year since Richelieu had died, and thus several months since my dearest Caroline had departed, and my dearest wife, for all I knew, been clapped into a debtor's prison.

This fellow would be able to reassure me that this had not happened, and might even, I thought, be of assistance to me in my plan to return home, as he would certainly have arranged a passage before being so unfortunate as to be overtaken by events. "In any event, as one Garneseyman to another," I told him, "welcome." I had, of course, to feel my way with caution. "It is, as you may know, some time since I have been in Garnesey. Is all well there? I had heard some talk of the island declaring for Parliament while the Lieutenant-Governor declared for the King."

"That is true, sir," Martel agreed. "And I wish you to know, Captain, how sad I am at your great misfortune, regardless of whose side one may be on."

I sat up, icy fingers clutching at my heart. "Misfortune? Of what misfortune do you speak?"

He cast me a quick glance, accompanied by a frown, and some evidence of alarm. "You have heard nothing from Garnesey, sir?"

"Nothing. I sent a messenger there several months ago but ... he has not yet returned. Speak, boy, speak."

Now he was definitely trembling. "Why, sir, it was the most terrible thing..."

I was on my feet. "Tell me!"

"Your home, Captain! L'Eree Farm! Burned to the ground."

"My God!" I sat down again. I had actually expected something worse.

But that was still to come. "And your wife and family ..." the poor fellow fell silent.

My head jerked. "They were inside?"

"Their bodies were found when the flames had died down."

I stared at him, uncomprehendingly. The words I spoke were those of any reasonable man. "Could they not leave? Even if they had been asleep, they would have awakened and left."

"That is the greatest tragedy of all, Captain. When they were examined, it was deduced that they had all died before the fire was started. Their bodies were torn to shreds, as if they had been assailed by a demon."

I began to feel as if *my* entire body was turning into molten lead.

"It was supposed, by the constables, that they had been attacked by vandals, because it had become known that you were serving the King ... but in truth, sir, no one knew that."

"Attacked by a demon," I whispered, the scales at last dropping from my mind and my eyes. A demon I had nurtured in my very bosom. Yet I had to be sure. "When did this happen?" I asked.

"Why, sir, it was just after last Christmas. A most unhappy time for such an event."

Just after Christmas, I thought. Just enough time for Caroline Bethlen to have gained Garnesey, and made her plans. But her plans had always been made. I had supposed myself safe, because had she wished to kill me she could have done so on our very first night together, while I was in a drunken stupor. But of course, as she was Richilde's daughter, the mere killing of me was only a part of the business. First she would enjoy me, and then reduce me to despair by destroying everyone who could possibly be dear to me. Only then would she come for me. But she would now come for me. Only in that understanding was there the least ray of consolation.

"I am most terribly sorry to be the bearer of such tidings, Captain," Martel said.

"If it was not you, it would have been someone else," I told him.

His gaze was curious. "What will you do?"

"Why," I said. "I will serve the King. And so will you, as my servant."

It was only after he had left me that I could allow myself to give way to my grief, throw myself on my cot and sob like a babe. But grief was only ever subservient to guilt. I had known almost from the moment of our first meeting that Caroline was a child of the Devil; indeed, she had admitted it. And in my besotted desire for her I had let her live. More, I had told her my innermost secrets, and finally, by giving her written *carte blanche*, I had made it possible for her to achieve the very end she had sought from the beginning – to avenge her own parent's death. Well, she had accomplished that – but only in part, I was certain. She had intended, from the start, to destroy me and mine, and with the deadly patience of the witch she was she had waited for the perfect opportunity. To destroy mine. But not yet me.

Therefore, as I had once sought her mother across half of Europe, so would she again be seeking me. She would no doubt begin by returning to East Anglia and the Cromwells. To be told that I had perished in the flaming ruin of O'Connell House? But she, with her supernatural powers, the powers which had guided her to me in Paris, would know that to be false, and would know, that if I had abandoned the Roundheads, there was only one place I would be found. But even if she accepted I was dead, and her quest ended, mine was only just beginning. I would seek her out, and destroy her as I had destroyed her mother. But to do that, I had first to destroy those who stood between me and her: the Roundhead army.

Thus was my loyalty to the King's cause at last assured, as my entire mind was once again bent to death and destruction.

And in the new year it seemed as if matters were at last moving to a crisis. Immediately after Christmas, the King felt so confident in his position – his army from Ireland had at last landed in the north-west and was marching to join us – that he issued writs for a parliament to be held at Oxford. Were this to be successful, then the parliament at Westminster, which continued to sit all this while and solemnly debate theological matters, would become entirely redundant, and Essex, Manchester, Fairfax and Cromwell no more than the leaders of robber bands. However, hardly had the writs been issued when we were assailed by a succession of evil tidings.

The first was that the Scottish army had crossed the Tweed and was advancing upon York. The second was that Parliament and the Scots had established a joint commission to govern the country. And the third, and most serious, was that our Irish troops, on which so much store had been set, had been routed by Fairfax at Nantwich, following which the Parliamentarian general had marched north to join in the siege of York, bottling up an army commanded by the Earl of Newcastle. These were serious matters, as Oxford was itself being masked by a Parliamentary army under the Earl of Manchester, and while as yet we had heard nothing more of Cromwell and his Ironsides, I was quite certain that they were there, and would be used most effectively when the time came. I was therefore relieved to be summoned by the King. "C-c-count," he said. "I consider that we are approaching a decisive moment. What is your estimate of the situation?"

"That the siege of York must be raised, Your Majesty, with all possible despatch. If we lose the north, we are

240

halfway to losing the war." I preferred not to tell him that I considered we were all but there already.

He nodded. "I am sure you are right. I am sending messengers to P-p-prince Rupert at Shrewsbury, commanding him to take his men and defeat Fairfax and his people."

As if it were as simple as that. But still, it promised action, which was all the pleasure I had left to me. "I shall leave immediately to join the Prince," I said.

"You? No, no, C-c-count. Your business is here. And elsewhere." He had this maddening habit of being deliberately obscure.

"Your Majesty?" I queried.

"Have you forgotten your first, your p-p-principal, your only d-d-duty with this army?"

I gulped. "As you have t-t-truly said," the King went on. "If we lose the north we are in dire straits. I have every confidence in Rupert, but war is ever a matter of chance, as you must know from your German experiences."

"There would be less chance if I were to be with the Prince, Your Majesty." These were bold words, but I was growing desperate.

"I have said, you have a greater d-d-duty. You are aware that Her Majesty has been brought to her bed?"

"The entire army has prayed for a successful delivery, Your Majesty."

"That is most g-g-gratifying of them, I am sure. However, the fact is that her life is in d-d-danger, and that of her b-b-baby d-d-daughter. She is still attainted by P-p-parliament, and I shudder to think what might happen if they were to g-g-get their filthy hands on her."

"In Exeter, Your Majesty? That is surely impossible. Do the Roundheads even know of her whereabouts?"

"Is anything impossible, C-c-count, in this benighted country?" He picked up a sheet of paper from the table. "Here is a report I received yesterday. It speaks of a woman in the t-t-town, asking questions about the-the whereabouts of Her Majesty."

I frowned, while my heart did a great leap. "T-t-take it

and study it," the King recommended. "I have t-t-two charges for you, C-c-count. The first is, find this woman, and find out who she is working for and what her intentions are. If they are sinister, then ... " he hesitated for a brief second. "She must be got rid of. D-d-do you understand me?"

"I do, Your Majesty," I said grimly. "It will be a pleasure."

"B-b-but C-c-count, the matter must be handled most c-c-carefully. There are many p-p-people, even in Oxford, who are opposed to me. Were a woman to be, ah, ill-treated without d-d-due p-p-process of law, there c-c-could be a riot."

"It will be done most carefully, Your Majesty," I assured him. I could hardly believe my ears, or my good fortune; if the woman was Caroline, as seemed likely, then this was one task I would rather carry out even than ride with Rupert. "You spoke of two commissions."

"Yes. I consider it is too dangerous for Her Majesty to remain any longer in Exeter, or even in England. Obviously she c-c-cannot be moved while in such a delicate condition, but the very moment she is able to travel, I wish you to t-t-take her to safety."

I had to gulp again at this, for here he was placing his all in the care of a man who had all but cuckolded him. Yet was I perfectly happy with the assignment, as it would come after I had dealt with the demon, and after that I had no further interest in this war. "Which place of safety did you have in mind, Your Majesty?" I asked.

"You will make that d-d-decision, C-c-count, as you will make all the arrangements, and you will keep them entirely to yourself. That is the only way we may be sure no one else will learn of them."

My heart swelled. "Your Majesty places a great responsibility on my shoulders."

"They are b-b-broad enough, are they not? Besides, Her Majesty trusts you, and she is not p-p-prepared to trust anyone else. I will wish you good fortune."

I bowed and withdrew, taking the report with me. It was from a provost marshal, who had found the inquiries made by the woman somewhat strange. I was more interested in his description of her, which was that she was very attractive, with curly dark hair, and a good figure. That certainly sounded like Caroline, even if he had also added that she was of less than medium height. Of course, in the absence of a tape measure, everyone has his own opinion as to height, but I would have described Caroline as tall for a woman.

In any event, I meant to have her. I summoned Martel, and bade him make discreet inquiries about this woman, and to discover where she was lodging. While he was gone, and partly in order to occupy my mind – for I was most powerfully affected by the coming confrontation in which I intended to avenge my family with all the vigour and brutality I could muster – I made some plans of my own.

Martel returned in an hour, with the disappointing information that the woman, who had called herself Mrs Trump, had left Oxford the previous day. "By herself?"

"No, sir. She had two people with her, a man and another woman. The landlord of the inn thought they were her servants."

"In which direction did they ride?"

"North-east."

"We must be after them." I had been given *carte blanche* by the King, and so handed over my duties to one of my captains, and within an hour Martel and I were on the road, hurrying north-east. Of course the demon had several hours' start – but she would not know she was being pursued. It was like my pursuit of her mother all over again, but now, instead of any longer being consumed with anger, I felt like a block of ice, determined to do what I had to do.

In fact our pursuit was a brief one, for the demon was apparently making no effort to conceal her tracks. The next village at which we stopped told us that a dark-haired lady and two servants had lunched there but three hours before. We hurried behind them, and rode into the next village just on dusk. I stamped into the taproom. "I seek a lady," I told the host. "She will have curling dark hair, be well-dressed, and very comely."

"Why, sir, there is a lady of that description staying here this very night," he told me. "That is her servant, over there."

I cast a hasty glance over my shoulder, and saw an ill-favoured lout sitting in a corner, drinking beer. "And the lady?" I asked.

"Why, sir, she is in her chamber, with her maid."

I took a gold piece from my wallet and slid it across the counter. "I would speak with this lady, privately, upon a matter of the utmost importance," I said. Obviously I dared not risk telling him I was on the King's business, because in the fuddled state that was England in 1644 there was no telling whether he supported King or Parliament. "Therefore do you not tell that fellow I am here."

He pocketed the coin. "I have never seen you before, sir," he said. "It is up the stairs and the second door on the left."

By this time Martel, having seen to the horses, had joined me, and I beckoned him with a nod to follow me up the stairs. He obeyed, but was clearly uneasy. "My lord?" he whispered, when we had gained the upper passage. "What are we about?"

"We are about to arrest a Roundhead spy," I told him, considering it best to keep the business as simple as possible. "She has a maid with her. Do you see to the maid, and I will see to the mistress."

"See to her?" he asked, more uneasily yet.

"In the first instance," I told him, "the pair of them must be seized and bound."

He gulped, and I recalled that while a promising soldier, he had never revealed any great interest in the opposite sex. Well, he would have to learn. "Now remember," I told him. "It will be necessary to act with great vigour and determination. Do not let yourself be put off by feminine trifles. Or feminine screams."

He nodded, and certainly gave every appearance of determination. I thus stood against the door and endeavoured to listen, but could hear nothing. I then applied my eye to the keyhole, but the key was in the lock.

While I was doing this a man came along the corridor, and paused to look at us most suspiciously. I gave him a toss of the head, and he went down the stairs. Then I knocked on the door. "Who is it?" someone asked. As I did not recognise the voice, I presumed it was the maid.

"An urgent message," I mumbled.

I heard the lock turn, and a moment later the door swung in.

"Now!" I told Martel, and hurled the wood back.

The woman, who was indeed the maidservant, gave a shriek and fell over. I left her to Martel – she was middle-aged and would surely not distress him too much – stepped over her supine body, hurled aside the screen which occupied the centre of the room, and faced Aimée Hubert.

CHAPTER 10

Having braced myself, both mentally and physically, for a confrontation with Caroline, I was totally taken aback. As was Aimée, perhaps even more so, for she had just completed her bath, and was indeed still standing in the tin tub, wearing only a towel, and that is putting it politely, for she had been in the act of drying her shoulders when I appeared, and all in all presented a most attractive sight.

We recovered in the same instant. She leapt backwards, and I leapt forward, treading in the tub as I did so to scatter water in every direction, and grasping the towel as I lost my balance. In the circumstances, Aimée decided to abandon her scanty protection in favour of killing me, so she turned away and ran to the dresser, on which there lay a pistol. But although I had stumbled I was too quick for her, gained her as she picked up the weapon, threw one arm round her waist and with the other seized her wrist. The pistol exploded with a huge sound but the bullet merely slammed into the ceiling, although the entire room seemed to shake.

"Garnesey bastard!" she shouted, attempting to hit me with the empty gun, but I evaded her blow easily enough and threw her across the bed, on her face, leaping after her to sit astride her buttocks and make it impossible for her to move, as I placed my hand between her shoulder-blades.

"My lord?" Martel inquired, in some distress. He had coped with the servant well enough, but was having to hang on to her as she endeavoured both to bite him and kick him, and he was looking thoroughly embarrassed.

"I just need to obtain one or two answers from this lady," I told him. Aimée, having fortunately run out of

246

breath so that she could no longer curse me, gave another futile heave.

"But should she not be dressed, my lord?" the gormless youth inquired.

"I think we will get on better this way," I assured him, and lowered my head until my lips were close to Aimée's ear. "Now listen to me very carefully, my dear. I wish to know why you were inquiring about the Queen's arrangements. To enable you to speak the more comfortably, I am going to roll you over, but should you scream or attempt to escape me, I am going to cut off your tits." I reasoned that this would be the most efficacious threat I could employ, as it was extended to her most prominent features.

She made no reply, and so I rolled her over, whereupon she lay on her back, pillowed in her hair, and glared at me. The objects of discussion heaved so violently I imagine I would have had trouble catching hold of them, even had I intended carrying out my dastardly threat. "Now," I said. "Your purpose."

Her response was to spit at me. She only managed to splatter my doublet, but even so it was a distasteful thing to do, and I was inclining towards placing her on her face again and bestowing some chastisement on to her splendid backside when I was distracted by a banging on the door. "Open up," someone was shouting. "Open up, sir. What are you doing in there?"

From the shouting and muttering, I gathered that the intruder was not unsupported. "Now you'll hang," said the servant. "Rape it will be. They hang for rape in these parts."

"My lord," Martel said, his voice trembling.

I realised that I would have to declare myself, which, if these people did have Roundhead sympathies, might even more rapidly lead to the gallows. "Look to your sword," I advised, "and open the door."

He obeyed, flattening himself against the wall as he did so, and just as well, for as he turned the key the door was almost hurled from its hinges by the thrust of eager men

247

and women bursting into the room. "Rape!" shrieked the beldam. "The foulest rape I ever saw."

I could not help but wonder just how many of these events she *had* seen, but I understood that I was in an invidious position, as Aimée was certainly naked, and on a bed, and if I was still fully dressed, I was kneeling astride the most carnal area of her body. While leading the throng were not only the ill-favoured manservant I had seen downstairs, and mine host, a large fellow, but also the gentleman who had looked upon Martel and me with disfavour when he had caught us attempting to peer through the keyhole. In their eyes I was already condemned.

"Save me, sirs, I beg of you," Aimée cried, in those dulcet tones she could use so well. "I am beset by a monster."

"By God, sir!" shouted mine host, waving a barrel stave, while the people at his back bayed for blood.

All save one, and as I looked at this fellow, who was tall enough to stand above those surrounding him, I realised I had discovered our salvation, and without having to indulge in politics. "Master Hopkins!" I cried. "What brings you to these parts? But no matter. Thank God you are here."

The mob was up to the bed by now, the men at least enjoying the view, but they checked at the possibility that I might be a friend of the one man they all feared. "Why, Captain L'Eree," Hopkins replied. "I am about my business. There are rumours of witches in these parts. But you, sir, why, I find this behaviour most indecent."

"What do you think I am about?" I demanded.

"Well, as to that, sir, it looks pretty obvious."

"Do you know this gentleman, Mr Hopkins?" inquired the host.

"We have an acquaintance," Hopkins said carefully.

"This woman is the foulest witch who ever walked the face of this earth," I said.

"What?" shouted her manservant.

"What?" shouted the beldam.

"What?" shouted the mob.

"What?" shouted Aimée.

"Can that be true, sir?" Hopkins inquired.

"Of course it is not true," Aimée shouted, making another futile effort to escape from beneath me. "This man would have his way with me."

"Lecher!" shrieked the beldam. The crowd bristled.

But I continued to look at Hopkins. "Come now, sir," I said. "Do I look as if I am committing rape? *Can* a man commit rape with his breeches on?"

"Hm," Hopkins said. "It would be difficult."

"This woman is a witch, whom I have tracked down for causing a great illness amongst my people," I told him. "Not knowing you were in the neighbourhood, I was examining her when these people burst in."

"Liar!" Aimée screamed, throwing herself about violently against my thighs.

"If you will send these people away, Mr Hopkins," I said. "I will prove the truth of my claim."

"Hm," Hopkins said again. But I had appealed to all that was vicious in his character; he enjoyed tormenting any woman, but a beautiful woman was obviously best of all. "Clear the room," he told his two companions, who as ever were at his shoulder.

"Out," they shouted. "Out!" And they began pushing people into the corridor. No one resisted. I realised that Mr Hopkins was worth a squadron of cavalry, where superstitious yokels were concerned.

Aimée saw with alarm that her support was vanishing.

"You cannot permit this!" she bawled.

"You as well, landlord," Hopkins commanded.

"And take that servant with you," I suggested.

"You are permitting murder," Aimée wailed.

But the door was closed and locked, and she was alone with Hopkins and his henchmen, myself, and poor Martel, who was shivering like a jelly. "I think you could release her now," Hopkins said. "We'll have no lewdity."

"Willingly." I swung my leg over Aimée's thighs and stood up. She immediately sat up, grasping the sheet to pull it against herself.

"Now, sir," Hopkins said. "You have accused this woman of being a witch."

"Indeed I have," I agreed. "Her spells are responsible for the deaths of four cattle belonging to my brother."

"How can you listen to such lies?" Aimée shouted. "His brother! If he has a brother, which I doubt, he lives in Garnesey, which is where this lout hails from. I have never been to Garnesey."

"Garnesey, you say." Hopkins stroked his chin. "I remember, you told me this, Captain. I have heard there is much witchcraft in that tiny island."

"Indeed, I have heard the same thing," I agreed. "Although it is years since I have lived there. Perhaps you should after all pay it a visit." And I would see that you never left again, I thought to myself.

"Hm," he commented. "Perhaps I shall. You say it is years since you were there? But ... when last we met, you were on your way there. With your wife."

I had forgotten that conversation. Now it was necessary to backtrack very rapidly. But I reasoned that a man like Hopkins, alike from his dress and his manner, not to mention his profession, had to be a supporter of Parliament rather than the King. "I changed my mind," I told him. "About returning. While awaiting a passage, I met an old friend of mine, Colonel Cromwell, and he persuaded me to serve with him in his regiment."

"Hm," Hopkins commented.

"Lies," Aimée cried. "All lies. He is a Royalist spy. It is Colonel Cromwell's greatest wish to seize him and hang him."

"Hm," Hopkins remarked. "But I have heard the tale of how you saved the Colonel's life, Captain."

"There you have it," I said triumphantly.

"Yet this woman accuses you of being a spy."

"Would you believe a witch?"

"How can I be a witch?" Aimée complained. "Do I look like a witch?"

"Witches come in all guises," Hopkins pointed out. "You spoke of proof, Count."

"Absolutely. She bears the Devil's mark."

"Well, that would decide it. Show me this mark."

"It is just beneath her right breast."

"Foul wretch!" Aimée screamed. "Devil's mark? It is nought but a mole! If you seek the Devil's accomplice, it is he you should examine." She was coming uncomfortably close to the truth.

But Hopkins was consumed with interest, as I had supposed he would be: examining Aimée was a far more attractive prospect than examining me. "You'll show me this mark, madam."

Aimée hugged the sheet tighter against herself. "Never! Do you expect me to expose myself to a bunch of men?"

"Do you, then, admit to possessing the mark?"

"Of course I do not. It is a matter of modesty."

"You must be examined." He beckoned his men, one of whom seized Aimée's ankles to pull them and stretch her out on the bed, while the other grasped her wrists and pulled them behind her and above her head.

"Bastards!" Aimée screamed. "Foul wretches!" And she went on to curse them most thoroughly in French, which fortunately only I could understand.

Not, I suspect, that Mr Hopkins would have been distracted even if he had known what she was calling him, as he now removed the sheet which had hitherto been concealing Aimée's charms. Delicately he found it necessary to lift her breast to peer at the mole beneath. "Hm," he said. "Hm."

Aimée had by now abandoned fighting in favour of panting, which again made his investigation a difficult matter, but by using both hands he managed. "It is a mole," she said. "Can you not see it is a mole?"

"The Devil's mark often resembles a mole," Mr Hopkins pontificated. "Now, we shall shave you."

Aimée let out another piercing scream at the thought. But I was appalled myself.

"My dear Hopkins," I said. "Would that not be a shame? Her hair is her crowning glory."

He pointed at me. "You are thinking lewd thoughts about this woman."

"And you are not?"

He went very red in the face. "We shall have to see," he muttered, and from his pocket he drew his little box, which he opened, to reveal the dreaded bodkin.

Aimée gave another most piteous howl.

"You'll not thrust that thing into me!"

"I must do my duty," Mr Hopkins said severely, and forthwith drove the needle into the brown eruption.

At this, Aimée's scream all but broke the windowpanes.

"Ah," I said, "I seem to have been mistaken." I spoke with some relief, for I was beginning to feel quite sorry for the poor woman, who surely had had as much manhandling as anyone could reasonably expect.

However, as I had invoked the Devil, who travels in many forms, I had now to sit out his frightful machinations. "Not necessarily," Mr Hopkins opined. "Sometimes these creatures' resistance is most devious. You'll observe that I have not drawn blood."

"My God, my God!" Aimée screamed. "You have wounded me to death."

"There may well be other marks," Mr Hopkins said, and proceeded to search for them, bodkin in hand. He poked and prodded, had his henchmen roll Aimée on her face, thrust the needle into her buttocks, after they had been suitably plumped, and drew another scream. Then it was a mole on her thigh which attracted his attention, and then, when she had been rolled on her back again, something which attracted him between her legs. But all the while he was watching and listening, and waiting, for he was the most diabolical scoundrel, and when he judged the time right, which was the moment Aimée had run completely out of breath and at the same time had been punctured in so many places she was clearly so consumed with pain she could not possibly identify any one source, he returned to the first mole. This time there was no response at all. "There," he said in triumph. "What did I tell you, Captain? She was truly devious, as one would expect of a succubus,

252

but we have found her out. She is clearly a witch. Dress yourself, woman," he commanded.

His men let Aimée go, whereupon she drew up her legs and folded her arms as if attempting to make herself into a ball. "Haste, woman, haste," Hopkins said. "I have not got all night." And he assisted her by pushing her off the bed, so that she fell to her hands and knees beside it, shuddering and sobbing.

"What do you mean to do with her?" I asked.

"Oh, she must be ducked, now that it is proven she is a witch."

I scratched my head. "Then, if you are going to throw her into the water anyway, why do you wish her to dress?" This procedure had indeed confused me with the Widow Litchen.

"My dear Captain," the villain said. "Would you have me permit this woman to appear before the mob in the altogether? That would be to inspire lewdity. This is not France, you know."

The absurdity of his attitude – seeing that the entire mob had already beheld Aimée in the nude – combined with his selfish point of view, was remarkable. But I had more important things on my mind. Earlier in this tale I confessed to not being a gentlemen, which is to say I care not a jot for the hypocrisies in which these creatures indulge to conceal their own shortcomings. Yet I will swear that my instincts have always *been* those of a gentleman, and this weakness of character has repeatedly got me into more trouble than I care to remember, beginning on that unforgettable day fourteen years ago when I had found myself unable to force Marguerite. So it was now. I had come here to beat the truth out of Aimée, and I had known that I might even have had to execute her. Yet now I felt that she had suffered far too much for one evening, nor was I about to stand by and allow her to be judicially murdered as had happened with that other unfortunate female I had been forced to watch suffer at Hopkins' hands. So here we go again, I thought sadly. "Haste, woman, haste," I said in apparent support of the witch-hunter.

Aimée dragged on her clothes, still sobbing, but regaining enough of her spirit to mutter, "I shall see you all burn in hell."

But now she had on her gown. I could wait no longer, principally because Hopkins would wait no longer. "Open the door," he commanded Martel. "And we shall take her down."

There was of course no time to bandy words or make suggestions; from the continuing racket outside I knew that the crowd was still gathered in the corridor. This suited my ambitions admirably, providing they were not allowed into the room. "Leave the door, Jonathan," I commanded.

The lad turned to look at me in surprise. So did Hopkins, thus presenting a perfect target for my fist. I may say that anyone struck by the fist of Helier L'Eree loses all interest in the proceedings for some considerable time. So it was with Hopkins, who collapsed as though dead, which he may very well have been, so far as I then knew. Unfortunately, as it later turned out, he was still very much alive. His two henchmen stared at me in consternation, and I levelled Aimée's pistol. They of course were unaware that this was empty, and hastily raised their arms. "Turn round," I suggested.

They obeyed, and I stepped up to them, reversing the pistol as I did so, and with two quick blows laid them both out as I had done their master. Now I found both Aimée and Jonathan staring at me with an equal consternation. "We have but a few seconds," I told them, and threw open the window. It was only a matter of twelve feet to the yard. "You go first, Jonathan, and catch Mademoiselle Hubert."

As was his wont, he obeyed me without question, hanging by his hands and dropping to the cobbles without mishap. "Now you," I told Aimée.

"You must think I am demented," she remarked. "Run away with *you*?"

"I will consider you demented if you do not," I pointed out. "Regardless of his feelings towards me, when he regains consciousness Mr Hopkins is certainly going to have you ducked as a witch, and that means you are going to drown."

"My servants..."

"Will obey Hopkins. For some reason, everyone always does. Now, it is up to you. I am leaving. You may precede me. Or you may stay here and take your chances."

That decided her. She climbed into the window, and with a faint shriek dropped into the arms of Jonathan. She was obviously heavier than she looked, because they collapsed together, but I was immediately with them, and we were at the stables before anyone at the inn realised what was happening.

"What do you intend for me?" Aimée asked, when we had ridden far enough to be safe from pursuit.

Well, what would you? I had spent a long five minutes wrestling with this young woman, her being naked, and in any event, I had marked her down as a most pleasing prospect from the moment of our first meeting. In addition, I felt it necessary to examine her most minutely, just in case Hopkins' bodkin had done her an injury. In the darkness of the wood where we had sought refuge, this was a matter of feel rather than sight, so I put Jonathan on guard while I carried out my medical duties, following which it was necessary to leave him on guard while I performed other duties, the principal one, as it was still early in the year and decidedly chill, being to warm the poor girl up again after her fresh exposure.

Understanding that she was entirely in my power, she raised no objection to all this, although I suspect her brain was tumbling away. Mine was also, but in an entirely different direction, until, exhausted, I remembered the reason for my being here and her being there. "Now, then, Aimée," I said. "You and I have some business together."

"Not again," she sighed, nestling into the bed we had made of our clothes in the bracken. "I have had an enervating evening."

"I am speaking of what you were doing in Oxford."

"You do not know I was in Oxford," she protested.

"As it happens, I do. You were identified. And if you do not tell me the truth of it, I shall be left with the choice of one of two courses. One will be to hang you, naked as you are, from that tree over there, and the other will be to return you to the care of Mr Hopkins. You may be sure I shall make my decision upon my reckoning of which, from your point of view, will be the more unpleasant."

"I had supposed you liked me," she complained.

"I do like you, Aimée. Very much. But I have never allowed my personal feelings to interfere with my duty."

This was of course a complete lie, but it convinced her. She gave a couple of huge sighs, and then told me what I needed to know. "It is felt by Mr Pym that the Queen is His Majesty's evil genius. And besides, she is under a Bill of Attainder, and is therefore an outlaw."

"And therefore subject to murder?"

"Our determination is to seize Her Majesty, and place her in a position of safety. It is then felt that the King will be more amenable to reason."

I was aghast. "You intended to kidnap the Queen?"

"Well, not me, personally. I was the agent sent to determine how it had best be done. Firstly, by discovering her exact whereabouts."

"Pym thought of this?"

"Well, the idea was put into his head, by one of Cromwell's officers, when we were on a visit to Huntingdon."

"Ireton," I growled. "By God..."

"No, no, it was not Mr Ireton, Helier. It was a young man who claims an acquaintance with you, or at least, that you have an acquaintance with his sister. As Mr Cromwell well knew."

My head jerked. "A young man ... with a sister ... " I seized her shoulders and shook her so that her teeth rattled. "What is this fellow's name?"

"He is a certain Charles Le Brock. A most handsome fellow. And an excellent soldier."

"Charles Le Brock," I muttered. "You say this Le Brock is serving with Cromwell?"

"He went to East Anglia searching for his sister. The

woman who was with you when I had you arrested, Helier. What have you done with her?"

"You mean Mr Le Brock could not tell you?"

"Well, he knew that you had sent her off to Garnesey. Mr Cromwell knew that too. But she has never been heard of since. And as Mr Le Brock was able to inform Mr Cromwell that you had not, after all, perished at O'Connell's Manor, but had escaped to rejoin the King's forces..."

"Mr Le Brock knew that, did he? Tell me how?"

"I have no idea."

"And no one thought to ask him?"

"It was the information which mattered. As I was saying, it was supposed that you had given Le Brock's sister, the woman Caroline, secret instructions merely to travel up the coast and rendezvous with you at an appropriate place."

"I see. And now Mr Le Brock devised this plan for kidnapping the Queen." Caroline supposed she was my mistress. The demon wished to strike down everyone she felt I might hold dear before she came for me personally. "But he would not carry it out himself."

"It was felt that would be unsafe; as he is acquainted with you, and it was known that you were in Oxford, it was deemed that another should spy out the land first."

"But are you not acquainted with me?"

"I volunteered. I was sure I could make the reconnaissance without being discovered."

"Which was an error."

"I was unlucky. Helier ... what are you going to do with me?"

"I *should* hang you from yonder tree. However, answer me another question, and you may just survive. You say Le Brock serves with Cromwell? In what capacity?"

"He is a cornet in the Ironsides. That is Cromwell's regiment of horse."

"I know of the Ironsides. I served with them myself. Very well, Aimée. I am going to let you go. I am even going to let you take a horse, and return to the Roundheads. Return to Cromwell, and Master Le Brock. Tell them of your misadventure, and of your encounter with me. And tell them that I look forward to encountering them, both of them, sword in hand, at the earliest possible opportunity."

It was a temptation, of course, to send by this woman a message to Cromwell to the effect that he was nurturing a witch in his very bosom. But in the first place, I doubted he would believe me, with Caroline there to deny it, and in the second, I wished to despatch her myself, just to make sure she stayed despatched. "And Aimée," I added, "you may tell Cromwell, and Mr Pym, that the next Roundhead spy or agent on whom I lay my hands I will personally hang, on the spot."

She grasped my hands. "Oh, Helier. I am grateful, believe me."

"And so you should be. Now, I recommend you depart immediately, remembering to stay out of the clutches of Mr Hopkins."

The poor girl was happy to obey; I do believe she could not quite bring herself to believe that she was still alive.

"Count," Jonathan said, as he mounted beside me. "I am totally confused."

"It is the safest way to be," I assured him.

I was not the least afraid that Aimée would regain the Parliamentary ranks and organise her attempt, or rather, Caroline's attempt, on the Queen before I had removed Her Majesty to a place of safety. This I regarded as my first duty. After that, I intended to devote the rest of my life to finding and destroying Caroline. Although I had every hope that she was going to come to me.

But first, the Queen.

Jonathan and I did not waste our time in returning to Oxford, but rode straight for Exeter. This was actually under a rough kind of siege by various Parliamentary units, but we evaded these without difficulty and I went to the Queen's quarters.

"L'Eree?" She looked alarmed, as she had not been informed of my coming, and thus immediately anticipated catastrophe. The baby princess, indeed, was still at her breast.

"Your Majesty." I made a leg. "I am from the King."

"With what news?"

"It is privy, Your Majesty."

"Leave us," she commanded.

There was less twittering than normal, although Jermyn, who was as usual in attendance, did some harrumphing, but they did remove the babe, and Henrietta dried her nipple. "Speak," she said.

I told her of the King's plans, both for himself and for herself. I did not bother her with my adventure with Aimée.

"And you are to take me to safety?" She gave a quick clap of her hands. "Oh, happy day. You understand that I do not wish to go, L'Eree. But if go I must, then I could ask for no better companion. You will accompany me to Holland?"

I had already taken the decision to disobey the King. I could not leave England without settling with Caroline. "Sadly, Your Majesty, no. My duty lies here. I am but to see you to safety."

"Ah," she said. "When do we leave?"

"As soon as I can arrange a ship, Your Majesty."

This was more easily said than done. The Navy was entirely in the hands of Parliament, and there were some men-of-war lying off the town, searching every vessel entering or leaving the port. I had to cast my net further afield, a slow business as it meant sneaking in and out of Exeter like a thief, but at last discovered a shipmaster in Falmouth who, on being liberally paid, agreed to undertake the task of transporting the Queen to Holland. Then it was necessary to move Henrietta, her babe – she had none of her other children with her, to her great distress, although her son James was already safely on the continent – her ladies and her dogs – she always had some of these around – not to mention the wretched Jermyn, to the smaller port, in, of course, the greatest secrecy.

It may be imagined that it was with decidedly mixed

259

feelings that I set off on this journey. I had scarce seen the Queen since our abortive set-to the previous summer, as we had been so widely separated. Now, while she seemed delighted to have me again in her company, I was a changed man. The laughing cavalier who had held her naked in his arms no longer existed. Over the winter, indeed, I had gained the reputation of a very dour fellow, never to be found over a pint of ale in any hostelry, never to be discovered pursuing any of the many wenches who flocked around us, interested only in drilling his men or in sitting alone in his room honing his sword.

In truth I was in hell, a hell composed of memories, those of my dearest, faithful Helga, my bonny children, now no more, and a hell dominated by that beautiful monster who had so completely encompassed my destruction.

I had insisted that Master Martel tell no one of my misfortune, and this injunction he had faithfully obeyed, thus every man had his own ideas on what had caused such a dreadful metamorphosis in so normally merry a fellow. And every woman too. Maureen had been quite put out, as, living with her father as she now was, she had endeavoured to encounter me at every opportunity, to receive not even a smile, much less an invitation to visit my chamber. At last, indeed, her Irish temper bubbled over, and she swore at me. "You are nothing but a rogue, Helier L'Eree," she bawled. "Who has his way with a woman and then discards her like a worn-out boot."

I let her have her say, and then stalk away from me. I knew she was much better off without me. It will thus be seen that my set-to with Aimée had been undertaken in something of the spirit of a monk who has got over the wall, but now that was behind me, I quickly reverted to my habitual, celibate gloom.

The Queen could also tell that something was amiss, and being a woman, she also assumed that it must be to do with her. We had barely set off, Henrietta in a carriage with her babe and her ladies, while Jermyn, Jonathan and I formed an escort around her and out in front, than she was smiling at me from the window, and when we stopped for the night

260

she summoned me to her tent – for I considered it best we avoid towns if we were indeed going to keep her departure a secret. "You know I would have sent for you if I could, L'Eree," she said.

"I never doubted it, Your Majesty."

"Thus there is no longer any reason for that grim visage and constantly angry demeanour," she pointed out.

"I shall endeavour to do better, Your Majesty."

At which *she* took offence. "Do you suppose," she demanded. "That you can vent your displeasure upon me? I am your queen, and you are my servant!"

"Then, with your leave, Your Majesty, your servant will withdraw."

"I do not give you that leave," she snapped. "You are my bodyguard. Then stay, and be my bodyguard."

I had to obey, but she could tell there was nothing in it for her, and soon sent me away. The rest of our journey was a silent one, as regards the two of us, and I was right pleased when it was completed, and the Queen was on board our ship. "When can you sail?" I asked the master.

"With the tide. That is two hours time."

It was then five of the afternoon. I visited Henrietta. "Your Majesty, God willing, you will be in Holland tomorrow morning."

"I would feel safer were you willing to come with me, L'Eree," she said, having decided to forgive me.

I kissed her hand. "It is my business now to fight for your husband's cause, Your Majesty. God willing, that too will be successful."

I bowed, clapped my hat on my head, and went ashore. I remained on the quayside until the vessel was clear of the river, then I summoned Jonathan and away we went. But I was almost happy. I was once again going to war, and to my destiny.

In fact, although I did not then know it, the war had been lost even before I had placed the Queen on that ship in Falmouth. Duly instructed by the King, Rupert had hurried north to the relief of Newcastle. His strategic campaign was a brilliant one, and despite the Roundhead attempts to block him, he evaded them, conquered Lancashire, and then united his forces with those of Newcastle. As I later learned, the Earl was against a battle, for the very good reason that, although the two sides were about equal in cavalry, around seven thousand men each, the Roundheads disposed of more than twenty thousand foot to the Royalist eleven. Rupert, of course, was all for fighting, as he continued to feel the most utter contempt for the Parliamentary forces. The battle took place at Marston Moor, and in terms of men engaged was the most formidable encounter of the war. It was also one of the most decisive, for the Royalists were soundly thrashed.

It will haunt me forever to suppose that this would not have happened had I been there. But I was not, and the battle was fought much as had been the encounter at Edge Hill, with one very important difference. While the Royalist cavalry under Rupert were routing the horse opposed to them, as at Edge Hill, and the Royalist foot were matching the Scots and Roundhead infantry, as at Edge Hill, the Roundhead right wing cavalry routed the Royalist left and then put the infantry to flight. When I heard this I had simply to inquire the name of the commander of that wing to know what had happened. His name was Cromwell, and his men were called Ironsides.

"Well, C-c-count," King Charles said when I regained him, and explained that I had determined to serve him to the end, having assured myself of the Queen's safety – he could hardly be annoyed at this. "It seems that your estimate of this fellow Cromwell was entirely accurate." His calm was amazing, for by now it was known that Rupert had managed to bring only six thousand men away from that dreadful field, and that Newcastle had abandoned hope, and fled to the continent.

Had I been a rational man, despite my assurances to the King, I would have done the same. Whatever catastrophe had overtaken me in Garnesey, I was still the Count d'Albret, with vast estates in Normandy awaiting me. But I was no longer a rational man. I wanted to fight, and kill. And I wanted to be where Caroline could find me.

As to fighting and killing, there was a lot of this to be done. Marston Moor and the loss of York had actually been mortal blows to the King's cause, but this was not readily apparent. The parliamentary forces had been concentrated in the north and east, and this exposed those of their people in the south and west. And thanks to the information I had been able to bring him, Charles himself now revealed some military ability, marched the remnants of his army down to the south-west, where Essex was endeavouring to establish a Parliamentary hold, and trapped that inept soldier at Lostwithiel. Essex managed to escape with his cavalry, but his infantry, eight thousand strong, were left to surrender.

In cold terms this was a victory to be set against the defeat at Marston, but it was in the wrong place and at the wrong time. The damage had been done, for while the King retained his hold over half of the country, the important half remained in Parliamentary hands. We fought several battles during the remainder of that year, and gave as good as we got, but never made any actual progress towards defeating the enemy. All the time we were receiving the grimmest news, that Cromwell, having proved what he could do with a single regiment of cavalry, had been given a mandate to raise an army, which the Roundheads boldly proclaimed to be The New Model Army, of fourteen thousand foot, six thousand cavalry, and a thousand mounted infantry, or dragoons. This whole formidable force was to be trained and disciplined as the Ironsides, and if the Royalist commanders continued to treat as nonsense the idea of a Roundhead army being worth a damn – and referred to this new force as the New Noddle Army – I at least had no doubt that it was going to be just about the most formidable army seen anywhere in Europe since the break-up of the magnificent Swedish army led by Gustavus.

Even more sinister, to my mind, was the general shake-up which took place of the Parliamentary com-

263

manders. This was done by means of what they called a Self-Denying Ordinance, proposed by Cromwell's friends, which established that no Member of Parliament should also hold a military command. This at a stroke removed the suspect generals, such as Essex and Manchester, and in their place elevated the Yorkshire quire, Sir Thomas Fairfax, as commander-in-chief – and Fairfax was a capable soldier. But then, what of Oliver, who was most definitely a Member of Parliament? The House, when it passed the rule, specifically excluded Colonel Cromwell from its effect. After Oliver's tremendous feat at Marston Moor, which had made him into a household name, they could hardly do less, but it was nonetheless a disturbing example of how Parliament would bend even their own rules to suit their purposes. It also left us with the prospect of facing men who were determined on our destruction, and had the means to accomplish it.

Needless to say the Royalist generals did not see it this way. They were still seeking excuses for their defeat at Marston, and put most of the blame on poor Goring, who had commanded the beaten wing.

I personally fought as hard as anyone, and with my great size and experience of warfare was several times commended, by both the King and Prince Rupert. But in truth, I was merely waiting, because I had nowhere to go, no one to go to ... and because I knew there was someone looking for me. Thus I lived from day to day, and fought and killed from day to day. Of women I had nothing. I was completely off the sex. I neither knew nor cared where Maureen had got to, or what Marguerite might be doing with the new ruler of France, another cardinal, this one an Italian named Mazarin. I was waiting on a demon.

In fact I thought my vigil was at an end that October, when the King's army, returning from its victories in the south-west, found its way blocked at Newbury by a vastly superior Parliamentary force. Our scouts reported with certainty that the enemy force included General Cromwell – as

Oliver was now called – and his Ironsides. And Cornet Le Brock? But that they did not know. Still, I felt in my bones that she was there, and was as anxious as even Rupert that we should give battle. As it happened, we did. It was a completely confused affair, in which not unnaturally we were bested, but the Self-Denying Ordinance had not yet been passed, and the Roundheads were still commanded by Manchester; thus they seemed even more confused than ourselves, and failed to follow up their advantage. We learned later that Cromwell was driven near mad by Manchester's incompetence.

But it was a frustrating time for us all. I was given no opportunity to close with the enemy. Nor were my feelings relieved when I interviewed one of the Roundhead troopers we had taken prisoner, and inquired about the whereabouts of Cornet Le Brock. "He would be a very handsome fellow," I explained. "Young, but wearing a moustache. A very private sort of fellow, keeps entirely to himself."

"Why, sir, I know the very man," the prisoner confessed. "At least, I know of him. But where he is now, why, that I do not know."

"I'll have no riddles from you," I informed him. "Does he not ride with General Cromwell?"

"No, your honour, he does not. He has gone. Disappeared it was. Just like that." He snapped his fingers. "It was presumed he had deserted. Or been killed in some skirmish and not noticed."

"Disappeared," I muttered. I had no doubt at all that Caroline was still alive: her sort are very difficult to kill.

"How now, Count," said Rupert, who had overheard the conversation. "Le Brock? Did you not report that he was killed defending O'Connell House?"

"I believed that to be the case, Your Highness. I lost track of him there. But then I learned that he had deserted to the Roundheads. Now it seems he is dead."

"And good riddance. You need to pick your servants more carefully," the Prince recommended.

I could not argue with that. But I was not finished with

the prisoner yet, and so waited until the Prince had withdrawn. Then I asked, "Know you of a Frenchwoman, named Hubert? Aimée Hubert?"

"Why, yes, your honour, I do," the fellow confessed.

"Then can you tell me where she is now?"

"Well, sir, it is an odd thing, but she has also disappeared. Indeed, she vanished the very night as did Mr Le Brock." He grinned. "There are some saying that the pair of them eloped together. But that will not save them if Mr Cromwell catches up with them. He was very angry at the suggestion."

"I will say Amen to that," I agreed.

Aimée and Caroline, together? I could have no doubt that Caroline had seduced Aimée, and equally that Aimée, under that influence, would very rapidly forget that she owed me her life, and only that she owed me her hatred. And they had disappeared together. There was catastrophe. Yet not utter. Because most of all I could have no doubt that they were looking for me. I could do nothing less than remain where they would know where to find me. I took every precaution, had Jonathan sleep in the same room with me with loaded pistols – he clearly put me down as a very nervous fellow for so famous a soldier, but as usual obeyed without question.

Meanwhile the King and his generals remained in a totally confused state. But then, so was the whole country, and the Roundheads. Following the Battle of Newbury, they sent commissioners to our camp, requesting a truce while they prepared a new set of proposals. Charles was delighted. "They know they are b-b-beaten men," he asserted, and agreed to the truce.

I complained to Rupert, privately. "This can only be a ruse, Your Highness," I said.

"A ruse, Count? What can they hope to achieve?"

"I will tell you, my lord Prince. This New Model Army they are recruiting and training, we saw nothing of it at Newbury."

"Cromwell's redcoats were there," Rupert pointed out.

"The Ironsides. A brigade of horse. But what of the foot? They are not yet ready for combat. They are being trained. That is why Parliament wishes some months of peace, to complete their preparations for the decisive battle."

"You think too deeply, and too sombrely, Count. Do you know why they are busily equipping their people with red jackets? So that they will not turn tail and run at the sight of the blood staining their neighbours. Ha ha! That will avail them nothing. Let them train as much as they wish, they will still be a rabble of shopkeepers and apprentices. While we will not again make the mistakes of Marston Moor. No, no, Count, you are depressed because you have been deserted by your little friend. I recommend you find another, of more orthodox tastes. Godsblood, you could have been hanged for it. Why do you not find that pretty little girl you rescued from the Roundheads, and give her a good tumble. That will restore your spirits. Or come hunting with me tomorrow."

I all but despaired. And indeed, over Christmas, I did go in search of Maureen O'Connell, who remained with the army, as her father was there, and like me she had nowhere else to go. But she was walking out with a captain of dragoons, and tossed her head most contemptuously at me.

In the new year my prognostications were proven correct, when news reached us that Archbishop Laud, had, like Strafford, been subjected to a Bill of Attainder and executed. This while Parliament was still 'negotiating' with the King, and envoys were constantly coming and going. This event made even Charles realise that he was being duped, and he commenced to draw up plans. I regarded this with a sinking heart, and in the event I was again proved right.

"We must d-d-defeat these p-p-people," the King declared, surveying the maps spread on front of him, and surrounded by his generals, amongst whom, of course, was myself. "And this c-c-can b-b-best b-b-be d-d-done b-b-by attacking him where we know we are well supported. That is, in the West c-c-country, and in Scotland."

This was true enough, for if this whole sorry affair had begun because of the King's determination to force episcopacy on the Scots and the Scots' refusal to accept it, certainly in the Lowlands, the Marquis of Montrose had nonetheless raised the Highlanders and had been carrying on a very successful campaign in the King's name. It was his proposals which staggered me. "How many men d-d-do we d-d-dispose of, General d-d-d'Albret?" he asked.

"We could put fifteen thousand men into the field within a month, Your Majesty."

"C-c-capital. We must strike as soon as the weather improves. Lord G-g-goring, you will take eight thousand men and march on the West Country. The rebels hold T-t-taunton. You will lay siege to the t-t-town and b-b-bring any relieving force to b-b-battle. Understood?"

"Understood, Your Majesty."

"P-p-prince Rupert, you will t-t-take seven thousand men and march north, to link up with Montrose and lay siege to York. We must have that b-b-back." He smiled. "You will gain your revenge for Marston Moor, eh, nephew?"

"I will do that, Uncle, you have my word," Rupert said.

I was struck dumb with consternation. Charles' plan, so confidently accepted by his commanders, broke the most important rule of warfare: concentration. Decisive battles are invariably won by the general who can concentrate the most men on a chosen field. Where dispersal is used, it must be used only as a means to an eventual decisive concentration. But there was the King blithely dividing his army into two and sending it to opposite ends of the country!

I could only ask, "And which army will you accompany, Sire?"

Charles gave another of his quiet smiles. "We shall see, C-c-count. We shall see. But you will accompany *me*."

Thus we began another muddled campaign. Needless to

say, nothing went according to plan, and the fact that the campaign dragged on as long as it did was because, initially, the Roundheads were as confused as we. Thus, they sent an army after Goring, which was according to our plans, but at the same time they sent Cromwell on a cavalry sweep up the Thames to disrupt Rupert's preparation for his march north. Rupert's ever-abiding necessity was of course horses, and thus he had moved to Hereford on the Welsh borders looking for remounts before beginning his march. Before he had properly begun, Cromwell had swept the country clear of horseflesh.

The Roundheads now at last began to realise what we were up to, and made the obvious decision; they would attack and seize the King's headquarters of Oxford, now virtually undefended. Their concentration, under Fairfax, brought everyone hurrying back, and there were Goring and Rupert swearing at each other for incompetence and generally upsetting everyone.

The upshot of all this was that the King determined to abandon Oxford, at least temporarily, and hopefully without Fairfax being aware of it, and by a wide march throw himself behind, ie, north, of Fairfax, and thereby put himself in a situation where his entire force could link up with the Scots.

Actually, although the plan was originally suggested by a soothsayer rather than any general, this was as good a strategic idea as he had ever devised, and had he embarked upon it with his entire army, who knows what we might have accomplished. But he again sent Goring into the West Country with a large proportion of our people. To say truth, he had personal reasons for doing this. The rivalry between Goring and Rupert had grown to such proportions that there was no possibility of the two men ever combining their efforts on the same field, but this admission is in itself evidence of the sorry state of affairs within the King's camp. In fact, Rupert had by now succeeded in antagonising so many of the Royalist commanders that the King was forced to appoint a new commander-in-chief, at least nominally – his fifteen-year-old son Charles.

Thus off we set with not more than eight thousand men. But all were in high spirits, as we felt we were about to steal a march on the rebels.

Our direction was first of all north-west. We left the city as stealthily as we could, and were away, certainly before the Roundheads knew of it, marching first for Woodstock, and then Evesham, where we crossed the Avon. We persisted in this direction for some time, until we reached Market Drayton. Here it became clear that we were *not* going to be joined by any Scottish contingents, and thus it was necessary to decide what we did next. But we remained in high spirits, and our scouts having informed us that Fairfax's people were unsure of our position, the King determined to attack the town of Leicester, where there was a Roundhead garrison, and more important, a considerable stock of arms and ammunition. Leicester lay only about fifty miles north of Oxford, so it will be understood that we had performed a considerable flank march to get at it, but as with our march on London three years before, which had resulted in the battle of Edge Hill, we felt confident that Fairfax would have to come up to relieve the town, and would then have to fight on our terms.

When I use the word 'we', I am referring of course to the collective Royalist leadership. I was far less sanguine, and unhappy on several points. One was the large numbers of camp-followers we had in our baggage train, ranging from 'ladies' like Maureen O'Connell all the way down to confessed whores. These females, a large proportion of whom were Irish, were not only apparently necessary to keep the army in fighting trim, but they had point blank refused to be abandoned in Oxford, as by now the Roundhead fashion of dealing in a most summary fashion with Cavalier prostitutes was well known. But the Royal army was beginning to remind me of the moving nation – albeit on a fractional scale – which had accompanied Tilly everywhere during the opening stages of the German war, and Tilly had been most roundly thrashed by the more controlled forces led by Gustavus Adolphus. This was a second cause of concern, the presence of the reincarnation of Gustavus in the Roundhead ranks. But was he there?

"We have heard nothing of General Cromwell," our scouts told us. "It is believed he has returned to East Anglia, recruiting."

This was the best bit of news I had heard for a long time. But I had yet a third worry: the overwhelming confidence of our people. Confidence when about to go into battle is an essential commodity, and should be indulged to the maximum in your common soldier. Generals also need confidence, but they also need to be aware of the skills, and strengths, which may lie on the other side of the fence. Our generals were totally careless of this. They did not even seem to feel that our position had been strengthened by the absence of Cromwell. And things continued to go our way. We arrived outside Leicester, and the King decided to take it by assault. As Quartermaster-General I was not required to participate in this fracas, but the assault was carried out with great élan, and although there were considerable casualties on both sides, by nightfall on 31 May Leicester was ours.

There followed an enormous celebration; one would have thought we had won the war. Well, I may have been less happy with the situation than anyone else, but I could celebrate as well as anyone, and I awoke the next morning with a distinct head. Nonetheless, I staggered off to the King's tent to discover what his plans were for today, and discovered that he was not there. "His Majesty and the princes have gone hunting," the secretary, Hyde, informed me. "If you had not been so drunk, Count, you could have gone with them."

"Hunting?" I was aghast.

"What else would you have them do, on such a fine morning?"

I felt the icy fingers of despair clutching at my heart. The army was in a state of disarray, and in fact had the Roundheads come upon us at that moment it would have been a massacre. But where were the Roundheads? Could they still be unaware of what was happening? I mounted and rode some miles to the south. It was most attractive, rolling, wooded country, and utterly peaceful, and the only living creatures to be seen were droves of sheep, and the occasional shepherd. But it was country across which we should be marching, I knew.

I returned to the town, and found the King and the princes, who had, it seemed, had a most enjoyable day. The King was in no mood to discuss business, even business which was so vital to his future, and indeed, as it turned out, his life. He remained totally confident, and I later learned that writing to Henrietta, he told her that his affairs had never been in better order. It was some days before I could get him to convene a council of war.

"Those rascals are still outside Oxford," Rupert said contemptuously.

"Then should we not go and find them, Your Highness?" I asked.

"They will come to us eventually," he asserted. "And then we will beat them, eventually."

I appealed to the King. "If we are so sure there will be a battle, on ground of our choosing, Your Majesty, then nothing else, and nowhere else, matters. I beg of you, send for General Goring and his people. Whatever they may be doing in the West Country is irrelevant to the course of this war. It is here that it will be won or lost, and it is here that we need every man who can carry a pike or wield a sword."

"Hm," the King remarked. "Hm." He looked at his nephew, somewhat nervously. "I suppose it can do no harm."

"Goring," Rupert said contemptuously.

But I pressed my point, and at last a messenger was sent. Then it was a question of whether he could get to us in time.

But we still seemed to have a great deal of time. There was no word of Fairfax, or Cromwell, and our people found the life around Leicester, with its abundant supplies of food and women, quite delightful after their long march. As the weather was now very fine, it being early June, the King and his lords spent nearly every day hunting.

I realised I had indeed made a stick for my own back in pressing for the recall of Goring, as now it seemed we would not move until he arrived. If only I knew what Fairfax was doing. I sent scouts south every morning, but they always brought back the same observation, that the Roundheads remained encamped north of Oxford, apparently waiting. What could they be waiting for, or who, save Cromwell and his New Model Army? My dilemma grew. I could have no doubt that Cromwell added to Fairfax would be a very difficult proposition, perhaps too difficult even for me. I would have preferred, as I had made clear from the beginning, to attack Fairfax immediately, with what we had. But that too would have been a difficult proposition, and now we were assured Goring was marching to join us. Then we might well outnumber Fairfax and be able to gain a decisive victory. But not if Cromwell got there first. "You will worry yourself into an early grave, Count," said a voice behind me.

I had been sitting my horse on the brow of a long, high ridge south of the village of Market Harborough, looking to the south. I spent much of every day doing this, for the ridge commanded a good view, and it was from there that the enemy would come. I had been in such a brown study that I had not heard the soft hoof-falls behind me on the springy turf, and now turned, to see Maureen O'Connell. "Had I been a Roundhead patrol, you were a dead man," she pointed out.,

"I sometimes wonder if the Roundheads actually exist," I countered. "Not having seen one for so long."

"Those devils exist," she said, coming closer.

She made a most attractive sight, for as it was a really splendid warm June day – it was the 12th – she was lightly clad, and her hair was loose beneath her broad-brimmed straw hat, which was tied beneath her chin with a length of blue silk ribbon. "And thus you also come looking for them?" I suggested.

She laughed. "And thus I come looking for you, Helier."

"There is a message? From the King?"

"From me," she said, with her customary boldness.

273

"I see. What has happened to your captain of dragoons?"

"He is a little fellow," she said, enigmatically. "And besides, you saved my life. Am I not therefore yours?"

"I doubt you would enjoy belonging to me."

"But I do belong to you. And I wish to enjoy it."

I sighed. How to tell this delightful but utterly amoral young woman that I was quite off her sex? It became more difficult, indeed, as she now dismounted, exposing a large amount of leg as she did so, and she did not appear to be wearing stockings or indeed any undergarment save for her shift. As I have said, it was a warm day. "Once you found me attractive," she said, leading her horse towards a little copse some short distance away.

"You are, most attractive," I said. "Unfortunately, I am preoccupied."

Yet had I also dismounted, and was following her, and would no doubt have surrendered to the calls of my libidinous nature, had I not been distracted by yet another arrival, and this fellow was at full gallop. "Count d'Albret!" he bellowed, while he was yet some distance off. "Count d'Albret!"

I turned towards him, and instinctively remounted; here was crisis. "Roundheads!" he shouted. "Thousands of them." He drew his horse to a halt in a lather of steam and sweat.

"Where?" I demanded. If they had just left Oxford, they had yet to be some distance away.

"Kislingbury," he panted.

"Kislingbury?!" That was hardly a dozen miles due south of where I was at that moment. "How the devil did they get to Kislingbury without my being informed?"

"I do not know, Count. I was on relief duty, and riding south, when I heard the noise, and approaching them privily, saw them."

I still could not believe that Fairfax had moved the bulk of his army so secretly that we had known nothing of it. "What were their numbers?"

"I would say not less than twelve thousand men, my lord, horse, foot and guns."

It was true then. They had caught us napping, not for the first time. Now we could do nothing but fight.

CHAPTER 11

I abandoned Maureen and galloped back to Market Harborough, there to receive news which nearly gave me a seizure: the King had taken most of our cavalry and had ridden down to Daventry, in search of the large flocks of sheep which had been reported in the vicinity – our supplies of meat were running low. Now, as a glance at a map will reveal, Daventry lies but eight miles west of Kislingbury. The King, and the princes, had ridden virtually into the jaws of the Parliamentary army, and for all I knew might already have been overwhelmed.

I had to find out. I begged Sir Jacob Astley, in command of the infantry – I had to beg because these fellows always refused to take orders from someone they considered an upstart – to assemble his men and prepare for battle, then went off down the road to Daventry. In mid-afternoon I was mightily relieved to hear the bleating of sheep, and there was the Royalist cavalry, shepherding their victims back towards us. I located the King, who listened to what I had to say with astonishment, and some scepticism. "Roundheads, C-c-count? We saw no Roundheads."

"Faith, Count, they must have heard us," Rupert laughed. "These sheep can be heard for miles."

I could not argue with the evidence of my own ears, and it remains to me a mystery to this day how Fairfax's people never became aware that they had the Royalist cause in their grasp. The only possible answer is that the Roundhead scouting was as incompetent as our own. In any event, the King now revealed some energy. We hastened back to Market Harborough, where he set about chasing his lords to mobilise their people, while Rupert took a squadron of

276

horse and galloped south to the next village, which was called Naseby, to see what he could discover. He was back in short order, having in fact encountered a patrol of Parliamentary horse.

The King's original intention, as proposed by the more faint-hearted of his people, was to retire on Leicester and await the enemy there. But Rupert felt that the ridge on which I had met Maureen that morning was a better position. We were all aware that we were outnumbered, if indeed Fairfax had managed to bring twelve thousand men up with him, and therefore understood that it would be necessary to stand on the defensive, if only for the start of the battle.

That was a busy night, with men rushing to and fro trying to find their regiments, so scattered had they carelessly become. What happened to Maureen I had no idea, as I was too busy with maps and various deployments even to think of her. I managed to snatch a few hours sleep just before dawn, to be awakened just after six by an agitated Jonathan. "Listen, my lord," he suggested.

I sat up to do so, and then got up to do so better, and went out of my tent. There was certainly a very loud noise welling up from the south, carried on the breeze. By now the entire Royalist encampment was aroused. "Those are men cheering," someone said.

"Roundheads," said another. "They are closer than we thought." That seemed likely.

"But why are they cheering so loudly, as if they had won a victory, when they have not yet *fought* the battle?" Jonathan wondered.

I had a terrible feeling that I knew why: it was because the Roundheads conceived that they *had* won the battle, even before it was fought. And there was only one event that would give them that amount of confidence – the arrival of Cromwell and his Ironsides. But I deemed it best not to discourage our people by telling them this.

As it happened, I was right, although no one suspected the truth until later. We spent that day in completing our preparations, and then, early on the morning of 14 June, marched out of Market Harborough and took up our initial positions on that highest portion of the ridge, lying between the villages of East Farndon and Oxenden Magna. Here Astley arranged his infantry, while the cavalry milled about. I describe this as our initial position, because, while we were ready for battle by seven o'clock, there was still no sign of any enemy. "Do you think they have gone home?" Rupert demanded with a laugh. "Count, do you go and find those fellows for me."

Because, our arrangements having been made, I was free to fight where I chose, and I had chosen to resume my original place at Rupert's shoulder, intending to keep the madcap under some control. However, I was happy enough to canter forward, Jonathan behind me, down from the ridge, past the various lower hillocks and protuberances which marked the ground, and up the farther side. Here I could make out several large bodies of men, at a couple of miles distant, and moving, it seemed away from our position, in an easterly direction. I waved my hat, and Rupert cantered forward to join me. "By God," he said. "They *are* going home."

"I do not think so, Your Highness," I said. "I would have said they are merely changing their positions."

"Bah," he said. "I know those dogs. They have no stomach for it. You, boy," he said to Jonathan, "ride back to the King and tell him to advance his people. The enemy are retreating."

Jonathan looked at me for confirmation. "Do you not think it might be wisest to wait until we are sure that is what they are doing, Your Highness?" I asked.

"The difference between a soldier, Count, and a general," Rupert said severely, "is that a general knows when it is the moment to strike, and a soldier does not. Off with you, lad."

"Off you go, Jonathan," I said. He crammed his hat on his head and kicked his horse into a gallop. Rupert and I followed more slowly. I knew by now of course that it was useless arguing with Rupert when he got an idea into his

278

head, and could only hope that this one did not turn out badly.

But it did. Jonathan duly regained the King, and gave him the Prince's message. Immediately the entire Royalist army began to advance, down the hill, inclining towards where the enemy had been reported, ie, the east, thus giving up its best possible position, and in such haste that even our few pieces of ordnance were left behind. They had not advanced very far, however, when the Roundheads reappeared, or rather, from the point of view of the majority of our people, appeared for the first time. They had, after all, merely been changing their original position for one their commanders – no doubt Cromwell himself – had decided would be stronger. Thus while we, thanks to Rupert's careless confidence, had weakened ourselves, our enemies had strengthened themselves.

Not that they appeared to need much assistance from the ground. From where I sat on my horse I could overlook the entire Roundhead position, and I reckoned they had not less than twelve thousand men. As it turned out, with the arrival of the Ironsides, they had even more than that. The Parliamentary army was drawn up as if on parade, in two orderly lines. The centre was composed of their infantry, wearing their new red jackets and commanded by Skippon himself. The cavalry, which I reckoned composed about half the total number, were conventionally on the wings, Ireton's on the left and Cromwell's on the right. In addition to these I could see that Fairfax, in overall command, had thrown forward a regiment of dragoons, who, dismounted, lined a series of hedgerows to protect his left flank; he would know that Rupert would command our right. However, I also observed that the main Roundhead force was on the reverse side of their hill – it was called Mill Hill – and would therefore still be invisible to our people.

We cantered back to the King's army, where at last some order was being introduced out of the earlier chaos. In truth we were only about half as numerous as the enemy, and looked fewer yet along the front as the King had opted for three lines. In the first he had placed Astley's infantry, with, again conventionally, cavalry on each wing, Rupert's as expected on the right, and Sir Marmaduke Langdale's on the left. The second line consisted of Howard's infantry, and in the third his own regiment of foot, another raised by Rupert himself, and his regiment of Royal Horse Guards. We actually had more cavalry than infantry.

The King had taken personal command of the army on this so vital occasion, and Rupert and I, with various other generals, rode up to his carriage to receive his orders. All this while those of the Roundheads that were visible did nothing but stand and watch us, which was either reassuring or ominous according to one's temperament. "They are afraid of us," Charles declared.

"Very possibly, Your Majesty," I agreed. "And are we not afraid of them?"

He gave me an impatient glance. "We will attack them," he declared.

I was not the only officer present who gave a little gulp at this. "With respect, Your Majesty," I protested, "what you can see is only a part of the Parliamentary force. The remainder are beyond the brow."

"So we are outnumbered," Charles said. "It is quality that counts. D-d-did not Alexander successfully attack three t-t-times his strength at Arbela, and gain the d-d-day most t-t-triumphantly?"

This was actually true. The point at issue was, was Charles a reincarnation of Alexander? If he was, he had kept it remarkably well concealed all of these years. "And our role, Your Majesty?" Rupert asked.

Charles pointed. "There will be no madcap charges, P-p-prince Rupert. We are going to fight this b-b-battle with new t-t-tactics. I b-b-believe our infantry can d-d-disperse that mob over there, and that is what we are going to d-d-do. Our only d-d-danger will come from flank attacks from their c-c-cavalry. You, P-p-prince Rupert will guard our right flank, and you, C-c-colonel Langdale, will do the same from our left. You will not charge, under any circumstances, until the enemy is b-b-broken and in d-d-disorder. I wish this c-c-clearly understood."

Both cavalry commanders saluted, and rode off to join

their men. I was in something of a quandary. My great desire was personally to oppose Cromwell, which meant I should ride with Langdale. On the other hand, the colonel was a sensible, level-headed fellow; he was not in the least likely to disobey the King, under any circumstances. Rupert was a different matter. Considering the way the King wanted the battle fought, victory would almost certainly depend upon a well-timed cavalry charge, just at the moment the enemy began to waver, and Rupert was the man to deliver that charge, if he could be restrained until that moment. I rode back with him, Jonathan following.

Rupert was in the highest of humours. "Today's the day, Count," he shouted. "I feel it in my bones. Today's the day."

I hoped he was right.

It was now mid-morning, and a beautiful day. The King gave the signal, and Astley pointed his sword. With drums beating and fifes playing, the Royalist infantry marched down the hill to the bottom of the slope, and commenced the ascent towards the Roundhead position. I do believe that to that moment our infantry had not even seen their enemies, but as they climbed the shallow slope the entire Parliamentarian army moved forward to the crest of the ridge, a most imposing sight, which for a moment gave our people pause. Then they recovered, set their rests, and delivered a volley.

This expert piece of military manoeuvring had a most unfortunate result. For with the Roundhead infantry had advanced their cavalry, like ours clearly deputed to protect their wings. From my position immediately behind Rupert I was looking at Ireton's brigade of Ironsides, all glittering steel breastplates and morions and red jackets, and could easily make out Ireton himself, riding at their head. Now, as I watched, he suddenly clutched at his chest and tumbled out of the saddle, clearly struck by a stray ball. "Who is that fallen?" Rupert demanded.

"Colonel Ireton," I replied. "Cromwell's protégé."

"By God," Rupert said. "We have them."

This was not because of Ireton's fall – he was not killed, but only badly wounded – but because his cavalry, seeing their commander hurt, suddenly lost cohesion. Some men clustered round the wounded officer, dismounting to see the extent of his injuries, others continued to maintain their position abreast the infantry, others urged their mounts down the slope as if determined to avenge their leader, and still others started to move to the rear, as if in search of a new one. "They are falling apart!" Rupert shouted. "Bugler, sound the charge."

"Your Highness," I protested. "His Majesty's orders!"

"Were to charge when the enemy start to break, Count. Are not those men breaking? Blow, bugler, blow!" The trumpet sounded, and with an immense roar the Royalist cavalry drew their swords and urged their horses forward. With them went Jonathan, and truth to tell, I never saw him again.

I pulled my mount aside and let them go, understanding that I had failed in my self-appointed duty. That Ireton's men were in disarray, at least momentarily, was undoubted. But equally was it undoubted that the King's command had referred to the whole Roundhead army giving way, not just one wing of it. I could only pray that the Prince had not undertaken another disastrous course.

Certainly initially all went as might have been expected. Ignoring the shot opened upon them by the dismounted dragoons, the Cavaliers crashed into Ireton's disorganised people, and drove them in a rout from the field. But behind the fleeing Roundheads galloped the cheering Cavaliers, and within a few minutes they were lost to view over the next hill. "Bring them back," I muttered. "For God's sake, bring them back!"

And now was the time they were truly needed, for in the centre our infantry were carrying all before them. Skippon himself fell, wounded while trying to rally his people, and although the Roundhead foot outnumbered ours by two to one yet they were being forced back. More important yet, they were starting to look over their shoulders, a sure sign that men are about to break. If Rupert's horse had been available to charge their exposed flank, the battle would have been won there and then.

But there remained Langdale, with two thousand fresh cavalry. He had, as commanded, advanced on the left in time to the infantry. Now, could he charge ... while overseeing this stage of the battle I had been riding back towards the King's headquarters. It was actually my intention to join Langdale and urge him into action, but before I had even reached the standard the battle on the left had been commenced. For Langdale was not faced by disorganised troops, but by Cromwell's Ironsides, and Cromwell himself. As at Marston Moor, Oliver could see that the battle was going badly, and needed retrieving. Thus as the colonel prepared to charge, the Ironsides came galloping down the slope and smashed into his people. As Langdale was also outnumbered by two to one, his men gave way, and found themselves forced back on to Rupert's Regiment of Foot, posted only a few yards to the left of the Royal carriage. "L'Eree," shouted the King as I galloped up to him. "Rally those men, for God's sake."

I saluted as I hurtled past, waving my sword to attract their attention, and then drawing rein. Had Cromwell been Rupert we might have had a chance, by launching a counter-attack against his troops before they could recover from their charge. But Cromwell never allowed his people to lose their cohesion, nor did he ever lose sight of the fact that he was here to win a battle, not a charge. He had thus brought his men to a halt when he saw that Langdale was no longer an immediate threat, took in the situation at a glance, and then sent but three squadrons to continue the harrying of our horse; the remainder of his brigade he swung in perfect order to his left, and sent them in a charge against Astley's now exposed flank. It was superb soldiering, not only from a tactical point of view, but from the quite marvellous discipline Oliver had instilled in his men, so that even in the heat of battle their officers looked only to their commander for instruction, and then carried out his orders without hesitation.

Only the most dramatic intervention was now going to

save Astley, and the battle. Of fresh troops we retained but the Royal Horse Guards and the King's Regiment of Foot. Seeing that Langdale was doing as well as any man to concentrate his beaten squadrons, I returned to the King, leaping from the saddle before his horse. "Your Majesty," I cried. "You must throw your reserves into the fight to extricate the infantry, or we are lost. Place yourself at our head, Your Majesty, and we can still gain the day."

"Are you mad?" Secretary Hyde shouted. "Would you send the King to his death?"

"L'Eree is right, Mr Hyde," Charles said. He had remained mounted, and now drew his sword. "Now is the time to d-d-do, and if we c-c-cannot d-d-do, then it is a t-t-time to d-d-die."

For the first time in the two and a half years I had been intimately connected with this man, I admired him. He suffered, as I have shown, too serious defects of heredity ever to have made a king, or even a soldier. But he did not lack courage. And in view of the future, it would have been a far more splendid death here on the field of Naseby than that humiliation which eventually awaited him. But as he raised his sword his arm was seized by one of the incompetent and cowardly lords who constantly surrounded the monarch. This man's name was the Earl of Carneforth, and he was a Scot. Now he shouted, "By God and the devil, you'll not go to your death," and pulled the King's horse round.

My admiration faded, for Charles made almost no effort to resist him. His remaining horse and foot witnessed this scene with stupefaction. Now someone decided to give them an order, to the effect that they would march off the field. Well, after that there was no saving anybody. The men looked at each other, and at their officers, and at the King who was now riding hard for the presumed safety of Leicester. Then they ran behind him. I was as stupefied as anyone. The truth of the matter is that in all my experiences, both in Germany and indeed in England, I had never in my life been on the losing side in a battle. I knew nothing of the absolute panic which can seize men and turn them from disciplined soldiers into arrant cowards, who will even throw away their weapons in their desperate anxiety not to have to fight any more.

I dashed into their midst, waving my sword and trying to rally them, but they ignored me. Worse, I had released my horse's bridle in the excitement of the moment, and some confounded rascal leapt into the saddle and galloped off. I ran to what had been our original front line, and saw Astley's and Howard's men crying out for quarter, now quite surrounded by Roundheads, horse and foot. I heard the thunder of hooves, and saw Rupert and his cavalry debouching from over the hill away to the left. Had they returned only a few minutes earlier ... but the Prince took in the situation at a glance, and without pausing led his men behind his uncle.

It went against my pride to shout for help from him, even if he could possibly have heard me above the din. But it was clear that I had to leave the field. I turned my face to the north, and was arrested by the screams coming from our baggage train, where there were more than a hundred women. These had not yet been assailed, but they anticipated the coming moments, as they had no hopes of moving the cumbersome wagons – the drivers had all run off. I knew of course that most of these females were whores, and that therefore for them to be raped by the victors would all be in the line of duty, as it were, and thus I might well have abandoned them to their fate had not one of them now left her wagon and run towards me, all streaming red hair. Needless to say it was Maureen, and I could do no less than pause to take her in my arms. "Save me, Helier, save me," she screamed.

"That I shall, if it is possible," I assured her.

But it was no longer possible, for we were already surrounded by the Roundhead cavalry. Amongst them was Cromwell, who sat his horse above me. "Well, Master L'Eree, or Count d'Albret, or whatever your true name is," he said. "I am right well pleased to see you again."

Before I could reply, a cornet arrived at his elbow. "We have seized the King's carriage, General."

"With him in it?" Cromwell seemed quite agitated.

"No, sir. But much that will interest you."

Cromwell nodded, then pointed at me. "Keep this man under close arrest."

"And the women, General?"

Cromwell looked towards the wagons, where the women had fallen silent. "You know what to do with them," he said, and rode off with the cornet.

His men gave a whoop, and, helpless as I was with a dozen muskets pointed at me, I understood I was to be witness to a gigantic debauch. But I was wrong. I was actually to be a witness to the most horrible scene of my experience, and remember that I had taken part in the sack of Magdeburg. The captain in command of the Ironside regiment, who for all their cheer remained under the strictest discipline, waved a dozen of his men to dismount and advance on the wagons. Unceremoniously they seized the first woman by the arms and dragged her out. She made no protest, anticipating rape, and was thrown to her knees before the captain. "How, now," he said. "Are you English or Irish? Speak, woman!"

"I am as English as you are, sir," she retorted with the spirit of her kind.

"Then you are a disgrace to the nation," he said, and nodded to his sergeant.

The woman's arms were still held, and before she even understood what was happening, the sergeant drew his knife and slashed both of her cheeks, with such violence that they were laid open to the bone. She uttered a most piercing scream, and was flung aside, where she writhed on the ground, pawing at her bleeding cheeks with her skirt. "You'll service no more Cavalier rascals," the captain remarked with satisfaction. "They'll run a mile at the sight of you."

The onlookers, women and surrendered Royalists as well as Helier L'Eree, were for the moment paralysed by this unheard-of savagery, and thus we were not prepared for what followed. For the next woman boldly declared herself to be Irish, and even presented her cheeks to the sergeant's knife. She was not so fortunate. Another nod and her throat was cut. "Oh, my God!" Maureen muttered, still in my arms. "Oh, my God!"

The ghastly work went on. Some of the women tried to run away, and were seized and dragged back. None of them was sexually assaulted, all suffered the far more terrible fate. Each one who spoke with an Irish accent was murdered on the spot; even one or two who cried out that they were Protestants were not spared. Everyone found to be English had her face slashed in such a way that she would forever be afraid to look in her own mirror.

And then it was Maureen's turn. She was dragged from my arms. "You cannot touch her," I shouted. "She is a lady."

"She is a whore!" the captain said. "And an Irish whore, at that."

"Bastard!" I started forward, careless of the bullets which I had to anticipate were about to slash into my body, and received instead a crashing blow on the head which stretched me senseless on the ground.

I was brought to by a bucket of water being emptied over my head. I rose to my knees, my brain still spinning from the blow I had received, to gaze at the girl stretched lifeless on the grass before me. I had experienced a great many catastrophes in my life, and with each one a piece of iron had entered my soul. Now I swear the metal composed the whole of it. I had never loved Maureen O'Connell. I am not sure I had even liked her. But she had turned to me in her hour of peril, and I had promised to save her. Now she lay dead at my feet. In my still dazed state I found myself weeping, but they were tears of fury. Then I was led away from the charnel field to where Cromwell and several officers were seated on the grass drinking ale and reading the King's papers.

"Ah, Helier," Cromwell said. "Sit you down and have a drink. You must be parched. Do you know what we have here? There are letters begging assistance from all the world, imploring foreign monarchs to land their armies on these shores and make war upon us, the people of England. Why, there is an army already gathering in Holland, commanded by the Count of Lorraine, and the Duke of Ormonde raises another in Ireland. That is sufficient to bring even Charles Stuart to book on a charge of treason."

"And what do you imagine will be the charges against you?" I demanded.

"Treason? Not now. We have gained the day. We have gained the war."

"I was thinking more of mass murder."

He raised his eyebrows. "Of a few Papist whores? Faith, I would hang the Pope himself could I but lay hands on him."

"You murder in the name of a God who spoke only of charity," I told him. "You are a despicable creature, your brain twisted with hate."

At this several of his officers started towards me, but Cromwell waved them back. "You saved my life," he said. "And for that I am eternally grateful. Yet are you as hateful to me as any Papist, for I do swear that you are an apostate and a heathen and a traitorous rogue. I am done with you. I sentence you to be hanged, at dawn tomorrow."

"I have not been tried, or found guilty, of any crime."

"You are an agnostic, sir. That is all the crime I need. As for a trial ... " he looked at his officers. "You have heard the case. What is your verdict?"

"Guilty," they answered without hesitation.

"And your sentence?"

"Death by hanging."

"At dawn," Cromwell repeated. "Let him have the night to brood upon his crimes, and upon the reception he will meet in the next world."

"I shall await you in hell, Oliver," I told him. "And there, the Devil willing, we will settle this business between us."

Brave words, of course, but I knew my situation to be utterly desperate. I was not afraid of death, although I could think of several better ways to go than by a rope.

288

With Helga and my children dead, I had little left to live for. Save vengeance. And now it seemed that even that was to be denied me.

Which but goes to show that it is never sensible to lose faith in the future.

I was taken under guard to a place some distance from the main Roundhead camp. Here, my wrists bound behind me like the commonest malefactor, I was placed against a tree, and another rope passed round my waist and secured on the far side, leaving me utterly helpless, unable even to attend to my necessaries. These were pressing, to be sure, but not so pressing as the other demands of my body. I had arrogantly refused Cromwell's offer of a drink. Now I was utterly parched, and my belly was empty, while the two men guarding me lit themselves a fire and settled down to what appeared a very hearty meal. "Am I not to be fed?" I demanded.

"That would be a waste," one of them pointed out. "Seeing as how you will be dead in twelve hours."

"Well, then, water, or I may well die of thirst before then."

"Water will only make you wish to pee, Count," the other guard explained, very reasonably. "And that will make you a nuisance to us. I will read you the Bible, if you wish?"

"In my situation, friend," I told him, "that would make you a nuisance to *me*."

He shrugged, and turned back to his meal, leaving me to some very unhappy reflections. It was a glorious evening, as the sun slowly drooped towards the western sky. There was some noise from the Roundhead camp, but it was not a celebratory sound, at least in the usual sense; they were not drinking to their victory over there, but rather praying. The ground around them was covered with men, who had at least died in battle, and women, who had been cruelly murdered. Occasionally a voice was raised, but soon subdued, and occasionally a horse would neigh; the doleful business of cutting the throats of those unhappy animals ruined by the fighting was completed by dusk.

With the night there came mostly silence. As their fire burned low, my two gaolers rapidly dozed off, confident in the strength of my bonds. They were fully justified in doing so, for strain as I might I could make no impression either upon those securing my wrists or that round my waist. I wondered what the King was doing now, with his every last hope cast into the dust? And where Rupert would take himself? For I had no doubt that madcap would survive. Then I thought of the Queen, now indeed an exile, refused entry into her beloved France, and separated forever from her faithful servant.

I wondered where Caroline Bethlen was, and if, with her marvellous powers, she would know of my predicament. If so, she would surely be smiling with pleasure. And then I found myself breaking out in a cold sweat, as I realised that if I were indeed to be hanged and sent to hell I would doubtless come face to face with her fearsome mother! There was very little prospect of my coming face to face with my Helga, who would surely be in heaven.

And then I thought of Aimée Hubert, surely an innocent pawn caught up in the wild game of life, unwise enough to meddle in the deadly game of politics. But she at least lived. At least I presumed she did, even if she was, now under Caroline's influence, truly a witch herself. I looked down at myself, as the rope securing me to the tree suddenly fell into my lap. "Do not speak," Aimée whispered, and I discovered her kneeling at my elbow, a sharp-bladed knife in her hands.

In truth, I was beyond speech, and only a moment later my wrists were freed. I promptly threw my arms round her to give her a hug, while the circulation prickled through my veins. "Quickly," she said, while not resisting me.

My guards continued to snore, as we stole away from them. She led me some distance, to a copse, where there were two horses. "We must walk these for a while," she said.

I saw to my great delight that the mounts were both

equipped with swords, muskets and pistols, for I was resolved not to be captured again. Thus we walked them away from the field of Naseby, into the night. "I owe you my life," I said. "Be certain that I shall never forget it. If you would tell me why, I would be most grateful."

"Do I not owe you mine?" she asked. "Every time I think of that witch-hunter I shudder."

"But yet I put you into danger in the first place," I said. "And before then."

"You did what you had to do," she said magnanimously. And then added, enigmatically, "As do we all. Are you thirsty?"

"I could drink the ocean dry."

She opened one of the saddlebags and gave me a skin of water. I had tasted much better, but I never enjoyed a drink more. "And hungry?"

"Lead me to it."

Another saddlebag produced a cold leg of lamb, to which I did full justice. "Now I think we are far enough away to ride a while," she decided. "it will be dawn in an hour."

"In which direction?" I asked.

"It is my ambition to return to France," Aimée said.

Well, that suited me well enough. I had come to England reluctantly, and had remained here even more reluctantly. The Queen I had been commanded to serve was already overseas, the King was lost. If indeed Oliver had won the war, then I was a hunted outlaw with not a friend to turn to, save this attractive young woman who was as much an outlaw as myself. But there remained Caroline Bethlen, the murderess of my wife and family. With whom there was a strong possibility this young woman was working, even if unknowing of her true horror. I needed to feel my way. "Those are my sentiments entirely," I told Aimée. "And I suggest we do that just as quickly as possible. However, there is a question I must ask you."

"Did you say that you would help me leave this accursed land?"

"Absolutely. When you have answered my question."

"Then ask it."

"Do you recall the woman who was with me when you denounced me to Hampden?"

"You understand I was only doing my duty?"

"I do. And forgive you. The woman."

"You mean Caroline Le Brock. Who returned to us as the Chevalier Le Brock."

I drew rein. "You knew this?"

"I recognised her at once. Do you suppose I am to be fooled by a moustache?"

"But you told no one?"

"I am a spy, am I not," she pointed out. "It is in my nature to wait, and watch. And see what I can learn."

"And what *did* you learn?"

"That she sought you. She was sadly disappointed to learn that you had deserted back to the King."

"But she remained with the Roundheads."

"Briefly." Aimée smiled. "They would have made her cut off her hair, for they said it made her look like a Cavalier. So she absconded."

"With you."

"Me?" Aimée turned her head. "Why should she do that? Or I do that, for that matter."

I brooded on this. Caroline had murdered my family. I had absolutely no doubt about that. Then she had returned to England to seek me out. But I was not where she had expected me to be, thus she had ... simply disappeared? I could understand her reluctance to return, as Charles Le Brock, to the King's encampment. Long before she gained me she would be recognised, and probably arrested as a deserter, and whether or not she could talk herself out of that serious charge, I would certainly know of her reappearance, and she had to assume I would by then have heard of Helga's death. But to do nothing? Disappear?

Then I realised that I was making the same mistake as would any man when considering that delectable body, those smiling, mocking eyes: I was trying to consider her possible movements and decisions as if she were a woman. But she was not a woman. She was a demon, trapped in a woman's body, perhaps, but with an utterly inhuman mind, to whom time and space were irrelevant so long as she achieved her objectives. And her objective was not merely the destruction of me: it was first of all the destruction of anything that might be dear to me.

My blood ran quite cold. I had no idea what had happened to Charles Stuart, or would happen in the future. But I knew that I could not permit any harm to befall the Queen. Caroline had already once had her in her sights, as it were. And in carelessly sending her back to Holland I had supposed she was going to safety! "Are you still known as a Roundhead agent?" I asked Aimée.

"Of course. I still *am* a Roundhead agent. Or was up to yesterday."

"What changed your mind?"

"Those poor women ... Cromwell is a devil."

"So some say. But he is the ruler of England now."

"Cromwell? He serves Parliament."

"He has now won, virtually single-handed, two great victories. He is not the man I know him to be if he does not now start serving himself. Certainly the army will serve no one but him."

She considered this as we rode towards the dawn. "The King will never surrender. He dare not."

"Then he will be hunted down, and probably locked up for life. Or become Cromwell's puppet. But that no longer concerns us. I wish to take ship from one of the east coast ports. Can you give me safe passage?"

"As long as I am at your side."

"I have already agreed to that."

"And afterwards?"

I drew rein to peer at her in the steadily lightening gloom. This was June, and early as it was, it would soon be broad daylight. "Aimée," I said. "I denounced you as a spy and caused you a great deal of inconvenience. Then I delivered you into the hands of Master Hopkins, and caused you even greater inconvenience..."

"But then you saved me from Master Hopkins, most convincingly," she pointed out.

"And so, despite all, you wish ...?" I had no idea what she was truly after.

"You and I, Helier, both began as agents for Richelieu," she reminded me. "Richelieu is now dead. Thus we are unemployed. That we continued to act as if we were employed was, I am sure you will agree, forced upon us by circumstances. Now circumstances are forcing us to reconsider our positions. But I think we should remain harnessed."

"But you betrayed your employment."

"It must have seemed so. But can you, knowing the Cardinal as well as you do, prove that? Did you not send me back to him, bound and with an escort, and did I not escape, without the least difficulty? How many people have escaped the Cardinal, when he did not wish it? I would claim to be the only one."

I was exhausted from the events of the past few days, and thus perhaps I was not thinking as clearly as I might have wished. But I did know it was not beyond the possibilities that Richelieu, with his well-known capacity for meddling in every direction, could have determined to have agents actively working for both sides in the English struggle. In any event, as far as I could see, that was irrelevant now. "And, of course, you know that I am the owner of a sizeable estate in Normandy," I remarked.

"And no one to manage it for you," she pointed out.

"You would undertake that charge?"

"Most willingly, sir."

"Well, well," I said. "Well, well, well."

"In return for seeing you safely out of this country," she added.

"Of course. However, suppose I were to tell you that, while my business with Richelieu may be ended, I have still some unfinished business which must be attended to."

"Here in England? It would be very dangerous for you to linger. Next time Cromwell will probably have you hanged on the spot."

"I do not think it is in England. It awaits me in Holland, I would say."

She shrugged. "I have no objection to going to Holland, first. Indeed, it will be simpler to find a ship for there than France."

"Before you make any rash decisions, I must tell you that this business is of a highly dangerous nature."

"You must tell me of it," she said equably. Clearly she had no idea of what I was speaking.

In fact I did not tell her anything more than I considered she need know, that I was pursuing the murderer of my wife and children. I did not inform her that this was Caroline Bethlen, and she did not ask very many questions; she clearly had no doubt that I could cope with any murderer. All of this entirely reassured me that she could hardly be working with the demon, as she seemed so unconcerned, and indeed, unknowledgeable regarding her.

Certainly she fulfilled her part of the bargain. She retained a large number of safe conducts signed by both Pym and Cromwell, and with these she saw us through the various Roundhead patrols that we encountered. We were, of course, and most fortunately, travelling ahead of the news of Naseby; in fact, we carried the news to the east of the country, and were thus received with the more acclamation by our audiences. I did not expect to get to the coast without some kind of trouble, as even if no one we encountered could yet know that I had been sentenced to hanging by Cromwell, I reckoned there had to be one or two who remembered me, and would remember too that after appearing to perish in the fire at O'Connell Manor, I had then rejoined the Royalist ranks and was thus only worthy of hanging in any event.

However, Aimée knew this country very well, carefully avoided the neighbourhood of Huntingdon, and brought me to the coast not at Great Yarmouth, but at a place called Harwich, from whence we easily obtained a ship for Holland. "Goodbye England," Aimée said, as our smack slipped out of the harbour. "I will not see you again." She turned her head. "And you?"

"I have long since given up attempting to foresee the

future," I told her, wrapping my cloak the more tightly round myself, for I was totally concerned with the immediate future, and was even hoping for a gale of wind, from the west, to be sure, to carry us the more quickly to Holland, whatever the effect on my stomach.

"But you can prognosticate," Aimée said. "What of the political future, for England? With Cromwell, if what you say is true, as ruler? King Oliver! That will look odd in the history books."

"King or no, he will remain the greatest usurper in English history. He is also the greatest Puritan in English history, and probably, because of his religious beliefs, the most violent man who has ever held power in England, when he considers that he is doing God's work. For this reason he will not last. The English will find him a far more unpleasant taskmaster than even the Stuarts. They will have a king, and drinking and damning and fornicating, back again just as soon as it is possible."

That was a considered opinion which has not been proved wrong by events. But would they have Henrietta Maria as queen?

We came ashore at Scheveningen, which is the port of The Hague, purchased ourselves horses, and rode like the wind for Amsterdam. I did not know what I would find there, and in the event was utterly surprised to find ... the Queen, safe and sound and surrounded by her ladies, and her dogs, her priests and her players, with her baby daughter in her arms. She stared at me in consternation. "L'Eree? What are you doing here?"

I had already given a quick glance around the room to make sure that Caroline had not managed to worm her way into the Queen's confidence, whether as man or woman. Now I fell to my knee before Her Majesty. "I bear the saddest of tidings," I said, and told her of Naseby.

She listened, her face slowly settling into the grimmest of expressions. "Then why are you here?" she asked when I had finished. "You have abandoned my Charlie, in his hour of need. You have abandoned Prince Charles! My son! Where is he?"

"Your Majesty, I do not know where the King or the Prince of Wales may be."

"And what of Henry and Elizabeth? Two small children! If their father is a fugitive ... but the cause cannot be decided upon one battle. There is still Rupert. There are still many loyal hearts in England. L'Eree, I command you: return at once, seek out my husband, and serve him, as you would me."

I stood up. "I am sorry, Your Majesty, but I must refuse."

"You? Refuse me?"

"Regretfully, I must. I undertook firstly to take you to safety; I have done that. I was commanded, secondly, to assist the King to victory. Sadly, no one alive can now do that. This adventure has cost me my wife, my children, and my home. All that is left to me is vengeance. This vengeance I intend to pursue."

She frowned. "You know who murdered your family?"

"Yes, Your Majesty. I do. It is the man Le Brock, whom I had assumed to be my friend. I will hunt him down. But Your Majesty, if either Le Brock or his sister – she cannot be mistaken, for the two are very alike: her name is Caroline – should appear here in Amsterdam, then I beg you, if you consider that I have ever served you, to execute him or her without a moment's hesitation."

"Le Brock," she muttered. "That handsome young man, a murderer?"

"Assisted by his sister," I reminded her. "And now, Your Majesty, I will bid you farewell. You will remain always an abiding memory, in both my mind and my heart. But I can no longer serve you."

She regarded me in silence for some seconds, and I feared an outburst, especially when she looked past me at Aimée, a spectator at the back of the room. "And that wretched woman? Why have you not strangled her? Why indeed do I not have *her* hanged here and now?"

"Principally because she has just saved my life, Your

Majesty. But the truth of the matter is, we are both servants of Cardinal Richelieu. Or were. Now that the Cardinal is dead, we must seek other employment, and we have chosen to do so together."

She considered this for some seconds, then she nodded. "Stout L'Eree. I have been selfish, and would be more so. Go, and gain your vengeance. Be sure that should anyone named Le Brock appear here in Amsterdam I shall have him, or her, dealt with. I wish you prosperity. Sadly, I cannot reward you as I would wish. However, I once gave you a ring. Do you still have it?"

"It was lost when I was forced to flee the Roundheads, Your Majesty."

"No matter. Here is its twin." She took it from her own finger to hold it out. "Try to keep this one." She gave me her hand to kiss.

"I would say that woman is very fond of you," Aimée remarked, as we rode south.

"I believe she is."

"Then do you not think you may have abandoned a great opportunity to rise at her side?"

"No. Because she is no longer going to rise. But that apart, I have business to complete."

"Vengeance." She gave a little shudder. "What will you do, return to Garnesey to trace the assassin?"

"I have not yet made that decision. Now ask me no more questions."

She held her counsel, as she realised I was in the grip of a powerful and consuming emotion. And indeed, although to avoid comment we travelled as man and wife, and slept in the same bed, we did not once tumble each other, nor had we since that night on the heath following her experience with Hopkins. We were both waiting, she on me, and I on the Devil. Because truth to tell, I knew not which way to turn. Caroline Bethlen had indeed disappeared, as into the air. Now I could reason that, considering my attraction to the Queen doomed to be unrequited, and no doubt aware that Henrietta had fled to Holland while I remained fighting with the King, she had not considered her worthy of her attention. But then, who was left for her to destroy, before me?

I clapped my hand to my head. There was only one other person alive to whom Caroline could suppose I was remotely attached: Marguerite! But where was Marguerite? She had disappeared as completely as had Caroline herself. Commonsense told me that she would have returned to Paris, to seek employment from Richelieu's successor, Mazarin. I did not intend to follow her. My sole desire was that Cardinal Mazarin should never learn of my existence. I had served enough, and suffered enough.

But whether or not Marguerite had found what she wanted, or had encountered Caroline and suffered a dreadful death, she was the end of the line for the demon. There was only me left, and she would know where to find me. And so we came to Albret.

We drew rein on the hilltop overlooking the valley, and feasted our eyes on the green fields and rustling trees beneath us, and upon the château, which was of an ancient design and more resembled a fortress than a country home. It should be recalled that it was now twelve years since I had last beheld this sight, much less entered that massive gateway. The difference was that while twelve years ago I had been on a mission similar to this, twelve years ago I had not been the Count d'Albret.

But obviously I was at least curious as to what sort of a reception I would receive, and was thus the more surprised by the sight of the blue and red banner of the Counts d'Albret flapping in the breeze above the watchtower – this should only be flown when the family was in residence, and as I had no family ... Aimée had also observed the odd phenomenon. "Are you expected?"

"Not to my knowledge. Let us investigate."

We cantered down the hill and along the bridle path between the apple orchards and the walnut fields. In both there were quite a few people, hard at work, because it was a fine late summer day, and the crops would soon be harvested. These people, men and women, ceased their labour to look at us, and those nearest the path touched their foreheads, for if none of them could possibly know they were looking at their new seigneur, they could tell from our dress – I had permitted Aimée to pause in Rouen in order to purchase herself a new gown, and had bought some new clothes for myself, having pawned the Queen's ring – that we were at least gentry. I smiled and nodded to them, and led Aimée up to the outer defences of the castle.

"Who comes?" shouted the watch.

"The Count d'Albret," I replied.

That caused some confusion. The sentry had a conversation with someone beneath him, no doubt his superior, and then there was obviously a good deal of coming and going, while we waited, patiently enough, as I could appreciate that my steward – who did not yet know he was my steward – would realise he was faced with a big decision. However, eventually the gates swung open and the portcullis was raised, and Aimée and I rode into the yard. Here a considerable number of people had gathered to receive us. A dozen of these were armed men, the rest were serving girls and scullery wenches, grooms and kitchen boys, all agape for a sight of their new master.

I dismounted, and one of the men, better dressed than the rest, hurried forward to bow before me. "Welcome home, my lord Count. Oh, welcome home."

"And who might you be?" I inquired.

"Martin Morin, your steward, my lord."

I assisted Aimée to dismount. "Well, tell me this, Morin: who informed you that I was coming home?"

"Why, no one, my lord. But we knew that you would, one day."

"And thus have flown that flag, every day, in anticipation?"

"Why, no, my lord. We have flown the flag since the return of the Countess."

"The Countess?" I frowned at him, for truth to tell I did not much care for his features. "What Countess?"

"Why, Helier," Marguerite said, speaking from the top

300

of the steps leading up to the knights' hall, down which she now came. "How nice to see you again."

For a moment I was utterly confounded, and then I realised that I was again guilty of estimating events entirely from my own point of view. Marguerite had been sent to the Queen's service by Richelieu; Marguerite had left the Queen's service before Richelieu's death: therefore Marguerite would have returned to Richelieu, and on his death, would have been passed on to Mazarin. Thus logic. But women are not logical creatures. From Marguerite's point of view, when she left the Queen, she had no longer been the widowed, landless Countess d'Albret: she now had a husband, at least in name, and through him had regained the use of her property. Why should she return to the employ, and possibly the embrace – I have never been sure of this – of another elderly priest? She would have ridden straight for Albret, and no doubt had been living here ever since, in the lap of luxury, while I had been suffering and nearly getting hanged into the bargain. She could see the thoughts going through my mind. "Well," she said. "Where else did you expect to find me?"

"Where else, indeed, my pet," I agreed. "You no doubt remember Mademoiselle Hubert?"

Up till then Marguerite had paid no attention to the woman at my side; she had known me long enough to understand that the time to comment would be when she encountered Helier L'Eree *without* a woman at his side. Now she peered at Aimée, and frowned. "The spy? My God! Helier, you have had your way with her."

I hesitated. I have never been very good at lying without some notice. And thus gave myself away. "You wretch," she shouted. "And a spy! She should be hanged."

"Oh, do be quiet," I said, and gave Aimée my arm. "We are both exceedingly tired, hungry, thirsty, and dirty. Do you organise us baths and then all the food and wine you possess."

"Well!" she commented, hands on hips.

"Or as you are my wife, I will beat you," I suggested.

"Well!" she said again. "I wonder what our guest will make of this."

Still holding Aimée's elbow, I had been climbing the steps to the doorway to the knights' hall, and had indeed just entered that mighty chamber. Now I checked to look over my shoulder, Marguerite being at our heels. "Guest? What guest?"

"Why, the mother of that lovely boy you were carrying on with in Holland," Marguerite said.

"The ... " I turned back again, and saw, coming down the grand staircase towards me, the most magnificent, terrifying, diabolical of sights: Richilde Bethlen, Princess von Hohengraffen.

At that moment I was not only struck dumb, but my limbs seemed to have turned to water. The last time I had seen Richilde she had been lying dead at my feet. Or so I had supposed. Yet I could not doubt the evidence of my own eyes. There was the tumbling auburn hair, the magnificent body hardly concealed by the loose pale blue gown ... and yet a body I had possessed time and again, and more recently than ten years ago. Just as the face, those green eyes, that short nose and pointed chin, and above all, those irresistible lips, had been mine too often during the past three years. Once again a series of curtains dropped away from my eyes. There had been no daughter. There had only ever been Richilde, alive and demonic, completely bewitching me, merely by changing the colour of her hair and appearing as younger than she was. But then, how old was Richilde? Fifty, a hundred, a thousand years?

But most of all had she bewitched me because I had wanted to be bewitched. While she had with her invariable deadly patience – what was time to Richilde Bethlen? – set about destroying everything I held dear. And enjoying my embraces, until she had been ready to come for me. But I had also come for her. The last time I had sought her I had been too besotted with desire to do the obvious, and cut off her head. Instead I had attempted to drown her, and failed miserably. But this time ... I whipped my sword from my

302

scabbard. But as I did so, there was a movement behind me, and I felt the prick of Aimée's knife point, a weapon I knew she was capable of using to the best advantage. "Drop your sword, Helier," she said softly.

How had I been tricked, betrayed, by my own libidity, led like a bull to market with a ring through my nose. Even as the sword slipped from my fingers, I looked at Marguerite, who for once in her life seemed lost for words. "You too?" I asked.

But immediately I knew I was wrong. Marguerite might have possessed every fault a woman could, but there was nothing supernatural about her; even less was there anything truly evil in her. Now she found her voice. "Will somebody tell me what is going on?" she demanded. "This is *my* house..."

"*Your* house, Countess?" Richilde inquired, her voice as low and musical as ever, as she finished descending the stairs and stood before us. "Any house in which the Princess von Hohengraffen resides, is *her* house."

"Why, you abominable creature," Marguerite declared. "I have a good mind..."

"You have no mind at all, any more, Countess," Richilde informed her. "Shut her up," she said, "and bind L'Eree securely. In that chair over there."

Without my being aware of it, the hall had become filled with men, six of them, headed by Morin. He now presented a pistol to my head, while two others marched me to the great dining table, placed me in a chair, and bound me to the arms with stout cords. I was still too confused to resist them, even had I been prepared to take on the pistol. But now I watched Marguerite being similarly manhandled, to her outrage. "Let me go, you foul beasts from the pit of hell!" she bawled.

This being her habitual way of addressing people who annoyed her, she was being far more accurate in her description than she knew. I was still confused. "Marguerite?" I asked. "Are these not your people?"

"Well, I thought they were," she said.

"They are my people," Richilde said quietly. "As Aimée

303

is mine. It was not difficult to gain entry, and disarm and dismiss the garrison and the servants; I showed them various letters patent I had obtained, from various sources."

"But ... Marguerite ... ?"

"I had not come yet, Helier," Marguerite explained. "When I arrived, the Princess was already here." Angry as she undoubtedly was, her tone of deference made me realise she still did not understand just who Richilde was; they had not met during my wild adventure of thirteen years before. "Well, I was surprised. But when she explained who she was, and explained further that she had been sent here by you to await your return, I was happy to entertain her as my guest. It never occurred to me that the people here were not ours. But now ... Your Highness, I must ask you to tell your men to release me, and give me an explanation of these events."

Richilde smiled, one of those terrible smiles which could bewitch and transfix at the same moment. "Why, Countess," she said, "or should I call you Marguerite? I have come here to kill you. And him. In the most disagreeable manner I can devise."

"You what?" Marguerite screamed.

"Oh, please do not waste your screams," Richilde begged. "You are going to need all of them. You are going to die first. But very slowly. Morin!"

Her steward produced a stout rope, which he threw over one of the beams above our head, making one end fast to the table leg beside me while the other dropped to the floor behind Marguerite. It looked as if the Princess intended to hang the unhappy woman, but I was certain that was far too quick and easy a death to satisfy Richilde Bethlen. "Aimée!" Richilde commanded.

Aimée stepped forward with her knife, and proceeded to cut away Marguerite's gown and petticoat and shift; as the weather was still warm she wore no stockings, and was thus left naked, no doubt a delightful sight but I had too many other things on my mind to appreciate her.

"Whatever are you doing?" Marguerite demanded, for as ever, she was not averse to being manhandled, or, appar-

304

ently, womanhandled. But then she looked down as Morin knelt at her feet and secured the rope to her ankles, bound together, whereupon he signalled his men, and four of them heaved on the rope to sweep Marguerite from her feet. She only just got her hands down in time to prevent herself receiving a nasty bump on the head, and then she was swinging clear of the floor, hoisted until her hair trailed. The violence of the upward movement plus her own reaction, had her spinning like a top, while she was for the moment entirely out of breath.

"Oh, stop her doing that," Richilde commanded, and Morin threw his arm round the rotating white body and brought it to a halt. Marguerite struck at him with her nails, but being upside down her aim was not good enough to do him any harm. "There," Richilde said. "Is she not a pretty sight, Helier? I can well understand why you were once willing to march the length of Germany to save her life. Well, I will keep her as a memento."

"Memento?" Marguerite shouted, having got her breath back.

"Or parts of you, anyway," Richilde conceded.

"Parts of me?" Marguerite screamed.

"I told you to save your breath," Richilde advised. "You are going to have to do a lot of screaming, very shortly. What I propose to do, you see, is flay you alive. Aimée!" Aimée hurried from the room.

"You . . . what!" Marguerite shrieked.

"I know," Richilde said sympathetically. "It is a most painful business for the person being flayed. But an exhilarating one of the person doing the flaying. Ah, Aimée."

Aimée had returned, having apparently known exactly where to go, although she had never been in this castle before, carrying a tray on which there were a variety of cutting tools, of every shape and size and form, but all razor-sharp. "I think you had better bind her wrists," Richilde decided.

Morin stepped forward, and after a brief struggle, as Marguerite, even naked and upside down, was quite prepared to fight him as long as her breath lasted, secured her

305

wrists together with a length of the same cord as was binding me to my chair. "You, Helier," Richilde said. "Will sit there and watch, and imagine what I am going to do to you, when I am ready. It will be far more interesting. Now let me see, I think we are supposed to start at the base of the spine. One works outwards, you know." She stepped up to Marguerite, who was again speechless, this time, I surmised, with fear, and examined those magnificent buttocks, then summoned Aimée and her tray, and picked up one of the scalpels. "This one, I think," she said.

At this, Marguerite let out the most piercing screech I had ever heard, at least to that moment, and I quite lost my temper. I will confess that for several minutes my brain had been numbed, both by the reappearance of Richilde, and the knowledge that I had been harbouring that most terrible of women in my bosom all of these years. Now I exploded. I was Helier L'Eree. There was no one bigger or stronger than me in the entire world! And I had allowed myself to be bedevilled by a woman whose neck I could at any time have snapped with a twist of my hands. Equally had I permitted her creature to live and beguile me, when I could have left her to the mercy of Hopkins.

I gave a roar, exerted every muscle I possessed and every ounce of mental concentration, and sprang to my feet, popping the cords holding me as if they had been string, which, relative to my strength, they were. My action caused consternation, as may be imagined. There were eight people in the room – apart from Marguerite and myself – and to a man, or a woman, they blanched. Even Richilde was distracted from her foul purpose, but even Richilde, who had known me for so many years, had not properly gauged my strength when truly aroused; the only time she had seen me in such a mood of violence had been when I had caught up with her after chasing her clear across Europe, and then there had been just she and I, and thus extreme strength had not been necessary. So now she still assumed the situation could be returned to normal, as it were. "Seize him," she snapped, "and this time do a better job of securing him."

Four of the men moved against me, and I remembered that it had been in this very hall that Richelieu had first tested my strength by sending three of his young men against me – and they had been armed with quarter staves. Now I gave a bellow of almost maniacal laughter, and as the first two men reached for me, I ignored their grasping hands to seize their heads and knock them together so hard that I swear I heard their brains addling. In any event they lost all further interest in the proceedings.

Their companions hesitated at the sight of this utter destruction, and before they could decide what to do next, I had seized one of them, also by the head, and using this alone, swung him from the floor. I heard his neck crack even as he slammed into the fourth fellow and sent him flying to the floor. By now Richilde had realised that she had aroused a monster, and that further enjoyment of the evening would have to be replaced by safety. "Shoot the villain," she commanded.

Surprisingly, the only persons in the room who were armed were the two women, and they had only knives, and Morin, who had the pistol stuck in his belt. This he now drew, but as he levelled it I picked up one of the very heavy chairs which accompanied the table and hurled it at him. The bullet struck the wood but did not in any way check its progress through the air, and Morin joined his comrades on the floor, quite brained. This decided the last remaining man to remain no longer. He ran for the door.

"Helier!" Marguerite screamed, her face crimson as all her blood was rushing to her head. "Save me!"

As if I was not in the act of doing this. In the event, her shout was unwise, as it reminded Richilde that she could settle at least part of the business. She turned back to her victim, knife in hand, no longer concerned with opening up her skin so much as to drive the weapon home. I was therefore forced to resort once again to missile tactics, seized a second chair, and hurled it at the pair of them. It struck Marguerite a most resounding thwack amidships, as it were, which caused her to swing to and fro most violently, putting a temporary end to her screaming; while doing this she cannoned into Richilde, on the side away from the knife, and thus sent the Princess sprawling, all flying skirts and kicking legs – but she had lost hold of the knife, which went scattering across the floor. "Aimée!" she panted.

I turned back just in time. Aimée had been slowly advancing towards me from behind. Now she lunged at me with her own dagger. I evaded the blow without difficulty, and struck down with all my force. Aimée gave a shriek herself as her forearm snapped. The knife fell from her grasp, and she turned and ran for the door. "Get help!" Richilde bawled, and scrabbled across the floor on her hands and knees, seeking her knife.

But I was now entirely in command of the situation. My sword lay where I had dropped it, and I picked it up, and reached the doors in three strides, before Aimée could get there, as she had collapsed to her hands and knees in agony. I slammed them shut, dropping the great bar into place and effectively cutting us off from the courtyard; there was a great deal of noise out there, as of course the surviving man would be telling his comrades about what was happening, but no one had as yet plucked up sufficient courage to challenge the mad monster within. That done I turned back to face my enemy.

Richilde had by now reached her weapon, and regained her feet. But she was some ten feet away from Marguerite, who was still swinging to and fro and bawling her heart out. And I was ten feet away on the other side. "You have no hope of escaping me," I told Richilde. "This time I shall finish it."

She tossed that magnificent head. "You thought to do so once before, Helier. And could not."

"Perhaps then, although I knew you were responsible for the deaths of my mistress and my child, I could still remember our hours together. But now you have murdered my wife and my children. I have no mercy for you now."

"No mercy," she sneered. "And what of our more recent hours together?"

"I regret them most bitterly."

"Well, then," she said. "What are you proposing? To drown me again? You were not very successful at *that*!"

"I propose to cut off your head, Princess," I said. "I am sure that will at least limit your activities. Now, it would be far more seemly, and dignified, for you to come over here and kneel before me, and be despatched with a single blow, than for me to have to hack at you, when you may well suffer before dying."

She stared at me, and saw the determination in my eyes. Then she looked at Marguerite, as if debating her chance of reaching her before I could get there. But she realised that was a certain way of dying. Thus she suddenly reversed the blade, hurled the knife at Marguerite, and ran for the inner doorway.

Marguerite shrieked, but a scalpel was never intended as a throwing weapon, and although it struck her, it did her no harm before falling to the floor. My immediate reaction was to run after Richilde, but I was checked by another scream from Marguerite. "Helier!"

I turned, sweeping my sword as I did so. behind me, Aimée, having recovered somewhat, had regained her knife and was again lunging at me, using her left hand. Truth to tell, I had not yet made up my mind what to do about Aimée, as executing females had never been my forté, but as it turned out the matter was settled for me. As I have said, I swept my sword as I swung round, with all my force, and my blade crunched into the already broken right arm, severing the limb completely and continuing through material and flesh to slice deeply into her side and then into her very middle. She made no sound, which leads me to suppose that she was dead long before she hit the floor, a mangled, bloody mess. I gazed at her in horror, for it is no slight thing to slay, certainly in such a fashion, someone with whom one has shared one's all.

"Oh, Helier," Marguerite commented. "You have slain her." She was given to such non *sequiturs*.

I was sorry to have so disposed of Aimée, but I was still concerned with the much bigger game, and looked left and right. Richilde had disappeared through the door leading to the sculleries. I started to run behind her, and was checked by another shout from Marguerite. "You cannot leave me so!"

I had to admit she could not be comfortable, and so stepped up to her, grasped her round the thighs, and with a single sweep of my sword cut the ropes above her. Then I laid her on the floor. "Free yourself," I told her, and ran to the inner door. Here I descended some steps into the huge kitchens, where the great cauldrons which were intended to provide dinner for the entire garrison of the château, such as it now was with six of its number – including Aimée – lying dead in the knights' hall, simmered over a huge fire, banked deep into the inner recesses of the great central chimney, and welling out of a glowing pit. the cooks and scullery wenches had all run outside, but a goodly crowd had gathered in the outer doorway, from whence they were peering, in the first instance, at their unholy mistress, who stood at the foot of the stairs, looking at them.

"Get up there and seize the monster!" she was shouting. "Bind him with chains, and then ..."

Her voice faded as she discovered that far from listening to her, her people were gazing at me, as I came down the steps.

"Have at me!" I shouted. "Before I have at you!"

Whereupon they gave a great shriek, and fled from the doorway, banging the door shut behind them.

Richilde looked after them in consternation, then left and right as if seeking a weapon. But for all the knives lying about there was nothing she dared pit against my blade, as I came closer. Save perhaps one of the spits that leaned against the wall. She gave a hasty glance at the door, but knew she could not reach it and open it before I would be upon her, and thus turned her back on me and ran to the fire, seizing one of these long, thin metal rods. But, hampered as she was by her skirts, she had to run round one of the great tables, whereas, by vaulting the same, I arrived beside her as she grasped the metal.

I reached out to seize her by the hair and thus expose her neck to the blow I was determined to deliver, but with a quick duck of her head she evaded my hand, and then swung back towards me. As she did so, however, her heels struck the edge of the stone grate, and she fell backwards. Richilde uttered a shriek such as will stay with me to my dying day, then, still falling, her head struck one of the cauldrons, and she plunged into the glowing pit of the fire.

In my horror, I dropped my sword and stood on the grate myself, peering down into the seething red. But she had already disappeared, unless a faint blueish eruption was part of her. But even that was gone in a moment. Richilde Bethlen, Princess von Hohengraffen, was finally dead.

Overcome by heat as well as emotional exhaustion, I staggered back and leaned against the table. I was panting and weeping, that after so many years my quest should have come to an end.

I was alerted by a sound, and sprang up, in the same instant scooping my sword from the floor. The door was again opening, and people were peering in. I faced them. "Your unholy mistress is dead," I told them. "So is Morin, and his crew. I will give you all ten minutes to leave this castle, or I shall commence slaying you as well."

As one man, or woman, they turned and ran. I went upstairs, to find Marguerite sitting in one of the chairs, examining herself. "Do you realise, Helier," she said severely, "that you gave me a very nasty bruise with that chair? I thought to have broken a rib, at the least. But it seems that I have been fortunate."

"Very," I agreed, and sank into a chair beside her. I was quite exhausted.

"Well, don't just sit there," she said. "Do you suppose I wish my knights' hall permanently littered with dead bodies? Summon the servants to remove them and clean up the blood. And what have you done with the Princess?"

"The Princess has returned to where she really belongs," I told her. "As for the servants, I have dismissed them all. We will have to clean up this place ourselves."

"Oh, really, Helier! Or do you intend to dismiss me as well?"

She bit her lip as she spoke, realising that she might have put the idea into my mind. "Helier!" She dropped to her knees beside my chair, an alluring sight, as she remained naked. "You cannot treat me so. Helier! You abducted me when I was but fifteen years old, and began this whole fearsome adventure. Helier! I would serve you most faithfully, in every way. Helier! We were made for each other!"

Taking everything into consideration, I realised she was probably right.

As to the future, no man can foretell that. If I felt that I had adventured enough, and suffered enough, and lost enough, to be left in some repose with the woman who, as she never tired of reminding me, had been with me, on and off, from the beginning of my adult life, there were yet those, both men and women, who were to find it necessary to call me back to arms, as the affairs of the Stuarts went from bad to worse.

But that is another tale, as is my next meeting with the despicable Hopkins.

As for the Witch of Hohengraffen, she was undoubtedly dead. Yet the next day, when the fire had burned itself out, I climbed down into the pit and poked into the ashes . . . and found not a bone. The heat had been extreme, and yet . . . having buried the various bodies lying around the place, I rode into the village and bought myself all the garlic they possessed. This I distributed around my château. Put me down as a superstitious man, after all. But it is better to be safe than sorry.